A JACK IN THE DARK

Also by Lesley L. Smith

Temporal Dreams
Neutrino Warning
Kat Cubed
Reality Alternatives
Conservation of Luck

The Space Operetta Series:
Book 1: *A Jack By Any Other Name*
Book 2: *A Jack In The Dark*
Book 3: *A Jack For All Seasons*

The Quantum Cop Series:
Book 1: *The Quantum Cop*
Book 2: *Quantum Murder*
Book 3: *Quantum Mayhem*

A Jack in the Dark

By Lesley L. Smith

Quarky Media
Boulder Colorado

A Jack in the Dark
Published by Quarky Media, PO Box 3332, Boulder, CO 80307
www.quarkymedia.com

Copyright © 2018 Lesley L. Smith
ISBN: 978-0-9973131-6-1 (ebook)
ISBN: 978-0-9973131-7-8 (print)

A JACK IN THE DARK

Chapter One

I leaned back in my chair in the dimmed theatre on Keplarr-452b. It was impossible to get comfortable in the high gravity. The thick planetary atmosphere almost felt like a blanket lying on a person; the humidity was impressive. I sucked in a dense breath.

My good friend and crewmate Ted, sitting next to me, glanced over. "You okay, Jack?" When I'd first arrived on our ship, the *Shakespeare*, he'd beguiled me with his extraordinarily long eyelashes.

I nodded.

The crew of the Terran Cultural Committee's flagship was putting on one of Earth's masterpieces, Hamlet, for the Keplarrians. It was an unusual experience for me to be in the audience since I was a huge star, but I was trying to make the most of it. I stared at the stage, letting the whole experience wash over me.

Lord Polonius, aka First Officer Carter Nillion, was talking. "*This above all: to thine own self be true. And it must follow, as the night the day, thou canst not then be false to any man. Farewell: my blessing season this in thee*!" Carter was doing a good job; he actually had some acting chops. Who knew? He did resemble a classically-handsome leading man, tall, with symmetric features--so it was good he could play a leading man.

I found this section particularly intriguing since I was a clone. Who was thine own self? Not the original Jack Jones--I hoped. He'd ended up being a dastardly thief and murderer, a brigand, and an evildoer of the highest order. I paused. Maybe I was getting a little carried away. At any rate, he was imprisoned back on Earth, so I didn't need to worry about him anymore. I cleared my throat.

"You could play any character in this, Jack," Ted whispered.

"I know, right?" I whispered back.

"Their loss," he said.

I nodded. "Yeah."

Somebody sitting behind us said, "Shh!" It must have been a human because it was doubtful the Keplarrians knew about shushing. Or could make that sound since they were snake-like creatures. I glanced back, but it was too dark to see who or what it was.

"Sorry, but my part's coming up," Ted said. "I have to go."

"Shh!" the mysterious audience member said again.

Ted stood.

"Down in front!"

Ted leaned over and crept away.

Yes, it was irksome that I was pretty much the only member of the *Shakespeare*'s crew not in or working on the show. Especially since the official mission of the *Shakespeare* was spreading Earth's awesome culture for the Terran Cultural Committee. The *Shakespeare*'s unofficial mission was spying on the rest of the galaxy for Earth.

Ophelia, aka Engineering Lieutenant Olivia Lee, said, "*My lord, he hath importuned me with love in honorable fashion.*" With her golden-hued skin and wide-set almond eyes, she made a great Ophelia.

I could imagine someone importuning her with love. I lost myself in the story...

At intermission, no one from the crew came out to say hi to me. Frankly, it was surprising. I'd made a point of staying near my seat so they could find me. "*Oft expectation fails,*" I muttered.

The theatre had a distinct cave-like vibe with walls, floor and ceiling made of what appeared to be gray rock. It wasn't the first non-Terran theatre I'd been to that reminded me of a big cave. On the other hand, all theatres looked pretty much the same with the house lights dimmed--especially from the stage.

As I lollygagged, I studied the crowd. I didn't see any sign of the annoying humans giving Ted grief earlier. I did see a few Tau-Ceto-ans with their gray scaly skin, powerful thick arms and legs, rounded backs, and gray-brown tunics. I'd been told not to say they resembled turtles, but come on. I'd had a bit of a mishap on Tau Ceto e--running from the law--but presumably, none of these Tau-Ceto-ans would hold it against me. Or even know about it.

I also saw a few Alpha-Catoblepans with their weak chins, prominent noses, big ears, and fur in shades from white to black. They also sported tunics. Why were tunics so popular? A couple of white-furred AC ladies(?) sitting behind me waved energetically as I turned around. I modestly waved back. They seemed thrilled. I'm sure I made their day since, on Alpha Catoblepas, I was renowned as a supremely gifted singer.

The Keplarrians resembled nothing so much as big snakes--wearing tunics. I guess when you have high gravity and a thick atmosphere, a snake is an economical body type. I nodded at the group to my right. They didn't respond--or if they did, it wasn't in any way I could discern.

I perused the crowd some more. There were quite a few species I didn't recognize, like that violet cloud over to the left and the rock-looking thing next to it.

Intermission can last a long time when you don't have anyone to talk to. I was just debating going over and chatting with my AC fans when the lights flickered, indicating the show would go on momentarily. I carefully set myself back down in the seat.

Sure enough, the lights soon dimmed...

Hamlet, aka Captain Gina Gomez, said, "*As thou'rt a man, give me the cup: let go; by heaven, I'll have't.*" Yes, it was an unusual choice to have a curvilicious woman playing Hamlet, but the captain was in charge of shows as well as the ship, and apparently, rank has its privileges.

Suddenly something was on my head blocking my vision, but when I tried to take it off, someone or something held my arms down. "Hey! Stop it! Let me go!"

Behind me, someone said, "Shh!"

In the background on stage, Gina said, "*Absent thee from felicity awhile...*"

I felt a small prick. That didn't seem right...

Everything went dark.

When I came to, it was pitch dark. I was lying on some kind of stone floor. "Hello? Anyone there?" I tried to get up and realized the strong gravity and thick soupy air meant I was still on Keplarr-452b. Was that a good thing or a bad thing?

Surely, the *Shakespeare* crew would be busting in any second to rescue me. Surely, they all missed me immensely by now. Surely.

"Hello?"

No one came.

"Anyone there? What do you want?"

No one answered.

"Help?"

Nothing.

It looked like it was up to me to get out of here. I tried to stand and, woozy, decided crawling was a more efficient means of locomotion. I crawled until I touched a wall. It was stone. I crawled the entire perimeter of my cell. It all felt like stone walls. Where was the door? How had I even ended up in here?

I lay back to regroup and come up with a plan.

I wracked my brain. Jeez, coming up with plans was tough, especially when one was woozy.

I lay on the floor for what seemed like forever. In the dark, with no sensory input whatsoever, it was impossible to tell how much time was passing. Eventually, my disquiet was replaced by boredom.

"Hey!" I yelled. "You can't just leave me here!"

I paused to listen.

Nothing.

Apparently, they could just leave me here.

I wracked my brain some more. Since I was technically less than a year old, it was doubtful this was about me. Either they wanted to use me as leverage somehow against the *Shakespeare,* or this had something to do with my original, the infamous Old Jack. I pondered. Yeah, it was most likely they thought I was Old Jack and I was in possession of his stolen goods, or he owed them money. Or he'd murdered one of them. The extent of Old Jack's crimes was still being investigated.

I'd had enough. If I couldn't escape right now, or come up with a plan, at least I could do something constructive: I could rehearse. The next time the *Shakespeare* put on Hamlet, I would play the Danish Prince.

I started to stand, but gravity was still very strong. Why use up my energy? I could rehearse lying down.

Let's see. What's my first line?

"*A little more than kin, and less than kind.*"

"*Not so, my lord; I am too much i' the sun.*"

Rehearsing was not super fun, with no one to run lines with you.

"*Ay, madam, it is common.*"

I heard a crash, and suddenly light streamed into the room. A section of the rock wall had collapsed.

Ted bounded in, grunting with the effort. "Jack! There you are! Are you all right?"

I felt my eyes fill with (manly) tears of relief. "Thank God, Ted."

Carter entered after him, looking like a hero, darn his classically-handsome looks. "Is someone else here? Captors?"

"No." I shook my head and reached for Ted. He leaned down and engulfed me in his arms. After so long alone in the dark, it was heavenly.

"So, you were talking to yourself?" Carter asked.

Eva strode in, her big brown eyes flashing. She was the weapons expert and trainer on the ship. "You got him? All right then." It was wonderful to see her; we were very close. Truth be told, it was always wonderful to see Eva: she was very fit and beautiful.

Ted said, "Let's get out of here."

"Yes, please." I let go of Ted. "How long's it been? How long have I been a prisoner?" He helped me off the floor, and I got a head rush as I ascended.

Eva looked at her fon. "Almost two hours."

I couldn't process that. Only two hours? That couldn't be right. It felt like two centuries.

Ted helped me to the door. "Yeah. We didn't know you were missing until after the show."

"You didn't show up at the after-party," Carter said. "In hindsight, that was suspicious. It's not like you to miss a party."

Ted shook his head. "I thought you were signing

autographs." We all started walking down the hall. "But then some AC ladies came looking for you and said they saw you leave wearing a hood over your head before the end of the show."

My prison was all nondescript familiar-looking gray stone walls and floors. The cell doors also seemed to be made of stone. "What is this place?" I asked. Then, Ted's words registered. "Did the ACs see who took me?"

"No," Ted said.

"The ACs were useless for intel," Eva said, striding in the front of the group. "Among other things, they didn't think there was anything weird about the hood."

"Didn't you see who took you?" Carter asked me.

"No." I shook my head, and everything spun. I remembered the little prick. "They, whoever or whatever they were, must have drugged me. And they put something over my head."

"The hood," Ted said helpfully.

I nodded. Head spin. I was officially putting a moratorium on head shakes and nods.

Eva stopped and turned around. "Who or what was it? What did they want with you?" She stared at me.

I had no idea. "I have no idea."

Gee, that wasn't ominous at all.

Chapter Two

The morning after my ordeal, I sat with Captain Gina Gomez in her pretty, rose-walled ready room. It was dominated by a large table and chairs; I now sat in one of the latter around the former. I knew from experience that the flowers in the vases were bolted down somehow. I hadn't quite deduced the mechanism yet but resisted the urge to investigate.

"I'm disappointed with you, Jack," she said. "It's not acceptable to be AWOL from the ship." She was the most voluptuous woman on board. Her combination of sexiness and power was almost intoxicating.

Wait. Was she blaming me for being kidnapped? "I was kidnapped!" I pointed at her. "You know I was kidnapped because your husband Carter was one of the people who rescued me!"

She frowned.

"I was in danger, real danger! It's not like some rabid fans took me for a fun orgy or something." I was a galactically-famous singer, so that scenario wasn't totally outside the realms of possibility. Of course, I was also a Terran spy, like everyone else on the ship--but did the aliens know that? I wasn't sure.

"Because of your unusual, ah, talent, I need to know where you are at all times," she said.

Sadly, the unusual talent she was referring to was not singing. Or even orgy-related talents. "But I thought my special skill was top secret, need-to-know."

"It is. But who knows who might have deduced it?" She frowned some more. "Or who you might have blabbed to."

To be fair, I was a little murky about who I'd told. A lot had happened in the last few months. "Well, how will you know where

I am at all times? It's not like you can hold me prisoner."

Her expression said, 'Yes, I can.'

"I'm a grown man!"

She wrinkled her brow. "Are you?" Technically, I'd only been decanted a few months ago.

"I am." We stared at each other for a few moments. She didn't seem convinced. "Come on, Gina. Give me a break. Aren't we *more than kin*?" Frankly, our relationship was confusing. She'd been married to the original me. Legally, I thought we were, in fact, still married.

She exhaled. "So, anyway, I won't assign you a guard if you promise to behave."

"Kidnapped!" I said.

"I know; I've got a team investigating." She paused. "In the meantime, we need to study your special skill. I'm assigning you to engineering; you can study with the engineers."

I knew a very sexy engineering ensign, Olivia Lee. "Olivia?"

"No," she said. "I'm not assigning you to work with a bimbo you can just flutter your eyelashes at and get in the sack." In point of fact, Olivia was surprisingly immune to my charms.

"Olivia's not a bimbo." Now I felt myself frown. "And that's not an appropriate thing to say about one of your crewmembers."

"You're right." She exhaled again. "I apologize to you and Olivia."

She didn't seem like herself. "You seem upset," I said. "Can I help?"

She hesitated.

"Do you need a hug?"

She looked like she might actually be considering it. "No, Jack. Just do your job. I'm assigning you to work with Chief Engineer Bello. Keep this all quiet. Report to engineering immediately."

She still looked like she needed a hug.

"Immediately," she said. "Do you not know what immediately means?"

So, no hugs. I got to my feet. "No, ma'am. I mean, yes, ma'am. I know what immediately means."

As I approached engineering, I appreciated the fascinating

14

mural on the hallway wall outside. It featured Hamlet and his father's ghost with lots of spooky fog and a dramatic full moon. I would play Hamlet some day.

Engineering was the same as ever, full of machines whirring and blinking lights. And full of engineers; they all looked cute in their form-fitting engineering uniforms.

Someone said, "Lieutenant Junior Grade Jones," as soon as I entered. He was an older man with gray hair and a trim gray beard. He was quite attractive, in a mature way. "We were expecting you earlier. I'm Commander Bello." The other engineers weren't paying any attention to us. They remained focused on their tasks--whatever they were. Maybe I'd learn more engineering being stationed here.

"It's nice to meet you. Please call me Jack. What should I call you?" I looked into his eyes. They were very nice, a strong gray-blue, the color of a stormy Terran sky.

"You should call me Commander Bello." Then, he looked back into my eyes.

I recalled what Gina'd said and fluttered my eyelashes. "Oh." I smiled. "Surely, you have a first name?"

"Dylan," he said as if in a daze.

I held out my hand, and we shook. "Very nice to meet you, Dylan." His hand felt strong and warm in mine. I liked this Dylan. "*More honor'd in the breach than the observance*."

Dylan withdrew his hand. "Ah, okay." He cleared his throat. "Perhaps we should get to work?"

"Sounds good, Dylan." I beamed at him.

"So, ah, anyway, we're supposed to investigate your 'special skill'? Can you enlighten me? What is this skill?"

I leaned towards him. "Are you sure you have the security clearance?"

"Yes. Gina already told me."

"Then why are you asking me?"

"It's pretty hard to believe." He paused. "What are you claiming?"

I took a step closer. He smelled nice, strong, like a powerful man. "I can make improbable things happen?"

He took a step away. "Seriously? I mean, that's what Gina said, but..."

I took a step towards him. "Seriously." I nodded.

He raised his eyebrows. "Well, I guess we'll see, won't we? I'm supposed to turn on the FTL drive?"

"Yes."

"All right." He turned around. "Follow me." I followed him deeper into engineering.

He paused in front of a featureless white ball, aka the mysterious FTL drive. It was about two feet in diameter. We humans knew almost nothing about how it worked. He accessed a computer near it. "So, I turn on the FTL drive? Are we going somewhere?"

"I'm no Engineer, but aren't we too close to Keplarr-452b? We're not supposed to try to jump near planets and stuff, right?"

"We've been flying through normal space at full speed since the crew returned last night. We should be far enough away."

I held up my hand. "Let's wait on jaunting across the universe for the moment. Is it on?"

"Yeah. Can't you tell?"

Tricky. Usually, I realized something wonky was going on with the FTL drive when my body started acting wonky. "Can we jump a few feet or something?" I asked.

He shrugged and fiddled with the machine. "Okay." He straightened and looked at me.

"What would you say if I asked you to kiss me?" I asked.

"I'd say you seem like a nice young man, but focus on your damn job."

"What if I said kissing you was part of my job?"

He stared at me.

"Go ahead. Check with Gina. I'll wait." I smiled and crossed my arms. It would be fun to kiss him.

Without saying a word, he took out his fon. "Gina? I'm standing here with Jack as you asked, and you wouldn't believe what he wants to do." He quieted, listening. He glanced at me. "Whatever he wants?" He listened. "Anything?" He listened. "Yes, ma'am." He hung up.

He stepped to me, held my face in his hand and planted a delicious kiss right on my lips. Wow. I lost track of space and time there for a moment.

But I didn't get aroused. That was very unlikely, considering

16

how attractive he was.

When we separated, he said, "So?"

"My special skill is working." I smiled. I needed to get to know this Dylan much, much better. "Do you have a wish? The more outlandish, the better."

He shook his head a little but then said, "I wish I was your age again."

I started to say his wish but stopped myself in time. "Ah, technically, I'm less than a year old. So, maybe that's not a great idea." I knew for sure Gina would be annoyed with me if I turned her chief engineer into a toddler.

Dylan's jaw dropped.

"Maybe we should wish you were eighteen years old again?"

He nodded.

"I wish handsome Dylan Bello here was eighteen years old." I stared at him.

He got kind of blurry, and then, suddenly, he looked much, much younger. If I'd thought old Dylan was attractive, young Dylan was really, really attractive. His stormy blue eyes were even more beautiful, framed by dark hair and smooth skin.

My skill worked. Of course. Yay, me.

"I feel different," he said. "I feel awesome. Energetic. Strong." He held up his hands. "My skin looks different."

He ran to a reflective piece of equipment. In the mirror-like surface, he beheld the eighteen-year-old version of himself. "What. The. Fuck?" Then he crumpled to the floor.

I got out my fon and called Dr. Sharma. "Hi, Dr. Sharma. This is Jack. I'm in engineering. I think Commander Bello fainted."

"What did you do to him?" Dr. Sharma asked.

"I didn't do anything!" Nothing bad, anyway. "Can you come over here or not?"

"All right," he said, sighing. "On my way." Why did people seem to sigh so often around me?

Soon, Dr. Sharma ran into the room with his medical bag. He was one of the oldest men on the ship, and it appeared his ancestors were from the Terran country India. Considering how old he was, he was a very good runner. He was also a very good doctor with an excellent bedside manner. Usually. Now, he pointed at Dylan lying on the floor. "Who's this?"

"Dylan Bello."

"I know Dylan," he said, frowning. "He's a fifty-five-year-old man. This isn't Dylan."

"Well, whoever he is, he fainted." I suppressed my own sigh. "Can you help him?"

"I should be able to." He knelt and leaned over him, taking his vital signs. He opened his bag and withdrew a vial. He opened the small container and waved it under Dylan's nose.

Dylan sputtered and opened his eyes. "What's going on? Why am I on the floor?"

"You just fainted, young man." Dr. Sharma put his equipment back in his bag. "But don't worry, you're going to be just fine. What's your name?"

Dylan stared. "What do you mean, what's my name? You know me, Sharma. I'm Bello, Dylan Bello." He struggled to get to his feet.

I lent him a hand. Because I was gallant like that.

Dylan bounced up. When he caught sight of his reflection again, he whispered. "Fuck."

Dr. Sharma stood. "What's going on here? What did you do, Jack?"

I couldn't recall if he knew about my special skill or not. "Why do you assume I did something?"

He gave me a smirk that said, 'Duh.'

"Top secret," I said.

"Change me back!" Dylan said.

"I wish Dylan was back to his usual fifty-five-year-old self," I said.

Nothing happened. Oops. My special skill was a little unreliable.

"Change me back!" Dylan said.

"I tried," I said. "It didn't work." I did not understand why it worked sometimes and didn't other times.

"What the hell is going on here?" Dr. Sharma said.

Good question.

Chapter Three

Gina, aka Captain Gomez, was calling me on the carpet. Again.

It felt like being summoned into the principal's office. I could remember that like it was yesterday--which was ironic since the last time I'd been called to the principal's was about forty years ago.

"What the hell, Jack!" Gina exclaimed, hands on her ample hips, fire practically shooting out of her eyeballs. "What did you do to Dylan?"

We were in her ready room. She was sexy when she was angry. But she was also more than a little scary.

"I made him eighteen again," I mumbled. I didn't understand why she was so mad. She'd told me to study my special skill, and I had. I also didn't understand why Dylan was so mad. Who wouldn't want to be young again?

"What?" she asked. "Speak up."

"I made him eighteen again!" I said. "You're the one who told me to experiment!"

"I also told you to keep it quiet." Her volume decreased slightly. "How are we supposed to explain this?"

"Isn't it obvious?" I waved my hand over my awesome bod. We could say Dylan was a clone, like me.

"What?" She shook her head. "You want to have sex with him?"

Why did everyone always assume I wanted to have sex with everything? I hadn't had sex in hours. In fact, I hadn't had sex in days.

"Jack!"

"Obviously, we tell everyone he's in a clone body," I said.

"How do we explain the fact that he wasn't in a clone body

fifteen minutes ago?"

"It's a secret clone body that we just transferred his memories to?"

"How do we explain the fact that we don't have the facilities to grow clones on the ship?"

"The clone body was in stasis or something?"

"Why did he transfer to a clone body?" she asked. It was a good question. "Did he die?"

"Okay," I said. "He died."

She took her hands off her hips and sat down in a chair. "Might work." She frowned. "I guess." She glanced at me. "Beggars can't be choosers."

"*Things without all remedy should be without regard: what's done is done*," I said.

"Maybe so." She sighed. "More like *the whirligig of time brings in his revenges*. But, all right. Secret clone body it is."

I stood up from my chair. "Are we done, then?"

"Where do you think you're going?" she asked.

"Back to engineering? Back to work?"

She looked at me.

"Aren't I?"

"Dylan refuses to work with you any more."

Aw. I knew things hadn't gone totally smoothly with Dylan, but I'd thought we'd had a connection. And I still didn't get why he didn't like being young again. "So what does that mean?"

She didn't answer me immediately.

"I thought figuring out the FTL drive was a priority?"

"It is," she said. "We need to let him cool down." She stood. "In the meantime, report to the cargo bay. Help Daniel do something."

The cargo bay was the largest open space on the ship, filled with boxes in various sizes from a few inches cubed to dozens of meters cubed. If there was a method for storing them, I hadn't deciphered it yet.

Surprisingly, my boss, Daniel, was not thrilled to see me. He was a guy about my age, well-built, with tan skin; if he wasn't usually annoyed with me, I might think he was hot.

"What?" I asked.

"You are the worst employee I've ever had," he said. "You're never here."

"I have other duties," I said.

"Everyone has other duties!" He scowled at me. "It's like you only come here to work when you're being punished or something." He wasn't wrong. But I didn't think agreeing with him would make him more agreeable.

"What would you like me to do, Boss?" I smiled deliberately. "I'm at your service."

"Oh, no," he said. "I don't want any sex acts."

Sex again? Why was everyone obsessed with sex around here? I mean, I was mighty f-i-n-e, but jeesh. "I wasn't offering sex acts--you should be so lucky." I grinned.

He looked hesitant for a second like he was considering sex acts. Then, he shook his head. "Okay." He pointed at a huge pile of boxes and crates. "Move that pile of stuff to--" he twirled his forefinger "--that empty spot there." He pointed at a big empty spot.

"Sir, yes, sir!" I smiled.

He started to smile back but caught himself. "The antigrav dolly's near the door." He pointed back towards the door.

I got to work. As I worked, I started out humming and ended up singing.

A few hours later, I noticed Daniel staring at me.

I'd been singing, "*Imagine there's no heaven...*" I stopped singing. "What? You got something against Lennon? He's one of the best Terran songwriters of all time." I grinned and sang, "*...and the universe will be as one.*"

"You may be a bad cargo handler, but you're not a bad singer," he said.

"Thank you, sir." Praise always felt nice. I couldn't help smiling.

"Go on, get out of here," he said. "Good job today."

"Sir, yes, sir!" I said and started pushing the dolly back towards the door.

He turned away, but I thought I saw a smile on his face before he did so.

I rested the dolly near the door. There was something important about the cargo bay, something that had been tickling my brain. Singing evidently facilitated my thinking processes. "Daniel, how do you think that stolen FTL drive got in here?" The two of us had found a secret stolen FTL drive in here a few weeks ago. FTL drives were super-valuable because the tech was top secret. If we could reverse-engineer one, we'd break the AC monopoly on FTL drives. (The AC sold FTL drives, but they didn't make them. We didn't know who made them.)

Daniel paused. "A question I'm more interested in is: how did the stolen FTL drive get out of here?"

I felt blood rush to my face. I had stolen the secret stolen FTL drive and installed it on the kind-of-stolen shuttle. "Ah," I said. "I think it was a secret mission for Captain Gina."

He took a step towards me. "You think, or you know?" The way he was walking, menacingly, I was pretty sure he knew that I knew.

"I, ah, know," I said convincingly.

"You're not very convincing," he said.

We stared at each other for a few moments.

Finally, I said, "I thought we were friends, Daniel." In point of fact, I'd paid Daniel handsomely to be my friend--albeit with some funds that had fallen into my lap via my special skill, but still.

He exhaled. "I may have some secret security footage of the cargo bay." He turned. "Come on." He waved at me to follow him.

We went to a little office space that was accessible through a door in the cargo bay. I hadn't even realized the room existed.

"How long has this been here?" I asked as Daniel sat down in front of a computer terminal.

I looked over his shoulder as he typed stuff on the keyboard. "A keyboard? How old-school."

He twisted around and looked up at me. "It's harder to hack."

He returned to his typing, and a view of the cargo bay appeared. He typed some more, and it started moving backward in time. There I was, singing and moving boxes around; I sounded great. He speeded it up, and the sound became unintelligible. Aw.

He stopped the recording when Olivia and I wheeled the

secret stolen FTL drive out of the cargo bay. He turned and gave me a long look.

"Captain Gina, I mean, Captain Gomez, told us to do it."

"Uh-huh," he said in a way that meant he didn't buy it for a second.

But he turned around and resumed looking at the recording. It sped by us in reverse on the screen.

"So, you said this was secret surveillance?" I asked. "That sounds unusual."

"You think so? Really?" he said without turning around. "This is a ship of spies, after all."

Oh, I knew that. The original Jack, my template, was supposedly a super-spy. But it turned out he was just working for himself.

Daniel stopped the recording when he and I discovered the drive. The antigrav dolly had been acting up, and the box holding the drive fell and cracked open. The recording showed Daniel and me peeking into the box and being amazed to see the drive inside.

On the recording, Daniel said, "I've never seen one not installed in a ship, but I think that's an FTL drive."

On the recording, I examined the item inside and said, "How can you tell? It doesn't look like anything." I looked good on screen, if I did say so myself.

"Yeah, mysterious, isn't it?" When he stood up on the recording, Daniel was smiling.

"It's surprising we get our FTL drives from AC," I said. "They don't seem smart enough to produce them."

"We don't, and they aren't," he said.

"So?" I asked onscreen. I was definitely photogenic.

Still grinning onscreen, he said, "I don't know what's going on. But it's very, very interesting."

"What does the paperwork say about the box?" I asked.

On the recording, he pointed his fon at the crate's label. "It's in AC."

In Daniel's office, I said, "That's enough." I seemed to recall something embarrassing coming up about my DNA on the drive. In hindsight, it was super obvious that the DNA was from Old Jack. We all should have been more suspicious of him. He must have stolen the drive.

Of course, in our defense, we thought he was dead at the time.

"So, did you ever track the crate?" I asked.

He shook his head slowly. "No. But it was high-security, so it should have been documented from the source." He glanced at me. "I'll investigate."

Yay. Exactly how Old Jack got the drive was a loose thread. Why? Hadn't they debriefed and even interrogated Old Jack?

What was so secret or horrible that he refused to admit it?

After doing physical labor all day, I was ready for dinner. The mess hall was a large space with beautiful Shakespearean forest and feast murals. It felt like entering a fairy wood, except for all the sturdy utilitarian tables and chairs. I was just sitting down to a couple of beautiful seitan steaks when Ted appeared at my elbow.

"Jack!" He fluttered his eyelashes. "Can I join you?" Clearly, he knew the power of his lovely lashes and was not afraid to use them.

I put a piece of steak in my mouth and started chewing. "Sure," I said with my mouth full.

He set his tray on the table and sat next to me. "I heard the craziest rumor that old Commander Bello suddenly got a new clone body."

"Wow." I swallowed. "Crazy."

"I've never heard of anybody getting a new clone body in the middle of a mission, have you?" he said.

Ted and I were probably the youngest members of the crew, so we hadn't heard much about anything. I shrugged and reached for another bite of steak.

Then the ship jerked, I heard a muffled thump, and the gravity turned off.

My plate floated away, and in my haste to grab it, I knocked it into the nearby wall. My dinner smacked into the wall and drifted away. Aw. I was hungry. On the bright side, the resulting splotch of sauce wasn't really noticeable in the forest scene, just making a group of leaves look a little more shadowed.

An alarm started blaring.

A JACK IN THE DARK

A voice came over the intercom, "Emergency in the cargo bay!"

Chapter Four

The ship's communication system blared, "Emergency personnel report to the cargo bay. Non-emergency personnel report to primary duty stations."

Still sitting in the mess hall, I had a moment of disorientation. What was my primary assignment?

Next to me, Ted said, "What do you think's happening in the cargo bay?"

I stood. "I don't know, but *it smells to heaven.*" I started floating/swimming/gyrating for the door. "I'm gonna find out."

"Wait for me!" Ted gyrated after me.

As we made our way down the halls, I started getting a bad feeling. What had happened in the cargo bay? Was Daniel okay? Could it have something to do with what we were just discussing?

I gyrated faster.

We didn't pass many other crewmembers in the hall. I guessed they were following orders and reporting to their primary duty stations.

An argument could be made that the cargo bay was my duty station.

But Ted's station was definitely security. I twisted around to look at him as I pushed off a wall. "Maybe you should report to security."

"What?" he said. "Why?"

"What if we're under attack or something? Don't they need you to do, you know, security stuff?"

He grabbed a wall and stopped. "Ah..."

We were in sight of the cargo bay now. A fine mist of particulates, smoke or something hung in the air. A group of security personnel was clustered around the doorway, blasters drawn.

The air scrubbers were getting quite a workout.

An older man saw us and called out, "Oh, there you are, Ted. You made good time. Nice job."

Ted smiled and pushed off to join his colleagues.

I realized Gina was floating there next to the doorway as well.

When she saw me, she frowned.

I followed Ted over to the group of security officers.

"So, what's going on, Gina?" I asked her quietly.

She ignored me. "Proceed when ready," she said to security.

"On my six, men!" the head security guy said. They all floated into the cargo bay. There was no sense of urgency. It may have been difficult to move decisively when you were floating.

"What's going on?" I asked Gina again.

She peered into her fon; it showed a room full of smoke. Was it the cargo bay? "There was an explosion in the cargo bay," she said.

"Explosion!" That did not sound good. "Are we under attack?"

"I don't think so," she said. "At least not from outside the ship."

"From inside the ship?" My voice squeaked a little.

"I don't know," she said.

"Why is gravity out?" I asked.

"I don't know," she said, still staring into her fon.

That was not good.

"I sent Carter to engineering," she said. "He's supposed to restore gravity. Too bad Dylan is out of commission at the moment."

Yikes. I was the reason Chief Engineer Bello was out of commission. "I'm sure Carter can handle--"

We dropped to the floor.

"--restoring gravity," I finished. "Ow." I'd landed badly, jarring my arm.

Gina landed gracefully.

I scrambled up.

"It was a bomb," a man's voice said over comms, "but specially designed for very localized damage."

It just demolished a small office in here." The man paused. "There's a body."

"Oh, no," I whispered. "Poor Daniel." My throat felt full. I knew in my heart our discussion of the FTL drive and Daniel's investigation had triggered the bomb.

I didn't know the details of how, but I knew why.

The man said, "There's, ah, not much left."

Gina stared at me. "What do you know, Jack? You didn't do this, did you?"

"Me? I didn't do it." I cleared my throat. "At least not directly."

She took a step towards me, narrowing her eyes. "And indirectly?"

I took a step back, rubbing my arm. "Uh. Daniel and I were investigating where the FTL drive came from."

Oh, no. Old Jack and his minion, Noah, had access to the cargo bay. Could they have planted the explosive somehow? To cover their tracks?

"Damn," she said quietly. More loudly, into her fon, she said, "We know who the body is. I'll send Sharma in for the remains. Scan the rest of the cargo bay for explosives. Hell, scan the whole ship for explosives. This shouldn't have happened."

"Yes, Captain," the man on the fon said.

She called Dr. Sharma and told him to report to the cargo bay with a body bag.

My face must have betrayed me because then she asked, "What? What are you thinking, Jack?"

"It could have been Old Jack or Noah who left some kind of booby-trap," I said. "Couldn't it...?" My voice trailed off at the end under the force of her glare.

"Shit!" She smacked her forehead with the palm of her hand. "I'm so stupid. We should have done a security sweep of the whole ship as soon as we found out Jack was still alive. Shit! I really dropped the ball."

"I understand, Gina," I said. "It's hard for you to think of him as a cold-blooded killer. He was your husband. It's hard for me to

28

think of him that way, too. For obvious reasons." Namely, he was me.

She squinted a little at me. "Honestly, you don't seem that much like him to me anymore. If you ever did." Since Old Jack and I were genetically identical, that was saying something.

I felt a little brighter at that pronouncement since Old Jack was a bad guy. I didn't want to think of myself as a bad guy. The corners of my mouth started to curl up.

Dr. Sharma showed up. Oh, right. Daniel was dead. My smile died.

"You said there's a body?" he asked. "What's going on? Are we under attack? Should I be preparing for more casualties or injuries?"

Gina shook her head. "I don't know." She punched a button on her fon. "Commander Lu, please report to me outside the cargo bay."

Dr. Sharma went inside.

Commander Lu (apparently) appeared. "Yes, Captain. What can I do for you?" He looked exactly like you'd expect a security commander to look: tall, strong, and determined. His perfectly turned-out uniform--including polished shoes--was capped by a severe crew cut. I knew instantly I didn't want to get on his bad side.

"We need to do a full security sweep of the entire ship, every cubic centimeter," she said. "ASAP."

"Yes, ma'am." He started barking orders into his fon.

Was Daniel's death my fault?

I would get to the bottom of this.

Later that evening, I was just starting to calm down. My cabin was similar to every other cabin on the ship, an approximately twenty-feet by ten-feet rectangle with a cot, small desk and chair, built-in storage compartments and a tiny bathroom. The original Jack had hung a bunch of pictures of him and other people over the desk. I still hadn't deduced who most of them were. If they were Old Jack's loved ones, they weren't anything to me.

Someone knocked on my door.

I got up from brooding on my bunk and nursing my sore arm

and answered it.

Eva. I couldn't help smiling. I'd hardly seen her since I'd been kidnapped.

She smiled back.

"Are you here to cheer me up?" I asked. "We could have a, uh, work out." When I'd first gotten to the ship, Eva and I had had a lot of nice workouts--both in the gym and in bed.

"Actually, Gina sent me to search Jack's cabin."

"Why didn't she just ask me to do it?"

"I think we've established you don't know as much about this cabin as I do." That was true. A few weeks ago, she'd revealed a huge cache of weapons I had no idea of. Embarrassing.

"Okay." I lay back down on my bunk and watched her work. She was one fine-looking lady in perfect shape. Her ass, in particular, was a thing of beauty.

"*For her own person, it beggar'd all description: she did lie in her pavilion--cloth of gold, of tissue--o'er-picturing that Venus where we see the fancy outwork nature,*" I said.

She glanced at me. "Did you just call me Venus?"

"Yes."

"Why?"

"You're beautiful," I said.

"How specifically?"

"Your, uh, eyes, in particular, are beautiful."

She smiled, and our eyes met for a moment. Did I detect a flush spreading over her cheeks?

She went back to work, and I went back to watching her. It was nice--not creepy at all.

In the weapons-cache-compartment, she did pull out a mysterious small box. "This isn't yours, is it?"

I shook my head no.

She carefully placed it on the desk.

"That was it." She approached the bed.

I held my breath, smiling. Time for a workout?

She sat down next to me. "Venus, huh?"

"Actually, you're more beautiful than the goddess of love." I leaned over and pressed my lips to hers.

She pressed her lips to mine right back. Hurray! The sex

drought was over. It had been days.

One thing led to another thing and then another thing...

Much, much later, after many lovely things, we lay together on my bunk.

Somehow, my arm didn't hurt at all anymore.

"You were great, Eva," I said, lying back, waiting for my own accolades.

"You were great, too, Jack."

I smiled. Of course, I was.

"What do you think that box is?" She gestured towards it.

It looked totally innocuous. "I don't know. What do you think?"

"I don't know, but after the bomb in the cargo bay, I don't think I'd want any of Old Jack's stuff about."

"Uh... Everything in here is Old Jack's stuff."

"But it's standard issue, right? You don't have any of his personal stuff, do you?"

"Pictures." I pointed at the wall. "And...do data cubes count?"

"Yes. I hope they're data cubes and not something else." She levered herself up on her elbow. "Where?"

I pointed down.

She got out of bed (aw), down on the floor, and looked under the bed. "I see something under the mattress. Is that it?"

"Yeah." I'd found some data cubes of Old Jack's and hid them there.

She extracted herself. "Not exactly an ingenious hiding place, Jack." She got to her feet. "I wish you'd mentioned this before."

I shrugged.

"Did you look at the data?"

"Some of it." I could only decrypt some of it.

"Now that we know, or at least suspect, he's good at explosives, I wouldn't want anything of Old Jack's under my bed," she said. "Where they might explode. When I, or a guest, were lying there."

Good point. Very good point. What if I couldn't decrypt the data cube because it wasn't a data cube?

I jumped off the bed and lifted the mattress, snatching the

31

cubes and putting them carefully on the desk.

The two of us stood staring at the found objects on the little desk's surface. My cabin wasn't very big, so we were standing quite close. I could feel the heat of her skin on my skin.

Considering what had just happened in the cargo bay, I had to admit I was a wee bit nervous as I stared at the mysterious object.

"You don't think it could be a bomb, do you?"

Chapter Five

I stared at one or more possible bombs on the desk in my cabin. I couldn't believe I'd been cavorting with Eva right on top of a possible bomb. I couldn't believe I had put her in danger. Heroes didn't put people in danger; they got people out of danger. And I was a hero, wasn't I?

For that matter, I'd done quite a bit of cavorting in that very bed with various bodacious people. I'd feel terrible if any of my cavortion partners blew up.

Of course, I'd probably be blown up, too, so maybe I wouldn't feel anything.

"Jack!" Eva tugged on my arm.

"What?" I asked.

"I've been trying to get your attention for several minutes now."

I shook my head. "Sorry. What?"

"I said we should call security to secure the possible bombs." She pointed at the mysterious objects now resting seemingly innocently on my desk.

"Sure, right," I said. "Let me call Ted." I dialed him up on my fon.

He answered right away. "Jack? Great minds think alike. I'm outside your cabin. Are you there?"

I heard a knocking sound. "Come in," I said. The door whisked open.

At the same time, Eva said, "Jack, wait."

I turned to look at her. "What?"

She gestured at her beautiful body. "Naked."

Ah. So was I. Oops. I turned towards the doorway.

Ted stood there with his lovely long eyelashes and

disappointment in his eyes. "Aw. You started without me."

"Sorry, buddy," Eva said. "That's not why we called you." She pointed at the desk. "We have some mysterious objects. We're not sure what they are. And considering what just happened in the cargo bay..."

"Bombs," I said.

Ted jerked back. "What!"

Eva shook her head. "We don't know what they are. But we don't want to take any chances with Old Jack's belongings after what happened to Daniel."

Ted seemed depressed that there would be no immediate cavorting with Eva and me. I couldn't blame him. Poor guy. "I guess I can put them in a stasis field." He turned. "I'll be right back."

Eva frowned. "For future reference, I generally don't get naked in front of junior officers."

"I'm a junior officer, aren't I?" I leaned in for a kiss. "Are you saying you don't enjoy getting naked with me?" Her lips pressed against mine, her body pressed against mine. We fit together like we were made for one another. "Mmm. *Speak low if you speak love*." I lost all track of time.

"Mmm," Eva said in return when we came up for breath. "Ready for round two, huh? I'm not sure we have time."

"Oh, I can be quick," I said. But something was awry. Not all of me was enjoying itself.

"I'm not sure quick is something to brag about," she said. "But, hmm." She looked down. "Maybe the FTL drive is on."

"Yes! That must be it!" We separated, and I tried to gather my thoughts. But I kept focusing on Eva's smooth skin, luscious lips, and curvaceous hips...

"So?" she asked. "Is it your special skill? What did you wish?"

"Uh." I couldn't concentrate. I really needed to make a list of wishes so I'd be ready when this happened.

Someone knocked on the door.

"Come in," I said. The door opened.

"Jack!" Eva said.

It was Ted again. He stepped inside. "So, you didn't get dressed?"

"Sorry," Eva reached for her clothes.

I needed a wish. Quick. A wish. Super quick. Somehow, telling myself to think quickly did not result in quick thoughts.

"So, I'll put these things in a stasis field, then." Ted leaned over the desk with some device.

"I wish nothing blows up!" I said.

The three of us looked at each other.

"Did it work?" Eva said.

"Or, maybe the stasis field stopped it," Ted said, glancing at his fon. "Oh, wait. I'm not sure the stasis field was completed."

"Or, it wasn't ever going to blow up," Eva said.

"Or, my wish wasn't outlandish enough," I said. "I wish I knew more about Old Jack." Was that outlandish?

One of the items on the desk began to float up in the air.

"Ack!" Ted jerked back.

"Did the stasis field do that?" Eva asked, now fully dressed. (Darn.)

It spun around, a strange whistling sound emanating from it.

"Definitely not. It's not the stasis field. They don't make things move around. They put things in, well, stasis, which means not moving around." Ted took a step towards the door.

"Jack," Eva asked. "Did you do that?" She gestured at the whistling, spinning, floating thing.

What was it doing? I shook my head. "I don't think so. I don't know."

We all took steps away from the desk.

The item in question started emitting some type of strange smoke.

Oh, no! It was a bomb! "Bomb!"

"Oh my God!" Ted ran towards the door. It whisked open. He ran out into the hall.

Eva and I followed him. The door whisked closed after us.

Ted started talking into his comms. "Security alert in Jack Jones' cabin!"

The three of us froze, staring at the closed cabin door.

"Maybe we should move further away," Eva said.

"Security's coming," Ted said.

We moved away from my cabin, still staring at the door.

Commander Lu rushed up. "You reported another bomb,

Ensign?" he asked Ted.

A phalanx of officers followed him. They snickered when they saw me. Really? Bombs were snicker-worthy?

Ted turned red. "I'm not sure what it is, sir. But it's inside." He pointed at my cabin.

Commander Lu calmly looked me up and down as he walked by. "You're out of uniform, Jones." He seemed unruffle-able like he could deal with anything. It was a good quality for a security commander.

I glanced down. Naked. Well, there was no help for it at this point. I smiled cockily. Let them all enjoy the view--as long as they didn't get distracted and did their important security jobs, of course.

Commander Lu approached my cabin. "Bertram, you have point." He pointed at the door. "Get ready to go on my command."

Oh, I knew Bertram. He'd helped me out before. I smiled and waved. "Hi, Bertram." Bertram's face was a bit horsey, but he was a good soul.

"Hi..." he said, with a hint of a smile as he passed me.

Commander Lu growled.

Bertram sobered. He approached the door with some kind of device. It looked like a ray-gun, with a hand grip and a flared opening at the other end. "Ready, sir."

The commander did something, and the door snicked open. "Go, go, go!"

Bertram ran inside with the device pointed in front of him.

We all peered after him.

Inside, he stopped abruptly.

"Well?" Commander Lu asked.

"I don't think it's a bomb," Bertram said.

Lu stuck his head inside my cabin. He snorted, stepped back into the hall and glared at Ted and me. "It's a hologram. Bertram, you're stuck with the paperwork." He started walking back the way they'd come. "Come on, men. False alarm." They all, except Bertram, departed.

"Thank you?" I called after them. "I appreciate your help." They were very brave. It could have been a true alarm, a bomb. They risked life and limb for me. "*There is special providence*

36

in the fall of a sparrow. If it be not now, yet it will come--the readiness is all."

They did not react to my words, just kept striding down the hall.

Bertram exited my cabin, punching buttons on his fon. "So, for the report, you called security because you thought a hologram was a bomb?" He glanced up at us.

"We didn't know it was a hologram when we called," I said.

"I guess we're a bit jumpy after what happened in the cargo bay," Ted said.

"With good reason," Eva said. "Boom."

"Yeah," I said. "Who knows how long that bomb was in the cargo bay?" Ugh. That was a horrible thought. Had the bomb been there a long time? Were we in danger without knowing it? Or had someone nefarious just placed the bomb there? Neither option was good.

"So, jumpy." Bertram continued punching buttons. "You were all jumpy."

"Can't you finish that later?" Ted asked.

We crept towards my cabin and peered inside.

Yep. Hologram. Check.

"Yeah," Bertram said. "I think so." He pocketed his fon.

Eva, Ted and I joined Bertram in my cabin.

Above one of the maybe-data-cubes was a life-sized hologram of Old Jack's head, complete with gray hair, beard and wrinkles. I would still be ruggedly handsome in my old age. He looked so real.

"Is it just me, or does that guy look like you, Jack?" Bertram asked.

Eva sighed. "It's Captain Jones."

"Oh, right," Bertram said. "The old guy that took the *Shakespeare* hostage a few weeks ago." He frowned. "He's not a good guy. Why do you have a hologram of him?"

"I do not know," I said, walking towards the desk.

"Why isn't it doing anything?" Ted asked.

"I do not know." I held my finger out and jabbed it. Holograms didn't feel like anything.

Eva said, "Maybe you shouldn't..."

It moved, and we all jerked back. "Jack, if you're seeing this,

37

you must have been successfully posted on the *Shakespeare* again. Who knew you, I, could be so successful after being decanted?"

Decanted? It made me sound like red wine or something. "I need a drink," I muttered.

"Pardon?" Old Jack's hologram said.

We all jerked back again.

"What is this thing?" Ted said.

Eva was shaking her head.

The hologram appeared to look at me. Then, it said, "Put on some clothes, Jack."

I jerked back again, but in my small cabin, there wasn't much room to jerk back into. I ended up falling on the bed. "What the hell?"

"Since when do holograms interact?" Bertram said without moving his lips like he was somehow trying to blend into the background.

"Stasis field," Eva whispered loudly, poking Ted.

"Uh, yeah," he said. "Totally." He took a device out of his pocket and pressed some buttons. A force-field surrounded each item, including the head, emitting a faint glow.

"Hello, Old Jack?" I asked experimentally.

"I think that stopped it, whatever it is," Eva said. "Jack, please get dressed."

I didn't have to be told twice, er, five times. I grabbed my clothes and pulled them on.

The four of us stared at the floating head inside the force field. My cabin was kind of small for so many people in it at once.

"What do you think it is?" Ted asked.

"It looks like a three-dimensional hologram," Bertram said.

"Yes, but I've never seen an interactive hologram before," Eva said.

I realized I didn't know much about holograms. Thirty-years ago, when my memories stopped, holograms hadn't been a big thing. And I hadn't had occasion to use any holograms since I'd been, uh, decanted. "So, this is unusual?"

Everyone nodded.

"Unlikely, even?" I asked.

They nodded again.

"Weird," Ted said.

"What do you think, Jack?" Eva asked.

I thought weird, unusual and unlikely were right up my alley. "I think it's a result of my special skill."

Chapter Six

The four of us stared at the head floating above my desk. It was surprisingly lifelike. And creepy. Lifelike floating heads were creepy.

"So what now?" Bertram asked.

"Holograms don't blow up, do they?" I asked.

Eva shook her head a little. "Not usually."

"I've never heard of it," Ted said.

"Remove the force field from the head," I said.

"Are you sure?" Bertram asked.

No. "Yes."

Bertram punched some buttons.

The glowy energy field faded.

"Hello?" I asked. "Jack?"

"Hello," it said, frowning. "Jack? Ah, good. You got dressed."

We all jerked back.

"What is this?" it asked, twisting its head as if looking around. "How am I talking to you?"

"How am I talking to you?" I asked.

"That's what I said," it said. "Get a clue, Jack." Beneath the gray whiskers, his teeth looked fabulous, white and straight.

I resisted the urge to caress my own pearly whites and leaned towards it. "Get a clue about what? What are you?"

"What am I? What do you mean what am I?" It sputtered. "Did something go awry with the cloning process? It must have. Good grief. I was never so imbecilic."

I didn't appreciate being berated by a hologram. I straightened and looked at Bertram. "Put the force field back."

He did. The head froze.

The four of us squished onto my bed, thigh to thigh, to thigh, to thigh. It was cozy.

"What do you think is going on?" Eva asked.

"What do you think is going on?" I asked her.

She exhaled. "I don't know. I'm asking you." Her fon pinged, and she glanced at it. "I'm supposed to be on duty. I'm late. I have to go."

"*What majesty should be, what duty is, what day is day, night, night, and time is time...*"

She stood up, ignoring my excellent Hamlet quote. "Let me know what you figure out." She exited.

"*Brevity is the soul of wit,*" I said under my breath.

Bertram said, "I don't think that means what you think it means. I played Polonius a few years back and--" He shut up.

When I glanced up, Ted was glaring at him. "So, anyway," Ted said.

I was tired of feeling confused. "Turn off the force field."

Bertram did so.

"Okay, Old Jack, where are you?" I asked.

"I'm in a TCC prison on Earth," he said slowly. "Why? Where do you think I am?"

"Where do you think I am?" I asked.

"I can see you're in my cabin on the *Shakespeare.*"

Ted and Bertram gasped. What were they so worked up about?

"So," I said. "You're saying you are the original Jack Jones, and ...we're having instantaneous communication across the galaxy?" Okay, that was a little gasp-worthy. I didn't know technology had advanced so much.

Old Jack's face blanched. "Instantaneous? Across the galaxy?"

"That's not possible," Ted said.

"Yeah," Bertram said.

I waved my hand at Old Jack. "Clearly it is."

"But how?" Old Jack said.

Can you say 'special skill'? "Who cares! I have a bone to pick with you! You just blew up Daniel and the cargo bay, you fiend!"

"Daniel's dead?" Old Jack's face crumpled. "Oh no. Poor Daniel."

41

"What do you mean 'poor Daniel?' *O villain, villain, smiling, damned villain!*"

Were those tears in his eyes? "I didn't do anything to Daniel or the cargo bay," he said, blinking. "Daniel was my friend, a good friend. I wouldn't blow him up." A holographic hand reached up and wiped his holographic eyes.

I said, "*Serpent's egg...*" but my heart wasn't in it. Old Jack seemed sincerely sorry that Daniel was gone. He looked super sad. "Force field on."

Bertram turned the force field back on.

The three of us stared at each other.

"If you're talking across the galaxy, you know, that's called an ansible," Bertram said. "That would be a neat invention."

I hadn't known. I glanced at Ted. He didn't seem to know either.

"Old Jack seems kind of sincere," Ted said.

"Yeah, I know," I said.

"So...," Bertram said. "There's some other villain on board?"

"With access to the cargo bay," I said.

"Maybe we should go check in with Commander Lu," Bertram said to Ted. Not a bad idea, considering they were both security guys.

"Yeah," Ted said. They both stood up.

"Wait," I said. "Can you transfer control of the force field to my fon?"

"Yes." Bertram fiddled with his device. "There. We should go."

Ted nodded.

They left.

Alone in my cabin, I stared at Old Jack's head, frozen in the act of wiping his eyes. He looked really sad. Poor guy. I shook my head. No! He wasn't a poor guy. He was a villain.

I should tell Gina what was going on.

But based on Ted and Bertram's reactions, she probably wouldn't believe me. Apparently, technology hadn't evolved to develop instantaneous holographic communication across the galaxy.

I didn't have the energy to deal with Gina right now. She was too intense. I lay back on my bunk and stared at the ceiling.

42

A JACK IN THE DARK

I didn't understand Old Jack. Why had he turned evil? I didn't think I was evil. I didn't think I was the serpent's egg.

What if we'd been wrong about him? What if he wasn't evil, or at least not totally evil?

I wanted to understand him better.

A few weeks ago, when we'd uncovered his plot, I had the opportunity to download the missing thirty years of his memories. I'd declined. That would make me him. I didn't want to be him. I wanted to be myself.

I yawned. Cavorting really took it out of you. Next thing you knew, I'd fall asleep. That wouldn't be good. I needed to do my job.

I couldn't avoid it any longer. Gina needed to know Old Jack didn't blow up the cargo bay. I accessed the comms on my fon. "Gina?"

She answered immediately, sighing. "That's Captain Gomez to you. What do you want?"

Yikes. She sounded ...intense. "There's been a development in my cabin. Can you come down here?"

"What the hell, Jack? Are you trying to get into my pants?"

"No. Why would you say that?"

"Are you in bed right now?"

"Well, technically..."

She growled.

"Fine," I said quickly. "Don't come down to my cabin. But I need to talk to you. It's important."

"I'm on the bridge. Come. But you better not be wasting my time, Jack." She hung up.

I decided to stop at the mess hall and get her a soothing chamomile tea on my way to the bridge.

At the bridge, the door whisked open. I hadn't been on the bridge for a few weeks. It was about thirty feet square and all business. There were special control computer consoles along all the walls. The four most senior officers all manned their bridge stations. The large front viewscreen wasn't on.

On the bridge, things seemed tense. Gina, First Officer Carter (her new husband and Old Jack's former best friend), Security Commander Lu, and Chief Engineer Bello all turned and practically snarled when I entered the room. Yikes. I should have

43

brought more tea.

I approached Gina. "Here. I brought you a soothing chamomile tea." I held out the cup.

Her face smoothed a little as she took it. "Thanks." She took a sip and seemed to relax a bit. "What's up?"

"I don't think Old Jack was responsible for the explosion in the cargo bay," I said.

She glanced at the other officers, who still seemed snarly. "Ah. Back to work, men." More softly, she said to me, "Why do you say that?"

"Uh." How to put it? "It has to do with my special skill."

"Do I want to hear this story?"

"Probably not."

She stared at me for a few moments and then exhaled. "Okay." She turned to Lu. "I think we need to issue a security alert."

"Yes, Captain, ma'am." He didn't ask any questions or anything. "Right away, ma'am." Wow. That was probably how you were supposed to do things.

He punched some keys on his console, and the red alarm lights started flashing. "Security alert," the comm system said calmly. "Security alert." I suppressed a yawn.

Carter said, "Should we emerge from FTL space?" Ah ha. The FTL drive was on. That's why the front screen wasn't on.

"Security alert," the ship's comms system alerted us.

"If an intruder is aboard, regular space is much easier to escape into," Lu said.

Commander Bello glared at me a bit before turning to Gina and saying, "Ready for your orders, ma'am." Even glaring, he wasn't bad looking. Frankly, I was surprised he was still mad at me. Who wouldn't want to look younger?

"Security alert. Security alert," the alert said.

"Turn the alert volume down a little," Gina said. It quieted. Carter said, "FTL?"

"No, don't leave FTL space," Gina said. "Maintain course."

"Where are we going again?" I asked.

"To our next planet," she said.

"Which is?"

She ground her teeth.

44

"Maybe drink some more tea," I said helpfully.

She took a sip and relaxed a little more. "Yeblypso. We have a new show."

I didn't yell 'yay' or jump up and down. It didn't seem dignified enough for the bridge. I wondered what the show was. I wondered what my part was. Something big, no doubt.

She looked at me. "I know you want to know what your part is. But put a pin in it. I have another idea."

I decided to take a page from Lu's book. "Yes, ma'am?"

"I need you to do your uniquely Jack thing and go around the ship and see if you can discover anything out of the ordinary."

"Yes, ma'am." I saluted her.

She wrinkled her brow. "What's that supposed to be?"

"Uh. I had an itch."

And, then, she smiled a little.

Nice. I felt myself smile in return.

All right. I liked this mission. Be uniquely Jack. I could do that.

But the rest of the bridge crew still seemed grumpy.

I would be uniquely Jack right after I got the rest of them some soothing chamomile tea.

Chapter Seven

After I brought the bridge crew some soothing tea, I decided to stop and get myself some caffeinated coffee. That would put a stop to my yawning.

Once that mission was successful, I started wandering around the ship. 'Do my unique Jack thing' was pretty vague. What did Gina want?

The ghost mural outside engineering caught my eye. How did they make the ramparts of Elsinore Castle so spooky? I leaned close to get a better look. It almost looked three-dimensional. Was there such a thing as holographic paint? Was the moon glowing in the background? I leaned closer. Were the creepy clouds coming out of the wall? I held my hand up. There seemed to be some mysterious mist in front of it. "Wow." It was very faint and only about a cubic foot in volume, but I saw it.

Up above my head, I heard a moan or maybe a muffled voice.

I jerked back. Unfortunately, I jerked right into Olivia as she was exiting engineering. My coffee ended up all over my shirt.

"Hey!" she said. "Please watch where you're going. What's wrong with you?" I didn't know what she was so upset about; she wasn't covered in coffee.

"Do you see smoke or something?" I asked.

She looked around the hall. "Maybe. It's a little hazy..." She coughed.

"No, up there, near the ghost," I said. "On the wall."

"What?"

"Did you just hear something?" I pointed up at the ghost mural. "I think I just heard the ghost say something."

She didn't look up; she gave me a pitying look. "So, you did get injured when you were kidnapped? They hit you in the head? I'm sorry." She scrunched up her nose. "Is it brain damage?" She rubbed my arm gently. I didn't appreciate her rude attitude, but her fingers on my arm were pretty nice.

"What?" I said. "No, I don't have brain damage. And that's not very nice."

Her eyebrows raised like she was surprised. Then, she said, "No, I guess you're right. I was joking. But it wasn't funny. Sorry."

I heard another moan and very quietly, "Mark me."

"Ack!" I shrieked.

Olivia stared at me. "Are you absolutely sure about the brain damage?"

"Didn't you hear that?" I pointed up. "It said 'Mark me.'"

"No, I didn't hear it." She smiled at me like I was an idiot. "But I can take you to the medical bay if you want."

"No." I pulled my arm out of her grasp. "Never mind." I waved my hand. "Just go about your business, please."

"Okay." She turned and walked away.

How could she just walk away like that? There was a fascinating mystery here. I stared up at the ghost. "Uh, sir, could you repeat that?"

Unfortunately, he didn't say anything else. I stared up at him for a while. No more talking. Not even any more moaning. If there had been clouds in the hall, they were gone now.

I got a lot of odd looks while standing there staring up at the ghost on the wall.

It was hard, even for me, to see how a talking ghost or some clouds could assist the crew in finding Daniel's murderer or do anything else helpful.

I yawned.

Okay. Enough of this. I started walking back to my cabin to change my shirt.

Unfortunately, when I got to my cabin, the force-fielded holographic Old Jack was not there. "Damn!" I looked on the floor, in all the drawers, and, yes, even under the bed. No sign of him or the mysterious cubes Eva'd helped me find. They had been right here on my desk. "I've been robbed!"

I looked in the secret passageway connected to my cabin. Nothing.

I tried the secret compartment Eva had found, but I couldn't get it open. "Damn."

I sat down on my bed. I took off my shirt.

I was still tired. Probably because I didn't get to drink my coffee. I lay back on my bed. What should I do next? What would a spy do? What would Old Jack do? Sadly, I had no idea what Old Jack would do.

Young-Jack was going to uniquely ask his good friend Ted what he thought he should do. I called him on my fon.

"Hey, Jack," he said. "How's it going? Have you and Old Jack been having a nice chat?"

"Not exactly," I said. "I went to the bridge and--"

"Oh, I knew that," he said. "Commander Bello stopped by and was in a much better mood than earlier. He said you brought him some tea. He said maybe you weren't an ass-- Uh, I mean..."

"Never mind all that," I said. "I've been robbed."

"Oh, no. When?"

"Just now, here on the ship."

"On the ship? Oh, no. What'd they take?"

"Well, they took Old Jack and the data cubes."

"Oh, no!" My friend Ted sounded genuinely concerned for me. He was a good guy. But I was getting a little tired of his 'oh nos.' He was a security professional. He should have some security ideas, like looking at the surveillance recordings.

"Do you think we could look at the surveillance recordings to see if anyone accessed my cabin this afternoon?" I asked.

"I was just about to suggest that," he said. "Yeah. Come to the security station near the brig, and we'll look."

"Sounds good." We hung up.

A little later, dressed in a clean, dry shirt and with a new unspilled cup of coffee, I arrived at the security station. I, of course, brought my buddy Ted a hot, invigorating cup of coffee. I was thoughtful like that.

"Wow." He seemed happy to get it if his smile was any indication. He was handsome when he smiled. His whole self seemed to light up; I was reminded of Oberon. I could imagine Ted playing Oberon. "Thanks!" He carefully took a sip.

"Be careful not to spill it," I said, very carefully taking my own sip.

After completing that minor mission successfully, I said, "Okay. Can we look at the security feed from right outside my cabin?"

Ted said, "I already queued it up." He pressed a button on his console. A holographic view of the hallway outside my cabin appeared. The door snicked open, and a small me came out and rushed down the corridor. I looked good.

I said, "I look good."

"Yeah, you do," he said. What a good friend. We smiled at each other.

We went back to watching the recording. People walked by my cabin. Back and forth. Sometimes alone, sometimes in a group. And on and on. Nothing else happened.

I yawned. "Can we speed it up?"

"Your wish is my command." He grinned.

Now we watched holos of people walking by quickly. Yawn.

"Well, this is boring," I said.

Ted diplomatically said nothing.

"No thieves, no brigands, no pirates," I said. "Can you speed it up some more?"

Now people zoomed past. No one stopped at my cabin. No one broke in. No one even waltzed in with a key.

Until a handsome man with a stained shirt rushed up. "Slow it down."

"That's you, isn't it?"

"Yes." I felt my brow furrow. "I don't get it. When I went into my cabin, Old Jack's head was gone."

"Huh," he said. "Yeah. That's weird because no one went in while you were gone."

The two of us stared at the empty corridor.

"What happened to your shirt?" Ted asked, pointing at the screen.

"Ooh!" We could look outside engineering and see if there was a cloud. "Can you reverse back to the same time frame and watch outside engineering?"

"Why would we do that?" he asked.

"I thought I saw something suspicious there."

49

"In that case, yes, we can!" He monkeyed with the controls for a few moments.

Then we were looking at a holo of the corridor outside engineering. People walked by. People entered engineering.

And, then, I arrived. I stood around for a few minutes, then jerked back and stared at the mural. I pointed at the image. "Do you see anything weird there?"

"Besides, you staring at the wall for no reason?" Ted squinted. "Weird, how?"

Olivia and I collided, and my coffee ended up all over my shirt.

"Spilling coffee isn't that weird."

"No." I leaned my head down and peered at the mural. "Near the wall. Do you see fog or something?"

Ted peered as well.

"Can you make it any bigger?" I asked.

"I can try."

"Zoom in on the wall."

We zoomed in. Zoom, zoom. It did look fuzzy. "There! That! Is that fog?" I thought I saw about a cubic foot of white-ish smoke.

Ted stared. "I'm not sure. It's blurry, but that might be because we're at the resolution limit."

"Bummer," I said. "I'm not sure, either." I leaned back. This was all seeming suspiciously like a dead end.

"Even if the environmental controls were messed up, how does that help us?" he asked.

I shook my head. "Good question." But my intuition was telling me there was something here. "What if it wasn't the environmental controls?" I did not say, 'What if it was a real-live (real-dead?) ghost?'

He shrugged. "So, who do you think stole Old Jack's head?"

I sighed. "I don't know. Are there any invisible species that can enter and exit a cabin without opening the door?" Oh, wait a minute...

"The door isn't the only way into my cabin," I said. "Let's check the entrances to the secret tunnel system."

"Okay. But you'll have to tell me where they are."

I did so, and we watched some of the secret tunnel

entrances. "Speed up." There was nothing to see. Until we switched to the disembarkation lounge. "Wait. Is that hatch open a little?" I pointed at the holo. "Do you see something?"

Ted zoomed it bigger. "Is that smoke?" He stared. "Could that be from the cargo bay explosion? I didn't hear anything about a new fire. Maybe there is something wrong with the environmental system or the air scrubbers."

The smoke, or whatever it was, was moving around the room in a cloud. Now it was more like a cubic yard in size and stretched out into a smoke stream as it moved around. "Slow it down."

We watched.

It flowed around the lounge to the tunnel entrance. Then the smoke flowed into the tunnel, like, well, smoke. And then, somehow, the hatch closed behind it.

"What the hell?" Ted whispered.

"It's like it's some kind of smoke-monster." I paused. *"We're all spirits, and are melted into air, into thin air. We are such stuff as dreams are made on. . ."*

"Could it be sentient?" he asked.

I shook my head. "It's sure acting sentient." I stared at it. Hello, Mr. Smoke-monster.

51

Chapter Eight

Smoke-monsters couldn't just steal my ansible and get away with it! I turned to Ted as we stood in the security station. "Let's get it!"

"Ah." He stared at me. "I'm not sure how to get a smoke-creature."

"Well, don't look at me. I don't know," I said. "You're the security officer. Surely, there's some weapon or protocol or something." I glanced around the security area. I could see the brig but no weapons caches or anything similar.

He raised his eyebrows high up his forehead but turned back to his computer terminal and started typing.

I resisted the urge to say, 'Hurry up, already.' I also resisted the urge to get some soothing chamomile for myself.

After a few interminable moments, he grunted and then said, "Huh. There is a special weapon." He pointed at the screen. "A disruptor. It's for vaporous creatures." The pictured disruptor looked like a shallow bowl with a handle on it.

Who knew vaporous creatures were a thing? "Cool," I said. "Let's get a couple and go after that thing."

He stood. "There's a weapons locker here at this station." He strode to the wall and did some complicated pressing thing, and a panel popped open. I would have never known there was something special about that panel if I hadn't just seen it.

He stuck his head in and rummaged around. He grunted.

I walked over. "Do you need some help there, buddy?"

He leaned out and looked at me with puppy-dog eyes. "Buddy?"

Was buddy bad? "Sorry." I gave him my most mesmerizing smile. "Do you need some help there, lover?"

He smiled back. "No. I got it. And technically, only security is supposed to have access to the weapons lockers." He returned to his task.

That piqued my curiosity. I stepped closer and stared inside. Every kind of weapon I could imagine was in there, and many I hadn't imagined yet. "What's that?" I reached for what looked like a gelatinous sparkly sack. "Is that a weapon?"

Ted slapped my hand away. "Top secret."

Reluctantly, I pulled my hand back. "How many of these weapons lockers are on the ship?"

"Oh, they're all over." He grunted. "It's a security measure. Readily accessible weapons are a good thing. You know this is a ship of spies--or did you forget? Here." He pulled out two of the dish weapons and handed me one. Then, he frowned. "Technically, only security officers are supposed to have access to weapons."

"I won't tell a soul," I promised immediately. I made a cross gesture over my heart.

"What's that?" he asked. "Why are you pointing at your chest? I mean, it's a nice chest and all, but..."

"Cross my heart and hope to die?" Huh. Kind of morbid.

"What?" He pressed the weapons hatch closed.

I guessed my childhood nursery rhymes weren't popular in his childhood, thirty or so years later. It was hard to remember that even though we were both nineteen, my nineteen years were significantly different from his nineteen years. "Never mind."

I turned and faced the hall. "Can we go? Or do you have to check in or something? You're on duty, aren't you?"

"Yes." He nodded. "I'll say I'm doing a security sweep. Captain Gomez's security alert hasn't been lifted yet." He went back to his console while I stood near the hallway, impatient. I shifted my weight from foot to foot. I lifted the weapon and stared at it. How the heck did this thing work? In the background, I was dimly aware of Ted talking to someone.

I flicked the red switch on the handle. I pressed the trigger.

A creaking sound came from the brig area. Then there was a deafening clang as a dozen bars crashed on the ground, leaving a huge gaping hole in the brig.

The dish portion of my weapon had been pointing at the

bars. Oops.

I flicked the switch off and tried to look casual. Gosh. Did something happen?

"Wha--what?" Ted sputtered. "What did you do?" He approached the brig, or, I guessed, it wasn't too briggy now-- what with the giant hole. He approached the former brig.

I walked over and put my arm around his shoulders. "Have I told you lately how great I think you are, lover?" I leaned over and planted a delicious kiss on his lips.

We both got into kissing for a few moments. I had half a mind to forget all this and take Ted back to my cabin.

When we separated, he said, "What was I saying?"

"I believe you were saying an intrusive, illegal vaporous creature flew through the brig area, and we attempted to shoot it with our disruptors." I smiled.

"Yes." He smiled back. "I was saying that."

We both turned and charged down the hall, disruptors raised.

"*Once more unto the breach, dear friends, once more!*" we said together as we ran.

"You realize this means we need to catch the creature, or I'm screwed, right?" he added. "And not in a good way."

I hadn't thought that far. "Of course." Our feet pounded the floor of the corridor in unison.

The disembarkation lounge was empty of crew, thank goodness. We wasted no time running to the secret tunnel hatch and entering said secret tunnel. I should probably quit calling it a secret tunnel at this point because who didn't know about it? I sneezed as Ted closed the hatch behind us. The non-secret tunnels still had a lot of dust in them.

"Now what?" he whispered.

"Now we find it," I whispered back, taking in the dimly-lit metal walls, floor and ceiling. The tunnel was like a giant duct. For all I knew, that's what it was.

He opened his eyes wide as if to say, 'How?'

I closed my eyes. I tried to do my uniquely-Jack thing. If I was a smoke-monster, where would I go? I started walking, holding the disruptor out in front of me. I sped up in a straight line. At some point in there, I opened my eyes. I recognized this

54

route. It led to the cargo bay. "Cargo bay," I whispered.

We raced to the cargo bay.

"Have you ever wondered why these tunnels have lights?" Ted whispered.

"No," I whispered. "Not until now."

"Why are these tunnels even here?"

"I guess, in case maintenance needs access to ...something." It was a spy ship. Who the heck knew why they did anything?

Ahead of us, I thought I saw a wisp of smoke. "Do you see something? Up ahead?"

"Maybe."

I hurried. Ted hurried after me.

As we approached the cargo bay, a cloud of smoke filled the tunnel ahead of us.

"Stop, brigand!" I yelled.

"Yeah, brigand!" Ted yelled. "Stop! Or we'll shoot."

We both held up our disruptors.

"Ack! No, please. Don't shoot," it said in a surprising Terran British accent. It still looked like a cloud of white-ish smoke.

Ted and I jerked back.

"It talks?" Ted said.

"In a British accent?" I said.

"Of course, I talk," it said. "What kind of person do you think I am?" It was getting closer and closer to the cargo bay hatch.

Ted and I glanced at each other. "Uh," I said. Clearly, we had no idea what kind of person it was.

The next thing we knew, it flowed through the fine mesh grate at the top of the cargo bay hatch.

My missing data cubes, or whatever they were, clattered to the tunnel floor. So that was one mystery solved. The smoke-creature stole my stuff.

"Yay," Ted said.

I leaned down and scooped them up. "Yeah, yay."

"Does the hologram thing of your sort-of dad still work?" he said.

"Good question." I started to fiddle with the holo-cube but stopped. "We need to catch that creature, don't we?"

"Oh, right." He popped the hatch and scuttled out.

Unfortunately, a diffuse layer of gray-ish smoke hung in the cargo bay air. If it was the smoke-creature we'd been chasing, it looked different. The rest of the cargo bay looked the same as it had earlier: a bunch of boxes of various sizes overlaid with explosion.

"What's with all the smoke?" He coughed a bit. "Is this still from the explosion?"

"I don't know," I said. "You'd think the air scrubbers would have cleared it out by now."

"Do you think it could be the creature?" he asked. "Spread out?"

"I don't know. Creature?" I called out. It had responded to a threat before. "*This misshapen knave--His mother was a witch... Thee have robb'd me, and this demi-devil--for he's a bastard...*"

I stopped talking and listened.

Nothing.

"*This thing of darkness...*" I said.

"It doesn't seem to be working," Ted said.

"Shh!" I listened some more.

I thought I heard something, a rustling or hissing, over on the far side of the cargo bay. "This way." We crept over. As we approached, the sound resolved itself into the sound of crying.

"It's crying?" Ted asked. "It's not a very good brigand if it's crying, is it?"

We crept around a last grouping of boxes and found an old man sitting there on a container, crying his eyes out. He had pure white hair, a craggy face, and a big nose--which was now quite red. Slumped over, he held his face in his hands.

I knew the guy. It was Bill, Daniel's partner in crime. Aw. He must be missing Daniel. "Are you all right?"

Ted walked up to him and poked his shoulder.

Bill jerked away. "What the hell?" he said through his tears.

"Relax, Ted," I said. "It's Bill. He works here in the cargo bay."

"I know it looks like Bill, and it sounds like Bill, but how do we know it's Bill?" Ted asked.

Was he implying a smoke-creature could impersonate Bill? "Uh..." I said.

"Who the hell else would I be, asshole?" Bill demanded.

I was getting a bad feeling. For Bill. "Uh, what's wrong, Bill? Are you okay?"

"No. I'm not okay!" He definitely seemed angry. "Daniel just died. He was blown to smithereens!"

Aw. Poor guy. Now here was a guy that needed some soothing chamomile tea. "I'm so sorry for your loss, Bill." I gave Ted my disruptor and walked to Bill, holding my arms out. "Do you need a hug?"

He squinted at me, grimacing, and shook his head. "Hell, no. Get away from me."

"Why are you so worked up?" Ted asked. "If you don't mind me asking, sir?"

"I mind," Bill said. "And why wouldn't I be worked up? He was my dad."

But Bill was old, and Daniel was young. Time stood still for a moment as I tried to process this new info. Suddenly, Old Jack's remark that he and Daniel had been friends made much more sense. They must have been contemporaries. When time resumed, my mouth was hanging open.

"I don't get it," Ted was saying.

"Daniel was in a clone body," I said. "Right?"

"Yeah," Bill said.

"Well, shit!" Ted stamped his foot. "How many damn clones are on this ship, anyway?"

Now it was Bill's turn to look surprised. "I don't know. How many?"

"Daniel was the only one," I said carefully. Ted did know I was in a clone body, right? But it was supposed to be a secret, right?

"And Eva," Ted said.

Oh, right. "Are we allowed to talk about that?" I'd lost track of whose cloneness was a secret and whose wasn't.

"Didn't I hear something about Dylan Bello?" Bill asked.

Oops. "And Dylan," I said.

When I glanced at Ted, it almost seemed like he was glaring at me. But he wouldn't do that, would he?

"Anyway, I think we're getting a little off-course," I said. "We were pursuing a smoke-creature, a vaporous entity. Did you see it?"

"An intruder?" Bill asked. "Is that what the security alert was about?"

"Uh," I said. "Yes."

He jumped to his feet. "Did this vaporous entity blow up my dad?"

Chapter Nine

Bertram appeared around one of the cargo boxes. "I thought I heard talking. What are you guys doing here?"

Ted stood up straight. It was cute how he tried to impress his co-worker. "We were pursuing a vaporous entity," he said.

"Here?" Bertram asked. "In the cargo bay?"

"It blew up my dad!" Bill said.

I held up my hands. "We don't know for sure that it's responsible for the bomb."

Ted had stepped closer to Bertram. "What are you doing here?" he asked quietly.

"We're still finishing up the, ah..." Bertram glanced at Bill. "Ah, crime scene," he said equally quietly. Then, more loudly, "But if you've detected an intruder, we need to find him."

"It," Ted said.

"Or he, or she," I said. I didn't know much about aliens, but I did know their voices didn't necessarily indicate gender. A while back on Alpha Catoblepas, I'd discovered the ACs--including the women--had very deep voices. It was particularly jarring since they resembled large mice. I shuddered a little. I don't know why, but it freaked me out.

Bertram was already fingering his fon. "Sir, Ted says he pursued an intruder, a vaporous entity, into the cargo bay," he said into it.

Some squawking came out in reply.

"Yes, we're in the cargo bay. In the back." Bertram paused. "Yes, sir." He hung up. "They're coming."

In seconds, Commander Lu came running around the boxes of cargo, with a bunch of other uniformed security guys and gals running after him.

I sighed. There was something attractive about a person in uniform...

Commander Lu said, "Which way did this intruder go, Ted?"

"Uh..." Ted sort of stuttered. "I'm, uh, not sure, sir."

Lu stared at him and then turned his headlight eyes to me. They bored into mine. Yikes.

"Uh..." I said, withering under the glare. He was intimidating; I wasn't afraid to admit it--to myself.

"You guys didn't pass us," Bertram said. "So...?"

"How'd you get in here?" Bill asked.

"Over here." Ted ran over to the tunnel entrance. "The creature flowed through the mesh here."

I was still trapped in the headlights.

Finally, Lu looked in Ted's direction. "How long ago was this?"

"I, uh, don't know," he said. "A few minutes."

"Spread out, men," Lu said. "Good job, Ted."

Ted beamed.

"Do you want to join the search?" Lu asked.

"Yes, sir," Ted said. He did everything but salute.

"What about you, Jack?" Lu turned his focus back to me.

"Uh..."

"Maybe you should leave it to the professionals?"

"Okay," I managed to eke out.

"I'll take that, then." Lu reached for the disruptor, and I let him take it.

"And when you find it, you're going to kill it, right?" Bill asked.

Lu frowned. "We'll see."

The four of them turned and followed the other security guys creeping about, pointing some detectors in front of them.

"So, I'll just go, then?" I said.

Ted said, "Yeah, see you later, Jack," without even turning around.

I muttered, "*Yet I should kill thee with much cherishing*," as I stalked for the door. I guessed the honeymoon with Ted was over.

My mood got even darker as I passed through the charred area of the bay. It smelled of burned hopes and dreams, and things on the floor crunched under my feet. It smelled of death. Poor Daniel.

I rushed back to my cabin.

I went in and whooshed the door closed behind me.

"All right." I was ready to get more answers out of Old Jack. I carefully set all the data cubes on my desk and stood over them. "Okay." I stood there some more.

Nothing happened.

How had I initiated it before? "I wish I knew more about Old Jack."

I stared at the items on the desk.

Nothing happened.

Had the smoke-monster broken it? Or...

I had a bad feeling. Maybe the ansible only worked when we were in FTL space? Had we come out of FTL space? I knew one way to find out. I ran out my cabin door.

In the hall, I stopped and turned around and ran back inside. Hadn't I learned anything today? I probably shouldn't leave mysterious and desirable tech out in my cabin. "So much for becoming a better spy." I went over to the area of the secret compartment Eva had found. After I had pressed a bunch on the wall panels, it snicked open. I put the cubes inside and closed it.

I ran out of my cabin, through the halls, to the bridge. I barged onto the bridge.

Gina was talking on the comms. "Yes, Commander Lu. Apprehend the suspect. Hold him for questioning."

The huge viewscreen showed a beautiful tableau of a star surrounded by planets. "Damn." So, not in FTL space; check.

"Setting a course for Planet Yeblypso, Captain," Carter said.

Gina turned around and looked at me. "Oh, all right! I'll tell you about the new show. It's *Hair*. Lu told me what just happened, by the way. Good job with the 'uniquely Jack' thing."

"*Hair*?" I was so surprised I hardly reveled in the praise--or at least not very much. "Is that dignified enough for us?"

"You're asking about dignity?" She chuckled. "I thought you'd be all over it, considering the nudity."

"Well, I am awesome in the nude." I smiled at her. "Are you going to be in it? That would be awesome, as well."

She blushed. Our intimidating powerful captain was

blushing.

I felt my smile spread further across my face. She looked sexy and beautiful. Suddenly, I saw what Old Jack must have seen in her.

"Ah, no," she said, clearing her throat. "So, ah, anyway, your part is..."

Say, Claude.

"Claude," she finished.

"Yes!" I said. I threw my fists in the air. I was so going to rock Claude.

"No!" Carter said. I twisted around to look at him. "That's my part."

"I need you here on the bridge, Carter," Gina said. "Jack's not good for anything but performing."

"Hey!" I said.

"Performing." Commander Bello snickered at his station.

"I'm good for lots of things," I said.

"Nothing useful," Bello muttered.

"I don't think sex counts," Gina said.

"What!" Carter jumped up.

Gina blushed some more.

I smiled.

"I just mean your secret spy skills leave something to be desired," she said.

"I'm a good shot," I said. "You can ask Ander." He'd been shocked at how good a shot I was, frankly.

"Your hand-to-hand combat skills are pathetic," Gina said.

"What!" Carter said. "How would you know?"

"I said hand-to-hand combat, not whatever sex thing you're thinking about." Gina looked at him. "I'm the captain; I need to know about people's skills. Eva told me."

Aw. Eva said I was pathetic? I felt my lower lip jut out.

"You need to relax, Carter," Gina said. "You're not acting like a first officer. You're acting like a jealous husband." She glanced my way. "I didn't act like that when I was first officer."

Carter still didn't look happy. He still hadn't sat down. "Maybe your captain wasn't so interested in crewmembers' sex lives and hand skills."

That didn't make sense. Old Jack, Gina's captain, was

sleeping with her, and Carter knew that. Poor Carter. He was irrational and jealous of me. And with good reason. Who wouldn't be? I darted over to him and wrapped my arms around him. After a few seconds, he seemed to relax into it. "It's all right, Carter. You're very sexy." I moved my head back and looked into his eyes. I puckered my lips and leaned in...

"Oh, good grief!" he pushed me away. "Not everyone wants to have sex with you, Jack!"

"That's what I said," Bello said.

I threw him a glance. I wasn't sure that was entirely true in his case. "I was just being friendly. I'm a friendly guy."

Gina shook her head a little and then smiled widely, looking at the two men. "Yeah, Carter. He's a friendly guy." She was clearly needling him.

"Get off the bridge, Jones!" Carter said. "I outrank you. Off. The. Bridge."

Gina laughed. "Go work out with Eva."

That did sound fun. I liked working out with Eva. I turned to the door.

"I mean hand-to-hand combat," Gina said. "If you can't take care of yourself, we might leave you with the kidnappers next time."

Yikes. That didn't sound very friendly.

And next time? Why assume I was going to get kidnapped again?

The gym was mostly empty. Considering it was one of the largest open spaces on the ship, that meant there was a lot of empty. Two built guys I didn't recognize were lifting weights in the back. I almost went over and introduced myself, but Gina was pretty clear about my orders. Work now, play later.

Eva was punching a big bag hanging from the ceiling.

Punch, punch, punch.

"Wow. What did that bag ever do to you?"

"What do you want? I'm busy, Jack."

I couldn't believe it. She was acting like she wasn't happy to see me. "Have I said lately how beautiful and sexy you are?"

She stopped punching. "No."

"And what an awesome teacher you are?"

She smiled. "Go on."

"The best hand-to-hand combat teacher for light years. The sexiest, most beautiful self-defense teacher for parsecs."

"Your kidnapping finally scared you enough to get serious about combat training?" She put her hands on her hips. "Or, Gina made you come?"

Or, both. But I wasn't about to admit that. "You drew me to you like..."

"Yeah, yeah, simmer down, lover-boy," she said, but she said it with a grin. "I'll whip you into shape in no time."

At the word 'whip,' our eyes met. Hers were twinkling.

"I leave myself in your capable hands," I said, twinkling right back.

Sadly, after all that talk of lover-boys and whipping, my work-out session with Eva just ended up being a bunch of hard work: hold, release, avoid, redirect, strike, and the like. Over and over.

After hours of effort, I was exhausted. I lay back on one of the workout mats in the gym, panting.

On the bright side, she lay panting next to me. "Huh," she said. "I'm a little surprised. Have you been practicing after all?"

"No." Breathe in. Breathe out. My whole body ached.

"You're so much better than that first session weeks ago. If I didn't know better, I'd say you were a black belt. You're clearly out of practice, but the skills and muscle memory seem to be there."

"Huh." Gradually, my breathing was evening out. "So, I'm not pathetic, after all?" I raised one eyebrow as I checked her out.

She had the grace to look a little embarrassed. She sat up and threw a towel at me. "Maybe not completely pathetic. I think you're almost ready for space karate."

I sat up and wiped some sweat off. "Space karate sounds awesome! How does that work? Is it in zero-g?"

She tried to keep a straight face but burst out laughing.

Aw. "So, no space karate?"

She shook her head as she kept laughing, slapping her palm against the mat.

Her good humor was a little contagious. It was nice to see such pure happiness. I couldn't help smiling.

Finally, her chortling wound down.

"Ander said a similar thing about my shooting," I said. "That I was surprisingly good." I paused. "Since you're a clone, can I ask you a clone question?"

"Shh!" She said, but there was no one near us in the gym to hear.

"You're a c-l-o-n-e."

She shook her head.

"Sorry," I said. "Is that secret?"

She nodded.

"Don't you remember all your hard-earned skills?" I asked quietly.

"Yes. But that's just it. I remember." She gave me a long look. "You don't have Old Jack's memories, so what's going on with you?"

That was a good question. I lay back down to consider it.

It was mysterious.

But maybe it was a mystery for another time. I glanced over at her. "*When the moon is in the Seventh House*," I sang. I'd done my work. I wanted to play.

"What?" she asked.

I grinned and waggled my eyebrows. "*And Jupiter aligns with Mars. Then peace will guide the planets and love will steer the stars...*"

Chapter Ten

Things were just getting really interesting with Eva in my cabin when my fon chimed.

She froze. Unfortunately. "Aren't you going to get that?"

I nuzzled her neck. "I wasn't planning on it," I whispered.

Chime, chime, chime. It seemed to be getting louder.

Eva sighed. "Do I have to tell you we're not on vacation? We all have to pitch in. We have jobs. We're supposed to be making the galaxy safer for Terrans."

Chime. Chime. Chime!

I felt a little bad. She had a good point, a very good point. I got out of bed (damn!) and answered my fon.

"Jack?" It was Bill. "You're on the duty roster for the cargo bay." A swarm of unpleasant replies flocked through my brain, but the poor guy had just lost his dad. So, I said only, "Oh?"

"Yeah. Can you come down and help me clean up the, ah, incident?" He sounded like he might start crying again any second.

Jeez. Making a guy clean up his own dad's explosion sounded c-o-l-d. I might have to have a stern word with Captain Gina.

"Jack?" he asked.

"Sorry, Bill," I said. "I'll be right down. Please leave it to me. You should go to the mess hall and have a soothing hot beverage."

"Really?" He sounded relieved.

"Yes. Please. I insist," I said. "I'll let you know when..." What? There's no more sign of your dad's brutal murder? Ugh. "I'll let you know when everything's, ah, shipshape again."

"Thanks, Jack. I appreciate it," he said. "You aren't as big a tool as everyone says." He ended the call.

Wait. What? Frowning, I turned back to Eva. "Do people think I'm a big tool?"

She laughed.

In the cargo bay, the security team was gone. I guess they got their man, er, smoke-monster.

I managed to find some cleaning equipment and got to work. Even though the explosion had been hot enough that there didn't seem to be any human remains, it was still a grisly job.

And the smell. Was I smelling burnt human? Ugh... I went and turned up the air scrubbers.

Back at work, I couldn't stop thinking about a vibrant life there one moment, gone the next. Daniel was the first crewmember I'd met when I'd come aboard the *Shakespeare,* and he'd been kind to me. He was a good guy. He didn't deserve this. My eyes grew heavy. I probably still had those gloves he'd loaned me somewhere. I had to stop working for a minute and get ahold of my emotions.

Daniel had been starting a new chapter of his life with a new clone body, and it had been cruelly cut short. How did he pay for his new body? Did TCC foot the bill? Or had he been scrimping and saving for years? Decades? What would happen now? Would he get a new clone?

And was Old Jack truly friends with him? Or had that been another scam of Old Jack's? Old Jack seemed sincere when I'd been talking to him on the ansible. On the other hand, he probably was a good actor.

I ended up turning up the air scrubbers three times. A small gale flowed through the cargo bay with a loud whoosh of moving air.

I cleaned up all the debris, but the floor panels in that section were damaged. It'd be nice if we could replace them so Bill wouldn't have to see a stark reminder of what'd happened. The trouble was: I didn't know who was supposed to do jobs like that.

I reviewed my list of crewmember friends and decided to call Carter. He'd know who to contact. And I didn't want to bother Gina with it. I called him.

He answered, "You better be calling to apologize for trying to kiss me."

"Ah." Why would I apologize for that? "No. You're an attractive guy and a good person--why wouldn't I want to kiss you?"

"But, er, I, ah..." He sputtered and ran out of steam. Finally, he said, "What do you want, Jack?"

"I'm cleaning the cargo bay, and the floor panels are damaged. Can we get someone down here to replace them now, so Bill doesn't have to look at them?"

He didn't answer right away. "Someone should have already taken care of this. I keep forgetting you're Jack Jones. He did have his act together before he turned to the dark side. You know he was my mentor and one of my best friends..."

"Yeah. You mentioned it," I said. "We should hang out sometime." I quickly added, "I promise, no kissing."

"Maybe." I could practically hear the frown through the fon. "Yes. I'll get a maintenance crew down to the cargo bay immediately."

"Thanks. While I've got you, are we going to do some kind of memorial for Daniel?"

"No," he said. "*Shakespeare* crew lost in the line of duty get new clones, courtesy of TCC. You, of all people, should know that."

That was a relief, at least. "But we lost Sam several weeks ago, and he hasn't been cloned yet, has he?" I asked.

He exhaled. "Generally, it takes several months to grow a new clone, implant recorded memories, do physical therapy and all the rest at the duplication facility on Earth."

I was reminded of Sophia, my favorite gorgeous dup engineer. She looked like a blonde Scandinavian goddess. How was she doing? I'd definitely have to look her up next time I was on Earth. In fact, maybe I should call her...

"Jack?" Carter said. "Are you listening to me?

No. "Yes."

"Oh," he said. "Good. We'll get Sam and Daniel back, but it'll take months."

We ended the call, and after several minutes a crew of five maintenance guys, complete with tools, ran into the bay. One of them ran over to me. "Why are the air scrubbers set so high?" he said, hair blowing in the wind. If I'd been in a better mood, I might have appreciated his fine muscular arms.

I just looked at him for a moment. Dumb question, right? Cooked-human-smell. But it was probably gone by now. "I'll turn them down."

He dipped his chin. "Good." He joined his crew, pulling up the damaged floor panels.

At the air controls, I heard a faint voice. "I say, mumble, mumble."

I turned down the scrubbers, and the whooshing noise stopped.

"I say, old chap!" a Terran-British-accented voice yelled. I recognized that voice. It was the vaporous sentience, aka the smoke-monster. I was struck again by the ludicrousness of a creature made of smoke sounding like a proper English gentleman.

The maintenance crew stopped working and stared at me. I waved and called out, "Just practicing my accents."

They variously rolled their eyes or shook their heads and went back to work.

I looked all around me and couldn't see anything. "Where are you?" I asked quietly.

"Near." It sounded like it came from the big cargo container on my right.

I was surprised the security team hadn't found it already. "What do you want?" I was pretty sure I shouldn't help it, whatever it wanted.

"I need your assistance."

Duh. "What, specifically?"

"I need access to your computer system."

Even a poor spy such as myself knew that was a bad idea. But what would a good spy do in this situation? Maybe string him along to try to find out what he really wanted? Or try to capture him? Distract him? Try to keep him talking, anyway.

"Just out of curiosity, do you guys have sex?" I asked. "Are you a guy? Or a girl? Or do you have something else?" It put a whole new twist on 'having a smoke.'

"What?" It/he/she sounded supremely annoyed. "Ah, why do

you ask, sir? What's your name?"

The capture option suddenly seemed more likely to succeed than the finding out what he wanted option.

"Uh, sure, buddy, I can give you access to our computer system." Not. "Stay right there, and I'll be back with some special, ah, equipment."

"I await your return with bated breath," it said. So, smoke-monsters were a little gullible. Good to know.

"Stay there. I'll be right back."

I jogged out of the cargo bay. Outside, I flicked my fon. "Ted?"

"Yeah," he said. "Hi, Jack. I can't talk now. We're still looking for the smoke mon--er, I mean the vaporous entity, er, sentience."

"Where are you?" I asked. If Ted helped me capture the entity, it could only help him, right? I was all about helping people.

"In the hall," he said. "Near the cargo bay."

"I'll be right there." I met up with him, and he did have access to a special 'capture apparatus' for vaporous entities--which looked a lot like a small vacuum cleaner of the sort you'd use to vacuum up dust. We hatched a plan and went back into the cargo bay.

Near the large box where I thought the creature was hiding, he said, "Hey, looks like the maintenance crew is almost done. You can't tell there even was an explosion in here." He was right. And Bill still wasn't around. Good. I'd contact him as soon as we got the smoke-monster.

"So, you sneak around the far side of the cargo container," I whispered, "and when I'm in position, you open it, and I'll suck him/her/it up in the vacuum."

"You mean in the vaporous entity capture app--" He paused. "Yeah, in the vac."

He started sneaking.

I went back to the cargo container. "Hey, uh, creature, I'm back."

"Good," it said.

It was weird to talk with a creature I couldn't see. "Was that you at the ghost mural? Did you say 'Mark me'?"

"Yes, indeed."

"How come my friend Olivia couldn't see you?"

"I can control how visible I am," it/he/she said.

Ted was on the other side of the container.

"This it/he/she business is awkward. What do I call you?" I held my fingers poised over the vac controls.

Ted reached the container's controls. I nodded, and he pressed the opener.

The container door opened with a crash, and I turned on the vac and shoved it at the smoke inside. The machine made a faint humming sound.

"I say, what are you doo--Ack." It got sucked up. "Help!"

"Ha," I said. "Got you! *Let it work, for 'tis sport to have the engineer hoist with his own petard.*"

Ted grinned, reaching for the vac.

"What's a petard?" it asked.

I grinned back at Ted as I handed him the vacuum containing the creature.

He said, "Commander Lu's going to be stoked!"

"I say, this is very rude." The creature had regained some of its composure. "I just wanted to talk to you, Jack. It is Jack, isn't it?" His voice was muffled inside the vacuum.

Jack? I felt my grin slip. "You know me?"

"This is rude?" Ted shook the vac a little. "Blowing people up is rude. You're in trouble now, you vaporous entity creature, you!"

"Blow up?" it said in a small female voice, losing its British accent. "But I didn't blow anyone up."

Uh oh.

71

Chapter Eleven

In the newly-repaired cargo bay, I should have been feeling proud of myself for facilitating the repairs, but I wasn't.

The smoke-monster had just been carried off, arrested for Daniel's murder. I should also be feeling good for capturing a nefarious criminal, but...

I was starting to get a bad feeling about everything. Where had the creature come from? Why had it stolen my stuff? Why did it seem to know me? Or at least know of me? Had it killed Daniel? And was it male or female? It was disconcerting not even knowing the gender of someone. I needed advice. Unfortunately, I wasn't sure who to turn to for said advice. I pondered it for a few moments.

Maybe Gina? She seemed old, so she must be wise, right? Plus, since I was officially Jack Jones again, I was pretty sure that meant we were married. That meant she had to be nice to me, didn't it? Of course, we hadn't talked about our marriage yet--much less done anything marriage-y. Yes, we'd been avoiding it.

After telling Bill the cargo bay was shipshape again, I marched over to the bridge and stuck my head in. "Captain, can we talk?"

The other bridge officers seemed startled by me. I didn't know if it was my sudden appearance, how hot I was, what I said, or what.

Carter, in particular, frowned.

But Gina stood. "Yes. It's overdue. Let's go to my quarters."

I nodded and popped back into the hall to wait for her. Outside the bridge, there, I enjoyed the mural of Twelfth Night. The shipwreck was beautifully rendered.

"Dramatic, huh?" she said, and I jumped.

"Yes." I turned to her. "Do you know how they decided what murals went where? I mean, why have a shipwreck right outside the bridge? And a ghost right outside engineering? And Puck right outside security?"

She stared at me for a second. "I keep forgetting you don't know anything. Short answer: irony. Come on, let's go to my cabin."

I glanced back in the direction of the bridge as we started walking down the hall. "Won't Carter mind?"

"*Let me not to the marriage of true minds admit impediments*," she said. But she looked a little sad.

"Are you saying you and Carter are soulmates, or aren't soulmates?" I wanted to know.

Exhaling loudly was her only response.

All too soon, we were at her cabin.

She opened the door, and we entered. Of course, all the cabins were essentially the same. Her cabin was slightly bigger to encompass her slightly larger double bed.

"I like the bed," I said. "Can I get one of these?"

She laughed as she sat down on it. "And yet, in some ways, you're the same as Jack, the other Jack." She paused. "What are we calling him?"

I sat next to her. Brigand? Evildoer? "Let's just call him Jack Senior," I said.

"All right. So, what did you want to talk about?"

I want a divorce. It was hard to say. She was so strong and lovely. "What were you saying about you and Carter?" She'd want a divorce if she was crazy in love with Carter.

"Quit avoiding the subject."

Avoiding the subject sounded good. "Ah, I don't think the smoke-monster blew up Daniel."

"The what?"

"The, ah, vaporous entity sentience, or whatever we're calling it."

"Okay," she said. "I hear you. We'll investigate."

Wow, that was easy. I thought we'd have to have a whole big discussion.

"Was that it?" she asked.

That was not it. "What do you say we get, ah, divorced?" I

said.

She blinked. "This was not where I thought this conversation was going to go."

"You don't like being a polygamist, do you?" I asked perfectly reasonably. "I don't like making you illegal."

She smiled. "Polygamy isn't illegal anymore."

What? "Since when?"

"Like, a quarter century ago." She shook her head and laughed a little. "I can see someone needs to put together some kind of guide or booklet for you that covers changes in the last thirty years."

"That would be great," I said. "I'd appreciate that." I scooted a little closer to her. "Are you saying you don't want to get divorced? 'Cuz I gotta say, you haven't been acting very wifely." No wifely duties had been performed, for one thing. I knew that for sure.

"I can *not* believe you'd say that!"

"Ah, what?" I asked. "You're saying you have done wifely duties?" She was luscious, and I'm sure I would have remembered anything like that.

"I've been protecting you since you got on the ship months ago," she said. "I let you steal the shuttle and go to Tau Ceto. You didn't get executed for being an illegal clone. Your special skill was kept secret. You got to keep your Jack Jones official identity, and your Jack Jones Junior cover identity. We rushed in and rescued you right away when you were kidnapped. I let you start investigating the *Shakespeare* FTL drive--and kept it secret."

Huh. That did sound like a lot. But, wasn't it captainly duties rather than wifely duties?

"Do you think TCC would do all that for just anyone?"

I had no idea what TCC would do. "No?"

"Damn right, no."

"So... you want to stay married?" Frankly, I couldn't blame her. I was pretty awesome. And, frankly, she was pretty awesome, as well. I hadn't known exactly how awesome until now.

I impulsively leaned over and hugged her. "Thank you for protecting me, Gina. I really appreciate it. You're awesome." We hugged for a few moments. For my part, it felt very comfortable and familiar. I appreciated all of her luscious curves in all the right places. Should I encourage her to perform her wifely duties? Sadly, I didn't think she'd go for it--right now, at least.

I wondered if I had any other wives I didn't know about but decided now was not the moment to ask.

Then she pushed me away. "You figured that out, finally." She smiled again.

"You have a very nice smile," I said. "And we're not getting divorced?"

"Not on my account," she said.

"What did you want to talk about, then?" I asked. I distinctly recalled her saying we should talk.

Her smile turned upside down. "I don't know if you know anything about TCC..."

I raised my eyebrows to say, 'I don't.'

"But there are a lot of internal politics in TCC and jockeying for power."

"I did not know."

"I've been trying to block Captain Wu from coming out here and getting involved in the study of the FTL drive and your special skill." I did recall Captain Wu as the captain of the super-sexy *Assyrian*. He'd brought me and my merry band from Tau Ceto when we'd been stranded there.

"Since we didn't officially divulge exactly everything that happened to TCC, he has some leverage over us," she said. "And Commander Bello has been adamant about not working with you." I still couldn't believe that.

She seemed very uncomfortable. My bad feeling started to come back."Just spit it out," I said.

"I think we should swap the *Shakespeare*'s FTL drive with the secret FTL drive on the shuttle. It would make studying your special skill easier, and I think the *Shakespeare* would be safer with a standard drive."

"Sounds good," I said. "I don't get what the problem is."

"Well, if we start monkeying around with the two drives, it will draw attention to them. I want to keep it as quiet as possible."

"A super-secret mission?" I asked. "Sounds fun."

"I don't think fun is the word," she said. "I'm serious. This has to remain super tip-top secret. I need to schedule things, so Bello and anyone else potentially troublesome is busy. When I do, can you swap the drives?"

"Me?" I said. "I'm not an engineer."

"I know, but you installed the drive on the shuttle, didn't you?"

"Yes," I said. "Technically. But I was very motivated. We were about to be suffocated to death."

"So, get motivated," she said. "Is there anyone you could ask to help you?"

I pondered. "Olivia was involved before," I said. "She's an engineer, and we know she can keep her mouth shut."

"Whatever you need," Gina said. "Let's schedule it for two a.m. tonight?"

Bummer. That would definitely cut into my lovemaking and cuddling schedule. "Do we have to do it then?"

"Two a.m. tonight, it is," she said. "I'll arrange the schedules. It should be as quiet as the grave, then."

"Okay." I tried not to think her metaphor was a little ominous. Foreshadowing anyone?

"Go talk to Olivia--and keep it quiet," she said.

"Yes, ma'am." I could recognize a dismissal when I heard one.

I made my way over to engineering, where I did find Olivia. "*Psst*," I said to her.

"What do you want now?" she asked. She didn't seem happy to see me.

"I need to talk to you in private," I said.

"What if I don't want to talk to you in private?"

"Just come on." I glared at her. I wanted to grab her arm and haul her out of there, but, of course, that wouldn't be gentlemanly.

Commander Bello appeared, walking around some equipment and staring at his fon. "Olivia--" When he looked up and saw me, he blanched. "Ugh. Jones. What are you doing here? Wait." He held up one hand. "Don't tell me. I don't want to know. Olivia, Captain Gomez has changed the duty schedule. You're off the rest of the day until two a.m." He shook his head.

"What?" she asked. "But Commander Bello, I don't want to work at two a.m."

"Don't look at me," he said. But he was quite nice to look at now. He must have thought the same of me because he was surely staring at me.

"*Aghh*!" Olivia stomped out of engineering. I followed her. Outside, near the ghost mural, she stopped. "This is you, right? You screwed up my schedule."

"Uh..." I wasn't sure what to say. "No?"

"*Aghh*!" She stomped down the hall.

I trailed after her. "I'm sorry your schedule got messed up. But I'm not the captain. It was Captain Gomez."

She kept on stomping.

I ran after her. "Has anyone ever told you you remind them of the Shrew?"

She stopped short and clenched her fist. Yikes. I recalled her arm punches were quite painful. I held up both my hands, palms out. "Katherine is a wonderful woman. Strong and beautiful. Just like you. You're strong and beautiful."

Her hand relaxed. "You think so?"

"Yes! Very strong. Very beautiful." I had to be careful not to get lost in her almond eyes.

"What's this about, then?"

"I have a super-secret mission from Gina, Captain Gomez, I need your help with."

"*Arghh*!!" She turned and started stomping down the hall again.

In all fairness, I had told her that several weeks ago and tricked her into helping me steal a shuttle. It turned out in that one instance, I was lying, sort of, okay, pretty much. Gina hadn't truly given me a super-secret mission that time. But this time was different. I ran after her. "This time, it's true. I swear!"

Before she could get out another one of those unique noises, I interrupted. "Can I buy you a soothing hot drink, and we can discuss it?"

She frowned. I sensed she was weakening a smidge.

"Chamomile tea is very soothing." I smiled engagingly.

"Tea does sound good," she said.

We went to the mess hall, got hot beverages, and sat at a

small table. No one was nearby. I got out my fon and contacted Gina.

Gina made her own loud, unique noise. "*Ugh*. What now, Jack?" she asked.

"Sorry for disturbing you," I said. "Can you just tell Olivia this is all official?"

"Fine," she said. "Put Olivia on."

I handed Olivia my fon.

They conversed.

I enjoyed my beverage. My eyes wandered to a young man sitting alone across the room. He was cute. I smiled. He smiled back. Who was he? I waved.

Olivia punched my arm.

"Ow!" I said, turning to her. "What was that for?"

"Quit flirting," she said and handed me back my fon.

"Who's flirting? I'm not flirting."

"Shut up," she said. "I'm in."

At the appointed two a.m. hour, I met Olivia in engineering. The overhead lights were dimmed, but the equipment still had various sundry lights. The area reminded me of a giant Christmas tree with all the sparkling, flickering multi-colored lights.

"Oh, there you are," she said. "I was hoping you'd oversleep and miss it."

I just smiled and whispered, "Strong. Beautiful."

"Oh, all right!" she said. "What do you want to do first?"

I whispered, "I think we should disconnect the FTL drive from the shuttle and bring it here to engineering so we can swap them out quickly."

"Not bad," she said. "It would be better to minimize the time frame when the *Shakespeare* doesn't have FTL capability."

"That's what I was thinking," I whispered.

"Why are you whispering? Everyone's asleep. We're the only ones here, probably the only ones on this deck."

Why was I whispering? "It's more fun." I grinned and waggled my eyebrows. I was all about the fun.

I caught a hint of a grin on her face. Ha.

We went to the cargo bay, got the anti-grav dolly and

pushed it to docking bay one, where the shuttle currently resided.

"I'm getting déjà vu," she said.

"I don't think it's déjà vu if you actually already did it," I said. "It's a memory." In point of fact, the two of us had pushed the secret FTL drive through these halls on the anti-grav dolly a few weeks ago.

She punched me on the shoulder. Hard.

"Ow!" When I glanced at her face, she was glaring.

Maybe this was more of a no-talking task. So, we quietly and successfully got to the shuttle, opened it up, and disconnected the FTL drive. We, oh, so, carefully loaded the drive on the dolly, exited the shuttle, and started back to engineering.

Suddenly, a huge cloud of smoke or mist or something billowed into the corridor, followed quickly by several security guards, including Ted.

Olivia and I froze, caught red-handed. So much for super tip-top secret.

But with all the smoke, it was getting difficult to see anything. Was this a failure of the environmental controls? Could the smoke hide us?

"Get it!" Ted cried, running up and waving the vacuum around.

Ah ha. The smoke had to be my old nemesis, the smoke-monster, but it hadn't acted like this before.

Olivia and I still hadn't moved or said anything. I could barely see the security officers anymore. Some of them started coughing. Some of the security team seemed to run into each other--judging by the assorted grunts and smacking sounds, and 'Ow!'s and 'Watch where you're going!'s.

A humming sound came from the direction of Ted. "I think I got it!" he said.

Gradually, the smoke cleared. Uh oh. What about our super-secret mission?

"Do something," Olivia whispered.

Some of the various TCC officers picked themselves up off the floor where they'd gotten tangled up with each other.

I pulled my shirt off and dropped it over the drive.

79

Olivia sighed.

The security officers finally took notice of us.

"Hey, Jack," Ted said, looking me up and down, noticing my shirtless status. "What'cha doing?"

"I demand to speak to Jack Jones," a stuffy British voice said from inside the vacuum.

"Back to the brig for you." But Ted's obvious elation at capturing the creature seemed to be ebbing. He looked from Olivia to me and back again. The light went out of his eyes. "Wait." He took a step towards me. "What's going on here?"

I felt bad since Ted seemed to be feeling bad. It was a very awkward moment, and I was a bundle of nerves. "I'm sorry, I can't tell you," I said.

"Jack!" the smoke-monster said. "Old chap, I have to talk to you! It's life or death!"

Chapter Twelve

The security team had taken the smoke-monster back to the brig.

None of the security officers had pursued exactly what Olivia and I were doing here in the hall, even with my shirt off. With the exception of Ted, they demonstrated a remarkable lack of curiosity. Maybe they thought it was some kind of sex game? If so, was that a common thing in the ship hallways? Clearly, I didn't know enough about the ship.

Of course, it may have had something to do with the fact it was two-thirty in the morning. Unlike engineering's skeleton crew, presumably, the bridge was fully manned as well as the security staff.

Unlike the security officers, however, I was a curious cat. Consequently, I was disquieted by the smoke-monster's life-or-death comment. What was that about? Why did it want to talk to me?

"Earth to Jack," Olivia said. "Are we doing this or what?" We stood in the middle of the hall with a secret FTL drive on an anti-grav dolly covered by my shirt. Talk about exposed.

"We're doing this." I nodded forcefully.

Taking in Olivia's slim but beautiful physique, my mind wandered. "What might 'or what' entail?" I asked. "Did you want to do something else with me?"

She glanced at me. "No. I don't even want to do this with you!"

She needed a soothing beverage if anyone ever did.

We finished moving the secret FTL drive to engineering. I saw no other crew members in the dark, gloomy area. Now, the twinkling little LED lights seemed to be saying, 'I see you. I see your secret activities.'

We dollied the drive right up to the *Shakespeare*'s FTL drive.

"Okay," Olivia said. "Go to it."

I nodded. "Sounds good." I stood there, waiting.

She stood there, waiting. Finally, she said, "What are you waiting for?"

"Me?" I asked. "What are you waiting for?"

"Me?" She pointed at the *Shakespeare*'s FTL drive. "Swap it out."

I broke out into a sweat. It suddenly felt like engineering was about three hundred degrees. "You want me to do it? I thought you were going to do it."

"I thought you were going to do it," she said.

Was it four hundred degrees in here now? "But I'm not an engineer."

She put her hands on her hips and stared at me.

I froze. I couldn't swap it out. What if I screwed up the *Shakespeare*'s FTL drive? Talk about life and death. I could put the lives of every single person, every man, woman, and other(?) on the ship at risk. The regular space engines were fine, and we were close to the Yeblypso planet, but still. "I'm not an engineer," I said again.

"But I've never done it," she said. "Commander Bello wouldn't let me touch it." She looked like I felt--terrified. "You did it before."

We stared at each other. Neither one of us made a move to do it. Time ticked by.

It was five hundred degrees now. "*The time is out of joint--O cursèd spite, that ever I was born to set it right!*" I said.

"Why are you so worried?" Olivia said.

"What if I break it?" I asked.

"Don't break it," she said.

I couldn't take the heat. "What about a compromise? We disconnect the *Shakespeare*'s FTL drive, take it, and leave this other one here. The FTL drive is no use this close to a planet." We used the regular engines in regular space.

"And then what?" she asked.

"And then you call in Commander Bello, and he installs this

drive." I pointed at the secret FTL drive.

"I like it," she said. "I know how to disconnect stuff. And we don't need the FTL drive right now." She leaned down and started disconnecting stuff.

And I could sneak off before Bello got here, and he wouldn't suspect anything.

Very soon, she stood up and said, "That's it. Help me move it."

We quickly moved the existing drive out of the way and popped the new drive in its place. We put the old drive on the dolly. "I can take this back to the shuttle," I said. "You call Bello." I was struck with inspiration. "You can tell him you had an idea of how to fix the drive."

She smiled. "And it'll be fixed because it's a different drive."

"He'll think you're a genius," I said.

"Yeah," she said. "Finally, helping you helps me instead of hurting me. I'll be the hero that helped fix the *Shakespeare*'s FTL drive."

I didn't like the sound of me being hurtful, but whatever. "Okay. Good luck." I reached for the dolly. "I'm out of here."

She reached for her fon.

I started for the hall. The FTL drive wasn't heavy, but it was bulky and did not corner well. I tried to move quickly, so I didn't inadvertently run into Bello. That's all I needed to get caught with a secret FTL drive. He was already pissed; who knew what he'd do?

I managed to get to the shuttlecraft without being caught. I dollied the FTL drive right inside and up to the front of the ship. I unloaded it. "*But you, O you, so perfect and so peerless, are created of every creature's best!*" Yay, me.

I kneeled to start connecting the drive in the shuttle, but what the smoke-monster had said was still bothering me. What if it was right and someone's life truly was in danger? If I could help someone, I would, wouldn't I? Yeah. That's what Jack Junior was about. I was all about the helping.

I stood up. It wouldn't hurt if I moseyed down to the brig for a few minutes to see what was what, right?

At 3:30 a.m., the ship was silent. No one was out and about, so no one stopped to question me.

At the security center, the officer on duty, Bertram, was asleep--if his loud snoring was any indication. I walked right up to the bars of the brig--which they'd somehow already repaired.

The smoke-monster was clearly not asleep because it rushed up to the bars.

"Hi, there, uh, vaporous..." I forgot what we were calling it. "Uh, sentient gaseous guy."

It zoomed around in front of the bars, but I couldn't hear anything.

I gingerly poked my finger between the bars and got a shock. Ah ha. They had a force field up. We couldn't hear each other if air couldn't pass through.

The creature made an arrow shape with its body, pointing at the security station.

I tiptoed over to the security station. Bertram was still snoring his head off. For a second, I wondered if I'd run such a loose ship when I was captain.

Focus, Jack! I carefully reached around him and accessed the computer station. I did know I shouldn't just take down the whole force field. See, I wasn't a total loss as a spy.

I searched the security protocols. They did have an option for serving meals to prisoners; it turned off a very small area of the force field to send food inside. That sounded perfect, so I implemented it.

Bertram didn't miss a snore.

I started walking the ten feet across the room back to the brig.

But the smoke-monster had already flowed out of the cell through the small opening in the force field. Oh. That's why they had it behind an impenetrable force field.

"Thank goodness, Jack," it said in its British accent. It resembled an opaque cloud bank with occasional colors and lights inside. It was pretty.

"Uh...I thought we were going to talk." This was not good. No one would be happy about me releasing a murderer or even a suspected murderer, or even a vaporous creature of interest.

"I knew I could count on you," it said.

"What did you want to talk to me about?" I said. "Did you want to confess to blowing up the cargo bay? If so, I'll try to help you get a nice deal." I was all about the nice.

"No," it said. "I don't know anything about that. I came here for you."

"For me?" Did he mean me, me, or other old me? "Have we met before?"

"Only by reputation," it said.

"Reputation?" I grinned. "My singing?"

"Sex," it said.

Of course. That made total sense. "My sex appeal knows no limits," I said. But did that make sense? Surely, my sex reputation wasn't intergalactic. "What planet are you from?"

"I need to have sex," it said. "It's life or death."

"I like sex as much as the next guy, but how is it life or death?"

"You want to," it said.

I didn't recall saying that. Or even implying it.

"You asked me all about it earlier," it said. "I need it."

I recalled asking it some questions while trying to waylay it. What had I asked?

I also recalled being called a speciesist in the past. I wasn't a speciesist, was I? It didn't sound like a good thing to me. "I might be interested." Suddenly, it was surrounding me, all around me. "Uh, what's involved in sex for you?"

It pressed in on all sides. It started moaning.

"Are we doing it now?" But as I spoke, smoke entered my nostrils, mouth, and probably everywhere else.

I tried to say, "Can humans breathe when they have sex with you?" But what came out was, "Mm mm mm mmm?"

Was it getting hard to breathe?

Chapter Thirteen

In the security area outside the brig, the smoke creature had completely enveloped me.

Waves of pleasure washed over me--although I could not have said from where. I spasmed with pleasure again and again.

Someone shook me. "Jack!" It was Bertram's voice.

I opened my eyes and found myself lying on the floor next to the brig. I had no idea how much time had passed. "Bertram?"

He nodded vigorously.

"What happened?" I asked.

Suddenly, I heard a mewling sound from the floor next to me.

My eyes whipped over to behold what appeared to be a flesh-colored slug about the size and shape of a loaf of bread. "What is that?" I pointed.

Bertram laughed.

I got a bad feeling. The longer he laughed, the worse my bad feeling got. When he finally stopped laughing for a moment to wipe the tears from his eyes, I quickly said, "Do you know what it is?"

That prompted another round of merriment.

Well, this was getting me nowhere.

Gingerly, I leaned over the thing. It pulsed in and out slowly as if it was breathing. I poked it with a finger. It felt warm and slightly yielding, like human flesh. I jerked back. What was it?

Bertram chuckled at my reaction. "Oh, you're killing me, kid." He sank to the floor next to me. "Let me guess. You let the prisoner out of the brig."

"Yes," I said slowly. "How'd you know?" I glanced back at

the empty brig. Okay, maybe that was a stupid question.

"And you had sex with it," he added.

"Uh..." I guessed I did have sex with it. I wasn't a speciesist, after all! That was good, at least.

"How'd you know?"

Now it was his turn to point at the slug, chuckling. "That's your baby."

I must have blacked out again because the next thing I knew, a whole big crowd of people stood around me as I still lay on the floor. Since they were all wearing security uniforms, I was guessing they were all security guys.

"I've never seen one before," someone said.

"They're pretty rare," another person said.

I didn't recognize anyone besides Bertram.

Until Ted ran up. "Jack! How could you?"

I couldn't very well claim nothing happened since the evidence was right there next to me for the whole world to see. "We never said we were exclusive, did we?" I finally managed to eke out.

"No, but, gosh, having kids with someone is pretty serious," Ted said, leaning over the thing, staring. He smiled. "It's kind of cute."

"Wait a minute." I held up my hand. "I don't understand what happened."

That motivated a lot of snickering amongst the crowd.

Bertram grinned. "When Mommy and Daddy love each other very much, they give each other a special hug..."

I sighed loudly. Good grief. "I know how sex works." I thought I had, anyway. On the bright side, now I knew more. "What I meant was, how can there be a baby already?" I asked. "And how can two different species make a baby?" I examined it. It didn't look like any kind of baby I'd ever seen. "And what the heck is it?"

The snickering turned into laughing. Not again.

The slug made that mewling sound again. Aw. I reached out and touched it lightly.

"Is it hungry?" I asked. "How do you take care of it?"

Uproarious laughter.

Even Ted couldn't help himself.

In my ear, I heard softly, "I knew I'd made the right choice." But the creature's voice sounded much higher than before. And the British accent was gone again.

I jerked my head that way. The smoke-monster, er, baby-daddy, whatever, creature was back. Its volume seemed considerably smaller, and it also seemed more transparent. "So, uh, is this your baby?" I asked.

"Yes," it said.

"Congratulations," I said, smiling. Babies were always a good thing, right?

It pulsed with light, and I somehow got the distinct impression of happiness from the creature. "Thanks."

The head security guy strode up. "What is going on here? Why is the prisoner out of the brig?"

Bertram just pointed at me and the slug-baby on the floor.

The boss already had his fon out. "Captain Gomez, there's been a...development."

The crowd snickered.

"You need to come to the brig," he said. "Yes. Jones. How'd you know?"

He ended the call and said, "Back in the brig with you, vaporous entity. You're our prisoner."

"I'll surrender if Jack takes care of the baby," it said. "You'll take care of the baby, Jack? Please. I'll owe you."

Someone had gotten out that portable vacuum thing that sucked up the creature before. He turned it on, and its hum approached us in a menacing manner.

"Jack?" The creature sounded panicky.

"Yes, I'll help you," I said. "I'll take care of the baby."

"Thank you," the creature said. "And I didn't have anything to do with any bomb. Will you put in a good word for me?"

As far as I knew, we still obeyed the law. "Don't worry, uh, creature. You're innocent until proven guilty. I'll get you a lawyer and stuff if you need it. You'll be safe here in the brig. And I'll make sure the baby's safe."

"Thanks, Jack," it said in a scared little voice. And then it flowed back into the brig of its own accord.

I picked up the slug-baby and cradled it in my arms. It felt about the same weight as a human baby.

"That's more like it," the boss said. "The rest of you lot, report to your duty stations."

"I was on my way to breakfast," one guy said.

"Me, too," another guy said.

"Well, then, go to breakfast!" the boss said.

The security officers, including Ted, scurried around a powerful Gina as she strode into the room. Something about her stance, solid build, and/or her intenseness made her seem like an Amazonian goddess.

"What the hell, Jack?" she said in her most strident voice as she approached us.

I tried not to quail.

When she got a load of what was in my arms, she stopped short. "Ah. I, uh, see." She glanced at the brig. The corners of her mouth started to turn up, but she forced them back down. "Ah." But she lost the battle, and a grin escaped. She forced it down again.

She stared at me and parted her lips. But then she laughed. "Sorry." More laughter. "Sorry."

"The creature escaped." The senior security officer stared at me. "Or something. But it surrendered."

"I'll say it surrendered." Gina looked at the brig. "Okay. Good to know." She turned to me. "Come on, Jack." She gestured towards the hall.

Still holding the baby, I managed to stand up.

She started walking away, and I followed.

"Where are we going?" I knew I wasn't going to the brig because we were walking away from it.

"The med bay, of course," she said. "Dr. Sharma can check out the baby and ensure it's okay. And give you instructions on how to take care of it."

I was all set to protest that I didn't know anything about taking care of babies--of any species--, but I had given the smoke-creature my word.

And we'd shared something especially intense. I felt myself blush, thinking about those powerful orgasms. Wow. I was definitely not a speciesist.

In the med bay, Dr. Sharma seemed to be waiting for us.

"Hello, there."

Gina said, "I guess you heard already." She pointed at the baby.

Dr. Sharma grinned. "This kind of news travels fast." Something in my expression made him add, "Good news." He patted my shoulder. "You did good, Jack."

Gina's fon pinged, and she looked at it. "I have to go." She pointed at me. "We're going to have a serious talk later, young man. About the birds and the bees." She turned for the door, guffawing.

Dr. Sharma patted one of the beds. "Put it here."

I gently set it down.

"Nice size." He took a stethoscope out of the pocket of his big white coat and pressed one end gently against the creature's skin. "Let's see how you're doing, little one." He listened.

I was still confused. What had happened? I wanted to ask Dr. Sharma; he seemed like he might know. I was sick of people laughing at me, but the only way to learn is to admit you don't know something.

"So, ah, I'm not completely familiar with this species," I said. "Is it okay? Healthy?"

Dr. Sharma threw me a glance while still listening. Then, he straightened up and smiled. "Yes. It seems very healthy, extraordinarily healthy."

"Good. That's good." I nodded. "Do you think you could tell me what happened?"

He smiled again, but he didn't laugh. "Sure. " He sat on one of the beds. "Take a seat."

I sat.

"So, this species is called the sldkfjfoisut."

Say what? But I didn't want to interrupt him. I nodded in what I hoped was a wise manner.

"They're essentially energy creatures," he said. "But they evolved from creatures very much like us. When they're ready to procreate, two sldkfjfoisut exchange genetic material, and then, one of them--you could think of it as the mom--looks for a member of a humanoid species to complete the process. The humanoid--you, in this case--acts as the catalyst to create the baby."

"Catalyst?" I asked. "So, is there any of my genetic material involved?"

"No." He smiled gently. "It's impossible for different species to procreate."

"Yeah," I said. "That's what I thought." I did think that.

"The catalyst is important, though. I've studied a little about the sldkfjfoisut in medical journals. Ideally, they want a catalyst with a good heart, someone open and willing to participate in the final sexual act. If a sldkfjfoisut is born out of an interaction with a stressed catalyst, the baby can be sickly or, possibly, even die. And since there aren't that many sldkfjfoisut left, that would be a real shame."

"And this slid..." I couldn't say the species' name. "This creature is healthy, for sure?"

"Very healthy, Jack," Dr. Sharma said. "I've never heard of such a large, calm baby sldkfjfoisut." He pointed at me. "If the TCC career doesn't work out, you should consider being a sldkfjfoisut midwife."

Despite the strangeness of all this, I felt a little bit proud. "Why does the baby look so different from its parents?"

"Right." He pointed at the baby. "The baby is basically in a chrysalis."

"Like a butterfly?"

"Yes. Very much like a butterfly. It will emerge from its chrysalis as a beautiful energy-creature. And that's all thanks to you, Jack."

"Neat." I smiled. It was really neat. I helped bring a new beautiful creature into the world.

Sharma nodded. "Very neat."

"So, how do I take care of it?"

"That's easy." He slid off the bed and grabbed a box from underneath. He pulled the linens off the bed and put them in the box, making a kind of nest. Gently, he picked up the baby and put it in the nest. "You just need to keep it in a cool, quiet, dark place."

I felt a little intimidated by the responsibility. "What about food and water?"

"Nope," he said. "Just a safe place." He gestured at the box.

"What?" I asked. "You want me to take it now?"

"Yes."

That didn't sound totally safe to me. "Don't you want to keep an eye on it? It is a newborn."

"It's perfectly safe for you to take it." His gentle demeanor slipped a bit. "I can't keep it in here; it's too hectic. It's your responsibility."

"But--"

"If you can't do the time, don't do the crime." I could tell he wasn't going to relent.

And I had promised to take care of the little baby. As I scooped up the box, I asked, "How tricky is this procreation process?"

"It's pretty tricky." But he said it like it was very tricky.

"Is there any chance the slid..., the creature, came to the *Shakespeare* solely to make a baby?"

"Huh." Sharma stilled for a moment. "Maybe." He nodded. "Maybe so."

Ha. I knew my baby-mommy wasn't a bomber.

Back at my cabin, I set the baby on the bed and caressed it gently with my fingertips. "*God mark thee to His grace! Thou was the prettiest babe that e'er I nursed*," I whispered. "*And might I live to see thee married once, I have my wish*." Did the slids marry? I just wanted it to grow up and have a good life.

Where to keep it? I glanced around my cabin. My favorite hiding spot seemed like a winner.

I slid the box under my bed.

Chapter Fourteen

Pounding woke me as I lay on the rumpled covers in my bed in my cabin. After staying up all night skulking around, I must have fallen asleep.

"Jack!" It was Eva's voice. She pounded on the door again.

I climbed out of bed and opened the door. "Morning, beautiful." She resembled a Norse goddess with her perfect physique. I couldn't help smiling.

But she jerked back a little when she saw me.

Surely, she wouldn't recoil from my nudity? I glanced down. Wow. I'd been so tired I hadn't even undressed.

"You look like crap." She strode into my cabin, looking around.

As I caught my reflection in the mirror, I knew there was a reason I preferred to sleep in the nude: fewer wrinkles. And more fun, too--of course!

I smiled some more. "*My heart love till now for sweared sight, for I never saw true beauty till this night.*"

Apparently satisfied, she plopped down on my bed. "I heard the craziest rumor today. Everyone's been saying you had a baby. Heh, heh." She snickered.

I plopped down right next to her. "I don't get why that's so funny." Our thighs touched, and I felt the delicious warmth of her skin through our clothing.

"It's just desserts for a player like you," she said, grinning. "Love 'em and leave 'em guys just waltz around fulfilling their own needs and never have to face any consequences. So, the idea of immediate and huge consequences seems funny." She snickered a little more.

I was hurt on multiple levels. I caressed her hand. "First

of all, I'm not a player. I love 'em and love 'em. I don't leave anyone. I would never leave anyone." Except for Sophia. But she had ordered me to go. "I would never leave you."

"Well, okay..." She looked a little uncertain.

"Second of all, I'm crushed to hear I've only met my own selfish need and haven't met your needs. I thought I was a considerate love-maker. " I turned my body to face hers on the bed. "I'm so sorry if I've left you wanting. Please tell me what to do to fulfill your desires. I want to fulfill your every desire. I want to make you happy." Making her happy would make me happy. I leaned in for a kiss, and we connected on every level.

When we separated, she said, "What was I saying?"

I frowned. "You were saying I'm a bad lover."

"Really?" Her brow furrowed. "Was I saying that?"

I leaned in and kissed her again.

"Ah..." she said. "I think you're convincing me that couldn't possibly be true." She grinned lasciviously. "But I need more data. Lots more data." She lay back on the bed and pulled me after her.

Good thing I'd had a nap!

Our souls joined as one as I kissed her all over.

"So why were people saying you had a baby?" she asked during a pause much later.

I kissed her eyelids. "Because I sort of did."

She pushed me away. "What?" And she said it in an angry, not loving, voice.

Suddenly I wished I had a teapot in my room. I sat up. "Do you need a hot soothing beverage?"

"No!" she said. "I need answers."

"I helped a slid-something couple have a baby."

"Do you mean sldkfjfoisut?"

That sounded about right. "Yes."

"Oh," she said in a softer voice, looking down at the bed. "They're endangered. If you helped them, that was nice of you."

Yay, me. But I just smiled modestly.

"If you have a baby sldkfjfoisut, where is it? Is Dr. Sharma taking care of it?"

"No. It's here."

She looked all around my cabin again. "But I don't see any

baby."

I pointed down. "It's under the bed."

She jumped off the bed like it was on fire. "What!" She crouched down to peer underneath the bed and pulled out the box. "It's, ah, cute?"

I peered over the edge of the bed into the box. "Super cute, right?"

She gave me a puzzled look.

Why hadn't Old Jack had any kids? They were adorable.

Hey, I could have kids. I looked at the baby. More kids. "Do you ever think about having kids, Eva?"

"What!" She shrieked and stood up.

"Shh," I said. But the little slid didn't stir. I reached out to caress it. "You need a name, don't you, little guy?" I glanced up at Eva. "What do you think of Slid as a name for it?"

Her mouth was hanging open.

I caressed little Slid. It moved ever so slightly under my fingertips. "It likes it."

I pushed Slid back under the bed. "Anyway, where were we?"

Eva's mouth hung open. Finally, she snapped it closed. "I'm not having sex inches from a baby."

Why not? "Is that bad?"

She stepped towards the door. "Ah, good for you for helping the sldkfjfoisut, but I have to get back to work." She opened the door and darted out.

"Okay, see you later," I called after her, but the door had already whisked shut behind her.

I pulled Slid back out from under the bed. "That was kind of weird, wasn't it, Slid?"

I thought it agreed with me.

"Women, you can't live with 'em, you can't love 'em enough."

Slid flexed slightly in agreement.

Then my fon demanded attention. "Jack!" It was Gina.

I picked it up off my desk. "Yes, O Captain, my Captain?"

She didn't miss a beat. "How's the sldkfjfoisut?"

I glanced down at it. "It seems good, very good."

She exhaled loudly. "Good. What about that other matter?"

she asked more quietly.

What matter was that? My aborted Eva sex? "Uh...?"

"Your secret mission," she whispered angrily.

I scanned my memories. Wow, a lot had happened in the last few days. "The FTL drive thing?"

"Yes! Commander Bello reported that the FTL drive in engineering had been disconnected. He was concerned about sabotage. I had to talk him down."

Sabotage? I hadn't even thought of that.

"Jack?"

"Uh, if you're asking if I successfully transferred the secret stolen FTL drive to engineering and took away the defective one, that would be a yes. But connecting the new FTL drive-- presumably not malfunctioning-- to the *Shakespeare* seemed intimidating. Olivia wouldn't help me, and we figured Bello could do it."

"I guess that makes sense. Sort of," she said. "Did you get the defective one hooked up in the shuttlecraft?"

My mind panned back. I'd taken the drive to the shuttle.

But then I'd gone to talk to the smoke-monster. Now that we'd made a baby together, I felt a little bad about calling it a monster. I also felt bad about the fact that we still hadn't actually had a conversation.

In addition, I did not complete my tip-top, super-secret, connect-the-FTL drive mission. Yikes. "I'm sorry to say, I did not. I got distracted by bringing a new life into the galaxy." That was even pretty much true. Might as well emphasize the positive.

"Damn," she said. "I was hoping you finished. We need you for rehearsal. We're supposed to do a whole run-through with costume--so to speak--of the new show."

Oh, right, the show. "When?"

"Now."

I shrugged. "Okay." I knew the show. It'd been one of my favorites as a kid.

"No," she said. "I don't think we should leave an FTL drive lying around. I'll push the rehearsal to tonight. Can you finish installing the drive by then?"

I'd done it before, so... "Of course." Positive, check.

"While doing so, practice the songs. I'm assuming you

haven't had much time to practice. Can you do that?"

"I can do it, but won't it draw attention to my super-secret mission? People will hear my wonderful singing and come investigate."

She made a suspiciously snicker-like noise. "I think we can risk it. Call me as soon as you get the drive connected." She hung up.

"Okay," I said to open air. People on this ship needed a refresher on manners.

Speaking of refreshers, I needed a shower.

I had to make a quick stop at the brig to reassure Slid's Mom it was okay. And maybe we could converse. I waved at Puck on the wall as I marched past him and into the security area.

Ted was on duty. Nice. I gave him a huge smile and sauntered up to him. "How's my favorite man?"

He simpered in pleasure. "I'm your favorite?"

I nodded. "Sure."

"How's the baby?" he asked.

"Good." I pointed back at the brig. "That's why I'm here. I wanted to have a confab with Mom."

"About how to take care of it?"

That sounded plausible. "Okay."

"I'm not sure," he said. "This sldkfjfoisut has given us a lot of trouble."

Could everyone pronounce the species' name except me?

I just smiled sweetly.

"On the other hand, taking care of a baby is important." He smiled back at me. "Oh, all right." He turned his attention to his computer. "I'm just opening a teeny-tiny spot in the energy field so you can talk."

"Thanks, sweetie." I turned and approached the brig.

The slid-whatever rushed up to one section of the energy field. In her high voice, she said, "Is the baby all right?"

"Yes, ma'am. It's doing well." I thought from what Sharma said, the creature in the brig must be a she.

"That's a relief," she said. "Thanks again for your help."

"We probably don't have much time. Can you tell me why

you're on the ship?"

"I was looking for you, Jack," she said.

"Me? Why?"

"That should be obvious at this point," she said.

"But how did you know about me? And how did you know I'd help?"

"Jack Jones' reputation is known throughout the galaxy."

I smiled. That sounded about right.

"I have some information to trade that I thought could convince you," she said.

Oooh. That sounded intriguing.

Loud footfalls approached from the distance.

"Ted! What the hell!" a man bellowed.

I whipped around to see what the commotion was.

Ted's boss stomped into the security area. "Close the energy field!" A faint shimmer appeared between the bars.

"To be continued!" I said to the creature, but I wasn't sure if she heard me or not.

Ted's boss glared at me. "You are a colossal pain in my ass. I'd shoot you if you weren't Captain Gomez's pet."

Captain Gomez's pet? What did that mean?

"Get out of here, Jones!"

I got.

I made it to the shuttle bay without further incident and got to work in the shuttle. The shuttle was utilitarian, with a command console in the front and a window above it. It contained four bolted-down chairs in two rows of two. The walls were all storage compartments and fold-down chairs and cots.

I livened up the plain space by singing. "*Harmony and understanding. Sympathy and trust abounding...*"

A little later, "*And I'm a genius, genius, I believe in God. And I believe that God believes in Claude...*"

I connected away.

By the time I got to "*Good morning starshine. The earth says hello...*" I thought I had the drive up and running.

Surprisingly, no one had come to investigate the marvelous singing. Score one for Gina there.

I examined the drive. How could I know for sure it worked?

98

I needed to know if its FTL capabilities worked. I also needed to know if my special skills still worked when it was engaged.

So, where could I go via an FTL drive? I could say hello to Earth and Sophia... She didn't think I'd loved her and left her, did she? It would break my heart if she thought I was a cad.

On the other hand, Gina would be pissed if I didn't make it back in time for rehearsal. I checked my fon. I might have enough time to get to Earth and back again. Hurray, FTL travel!

I sat down in the shuttle's captain's chair. The wise thing to do would be to stay here. I knew that, at least.

But since when were eighteen-year-olds wise?

Plus, I was a hero after helping create little Slid.

It was easier to ask for forgiveness than permission.

I texted Eva and said if anything happened to me, she should take care of little Slid. She called me back immediately, wanting to talk. I didn't answer. Yeah, it was a little bit chicken of me.

I closed the shuttle doors and ran down the takeoff checklist. Everything was shipshape. I engaged the sub-light engines and flew the shuttle out of the *Shakespeare.*

Immediately my comms lit up. "Shuttle one? I detect an unauthorized--" one of the *Shakespeare*'s crew said.

I turned off comms in the middle of a powerfully strong feeling of déjà vu.

I flew away from the ship.

I reached for the FTL Drive.

"Here goes something." Hopefully.

I engaged.

Chapter Fifteen

On the shuttlecraft with the special FTL drive, I was kicking back on my short jaunt to Earth. I'd set a course in FTL space to arrive in orbit around my favorite planet. Once in orbit, I would take over navigational control and land the shuttle near scrumptious Sophia. Or not. I could do what I wanted.

I leaned back in the captain's chair, thinking about Sophia with my hands behind my head. She was my first real friend. She was a good person with a generous heart and generous in other ways...

She was sooo beautiful. Like a Scandinavian goddess. I remembered kissing her all over. I remembered lots of things we'd done in her apartment. I wished I was with her now.

And then I fell on the floor, a hard, cold, tile-covered floor, next to a woman in a medical coverall. What the heck?

The woman leaned down to examine me on the ground. "Jack? Where'd you come from?" The small opening in the coverall-mask combo featured stunning cornflower-blue eyes. It was Sophia, beautiful Sophia.

"Hi, Soph." I smiled and waved from my spot on the floor. I knew immediately what must have happened. The FTL drive was malfunctioning, and the improbabilities must have been leaking out--which is exactly what I'd been hoping for. Consequently, when I wished I was with Sophia, I instantiated that improbable reality to transport myself to her. Nice.

I scrambled to my feet. "*My heart love till now for sweared sight, for I never saw true beauty till this night.*"

Sophia, now smiling, stood in front of a large person-sized vat with her hands inside it. "You really shouldn't be in here. It's supposed to be sterile."

I glanced inside the vat and was sorry I had. It contained a disgusting-looking proto-human, apparently in the process of growing and not very far into the process, judging by its spindly, bloody limbs. "Yuck." Obviously, she was working on a new clone. Had I once looked like that? If so, how could she have had sex with me? She was even more generous than I'd known.

"Jack?" She made an impatient face. Was she impatient with me? Impossible.

"What?"

"Please leave." She gestured at the doorway with her shoulder, not taking her hands out of the vat. "I'm working. I'll meet up with you when I can."

"Really?" I asked. "You want me to leave?"

"Yes," she said quickly but then smiled. "Horace, here, is at a difficult stage. I have to focus." She inclined her head at the door.

"Yes, ma'am." I saluted her. "As you wish. Call me when you're available." Luckily, I still had my fon in my pocket. I smiled handsomely, twirled and exited.

Outside in the hall, I stopped. What now? "I wish I knew what to do now," I said.

Nothing strange happened. I looked around the duplication facility's bland, boring, all-white hall.

It was slowly dawning on me that I was not in the best predicament. I couldn't use the shuttle FTL's special power, apparently, if I was physically separated from it.

I didn't even know where in the galaxy the shuttle was.

Would it continue on its course here to Earth and enter orbit? Hopefully.

But how would I find it in orbit? Earth orbit was a very large place.

And how would I get to it in orbit when I found it?

And I was clearly going to miss rehearsal. Gina would be pissed. She might even give my role away to someone else. That would be a disaster.

I stood there in the hall for a while, frowning and, okay, berating myself. I should have known better than to make a wish while that special FTL drive was operating--especially since I'd been thinking sexy thoughts about Sophia and hadn't physically reacted. I should have known better. I should have known much, much better.

Well, hopefully, lesson learned.

Besides sexy Sophia, the only people I knew on Earth were Noah Anderson and his best friend, my older criminal self; they were both in a secret TCC prison. I had a lot of questions for Old Jack, chief among them: did he blow up the cargo bay?

I did know where the secret TCC prison was.

With my improbably-gotten monetary gains still in my account, I had no problem catching a ride to Paris, the city of lights. This was my first visit to Paris in this body, although I remembered a high school museum field trip. Many people believed Paris to be the cultural center of Earth.

I walked along the cobblestones taking it all in, the cafes, the small shops, beautiful green trees and scores of people--mostly human and mostly dressed in fashionable black. I inhaled lustily; I loved how Earth smelled: damp, full of billions of wonderful living creatures, full of hopes and dreams, full of life.

I passed a gorgeous woman, all dancing eyes, luscious lips and upturned nose, and smiled broadly.

She tossed her thick mane of brunette hair and smiled back. Of course. Hello, cultural center!

"*What is the city but the people*?" I pulled out my fon to double-check directions to the secret prison.

"You know that won't work here," the brunette beauty said with a lovely French accent.

Sure enough, my fon had only the most limited functionality. "Right. I know that," I said. "Why is that again?"

She laughed. "We're preserving our French culture. Nothing too modern is allowed. It's a no-tech zone."

"Right," I said, nodding wisely. "I knew that." Well, now I did. I also knew the secret TCC prison was located near the Eiffel Tower. "I'm looking for the Eiffel Tower."

"Of course you are. Everyone's always looking for the Eiffel Tower." She grinned. "You should just take a taxi."

"A taxi." I nodded. "Sure. Right."

"*Bon chance. Au revoir.*" She waved and glided away.

I found a taxi and did my own gliding of a fashion. I had the guy let me out at the Parc du Champ de Mars. The entrance to the large underground TCC complex was a small unobtrusive maintenance building in the park.

I strolled along the gravel walkway, feeling the sun shine on my skin. I loved sunshine. I loved Earth. The young people sitting on the lawn all seemed happy and healthy. I loved humans.

I almost plopped down next to a bevy of beauties and asked to share their baguette and wine, but I was on a mission. This was my chance to interrogate Old Jack and his partner-in-crime, Noah.

And to find out if TCC would help me find my missing shuttle.

That would be a delicate ask.

Eventually, I did spy a very small unobtrusive-looking maintenance-type building. I walked right up to the door and knocked firmly.

From a speaker near the upper corner of the door, I heard, "Jones? Oh, *mon dieu.*" There was a buzzing noise, a clink, and then the door swung open. From inside, I heard, "Get in here, quick!"

I darted inside.

The door swung closed behind me, leaving me in pitch dark. I couldn't see a thing after the bright sunshine outside. "Hello?" I asked. "Is anyone there?"

"Jones, what are you doing here?" a male voice said. "How did you even get here? You're supposed to be on the *Shakespeare.*" The voice was familiar.

"Is there any chance you could turn on a light?"

I heard some muttering, but then another light flipped on. A man stood in front of me: Captain Wu of the *Assyrian.* I'd met him briefly during my earlier escapades. He still looked fierce, like he could cut me in half with his sword if he had one.

The room we were in resembled a dingy broom closet and contained only some ancient gardening equipment. I'd never been to the Terran Cultural Committee headquarters before (that I recalled), but I had been expecting something more magnificent.

"Captain Wu!" I said. "Nice to see you again. What are you doing here?" Did he have a sword?

"I just dropped off another prisoner," he said, looking somewhat exasperated. "I say again--what are you doing here?"

"I wanted to interrogate the, ah, former Jack Jones and his partner in crime, Noah Anderson." I needed to quit thinking about swords.

"I meant, what are you doing here on Earth?"

If memory served, he was one of the people who knew about the stolen FTL drive. Gina had sworn him to secrecy. I had no idea how she'd pulled that off.

I stepped closer to him. "Between you and me, I installed the, ah, extra FTL drive in a shuttle and popped over here from the *Shakespeare*." Belatedly, I recalled Gina said something about political machinations and Captain Wu.

"Gina approved that?" His eyebrows were making a big skeptical V on his forehead.

"Yes," I said. "Of course. You can call her and check if you want." I didn't want him to call her and check, but I knew it would take at least a couple of days for them to communicate since she was so far away. If he had a sword, he didn't appear to have it with him.

"I can't call her. No-tech zone, up here anyway." He relaxed. "I already knew about the drive, remember? I was the one who rescued you from Tau Ceto."

"Yes. Thank you again. I appreciate it." I glanced around the little room. "So, how do we get to the prison area?" Or any TCC area because this didn't seem like TCC.

He sighed and pressed something on the wall, and then a section of the wall swung open.

"Neat!" I zoomed through the doorway and started down the long expanse of concrete stairs before he changed his mind. Where did sword-owners typically keep their blades?

"I better keep an eye on you." He stepped through the door and did something, and the door swung closed behind him.

I descended the stairs. "So, how've you been?"

"Fine." He clomped after me.

My mind was racing, trying to think of something to say, some small talk, but all I could think of were swords. "Uh, so how about those crazy French? What do they have against technology?"

104

He sighed again. Why did folks always seem to sigh around me? "Obviously, it's TCC's policy. They have jammers and other tech in place, so extra-terrestrials can't penetrate the security of this base."

"TCC policy?" I turned back to look at him and almost stumbled on the stairs. "Really? I figured it was a French policy. The French have always been strict about preserving their culture. They legislate baby names, the language, wine, food, and everything else." At least from what I remembered back on that field trip thirty-some-odd years ago.

"Yeah. It's pretty brilliant," Wu said. "French people are brilliant." He said it with pride.

"Are you French?" I asked, surprised.

"Yeah," he said. "Why do you ask it like that?"

We'd finally reached the bottom of the stairs.

"Uh, you don't have an accent."

He shook his head. "*Mon dieu*." He said it in what sounded to me like a flawless French accent.

He stepped around me and pressed something on the wall, and another door swung open. "I am a TCC agent." He pointed through the door. "We're *supposed* to blend in. You could work on your blending in, you know, Jack."

Who would want to blend in? I wanted to stand out. "Ah, good idea," I said. "Thanks."

I stepped into some high-tech nirvana. Everything was bright white; walls, desks, uniforms, electronics. There must have been over fifty TCC officers sitting in front of the latest bleeding-edge computers hard at work. So, clearly down here was not a no-tech zone.

None of the workers turned to look at us.

I was a little insulted. Who wouldn't want to look at me?

Wu closed the door behind us. "Come on." He walked around the desks.

We tramped to an office in the back and entered.

"Wu?" A woman said. She was older, with white hair, but with her smooth skin and bright eyes, she was still very beautiful. If I had to guess, I'd say she was Latina. I glanced at Wu. And French. "I thought you left. What are you doing back here?"

"I ran into Jones, here, entering." He sort of smiled. "Since it's his first time here, I thought I'd show him around." I knew he meant 'keep him out of trouble.'

The woman stood and stared at me. "Jack Jones?"

I dipped my head. "Yes, ma'am."

"What's your mission?" she asked.

Wu interrupted. "Captain Gomez sent him."

"Yes, ma'am. To, ah, interrogate the former Jack Jones and his accomplice, Noah Anderson." It sounded plausible. Sort of.

"It seems a little unusual since I didn't hear anything about it in advance." She turned and looked at something on her console. "But DNA shows you are Jack Jones. And created in one of our TCC cloning facilities."

Did my DNA show that? "How--"

And then the lights turned from white to red, and an alarm started beeping. A voice over some kind of PA system said, "Alert! Unauthorized craft entering orbit! Not responding to hails! Earth is under attack!"

Uh oh. That couldn't be my secret shuttlecraft, could it? It couldn't answer hails because there was no one on board.

Wu looked at me. "Jack?"

"Uh..."

Chapter Sixteen

I stood underground, underneath the Eiffel Tower, surrounded by stressed-out TCC officers and blaring alarms. They seemed to be about to shoot my spaceship out of the sky.

I really didn't want them to shoot my spaceship out of the sky.

Awkward.

To make matters worse, I was getting stressed out myself and having a little trouble concentrating, what with all the blaring and scowling around me.

Where was a soothing hot beverage when you needed it?

"Uh," I said. "Please don't shoot the ship. It's my ship."

The as-yet-unnamed beautiful older Latina turned to me. "Your ship? What ship? How do you have a ship?" This one was good at asking questions.

It was a shuttle from the *Shakespeare,* but I didn't want to say that because it would raise questions like 'how did I travel across the galaxy in a shuttle?' and, even worse, 'how did I get down to the surface if my ship was still in orbit?' The shuttle's FTL drive was supposed to be secret. My special skills were supposed to be secret.

"It's my ship," I said.

"You bought it, right?" Captain Wu said. He knew a little of my backstory but not everything.

No. "Yes." Buying a ship was as good a story as any. "I bought it. At, the, ah, spaceship store."

Wu frowned.

A man in one of those white uniforms rushed in. "The ship does have a TCC transponder."

Beautiful-Latina looked at me like she didn't believe it. But she turned back to her console. "Cancel alert. Stand down, everyone." Her voice echoed out over the loudspeakers. The alarm quieted.

Thank goodness. My pulse quieted in turn.

Everyone seemed to relax a bit. The uniformed man left the room, presumably returning to his desk.

I smiled at the beautiful Latina. "Hi, beautiful. We haven't officially met yet. I'm Jack Jones, the intergalactically renowned singer." I held out my hand.

She smiled and held out her hand. "I know who you are, Jack."

I grabbed her hand, leaned over it and kissed it. "It's always a pleasure to meet a fan." Then, I said, "It's a real honor to meet you. If I'd known TCC senior officers were so gorgeous, I would have visited before."

Wu sighed.

But she made a noise that sounded suspiciously like a giggle and said, "Thank you. You can call me Katarina."

Standing beside me, Captain Wu stiffened, but he only said, "He's here to interrogate the former Jack Jones and Noah Anderson."

The former Jack Jones was a pretty awkward appellation, but when you fake your death, causing your clone to be illegally born--or decanted--and then commit a bunch more crimes, you get what you get. Old Jack lost the right to be Jack Jones.

My mind focused on the word decanted for a few seconds as I recalled that poor creature Sophia had been working on. I shuddered. Focus, Jack.

I was the official Jack Jones. I was on a fact-finding mission.

"That sounds fine," Katarina said. "Captain Wu, can you escort him to the cells?"

"I guess so." He faced me. "Come on, Jack."

The two of us walked back through the busy, cavernous, white room to a closed door in the back. Wu faced the retinal scanner, there was a beep, and the door opened. Through the door was another staircase. We descended.

"How do you do that?" Wu asked.

"Do what?"

"Get people, women, to like you so much? I've known the

commander for years, and she's never asked me to call her Katarina."

"Well, I am pretty awesome." I smiled, but Wu couldn't see it from behind me. "But you're pretty awesome, too. There's no reason why she shouldn't take a shine to you."

"But, seriously, how do you do it?"

How did other people not do it? "I guess... I like and appreciate other people, and I'm not shy about telling them. They pick up on my sincerity and positiveness." I glanced back at him for a split-second. "You could stand to be a little more positive."

He didn't answer me.

"This complex is huge," I said. "How did all this get here?"

"TCC built it using the latest tech and equipment." Wu grunted. "A better question is: how did you get here? Your ship is a shuttlecraft from the *Shakespeare*, right? It has an FTL drive, right?" Clearly, he knew a lot. Darn it.

"How did you get down to the surface?" He was suspicious. But I guessed that made sense. He was a captain in a huge spy organization.

My mind raced. I didn't want to emphasize my special skill. "I caught a ride?" I said.

"Are you asking me or telling me?"

"Telling you, of course," I said. "Asking wouldn't make sense. I'm not asking."

We got to the bottom of the stairs, and he pointed ahead of us down the dimly-lit hall. We traipsed down the hall. On either side of us were detention cells with old-fashioned-looking vertical metal bars. From what I could tell, they were all empty. As we walked, the light brightened above us.

He stopped in front of one of the cells. This one wasn't empty. "Here's Anderson." He pointed inside and then typed something on the keypad. An almost imperceptible shimmer between the bars disappeared.

"Hello?" Noah stood and called out. He was a big burly guy with a huge chest and a mop of gray, curly hair. When I'd first met him, he'd reminded me of a bear, and he still did.

Wu stepped down to the next cell, which was also not empty. "Here's the other guy, whatever we're calling him now." He typed something on that keypad.

"Hello?" Old Jack said, standing. "Wu, is that you?" Old Jack was also fifty-ish with gray hair, but on him, it looked handsome and distinguished rather than ursine.

Wu didn't answer Old Jack. He said to me, "I'll be back."

I nodded. The adjacent cells were empty. I guessed TCC didn't have many prisoners.

He spun around and marched back the way we'd come.

Noah and Old Jack had walked up to the bars and grasped them as they stared at me.

"Jack?" Noah asked. "What are you doing here?"

"TCC authorized you to come here?" Old Jack asked. "Or is something else going on?"

"Something else?" Noah asked, staring at Old Jack. "What else would be going on?"

"Is Daniel truly gone?" Old Jack asked.

Noah gasped.

I felt very tired all of a sudden. I sank to the floor against the wall opposite their cells.

"Jack?" Old Jack asked, staring at me.

"Jack?" Noah asked, staring at me.

"Answer me," Old Jack asked. "How did you contact me before?"

These old guys were too bossy. What gave them the right to question me? Nothing, that's what. They were criminals.

"When did he contact you?" Noah asked.

"How'd you do that ansible thing earlier?" Old Jack asked. "How'd it get through the forcefield?"

"What ansible thing?" Noah asked.

I gathered in my own bossiness. "Shut up. I'm the one asking the questions here." Coming to Earth had been an impulse, but that didn't mean I couldn't take advantage of it. I glanced at my fon. Rehearsal should be starting about now on the *Shakespeare*.

The two old men both shut up and looked at me.

What was I most concerned about right now? "What do you know about Daniel's death?"

"Daniel's dead?" Noah asked.

"We didn't have anything to do with it," Old Jack said. "It's a pity. Daniel is, er, he was, a good man."

"So, you're both claiming you had nothing to do with it?" I asked.

"We're incarcerated," Old Jack said. "We're good, but we're not that good. How could we have something to do with it?"

"Obviously, I know you weren't on the *Shakespeare* yourselves, but you could have hired someone or something," I said. "Maybe you left a booby trap? Or you might know something. It could have something to do with..." I paused and looked around. What were the chances that we were being recorded? About a hundred percent, I was guessing. "Something to do with the events of the previous months, with the events that led you to these cells."

"What are you talking about?" Noah ran his hand through his already messy hair.

"I'm asking the questions here." My mind raced. What was the question? "Who knew about your stolen cargo in the cargo bay?"

"No one," Old Jack said.

"I didn't tell anyone," Noah said. So, Noah knew.

"Did Daniel know anything about your cargo?" I asked. Thinking back, he'd seemed pretty surprised when he and I found the secret FTL drive a few months ago.

"No," Old Jack said. "And I don't see how anything I, or we, did months ago could cause Daniel to be murdered now."

I stared at them. They did seem sincere. But how the hell would I know? If my short life had taught me anything, it was that I was not a good judge of people. I hadn't known Noah, here, was a villain. And I hadn't even known Old Jack still existed.

Maybe I was too positive.

"Okay," I said. "New topic. Do you have any ideas on who kidnapped me and why?"

"You were kidnapped?" Old Jack asked.

"You were kidnapped?" Noah said.

"What happened?" Old Jack asked. "Tell me what happened."

So, we were all in the dark, all three of us. Ugh. "I was on Keplarr-452b watching the *Shakespeare*'s show," I said, "And somebody drugged me and grabbed me and threw me in a hole. The *Shakespeare's* crew found me after a couple of hours."

"Keplarr-452b?" The blood seemed to drain from Old Jack's face. He looked haunted. Gee, that wasn't suspicious at all. My mind started to go back to the dark place when I didn't know if I'd be saved, tortured, or executed, but I forced it away.

The lights in the hall dimmed. Yikes. I didn't want to be literally in the dark again; metaphorically in the dark was bad enough. I waved my arms around, and the motion sensors flipped the light back on. Phew.

In the meantime, the two men had exchanged a look.

"Nothing," Old Jack said. "We don't know anything."

So, they knew something. Check. "I can tell you know something. What?"

"Nope," Old Jack said. "Don't know anything."

I exhaled and stood up. What an asshole. How could he just keep me in the dark? "You're lying!" I yelled. "Tell me!"

They didn't answer.

Why did so many people keep me in the dark? Even that stupid sldkfjfoisut creature had kept me in the dark. It, she, I guess, had just made a baby with me--without even asking my permission. And she'd said she had information for me but never told me what it was.

"Tell me what you know about the sldkfjfoisut!" I said.

"The sldkfjfoisut?" Noah asked, his face turning red. He glanced at Old Jack. "Rare species. How do you know about them?"

"Tell me!" I may have jumped up and down a little. "I demand you tell me. Now!"

After looking at Noah, Old Jack finally said, "A couple of renegade sldkfjfoisut were my brokers for the stolen FTL drive."

"Renegade sldkfjfoisut? I thought they were practically extinct," I said. "What does brokers mean? Like pawnbrokers? They sold you the stolen drive?"

"Yeah," Old Jack said. He looked a little ashamed. Good. He should feel ashamed about encouraging practically-extinct creatures to commit crimes. "I can't believe you know about the sldkfjfoisut."

"How did you even find out about them, er, young Jack?" Noah asked. "They don't generally interact with humans. I'm not sure they're even allowed on Earth."

Clearly, sometimes they interacted with humans--if little Slid was any indication.

"I'm asking the questions here!" I said. And, yay, me. I'd actually learned something.

"Now tell me what you told TCC when they interrogated you before," I said, now full of confidence.

Noah shuffled his feet. "We didn't tell them anything." I couldn't tell if he was being sincere or not.

I took a step towards his cell. Didn't he have a crush on me? I smiled handsomely. "Are you sure about that, Noah?" I said in a tender voice. "If you help me, maybe I can help you."

Old Jack gave me an odd look.

Noah took a step back.

I took a step forward. Would it be possible to kiss someone through the bars? I bet it would.

Captain Wu said, "Ready?"

I jumped. Where had he come from?

I looked from Noah to Old Jack and back again. They didn't look like they were going to spill any more secrets. Finally, I said, "Yeah. These assholes haven't been very helpful."

Wu was already typing on keypads. "I'm not surprised." The shimmering between the bars returned.

Old Jack moved his lips, but I now couldn't hear anything. Too late. He lost his chance to do the right thing.

Wu turned and started walking back down the hall.

I hurried to catch up to him.

"I'm taking off with the *Assyrian*." He glanced at me sidelong, like he was suspicious of me.

Brainstorm. He had a ship taking off from the Earth's surface. I needed a ride from Earth's surface. "Can you give me a ride to my ship?"

He grunted. "You were nice enough to answer my personal question, so, I guess."

I glanced at my fon. Rehearsal might still be going on. But what about Sophia?

"Can we stop in North America?" I asked. "I want to say goodbye to someone."

Wu exhaled. Loudly. "Now you're pushing it, Jones."

"Pretty please?" I fluttered my eyelashes engagingly.

He exhaled loudly. "I guess."

Once we exited the TCC facility and the tech-dampening field, I dialed Sophia.

"Jack?" she asked. "I've been trying to call. Are you still on Earth? Do you want to get together?"

"Of course, I'm still here, beautiful. I want to meet up to say goodbye and a proper hello."

I glanced at Wu. He was frowning.

A little later, I entered the front doors of the Duplication facility. The front hallway looked like every other sterile medical facility hallway on the planet, all clean and white.

Wu had stayed behind in his small shuttlecraft. Apparently, the small *Assyrian* had small shuttles to go with it.

Sophia saw me immediately and squealed. Her blonde curls and other parts of her bounced deliciously. She ran up to me and gave me a big old hug. She felt wonderful in my arms.

I gave her a juicy kiss.

She kissed me back enthusiastically.

When we finally separated, all too soon, she said, "What are you doing here on Earth, Jack?"

"It's a secret TCC mission. Sorry, I can't tell you." I sighed on the inside. I was getting entirely too good at lying. "But since I was here, I had to stop and say hello to my favorite Earthling."

"That was hello?" She beamed. "I liked it."

"Sadly," I said, "Now I have to say goodbye."

She reached for me. "If it's anything like hello, I'm all for it."

We kissed some more.

We were rudely interrupted by Commander Wu walking into the Dupe facility. "What's taking so long, Jones?"

Sophia and I separated, staring at him. Where had he come from? He was like a ninja the way he kept sneaking up on me.

He exhaled a lungful of smoke. Upon closer inspection, he was smoking one of those brown French-type cigarettes. It smelled awful.

"Huh..." Sophia said.

I turned back to her. "What?"

"I forgot until now, but when I was working on you, when you were at Horace's stage--" she inclined her head back towards

114

her lab"--there was some smoke or something in the lab."

Smoke? Maybe it was because I had sldkfjfoisut on my mind after talking to Old Jack, but what if it hadn't been smoke in Sophia's lab? What if it had really been a smoke-monster? I resisted the urge to whisper *Mark me*.

"Let's go," Commander Wu said.

I held Sophia's hands in my hands. "*It were a grief... to part with thee. Farewell,*" I said.

"*Parting is such sweet sorrow,*" she said.

"*Farewell! thou are too dear for my possessing,*" I said.

She started to say something else, but I pressed my lips to hers before she could do so.

And then I quickly twirled, in a manly way, and exited the building.

My ride on Wu's ship up to the *Shakespeare*'s shuttle was uneventful. No kissing. No Shakespeare quotes. Captain Wu didn't even say goodbye when he dropped me off.

For my part, I was glad to get back to my familiar shuttle. I had mixed feelings about my little jaunt to Earth. Seeing Sophia had been heavenly, and I did learn some sldkfjfoisut were involved in Old Jack's evil plot.

But...I realized I probably shouldn't have gone. It was too impulsive. I was several months old now and should have known better.

My FTL trip back to the *Shakespeare* was uneventful. I very carefully did not wish I was anywhere else.

When I came out of FTL space, I found ...nothing.

There was no sign of the *Shakespeare*.

I floated in outer space in a shuttle, surrounded by the vast empty reaches of vacuum.

I was alone in the dark.

Again.

Chapter Seventeen

Sitting alone in my shuttle, alone in outer space, I pondered: if I was a giant missing spaceship, where would I be?

For a second, my breath caught in my throat. Things hadn't been going smoothly on the *Shakespeare*. What if something bad happened?

What if it wasn't anywhere? What if it'd blown up?

But if that had happened, there'd be a debris field. I accessed the sensors. No debris. Phew.

I leaned back in the captain's chair. Where were they?

Gina had said something, hadn't she? Something about them leaving the area...

I couldn't recall what it was.

I pulled my memory-recording rig and the data cube with my memories on it out of my pocket. Ha. I wasn't going to get caught memoryless again.

I could use the rig to access my memories of the other day.

I fired it up and soon got lost in the sex with the smoke-monster. I re-experienced waves of pure pleasure washing over me, over and over again. When it finally stopped, I was gasping for breath. "Wow." I had to try that again.

Waves of pleasure overtook me.

After I didn't know how long, I became aware of myself again.

"Wow." I tried to calm down and catch my breath.

What had I been doing? I glanced around. I was on a shuttle. I was lost in space.

Oh, yeah. I was trying to recall where the *Shakespeare* was bound.

I glanced around again. I was not in a good situation. I

hadn't even checked how much air, fuel, or other supplies I had. I couldn't afford to sit here and re-experience memories repeatedly--no matter how awesome they were.

I glanced at my fon. Oh, no! According to my fon, several hours had passed.

Suddenly, I felt afraid. That was a close one. I could have sat here, lost in memories until I died. I could have run out of oxygen and not even known it.

I hadn't realized memories could be dangerous.

I deliberately checked the shuttle's front control panel. The air and fuel gauges were large, obvious, and both at about fifty percent. Phew.

I carefully accessed my memory rig again, fast-forwarding past the sexcapades.

I remembered the huge viewscreen on the bridge showing a beautiful tableau of a star surrounded by planets.

At his duty station, Carter said, "Setting a course for Planet Yeblypso, Captain."

In the captain's chair, Gina turned around and looked at me. "Oh, all right! I'll tell you about the new show. It's *Hair*."

I quickly extracted myself from memory.

I set a course for Planet Yeblypso.

Once I was underway, only a few hours away from Yeblypso, I winced and checked the air, fuel, water, and food supplies.

Phew. I had just enough air, fuel and water. But no food. Who needed food?

Suddenly I was starving. I couldn't even remember the last time I'd eaten. I resisted the urge to check my memories to find out.

I took a few very slow sips of water and settled in to wait.

At planet Yeblypso I could see the *Shakespeare* in orbit. My plan was: I was going to throw myself on the mercy of the court and beg Gina for forgiveness.

I hailed the *Shakespeare*. "This is shuttlecraft one, requesting communication with Captain Gomez."

The comms officer answered, "You're cleared to dock, Ensign Jones. Then, report immediately to the brig." She had kind of a sexy, sultry voice. Had I ever met the comms officer?

Why did she call me ensign? I'd been promoted. I wasn't an ensign any more.

And brig? I didn't want to report to the brig. I'd experienced the brig, and I didn't like it.

"Uh, come again, ma'am?"

"Dock, Jones. Report to the brig." Hmm. Maybe it wasn't such a sexy voice after all.

"Can I talk to Captain Gomez?"

"No." Nah. It wasn't sexy.

"Please?" I asked.

"No." It was a scary voice.

"Pretty please?" I found myself fluttering my eyelashes even though I knew she couldn't see them.

"Give me a break!" she said. "Captain Gomez isn't even on the ship. She's down on the planet preparing for the show."

"Thanks," I said. "Jones out."

"What are you--" the comms officer started to say, but I cut her off.

Surface, here I come! I could easily throw myself on Gina's mercy on the surface. Surely, she'd see reason.

I landed the shuttle at the space port. They approved me immediately when they registered I was a shuttle from the *Shakespeare*.

I exited the shuttle. This planet was very humid. There was so much moisture in the air that it practically felt like I was swimming as I walked through the port. It was a huge sun-filled room with a lot of windows in the ceiling, seemingly large enough to park a spaceship in.

The space port had an unusual number of different species perambulating around. I only recognized a few of them, such as the mouse-like and turtle-like creatures of previous missions. Had I seen one of those giant slugs at another space port? I carefully stepped around its slime trail; it looked slippery.

I debated texting Eva and inquiring about the venue but saw a neat poster: '*Hair*! The Terran Musical! Today! Featuring galactically-renowned singer Jack Jones as Claude! Human Adventures and Antics! Human nudity! Yeblypso Amphitheatre next to the space port!'

Judging by all the exclamation points, they were excited. And, of course, they were excited. Probably everyone on the planet was excited.

I stood there for a few moments, drinking it all in.

From behind me, I heard, "Hey, human..."

I twirled. Some creatures that reminded me of monkeys sat in a kind of golf-cart machine. They had slight physiques, big chins covered in thin brownish-orange fur, and ears that stuck out.

"Yes, it's me," I said, smiling. "Would you like an autograph?"

The driver said, "No. Move! You're blocking the way!"

I stepped closer to the wall.

As they zoomed past me, it almost sounded like they said something like, 'Stupid humans...' But that couldn't be right.

Galactically-renowned singer Jack Jones held his head high, smiled, and stepped lively to the Yeblypso Amphitheatre.

When I got to the theater, the sentient at the door, also resembling a monkey, had the gall to ask me if I had a ticket. After explaining I was in the show, I had to elbow my way inside. I marched right up to the stage door.

With long spindly limbs, the guard had the nerve not to step aside when I asked him to let me backstage. "No," he (?) growled. With his small black eyes, flat nose, wide mouth, and thin brown-orange fur, he reminded me of a chimpanzee even more than the other natives I'd met.

"I assure you, good sir, I'm in the show. They need me backstage." I reached for the door.

"No," he said, pulling out a device that buzzed. I didn't know anything about Yeblypso devices, but it definitely gave off a stun-gun vibe.

I took a step back and rubbed my arms. I'd been stun-gunned. It was not fun.

"Seriously," I said. "I'm in the show. I need to get back there."

"No." He smiled, showing off a very long row of pointy teeth. "And that's your last warning."

I took a step back.

The lights flickered, indicating the show was about to start.

How could it start? I wasn't backstage!

The guard extended his buzzy device in my direction.

I stepped back some more. "Seriously?"

He showed off his teeth again and nodded.

Well, I never. These Yeblypso people were very rude.

I turned around and marched back to the seating area. As I stared out over the mostly-full seats, the lights dimmed. When I looked toward the stage, the entire cast already stood there.

I couldn't believe it. They were doing the show without me. Who was playing Claude?

Another one of the chimpanzee guard types appeared at my side. "Find your seat, sir."

I jumped. At least he 'sir'ed me. That was better than electrocuting me.

I frowned and elbowed my way to an empty seat as the lights went up on stage.

A diminutive creature with a kind of feathery down on its face said, "I don't think that's your seat, sir."

I smiled and said, "I think it is my seat, sir."

The downy creature didn't reply, sinking down in its seat.

"*When the moon is in the seventh house...*" the entire cast sang.

I soon lost myself in the show. That opening number was beautiful.

And then Carter was spotlighted. He said, "My name is Claude. Claude Hooper..."

"Ack!" I said.

Sentients behind me said, "*Shh!*"

Carter was Claude? Inconceivable!

He started singing, "*Manchester England England...*"

"No way!" I whispered. That was my role.

"*Shh!*"

And then I felt a little prick, a familiar prick. I was getting a whole déjà vu thing. Déjà vu from when I got kidnapped!

I started screaming at the top of my lungs. "Help! Help! *Aaaaghh!*" But I started feeling woozy.

Sentients lifted me out of my seat.

"Help! I'm being kidnapped! Help!" But I was running out of juice as the drugs or whatever kicked in. "Help!" but it petered out.

"Help... " I really shouldn't watch the *Shakespeare*'s shows from the audience. It never seemed to end well for me.

In the background, I was dimly aware of the show stopping, of the house lights coming up...

When I came to, I was in a cavernous humid room. Gina was there, and she was livid; I could practically see steam coming out of her ears. There were several of those chimpanzee-type creatures there.

There was probably a mission briefing I should have read on planet Yeblypso.

I looked around the room. It was filled with plants, green leaves and vines everywhere. The floor seemed to be covered with a kind of short verdant grass. But there was a ceiling. How did they keep all these plants alive inside? Was that a bird over there? It smelled luscious, like a jungle.

I was guessing my attempted kidnapping had been foiled.

"So this is Jack Jones? The so-called galactically-renowned singer?" A deep voice, an authoritarian voice, interrupted my sightseeing. "He's littler than I expected."

The crowd parted, and I saw what looked like a large chimp wearing a cape and crown and sitting on a throne.

I couldn't help it, I started laughing. I laughed and laughed. I laughed until tears ran down my face.

Peripherally, I realized Gina started looking madder and madder. She kept glancing at the King Chimp.

But as I continued to laugh, her angry look turned fearful as she stared at King Chimp.

The chimps surrounded me. Several of them held those buzzy, stunny devices. They showed off their teeth as they approached.

"Jack," Gina said. "Get a hold of yourself. You're being disrespectful." She turned to the king. "I think he's sick or something. He doesn't mean to disrespect you. We respect you, sir. Terrans respect you a lot." Her smile looked forced.

But I couldn't seem to stop laughing. Laugh. Laugh. Laugh. It must have been the drugs.

And then electricity coursed through my body. I stopped

laughing. "*Ooowww*! Ow..."

When I came to, I was in a cell. It seemed chiseled out of rock with crisscrossed bars made of wood.

Not again.

It was still humid.

Gina was there, and she looked tired. "Oh, you're awake."

I sat up, wincing. The chimp's stun gun engendered a dull ache all over my body. I also had a headache--probably from the drugs. "Ouch."

She sighed. "What's wrong with you, Jack?"

I was guessing that was a rhetorical question.

"Were you trying to cause an interplanetary incident?" She shook her head.

"Wait a minute," I said. "Why are you in a cell?"

"Inter. Planetary. Incident," she said, enunciating each syllable.

"It wasn't my fault," I said. "Plus, come on, a Chimp King." I felt my lips grin. "That's funny."

She growled. "Do I have to remind you again about convergent evolution?"

She'd reminded me about that? What was that? And when had she told me about it?

I must have looked confused because she said, "Obviously, they aren't chimpanzees. They only look like chimps. Different planets have different species and different biospheres. They're bipedal humanoids whose ancestors evolved in trees."

I shrugged. "It wasn't my fault. I was under the influence of drugs. I got drugged."

"Drugged?" she asked.

"Yes," I said. "I have proof. Look. There's got to be a puncture mark on my neck." I craned my neck in her direction.

She got up and stared down at me. "Hmm. I do see a mark. But why do people keep drugging and kidnapping you?"

"Some kind of nefarious plan?" I said.

She curled her lip.

"Or maybe they weren't trying to kidnap me. Maybe somebody's out-maneuvering the Terran spies, trying to cause an incident." Now that I'd said it, it made a kind of sense.

Or, maybe not. Maybe they *were* trying to kidnap me. Who the hell knew?

Her sensuous lips said, "We need to get to the bottom of this. If Terran spies are at risk, planet Earth could be at risk."

Yikes. I hadn't even thought of that. Planet Earth at risk? Oh no.

Chapter Eighteen

Gina and I spent a long quiet afternoon in the Yeblypso jail. Whenever I tried to start a conversation, she pointed at the ceiling and shook her head.

When they brought us a dinner of bananas, I couldn't help laughing again. I mean, come on.

"They're not bananas," Gina said. "They're convergently evolved banana-like plants--" right before she broke down and started laughing herself.

"I'm still mad at you," she said when she finished laughing.

I nodded. "Fair enough."

"What happened to you yesterday?" she asked. "Did you, ah, fulfill your mission in the shuttle bay?" She glanced around the cell.

Did she think the cell was bugged? It was a reasonable assumption.

"I did fulfill my mission," I said.

"And then what happened?"

"I tested out the, ah, apparatus."

She curled her lip. I could tell she was dying to ask me where I went but didn't want the Yeblypso natives to know about our secret FTL drive. "What happened? No. Don't tell me now. Tell me later."

I shrugged.

"Why are you in here with me, anyway?" I asked.

She exhaled loudly, and I could tell she was refraining from one of her carefully enunciated sentences. Finally, she said, "You accused the Yeblypso people of being unable to keep their guests safe. Honor is very important to them. I was in the throne room to try to smooth things over. Then, when you disrespected the king, they got so pissed off that they threw me in the cell with you." She paused. "So, thanks for that."

Yikes.

We sat there in silence for a few moments. She still looked very luscious.

We couldn't save Earth at the moment. "Wanna make out?" I asked.

She shook her head, but I saw her smile, too.

"*Thy husband is...*" I said.

"Careful," she said, no doubt thinking about the obedience stuff. But I wasn't a total idiot.

"*Thy husband is one that cares for thee, and for thy maintenance commits his body...*" I waggled my eyebrows. "*To painful labour both by sea and land,*" I said, "*to watch the night in storms, the day in cold, and craves no other tribute at thy hands but love, fair looks...*"

"*Too little payment for so great a debt,*" she whispered. And then she got up and kissed me. On the lips.

"*Mmmm,*" I said. I'd been right. She was a fabulous kisser. Our souls melded together as if we'd always been one.

The evening passed much more pleasurably.

Right up until Carter showed up. "Oh, Jesus Christ!" He stood outside the cell with one of those not-a-chimps. His face was all flushed.

"Oh, thank God." Gina bolted up, straightening her clothing.

Thank God?

"Are you sure you even want out?" Carter said in a kind of peevish voice.

Was I sure? No. "Ah..." I said. "Maybe you could give us a little more time..."

"Yes. Hurry up!" Gina said.

Hurry up?

She glanced back at me. "Get it together, Jack!"

I slowly stood up as the non-chimp unlocked the cell.

"What happened with the show?" Gina asked as she strode out.

"We started over," Carter said, seemingly calming. "It was fine."

I still couldn't believe Gina had given Carter my part. I may

125

have been gaping at him a little. How could it have gone fine without me?

"Jack!" Gina said. "Let's go!"

I stumbled after them, adjusting my own clothing. Walking and buttoning were a little difficult to do at the same time. It was too humid on this planet, anyway. I decide to forego buttoning my shirt.

"Only fine?" Gina asked.

"Okay, it was fabulous," Carter said, glancing back at me and frowning. "The natives were thrilled."

"How'd you manage to get us out?" Gina asked.

"Jack's friend helped," Carter said.

As we turned a corner, I saw a familiar smoky creature standing with a small group of non-chimps. "Jack!" she said and sparkled a little.

"How's Slid?" I asked, overcome with guilt that I hadn't thought of it until now. "Did Eva take good care of him? Her?"

"Yes, Jack," the creature said. "My offspring is doing great."

"Why are you out of the brig?" Gina asked the smoke-creature.

The non-chimps looked unhappy.

"Out of the dancing rig?" Carter asked. "Yes, the ambassador here got tired of dancing."

Ambassador?

The smoke-creature sparkled.

Gina looked confused for a moment, but then, super-spy that she was, she rallied. "Well, thank you so much for your generous accommodations, but we need to get back to the *Shakespeare* ASAP."

One of the non-chimps said, "What's ASAP?"

The smoke-creature sparkled and said, "It's a human thing. Yes, I need them to return to their ship with me since I'm an important ambassador and all."

The non-chimps stepped back. One of them waved towards the exit.

The smoke-creature flowed that way. Carter and Gina, and I quickly followed.

Carter opened the door to reveal the space port. Convenient.

126

"Back to the ship ASAP," Gina said. "We'll debrief there." She glanced at Carter. "Good job getting us out of there. Thank you." She turned to me. "If you get the shuttle, can I trust you to return to the ship?"

"Of course!" I said. How could she imply I wasn't trustworthy?

"I'll go with Jack," the smoke-creature said.

"Okay, Ambassador," Gina said slowly. Then, Gina and Carter turned and speed-walked away.

I started walking to my shuttle with the smoke-creature flowing beside me. "Uh, this is a little awkward considering everything we've been through already." My mind dipped back to our sexcapades, and I almost climaxed right then and there. Focus, Jack! "Are you truly an ambassador? What's your name? And are you a girl or what?"

The smoke-creature made a sound like a laugh as we approached the shuttle. "Our species doesn't have males and females as you understand them, but I accepted my mate's genetic material and carried it until a suitable facilitator was found, and I brought the new offspring into the world. You can consider me female if it helps."

We reached the shuttle. "And your name?" I pressed my palm to the DNA reader and my eye near the eye-reader.

She said, "Adfsodiaotuaorh."

Oh, good grief. There was no way I could say that. The shuttle doors snicked open.

"Can I call you, ah, Addie?" We stepped or flowed into the shuttle. I closed the door.

"Why? That's not my name," she said.

"As a sign of affection. Humans would call it a pet name. We've been through so much, after all." Focus, Jack!

"I've never had a pet name," she sounded pleased. "How nice. I don't care what other species say; humans are nice."

I was strapping into the pilot's chair. "Wait. What do other species say about us?" I glanced at her. "I don't know if you can strap in, but get ready for takeoff."

I initiated the takeoff procedure. We took off. I set a course for the *Shakespeare*. Through the viewport, Yeblypso was a vibrant green marble.

When I looked around for Addie, she was floating this way and that, definitely not strapped in.

"What do other species say about us?" I asked again.

She made her laughing sound again. "Well, among other things, they say humans are stupid."

I raised my eyebrows. I had no idea where we stood in the galaxy's intellectual pecking order.

She flowed up to the front of the ship. "My, my, my. Is this the FTL drive?" She flowed towards me a little. I tried not to get excited. "Maybe you are less stupid than other humans?"

We approached the *Shakespeare*.

Talk about a backhanded compliment.

The comms officer said, "Ensign Jones, you're cleared for approach. Enter shuttle bay one."

Ensign? I was still an ensign? Bummer. I felt my lips curl down.

Now I was definitely in a bad mood. "Addie, please don't insult my species. And come to think of it, you said you had information to trade with me. I want that information. "

She flowed into the co-pilot's chair. "Apologies. I didn't mean to insult your species. I am grateful to you for helping me procreate. Let me make it up to you. We can copulate again. It will not result in offspring, but you will still enjoy it."

Whoa. That was an offer that was hard to refuse. Hard. Heh, heh.

Focus, Jack! "Thank you for the offer, but no. Spill the info you promised me." We flew into shuttle bay one.

"I am an ambassador for my species," she said.

"I already figured that out. You owe me more than that."

"I am an alien expert among my people," she said.

I stopped the shuttle and powered it off. "Continue."

"I've heard rumors..." She trailed off.

My fon trilled. It was a text from Gina. 'Jack, bring the sldkfjfoisut ambassador and report to my ready room.'

I didn't get up. "Addie, tell me what's going on. Now. I need to know."

"But it's just rumors," she said in a little voice.

"Tell me."

The shuttle made some soft, pinging noises as it warmed up

128

in the shuttle bay.

"There may be a problem," she said.

"A problem? What kind of problem?"

"A problem with the FTL drives."

I felt my eyebrows crawl up my forehead like some kind of creatures. "What?"

My fon trilled again. 'Now, Jack!'

"What kind of problem with the FTL drives?" I asked.

"A problem like they could all stop working."

I jumped out of my chair. "What! They're defective? That could strand people across the galaxy! That could kill people! That could kill a lot of people!"

"They're not defective," Addie continued in her small, scared-sounding voice. "They were designed that way."

"What!"

My fon said, "Jack! Report!" in Gina's strident voice.

I glanced at it in annoyance.

I tried to calm down. Screaming at Addie didn't seem to be helping anything. I focused on calm breathing. "I don't understand, Addie. What are you saying?" I said in a more reasonable tone.

"That's the rumor," she said in a more regular tone. "The designers built in an off switch. They control all the drives."

"Who are the designers?" I asked.

"I don't know," she said.

"How does the off switch work?"

"I don't know."

"Will they turn them off?"

"I don't know."

"When would they turn them off?"

"I don't know."

The shuttle door snicked open. Gina stood in the doorway, fuming. "I can't believe you're blowing me off. Especially after what we just ...shared."

I looked from Addie to Gina and back again. Two women I'd shared carnal delights with. Recently.

"Is this your mate, Jack?" Addie asked.

Awkward.

"Don't change the subject, Addie. You have to tell Gina what you just told me."

But Addie just flowed around the shuttle cabin, not sparkly at all. In fact, she looked kind of gray and blah.

"What did she just tell you?" Gina asked, less angry.

I stared at Addie, but she wasn't forthcoming. "She said all the FTL drives are vulnerable to being turned off ...at any time."

Addie bounced up and down as if she were nodding in agreement.

"But why?" Gina looked thoughtful.

After a few moments, Gina slowly said, "War?"

Addie bobbed up and down a little more, looking gray and stormy, before saying, "Yes."

Chapter Nineteen

My lover Ambassador Addie had just dropped a bombshell. All the FTL drives could be turned off at any time without notice.

She bobbed in the hall of the *Shakespeare*, all gray and smoky. I was deciphering that was what she looked like when she was unhappy.

The bleak winter landscape mural on the wall matched her mood. I stared at it for a moment. What was it supposed to be? The setting of King Lear? I muttered, "*Unhappy that I am...*"

My lover (sort of), Captain Gina, also stood in the hall, also looking unhappy.

Huh. I had some distinguished lovers.

Gina frowned at me as she pulled out her fon. "All senior officers report to the captain's ready room immediately." She turned and started storming off down the hall.

Then, she stopped and turned back. "Well? Aren't you guys coming?"

Addie bobbed up and down, which I knew meant yes.

"Yes," I said, bobbing up and down on the balls of my feet.

Addie and I raced after Captain Gina. I let her stay ahead of us. Truth be told, even after our recent makeout session, I was still a little intimidated by her.

The senior officers were already there when we got to the ready room. Handsome, young-looking Commander Bello of engineering was there. Handsome First Officer Carter was there. Security Commander Lu was there. Even Doctor Sharma was there. I hadn't known he was a senior officer.

At any rate, they all pretty much glared at me as I entered. For a fleeting moment, I wondered if they thought I was handsome.

"What's Jones doing here?" Commander Bello asked.

Gina silenced him with a look as she sat down at the table.

"Yeah, since when do ensigns..." Carter started to say.

Gina silenced him with just the beginning of a look. "So, Ambassador, ah..."

Carter said, "Adfsodiaotuaorh."

Gina said, "Ambassador Adfsodiaotuaorh has something to tell us."

Oh, good grief. Why was everyone but me so good at saying alien names?

Gina leaned over the table towards Addie with eyes narrowed. "First, why don't you explain why you didn't tell us initially that you were an ambassador?"

Considering the fates of all sentients in the galaxy were basically at stake, I said, "Is that really what we should focus on now?"

Everyone froze for a moment.

Then, Gina cleared her throat and said, "Okay. Tell them what you said about the FTL drives."

Addie said in her little, scared voice, "The FTL drives can be turned off remotely."

Everyone sitting around the table jerked back.

"What!"

I didn't catch who said that.

"Oh no," Carter said.

"Are you sure?" Commander Bello asked. "Remotely? By someone other than the operator?"

Gina grimaced. "Continue, Ambassador Adfsodiaotuaorh."

"Yes," Addie said. "I haven't seen it happen myself, but we have intelligence that the FTL drives can be remotely turned off."

"But that could strand the ships anywhere," Commander Bello said. "It could kill everyone."

Gina nodded. "Yes. You've grasped the primary problem."

"But, that..." Carter stuttered like he didn't know what to say.

"Why?" Commander Lu asked.

Addie turned an even darker gray. "We surmise the species that built the FTL drives wants control of the galaxy."

"Why surmise this?" I asked. "Do you have evidence?"

Addie didn't answer me.

"But people won't accept that," Carter said. "We won't let others control us."

"What can we or anyone else do about it?" Commander Lu asked. "Start a war?"

"Yes," Gina said.

"We think intergalactic war is coming," Addie said in her scared voice.

"Against who?" Lu said. "We don't even know who the enemy is."

"Why war?" I asked. "What's there to gain by a war?"

Doctor Sharma said, "War would be bad," frowning and shaking his head.

"*I'll not weep*," I said. "*I have full cause of weeping, but this heart shall break into a hundred thousand flaws, or ere I'll weep.*"

Addie said, "*As flies to wanton boys are we to the gods; they kill us for their sport.*" My lover Addie knew the bard! Nice.

"Quit with the *King Lear*," Gina said. "It's not helping anything."

She was right. What would help? Knowing who the enemy was would help. I glanced sidelong at Addie; was she telling us the truth, the whole truth and nothing but the truth? Did she have any evidence of all this? Did she know who built the FTL drives? Where had the rumors come from? "Can you tell us anything else, Addie?"

"No," she said.

"Shouldn't we send out a warning to the rest of the TCC fleet?" Commander Lu asked.

Gina nodded.

"Shouldn't we warn everyone, other species?" I asked. "We don't want anyone to die, do we?"

All the human officers glanced at each other, exchanging a look, like 'what are we going to do with this kid?'

"Hey!" I said. "I'm not a kid! And I know saving sentients is the right thing to do. We're going to do that, right? Save all the sentients?"

Addie's color brightened to a midnight blue, and she bobbed over next to me.

"Well..." Commander Lu said. I wasn't sure I liked security commanders.

Doctor Sharma said, "Young Jack is correct. I took an oath to help sentients, all sentients. What does TCC stand for if not humanity? The best of humanity? Doesn't that mean helping sentients if we can?"

Carter grabbed Gina's hand. "What do you think?"

She looked into his eyes for a moment, and her expression softened. "It's dangerous. And it's just a rumor at this point."

"I concur. That would put us on the bad guys' radar," Commander Lu said. "It might even cause them to turn off all the FTL drives immediately."

If only we knew who the bad guys were.

Gina nodded her head assertively. "Let's notify everyone quietly, using back channels."

Addie turned a kind of royal blue with a little bit of sparkle. "I might like humans after all."

"Isn't there some way we can detect who built the FTL drive?" I asked.

Everyone turned to examine me.

"Can't we scan the drive for DNA?" I asked.

"We already scanned our drive," Commander Bello said. "It's standard practice when TCC takes delivery of a drive. We are trying to find out who built them, after all." It was one of the best-kept secrets of the galaxy.

But my brain was zinging. The drive in engineering right now was a different drive than the one they'd scanned. And it hadn't come through official channels. What if it had some DNA on it?

Gina was looking at me like she knew I was onto something. "Jack?"

"Commander Bello," I said, "I think you should scan the *Shakespeare*'s FTL drive again."

"What's the point?" he said. "I already did."

Gina interrupted him. "No. Jack's right. Scan it again. Scan it with every device we've got." She stood up. "Jack, help him."

"But..." Commander Bello said.

She silenced him with her expression.

"Yes, ma'am," he said as he stood.

I stood as well. "Yes, ma'am."

Operation 'Find the Bad Guys' was about to begin in

earnest.

Chapter Twenty

I was dying of curiosity about the secret FTL drive, so I accompanied Commander Bello to engineering. Of course, technically, I was also ordered to accompany him, so it was a win-win.

He scowled at me but didn't object. Once in engineering, he rummaged around in some storage bay for a while and finally pulled out what looked like a giant fon. He blew the dust off it, marched over to the FTL drive, flipped on the device and pointed it at the drive.

It immediately lit up with lots of flashing lights and beeps and such.

As he stared at the device, his scowl deepened more and more. A person could practically fall into that scowl, it was so deep.

"You are a very good scowler," I said.

When he looked at me and glared, I added, "Sir."

He expelled a big bunch of air, like a spaceship using its thrusters.

I really wondered what he'd detected.

"Olivia!" he bellowed.

I snickered a little at the thought of Commander Bello bellowing.

"Olivia!"

The beautiful and mysterious Olivia appeared around some equipment. "Sir?" She was mysterious because she was one of the few people that didn't seem to like me. I needed to remedy that.

I bowed deeply to her. "*I never saw true beauty till this night,* Fair Olivia."

She ignored me. How could that be?

"Sir?" she said again to Bello. "What can I do for you?"

"Since your DNA is all over the FTL drive, along with Jack's, I'm guessing you two were the ones who disconnected the drive."

Her face paled and she gulped.

I gulped.

"I, ah, was trying to fix the drive, sir," she said. "I apologize, sir. I meant well."

Oh, right. That was our cover story. "Sir, Olivia did fix the drive," I said. "It hasn't experienced any problems since then, has it?"

"Well, no..." he said.

"That's not a coincidence," I said. "Olivia should be commended."

Bello turned to face me. "The fact that you say she should be commended makes me think that she shouldn't be commended. I don't trust you. I've got my eye on you."

As well he should. I looked good. I smiled and waggled my eyebrows a bit.

He blushed and looked away.

Huh. He was acting like he was interested in me and embarrassed about that. But why? What was there to be embarrassed about? Who wouldn't be interested in me? My eyes migrated to Olivia. She was a riddle wrapped in an enigma with a juicy core of hottie.

"Jack, don't look at me like that," she said. Now she was blushing.

Commander Bello had pulled out his fon. "Captain?" He paused. "Yes, there is DNA on the FTL drive. But I'm sorry to say it's all human." He paused. "Yes. Jack's DNA. And Olivia's." He glanced at me while still speaking into his fon. "How did you know, ma'am?" He paused. "So, we can't just put him in the br--?" He quieted. "Yes, ma'am." He turned off his fon.

He turned away from me, flicking off the DNA detection device. "Get out of here, Jones," he growled.

I got.

In the hallway, my brain tingled. Why couldn't I just go to the shuttle, turn on the FTL drive, and imagine I knew what species built the FTL drives? My special skill might let me know somehow. It was worth a try.

I ran down to the shuttle bay, only colliding with one crewmember on the way.

I opened the shuttle door and ran inside. I sat down in the captain's chair and closed the shuttle door. I turned on the FTL drive.

Was my special skill activated? I couldn't tell. Did I need to take a little FTL jaunt somewhere?

"Jack," Addie said, and I jumped out of my chair and almost jumped out of my skin.

"Addie!" I twisted around, looking for her. I couldn't really see anything. "Where are you?"

Seemingly out of nowhere, she opaquified. She wasn't there one second, and then, there in the middle of the shuttle, there was a bunch of white smoke all of a sudden.

"What are you doing?" she asked.

"What are you doing?" I asked at the same time.

"I saw you running, so I followed you," she said.

"I'm, uh, thinking," I said. I couldn't recall who knew about my special skill and who didn't. "I needed a quiet place to think."

"What about your cabin?" she asked.

Oh no. I'd been on the ship for almost an hour and hadn't gone to check on little Slid yet. I was a horrible catalyst, foster father, babysitter, or whatever I was.

"What's wrong?" she asked.

"I forgot to check on baby Slid," I said quietly, ashamed.

"I just checked on him," she said. "He's fine." So Slid was male? Good to know.

"Good." My guilt dissipated a bit.

I glanced at the front panel. The light on the FTL drive was definitely on. I couldn't tell if my special skill had kicked in or not.

I glanced at Addie. "Do you want to make out?"

She didn't answer immediately. Then she said, "If you mean 'Do I want to mate?' I could do that."

Before I could comment further, a white cloud floated toward me, enveloping me.

I immediately felt uncontrollable excitement.

With extreme difficulty, I managed to say, "Wait! Stop!"

Addie flowed away. "Why?"

"Just a second," I said. "Let me think."

She hovered right in front of me. My mind couldn't seem to focus. I kept thinking about mating with her.

"Maybe move further away from me."

She did so, and my brain started working again. I was supposed to be thinking about the FTL drive. How did it get my special skill to engage? The quantum stuff had to start. Did that mean we needed to go somewhere with the drive? Maybe so.

"Are you still thinking?" Addie asked.

"Yes. *Shhh*." What was the smallest FTL jump we could take? "Do you think we could use the FTL drive to jump a millimeter away here in the shuttle bay?"

"Yeah," she said. "But why would anyone do that?"

"*Shhh*. Thinking."

"If you want me to *shhh*, quit asking me questions." She sort of snorted, and then she was quiet.

I leaned over the control console. I programmed an FTL jump of one millimeter. I got ready to engage the drive, holding my finger over the FTL button.

In my mind, I started thinking, 'I know what species builds the FTL drives. I know what species builds the FTL drives.' I pushed the button.

And then I did know. It was the Quihiri! They built the FTL drives!

"I know what species builds the FTL drives!" I said.

"Who?"

"Quihiri!"

139

Chapter Twenty-One

In the shuttle, I jumped out of the captain's chair, punched the door release, and pulled out my fon. The door whooshed open, and I accessed the ship's public address system. "Senior officers report to the captain's ready room immediately."

Gina answered right away, calling me privately. "Jack? Since when do you order senior officers around?"

Well, technically, I'd been ordering senior officers around for the last twenty or so years--with the exception of the past few months. "Do you want to know what species builds the FTL drives or not?"

"Yes!" she said. "Tell me now."

I ran full-out down the hall. "In your ready room."

She exhaled loudly. "Fine." Over the comms system, I heard her say, "Senior officers to captain's ready room immediately."

As I was running, from directly behind my head, I heard, "What are you going to do, Jack?" It was Addie. If you've never had an entity talk to you from right behind your head, it's disconcerting, let me tell you.

Thus, I screamed and jumped a little, looking around. A white-ish, slightly sparkly cloud followed me, enveloping all sides of me except in front. I kept running.

"What's wrong, Jack?" she asked.

"Nothing wrong except you startled me," I said. "But, never mind. Be quiet, please. I need to think."

We needed to go to Quihiri and spy on them. Doing a show was an obvious scheme. It would get us to Quihiri and give us cover while we were there. Ideally, we could get there early and scope out the place first. Maybe we could take some R & R there or on another planet in their system.

I ran the rest of the way to the ready room, my brain buzzing.

Addie and I were the last people there.

"Wow. You guys are fast," I said to Gina, Carter, Dr. Sharma, Lu and Bello. They looked annoyed.

Gina said, "It's called the captain's ready room for a reason." I must have looked blank because she added, "It's right next to the bridge."

"Oh, right," I said.

Commander Lu said, "What's that sldkfjfoisut doing here? It's a security threat."

I glanced at Addie bobbing next to the table. A moment ago, she had been pink and orange and sparkly, but now her color dimmed to white, and her sparkles diminished.

"Relax," I said. "She, ah, helped me get this piece of intelligence." As in, she didn't distract me too badly.

"Tell us already, Jack," Gina said. "Who builds the FTL drives?"

"Quihiri!" Addie said. She seemed very sure.

Jeez. Way to steal my thunder. I glared at Addie until her cloud-like appearance hit me, and then I had to stop giggling. Cloud. Thunder. Heh. Heh.

"Is this true, Jack?" Gina asked.

"Yes," I said. "I, uh, divined it using my special skill."

Commander Bello nodded. "Fascinating."

"Where'd you get this information?" Commander Lu asked.

"It's not important," Carter said. He knew how my gift worked.

"I, ah, agree," Commander Bello said. He also knew how my gift worked first-hand.

"If this is true--" Gina started to say.

"It is," I said.

"If this is true, this is huge," she said. "We've been on the track of the FTL drive-builders for years. We have to keep this new info very, very quiet."

Everyone nodded solemnly. Addie bobbed up and down solemnly.

"And we have to get to Quihiri," I said.

"Quietly." Gina was looking up something on her fon.

"Yes," Commander Lu said. "If they figure out we're on to them, they could move up their time table and turn off all the FTL drives--if that's their plan."

"It is," Addie said. It was a little odd that she knew of the plan but didn't know which species hatched the plan. We needed more info and corroboration.

"So, we're going to sneak into Quihiri to investigate this?" I asked. Sneaking sounded fun. I had a feeling I'd be a good sneaker.

"Risky," Commander Lu said.

"Yes," Gina said. "It would be better to be there for a legitimate reason and do our usual secret mission on the side." The usual secret mission was news to me. What secret stuff had they already done on the trip?

Addie made an odd noise. Why? Maybe she didn't know about secret stuff either.

"They're on our tour," Gina said. "We're supposed to perform *Don Giovanni* there in five months."

Carter, Dr. Sharma, Commander Bello and Commander Lu all exhaled loudly and simultaneously.

"What?" I said. "You guys don't like *Don Giovanni?* I love *Don Giovanni.* I was born to play Don Giovanni."

Carter snorted.

Commander Bello stared at me and then looked away. "Maybe so."

Dr. Sharma looked concerned. "Are you still acting like a libertine and seducer, Jack?" Yikes. I threw him a dirty look. So much for doctor-patient confidentiality.

"Maybe you were born to play him," Gina said, "but you're not ready to play him. And the orchestra's not ready yet either."

"We work our way up to the operas on tour," Carter said. "Or haven't you noticed how easy the shows have been? I mean, seriously, *Hair?*"

"I like *Hair*," Addie said. "It's fun."

"Yeah," I said. And Addie would know fun; she was fun. I liked Addie.

"Furthermore, who says Jack gets to play Don Giovanni?" Carter said. "I could play Giovanni." The people in the room froze for a moment as if everyone was embarrassed for him.

"I'm not ready," Gina said. "No one's ready. We have to do some serious rehearsing for *Don Giovanni*." I wondered what her role was.

"I feel like I should mention we don't have to do the show," Commander Lu said. "After we foil the Quihiri's intragalactic plot, they won't want us to do the show. We'll be lucky to get out of there alive."

I gulped. I hadn't connected the dots yet. They'd definitely want to kill us if we foiled a plot so many years in the making.

"Good point," Commander Bello said, nodding. "But it also raises the question: how do we foil their plot?"

They all turned to look at me. I resisted the urge to say, 'Why are you all looking at me?' Instead, I said, "I guess…."

They leaned toward me.

"I guess if we figure out how to turn the FTL drives back on, we'll foil them, won't we?" I said.

"Assuming we have the technical expertise to turn them back on," Commander Bello said. "And assuming any of this is true."

"So, the plan is," I said, "we go to Quihiri for a fake show of *Don Giovanni* and uncover their super-secret FTL technology, including how to turn on the drives after they've been nefariously turned off."

We all looked at one another. I don't know what they were thinking, but for my part, I was thinking that sounded pretty difficult.

Addie poked me.

I jumped.

She whispered right in my ear. "Why don't you use your special skill to figure out how to turn on the drives?"

Gee, no pressure. But it was a good idea.

"There's no time to lose," Carter said.

"Commander Nillion's right," Commander Lu said. "Things might be in motion. They might have been involved in Jack Jones Senior's murder." But Jack Jones Senior hadn't been murdered. I couldn't recall who knew that at this point. I looked around the table. Everyone else was also looking around the table as if also trying to ascertain who knew what.

"I'll contact Quihiri," Gina said, "and tell them we need to change the performance date for *Don Giovanni*." She put her palms on the table and stood up. "Dismissed."

"*Why then tonight let us assay our plot*," I said.

"I just hope it's *all's well that ends well*," Addie said.

Everyone filed out, with Addie and me last. I turned to her. "Okay. Let's go try what you suggested."

We ran back to the shuttle. I repeated the millimeter move while thinking, 'I know how to turn on the FTL drives after the Quihiri have turned them off.'

Nothing came to me. I didn't have any sudden epiphanies. Or even any regular epiphanies.

"Is it working?" she asked.

"No," I said.

"Why not?"

"I don't know."

Chapter Twenty-Two

Addie and I were in the shuttle bay, and absolutely nothing was happening.

"Do you need to mate with me again?" she asked.

I was sorely tempted, but I hadn't actually mated with her last time--when it worked--so I didn't think mating was the issue.

And after all the recent excitement, I was definitely ready for some down time. And I was hungry. For food. "Thanks for the offer, but no." Ha! Take that, Dr. Sharma.

"Should we visit with my offspring, then?" she asked.

Ugh. I felt guilt attack me like a hungry fire eel coming out of hibernation. I hadn't checked on little Slid yet. Bad Jack. My stomach rumbled. "Of course, Ambassador. Let's go visit your offspring post haste."

We perambulated back to my cabin. Inside, under my bed, Slid was snoozing (or whatever) away as usual. Phew.

Addie flowed down and around and inside the box, encapsulating Slid. What was that about? I had no idea.

"So, ah." I started backing away from them, moving towards the door. "Why don't you guys have some family time? You can stay in my cabin as long as you like."

They both ignored me. That was fine with me. I stepped outside and closed the door behind me. Mess hall, here I come! On my way there, I texted Eva: 'Buy you dinner?'

She texted me back a smiley-face holo.

In the mess hall, I sat down with my tray of food, smiling. I'd dialed up a baguette, French onion soup, French fries and French wine. Yes, I was sorry I hadn't had a chance to taste any of the cuisine on my short Earth trip to Paris.

Eva slid into the seat next to me as I took my first bit of

cheesy, oniony soup. The strings of cheese were going all over the place. She laughed. "Eat much, Jack?"

I chewed and swallowed. "Not nearly enough."

She smiled and took a bite of her nondescript meal. Tofu something?

I broke off a piece of baguette, and bread crumbs spewed all over the table.

After she swallowed, she said, "I heard a rumor we're going to Quihiri early."

So much for super-secret. But I only said, "Oh?"

She furrowed her eyebrows. "What's that look? You know something. Spill. What do you know?"

"I know you heard a rumor we're going to Quihiri." I smiled sweetly. See. Look at me. I could keep secrets like a real spy. I was a real spy, dammit!

"If you tell me what you know, you can come back to my cabin and spend the night with me," she said sweetly.

Ooh. She played to win. But I'd promised to keep the new mission under wraps.

"Is the ambassador staying in your cabin?" she asked. "And her baby? It must be pretty crowded in there." She made a lot of good points, but I was trying not to succumb.

Out, damn'd spot! Out, I say!

On the other hand, Eva was one of the good guys. In point of fact, she was very, very good at many things.

She leaned over and kissed my neck. Wowsa... One of the very good guys. And everyone in the crew would know of the Quihiri mission soon enough.

"Okay, okay," I said. I leaned over and whispered in her ear. "The Quihiri make the FTL drives. They have a secret off switch, and we're going there to spy on them and find out how to foil their nefarious plot for intragalactic war." I paused. Possibly I used the words 'foil' and 'nefarious' too much.

She straightened her back as her mouth fell open. Finally, she said, "That's... I had no idea... wow."

She seemed sincere. I was reassured that telling her had been the right thing to do. She wouldn't have been so surprised if she'd been a Quihiri spy.

I picked up my glass of wine. "To a successful, ah," I

glanced around the mess hall. Could one of my crewmates be a spy for someone besides TCC? Based on what I knew of spies: yes.

I raised my glass. "To a successful show on Quihiri."

Eva toasted with me, and then we both sipped our respective beverages.

"Isn't Quihiri supposed to be secret?" she asked, grinning.

Oh, shoot. I wasn't at my best when I was hungry. I dug into my dinner with gusto.

Later, in her cabin, she kissed me again, and I felt it all over. It turned out I *was* at my best after a nice filling dinner and some French wine...

First thing in the morning, my fon pinged.

Eva's fon pinged at about the same time.

We had updated duty assignments. Mine was rehearse, rehearse, rehearse.

"*Don Giovanni*?" she said, looking at her fon. Then, she glanced at me.

According to my fon, the Shakespeare jumped to Quihiri space sometime during the night using the FTL drive. We didn't have any problems with it. So, presumably, the Quihiri weren't on to us yet.

"We're not ready for *Don Giovanni*," she said. "We haven't rehearsed at all."

I was feeling guilty again, this time for spilling the beans to Eva about the Quihiri. I resolved not to spill any more about the plan if I could help it.

I stared back at my fon and its information. "It looks like we're here for an extended time so we can rehearse."

She narrowed her eyes. "What's going on, Jack?"

"Gosh, I, ah, don't know."

"Jack?" She smiled and reached for me.

I jumped out of bed. "Gosh. I better get to work. Got a lot to do. A lot to do!" I opened the cabin door and stepped into the hall.

In the hall, someone walking by snickered.

From inside her cabin, Eva called out, "Clothes. Jack."

Oops.

After I got dressed, I went back to the mess hall. I'd worked up quite an appetite last night.

And who did I spy there but Gina?

I sat down next to her with my food. "Gina!" I needed my real orders. What special assignment was she giving me? Something super-important, no doubt.

She gave me a baleful stare.

"What?" I said nervously. I'd thought after our makeout session we were past all this.

"I think you mean Captain Gomez, don't you?" she said slowly.

"Sure. Whatever." I leaned towards her. "What are my real orders?"

"Real orders?" She leaned away. "You got your real orders. You need to rehearse."

"I know that's the story," I whispered. "But what do you really want me to do?"

"Rehearse," she said. "For the show. That we are putting on."

"No, really," I whispered.

"Really." She stood up. "Get with the program, Ensign." She walked away.

She couldn't truly want me to rehearse, could she? No. Couldn't be. Rehearsing was just my cover.

I turned my attention back to my breakfast.

"Jack!" A tray appeared on the table next to me, held by my dear friend Ted.

I missed Ted. "Where have you been?" I asked.

"Where have I been?" he asked. "Where have you been?"

Secret senior officer meetings. Earth. I really wanted to tell him.

But I didn't.

"Kind of crazy how we changed the schedule so suddenly, huh?" he said, taking a bite of eggs.

I leaned towards him. "How would you like to help me with a secret mission?"

Chapter Twenty-Three

Unfortunately, when it came time to disembark at Quihiri, Gina insisted I join her and Carter in the disembarkation lounge. I had been planning on disembarking with Ted later with the nonsenior officers. Last night I'd only asked him to help me out on the planet on an unspecified mission. Look at me, holding my cards close to the vest like a real spy!

I took out my fon to text Ted so we could figure out where to meet somewhere on the planet.

Gina narrowed her eyes at me. "What are you doing?"

Come up with a good excuse, Jack..."Texting Ted," I said, wilting under her glare. Damn. Clearly, my spy skills still needed some work.

"You don't have time for Ted," she said. "You're coming with Carter and me to the embassy. Since I assume you didn't read the mission briefing, the embassy's what they call their government headquarters. And whatever I say or do, go along with it."

Gee, that didn't sound ominous at all. And, oops, I should have read the mission briefing.

The embassy sounded pretty interesting, but if I was with Gina the whole time, how would I do any secret sleuthing? This trip was going to be more challenging than I'd thought.

The light on Quihiri was oranger than I was used to. Quihiri was also humid but cold. Somehow the cold humidity here was different than the hot humidity we'd experienced on the non-chimp planet. And why were so many planets so humid?

If gravity differed from Earth-normal here, I couldn't tell.

I sniffed. There was an unusual smell in the air. It reminded me of ... something familiar. The ocean? Yeah, it reminded me of the Terran ocean: salty, fishy, and seaweedy.

The space port was in the same complex of buildings as the embassy, so we didn't get to see what the outside looked like. In the space port, hallways and doorways were clustered in groups of three. Weird.

The Quihiri natives were odd, odder than any species we'd come across before--with the possible exception of Addie and her kin. The Quihiri reminded me of a cross between a three-legged stool and an octopus. They were gray, with three leg-like appendages, three long arms, and three-fingered hands on the end. Their torsos just flowed into their heads with no delineation. They had three eyes and three nostrils. I was sensing a pattern: threes. At least they only had one mouth on their one head.

I tried to stay nonchalant and not gape too much as we entered the embassy. I saw round tables with three chairs around them, conversational groupings of three Quihiri natives. Everywhere I looked: three, three, three.

One of the Quihiri escorted us into a plush office with three desks, complete with three natives sitting at them.

The largest of these stood up. He/she/it was significantly larger than the other two. "Captain Gomez?" If he(?) had a translator, I didn't see it. His voice came from his mouth, and he didn't even have a discernible accent. If I'd just been listening, I would have guessed an adult Terran male was talking.

"Yes, Ambassador," she said, dipping her head. "It's an honor for you to receive us." She raised her head. "Thank you for accommodating our schedule change."

"It's no problem," the Quihiri ambassador said. "We enjoy the Terran culture." Barely moving his head, he seemed to turn his attention to his smaller colleagues. "In fact, my mates are big fans of Jack Jones. That's the correct idiom, is it not? Fan?"

I straightened. Of course, they were fans!

"Yes, Ambassador," Gina said. "Your command of English is impressive." I may have detected a hint of a curled lip--as if she didn't like people fussing over me more than her.

"May I introduce my mates?" the ambassador asked.

"Of course," Gina said. "My mates accompany me as well. May I present my husband, Carter Nillion, and my husband, Jack

Jones." She pointed at each of us in turn.

The smaller Quihiri seemed to be getting restless.

Mates? Technically, that was true. We were both her husband. Huh.

The ambassador's gray skin had taken on a viridian green tone. "You brought your triple, Captain Gomez? We are honored. We have never met a Terran triple before."

Carter nodded his head regally. Apparently, two husbands were good on Quihiri.

I copied his regality.

The ambassador gestured at the seated Quihiri with one of his tentacles.

His two mates jumped up from their desks and approached us. He pointed a tentacle at the slightly smaller Quihiri. "This is my husband." He pointed a tentacle at the other. "This is my wife." His skin had turned even more greenish. What did that mean?

I was suddenly transfixed by the question: if the smaller Quihiri were his/her/its husband and wife, what gender was the ambassador? Could the ambassador be a gender not found on Earth?

And, yes, I knew I should know the answer to that question. I'd planned on reading the Quihiri briefings last night, but Ted had distracted me with his sweet, sweet love.

Thus, I was slightly surprised when the two smaller Quihiri rushed me. "Can we have your autograph, Jack?" one said.

"Will you sing something for us, Jack?" the other said.

"Of course." I smiled broadly. Hopefully, that wasn't offensive on this planet. I would have to start reading the mission briefings one of these days.

"Certainly he will," Gina said. "Go ahead, Jack."

The smaller of the ambassador's spouses shoved a piece of paper and pen in my face. I grabbed them and scrawled my name with an artistic flourish.

"Wow." The small husband's skin changed color, morphing from boring gray to royal blue. I was guessing that was good--- because who wouldn't react to me in a good way?

"Now me! Now me!" the wife said. "Please sing!" Her skin started shading into celadon tones.

I cleared my throat. *"Donna folle. Indarno gridi, chi son io tu non saprai,"* I sang.

The wife made a squealing noise.

Gina put a hand on my arm. "That's enough."

All the Quihiri turned a blue color. What did that mean? I was sensing that it meant something. I was not sensing nefarious plots. These folks seemed like friendly music lovers, not bad guys.

Carter was grimacing, but he quickly replaced it with a neutral expression. Was he jealous of my talent? That was probably it.

"So, I'm guessing you need a rehearsal space," the ambassador said, his tone fading to gray.

"Yes," Gina said. "We need to rehearse." She glanced at me.

Did she think I needed to rehearse? I felt my own skin color morph into a red color.

"We appreciate your assistance in this matter," she continued.

The ambassador pointed a tentacle back at the smaller desks, and its spouses slid back to their desks. The small husband accessed a machine on said desk. After a few moments, he said, "The Magnificent Atrium here in the embassy complex is available."

"Ah." The ambassador's skin brightened to cerulean. "Excellent. Yes, let's let them use The Magnificent Atrium. Then, the Terran triple can reside in the artist's quarters there."

Wait a minute. Did that mean I was stuck here inside the embassy? How would I meet up with Ted? How would I investigate stuff?

Was this all part of Gina's plan? I tried to scrutinize Gina's and Carter's expressions without seeming to scrutinize them. Sadly, my nascent spy skills were not up to the task.

Gina inclined her head. "You are most generous, Ambassador." If this wasn't part of the plan, she was covering it well.

"Can I give them the tour of our enchanting embassy?" the wife asked, a tinge of citrine in her skin.

"Yes, wife," the ambassador said, shading to sky-blue.

"Please proceed. But bring them back here promptly for lunch."

The wife was now fully citrine. I was starting to get the hang of reading their skin. Blue and green were both somehow good. Black was bad. Could green be associated with lust or love?

The wife glided towards us. "Please follow me, Terrans." She glided out the door.

"Thank you for everything, Ambassador," Gina said before following the wife out the door.

I got a text from Ted. 'I'm on the surface. Where are you?'

I slowly trailed after Gina, Carter and the green wife.

I started to text Ted back. 'I'm stuck in the embassy. Our plan's on hold.' I glanced up, realizing I was pretty much surrounded by gray Quihiri. I erased the text and replaced it with, 'I'm honored to remain in the embassy. I will see you sometime later.'

I hurried to catch up with Gina, Carter, and the ambassador's wife, who was now shaded cyan. As I got even with her, her cyan shaded more green. I wanted to ask her about her colors, but I knew Gina and Carter would chastise me for not reading the planet dossier.

"As I was saying," the wife waved her tentacles around, "this is the extra-terrestrial diplomatic core." Extra-terrestrial?

Carter whispered, "Extra-terrestrial means not native to Quihiri."

Ah ha. But I gave him a look that said, 'Duh. I knew that.'

The wife showed us many rooms of gray Quihiri sitting at desks in groupings of three. Offices and office workers are boring on every world.

She brought us back to the ambassador's office at lunchtime, where a large seafood feast was laid out. It was delicious. I enjoyed the shrimp, crab, and fish eggs the most--or, rather, the shrimp-like, crab-like, and fish-egg-like food. See, I was learning.

After lunch, the tour continued, and the wife took us to a humid, empty foyer. "And here's the Glorious Aquarium." They did like their grandiose names here on this planet.

She threw open one of the tall triple doors, and it suddenly got even more humid. A vast body of water spread out in front of us about ten feet away. It smelled like Earth's oceans: salt, seaweed, and a faint fishy odor. I couldn't see the far edge of the aquarium. I wanted to ask how they got the sea inside the embassy and what the significance was, but I didn't want my wife to know I hadn't done my homework.

I walked towards the water, peering. My feet sunk into the sand. Yep. It seemed like I was on the beach approaching the ocean.

The wife followed, turning a brighter and brighter shade of green. Could the Glorious Aquarium be for mating? It would make sense if the Quihiri were descended from octopus-like creatures.

"You are welcome to partake in the Glorious Aquarium!" the wife said.

I stared at her.

Gina looked a little confused, but she said, "Not right now."

The wife froze for a moment as if she was surprised. Aliens were confusing.

Was she insulted that we didn't appreciate the offer? "Thank you?" I said. "We're honored?"

The wife shaded back to cyan and then to sky-blue. So, was blue happy?

Gina was frowning at me. "Can we please see the Atrium now?"

"The Magnificent Atrium? Yes." We followed the wife out of the gloriousity.

She led us through more rooms of triply-arranged furniture. The Quihiri embassy was huge. I couldn't believe it, but I was getting bored.

The wife's hue had faded back to gray. Did that mean she was getting bored? I wasn't going to ask, that was for sure.

Eventually, we reached another tall set of triple doors. The wife threw them open, shading to a navy blue. "The Magnificent Atrium!"

The room was huge, with a glass ceiling soaring fifty feet above us. From between the clouds, rays from an orange sun pierced the space. It was magnificent. I stepped inside. It reminded me of how I'd imagined heaven as a kid. "Wow," I said.

"This will do," Gina said. I didn't know all of Gina's expressions, but I was pretty sure this was her impressed face.

I faced the wife. "Thank you, ma'am. We're honored to use this space."

Carter just stood there, staring at the giant space.

"Would you like to see your quarters now?" our guide asked.

"Sure," Gina said.

The four of us walked along the back wall to another triple set of doors. Our guide opened one and led us into what could only be considered a large bedroom, with muted lighting, thick carpeting, a small table with three chairs, and one giant round bed. The table had what looked like another seafood-like feast laid out on it.

"Is this sufficient?" our guide asked. "There is a multi-species compatible washroom through those doors."

"Thank you for access to these fine rooms," Gina said.

"If you could just show us to the embassy entrance, we'll be on our way," Carter said. "We'll return tomorrow and start rehearsals."

"No." The wife's hue was shading to orange. I hadn't seen that color yet. What did it mean? I was guessing it was nothing good.

"Yes," Gina said.

"Uh," I said. "Thank you. We sincerely appreciate it."

Her orange shade faded.

I didn't know why Gina was risking an interstellar incident--or at the least, pissing off our hosts--but it wouldn't help our investigation. "We would be honored to stay here," I quickly added.

It would be easier to investigate the Quihiri if we were on Quihiri.

Now the wife was more of a navy color.

"Good," she said. "Your bags have been brought here." Then, she pointed a tentacle at the table. "We prepared an evening meal for you."

"Thanks again," I said. "You are a very lovely Quihiri, if I may say so." I smiled.

She turned green. Of course.

"Is there anything else I can help you with?" she asked. "Especially you, Jack Jones. Can I help you?"

I stepped closer to her. She had some small dark spots on

her head, like freckles. They were cute. "You have helped us so much already. Thank you. You're my favorite Quihiri. I look forward to seeing you again."

Bright green.

She glided out of the room.

"What was that? Why did you act that way with the wife?" Gina asked me as soon as the door closed behind her.

"I was just expressing my appreciation," I said. "I thought you guys were supposed to be diplomats. I was being diplomatic."

Carter plopped down on the bed. "I can't believe we're all stuck here."

I grinned. "What will the sleeping arrangements be?"

They both stared at me.

After a few moments, it got awkward.

At least they didn't say anything like 'Yuck. We would never sleep with you, Jack.'

I knew, deep down, they both wanted to, even if they wouldn't admit it to themselves or each other.

I went and sat down at the table. More yummy seafood. There was also some golden liquid. Intriguing. I poured myself a glass. Delicious. It was like drinking liquid sunshine, warm and silky in my mouth and throat. "I love this! You guys have to try this!"

"Jack, why did you act like that?" Gina finally said. "You derailed the mission. Yes, we're investigating the Quihiri, but we need to be able to go back to the ship."

I took another sip and then waved my hand around. "She was turning orange. I wanted her to turn green, or blue would have been okay, too."

"What?" Gina asked.

"What the hell are you talking about, Jack?" Carter asked.

"You're acting like their colors mean something," Gina said. "They don't. Didn't you read the mission briefing?"

"I bet he didn't read the briefing," Carter said. "It clearly says their colors are meaningless. Many Earth scientists have studied the Quihiri. They all agree. The colors are random."

"I, uh, read the briefing," I said. "But, evidently, many Earth scientists are stupid. Green is horny. Blue is happy. And orange is, well, I'm not completely sure what orange is, angry maybe. It was obvious!"

They both stared at me some more. It was obvious they were good at staring.

"I'm sure about this," I said. "If there's one thing I can do, it's read people--even Quihiri people."

I smiled and pointed at the bed. "So anyway, boy, girl, boy? Boy, boy, girl? What do you think?" I'd waited a surprisingly long time to make love with Gina and Carter, especially since we were all married. "*If music be the food of love, play on...*"

Chapter Twenty-Four

After all my bragging about being able to read people, I did not manage to have a ménage à trois with my wife and my brother husband. Disappointing.

I lay on the edge of the big bed, not sleeping.

Gina and Carter didn't seem to have the same problem--if their snoring was any indication.

This situation was very frustrating.

I slowly sat up, swung my legs over the edge of the bed and very carefully got out of bed. Gina and Carter didn't stir.

I checked my fon for texts. Nothing new. Since it was 2:00 a.m. local time, I decided against texting Ted. I paced back and forth on the thick carpeting in front of the bed. It muffled all sounds.

Wait a minute. Sound muffling! That could come in handy. Maybe now was a perfect opportunity to investigate Quihiri.

I went to the bedroom's exterior doors and quietly snicked one open. We weren't locked in the bedroom; that was good.

But we were basically stuck in the embassy because we didn't know the way out--and who knew if we could get out, even if we knew the way. There might be any number of obstacles between here and our ship.

Plus, Gina didn't want to offend our hosts. She had a point; it was pretty tough to sneak around and investigate sentients if they were pissed at you.

I peeked out into the atrium. The light from three moons shone into it. I had to suppress a gasp. Three shades of silver rays filled the space. Beautiful. I stepped into the atrium and closed the bedroom door quietly behind me; the snoring sounds disappeared.

I stared up at the moons. What was it about stuff in the sky, like stars and moons, that was so moving?

"*No one can stop us now 'cause we are all made of stars*," I whisper-sang.

I found a chair and sat down and watched the silver moons and some clouds sail overhead. The beauty of the space filled with silver light was mesmerizing. I felt like I was on some fantastical world where anything could happen.

After I didn't know how long, I got up and paced around the atrium. There were several more sets of triple doors--containing more bedrooms when I peeked inside.

I had to suppress a giggle. If only Gina and Carter had known we didn't have to sleep together.

There was a stage at the front end of the large atrium, only about a foot higher than the rest of the space.

I arrived back at the rear of the atrium near our bedroom. But instead of choosing one of the doors of my triple bedroom, I chose one of the giant doors out of the atrium.

Not locked. I grinned in the moonlight.

Outside, I stood in the empty foyer. Somehow, the silvery moonlight made it seem more alien. Something about the light--the color or the glow--had a quality I'd never experienced on Earth.

I was on an alien planet. In an alien embassy. It was pretty amazing when I stopped to think about it.

Through the foyer and back in the office areas, I wandered between sets-of-three office furniture, realizing the walls had a faint silver-blue luminescence that resembled moonlight.

I approached one of the walls and touched it gingerly. I couldn't tell if it was special paint or algae or what.

"*No one can stop us now 'cause we are all made of stars...*"

It all seemed quite ...alien.

I continued to explore.

In the office complex, I spied some golden light at the end of a long hall. It stood out since the rest of the embassy complex was so dimly lit. Barefoot, I walked towards it, curious.

When I was still over fifty feet away, I saw a Quihiri approach the light, gliding right up to it. Then, the light disappeared. Then, it appeared again, but the Quihiri was gone.

Carefully, I crept up to the golden light.

Strange. All the light was coming from a six-inch-diameter hole in the wall. There did not appear to be any kind of door, hatch, or even a larger window in the wall. Where had the Quihiri gone? I scrutinized the wall and the floor. I turned around and scrutinized the ceiling.

It was only by the merest of chances that I was facing in the right direction when another Quihiri approached.

Quickly, I ducked down behind a desk.

The Quihiri glided right up to the hole and then, somehow, squished itself through. I never saw anything like it. How could a roughly human-sized creature fit through a six-inch hole?

Bizarre.

Trying to keep one eye open behind me to watch for more Quihiri, I glided up to the hole and peered through it.

Inside, I saw a cavernous warehouse-type space filled with Quihiri workers dollying featureless white spheres from one place to another.

I knew those featureless white spheres. They were FTL drives.

In the past, I'd discovered the recessed ports of FTL drives and connected one to a shuttle.

In the middle of the warehouse, I saw some open spheres. I craned my neck. How did they open? Inside the spheres were a mass of wires and ...goo.

At the far end of the warehouse, I saw what appeared to be a golden-yellow sun shining through some kind of portal. Wow. It was quite bright--like a real sun.

Could there be a wormhole to another star system? If so, was it related to the FTL drives? If so, how?

An announcement was made over a public address system in the warehouse. It wasn't in English, so I couldn't make heads or tails of it.

And then, the portal closed with a whoosh of spacetime or something. The golden light went away.

Now, the lighting in the warehouse was the typical Quihiri orange.

Apparently, I had found the much sought-after FTL drive factory. It was on Quihiri, in their embassy complex. Wow. Who would have guessed?

Yay, me! I stood there staring through the small hole and feeling good about myself. Who said I wasn't an awesome spy? Not me.

The FTL drive factory was the most closely guarded secret of the galaxy. I started getting nervous. Why had I been able to find the FTL drive factory? Why hadn't the Quihiri locked me and the rest of my triple up or, at least, guarded us?

What would the Quihiri do if they found me here? What would they do if they knew I'd seen this? Was the *Shakespeare* in danger? Was Earth in danger?

I ducked behind the desk to gather my thoughts and calm my nerves.

I breathed in through my nose and out through my mouth. Somebody had told me once that was a way to calm down. Calm. I'm calm. I'm super calm.

What did I really know about FTL drives? I knew my original, Old Jack, had faked his death to get his hands on an FTL drive. I knew the broken FTL drive on the shuttle gave me, and presumably Old Jack, special skills.

Addie had told us the drive makers had put an off switch in the FTL drives. But did I really know that? Was Addie trustworthy? Why hadn't she known the Quihiri were the species responsible? And why had she believed me so easily when I mentioned the Quihiri?

Gina and the rest of the *Shakespeare*'s crew also seemed to believe the disable-the-FTL drives scheme. But Gina and her crew of spies always seemed to be ready to believe the worst in people. They were definitely cynical.

Why had I believed Addie? Because we'd had sex? Because we'd made a baby? What did I really know about her?

A good spy wouldn't let his feelings--whether good or bad-- get in the way of his data and conclusions.

I needed more information. Was there an off switch? What would its purpose be?

I glanced over at the minuscule six-inch door. Talk about good security. No other species could get into their factory.

If that was the only door.

I stared at the door so long I yawned, getting sleepy.

I shook it off, got up, and snuck back down the hall the way I'd come.

I was very nervous that one of the Quihiri would find me up and wandering around.

When I finally got back to the area of the atrium, I relaxed a little. I could see the large foyer outside the atrium in the distance.

I hummed, "*No one can stop us now 'cause we are all made of stars...*" as I stepped into the foyer.

"Jack?" someone said, and I jumped sky-high.

"Ack!" When I looked around, I spied the cute little ambassador's wife, green skin quickly shading to black. Oh, no. Was I busted?

"Ah, greetings, honored ambassador's wife," I said when my feet touched the ground again. I smiled. "You have me at a disadvantage. I don't know your name."

Her skin shaded to green again. "You can call me Quinta." Was the little lady pining for some Jack?

"What a pretty name, Quinta," I said with a smile. "What can I do for you?"

"What are you doing outside the atrium?"

"I was stretching my legs a little. I couldn't sleep."

"Are your accommodations not to your liking?"

"Yes, of course," I said. "Your moons are especially beautiful. Would you like to come inside the atrium and admire them with me?"

Her skin turned bright green, even glowing a little. "Yes." Pining, check. Whatever she had in mind, I would go with it. I was guessing it was better than being captured, jailed, and/or tortured by evil octopi.

The two of us entered the atrium together. The silvery light was still magical.

"Your planet is very beautiful," I said.

"Thank you," she said.

My mind was racing; what did I know about octopus reproduction? I couldn't remember a single thing. Apparently, it hadn't come up in my first eighteen years on Earth.

"Would you like to try an Earth custom, Quinta?" I asked.

She'd come to me; she must want a romantic adventure.

"Possibly..." she said. "What custom would that be?"

"We have something we call kissing," I said. "When two sentient creatures take a liking to each other, they press their mouths together to show how they feel."

She made a sound that resembled a giggle. "Oh, you're bad, Jack. Two creatures! That's very naughty." But her green glow was brighter, if anything.

"I think you'll like it." I leaned in and planted a kiss on her lips.

She pressed back enthusiastically. It felt exactly as I would have imagined kissing a sentient octopus would. She smelled faintly of fish and seaweed, but it wasn't unpleasant.

After a few moments, we separated.

Her skin was shading into yellow. What did that mean?

"You can't tell anyone we did that, Jack," she said softly.

"*Speak low if you speak love,*" I said.

Now she was a bright yellow.

"I won't tell," I said. "A gentleman doesn't kiss and tell."

"You seem different from other humans," she said. "I could tell right away."

I yawned again. Sneaking around an alien planet and kissing said aliens in the middle of the night really took it out of you.

"Thank you, Quinta." I smiled. "I must admit we humans get tired at this time of night. Perhaps you'd care to join me in one of the artist's quarters, to sleep?"

Neon yellow.

"Don't humans mate on dry land?" she said. "It's dry in the artist's quarters. I shouldn't mate with you."

"Don't Quihiri mate in the ocean?" I said. "We aren't in the ocean. You can't mate, right?"

"Yes," she said. Phew. Good guess.

"So, no mating tonight," I said. "Just sleeping. Quihiri sleep, don't they?"

"Yes." Now she was more of a light yellow-green.

"Come on, then," I said. "It'll be an adventure. Something to tell your friends."

Turning green again, she followed me into one of the empty

bedrooms.

The two of us lay down on the giant bed.

Too late, I realized this was the spouse of the ambassador. This could end up being a little troublesome. On the other hand, a sex scandal could distract people from an FTL drive scandal.

I lay on my back, eyes closed, yawning. "Quinta, what's the relationship between the Quihiri and the sldkfjfoisut?" Yay. I said it.

She made a yawning sound. "Oh, we're mortal enemies. Have been for thousands of years..."

Chapter Twenty-Five

"Jack!" Gina yelled. "What have you done!"

I opened my eyes and spied my wife standing in the doorway. She was fully dressed and quite impressive with her powerful physique and obvious passion. We were in one of the bedrooms off the Quihiri's Magnificent Atrium.

"Oops," came from the other side of me--in the bed. Oh, right. It was cute little Quinta. "Morning, Jack," she said. "You're right. This has been fun." She hopped out of bed, glowing blue, and sauntered past Gina.

I said, "*Journey's end in lovers meeting, every wise man's son doth know.*"

Carter appeared (also dressed) behind Gina. "What's all the yelling?" he said as he swiveled to watch Quinta glide away. "Wait. What's going on here?" He turned back to me. "Jack! You didn't."

I got out of bed and was a little surprised to note I was wearing my underpants. I indicated them with a flourish. "Obviously, nothing happened."

Gina was still fuming if the smoke practically coming out of her ears was any indication.

"Why are you so worked up?" I asked.

"Yeah, why are you so worked up?" Carter asked, staring at her and frowning. Did he think she was hot for me? Was he jealous? Probably. Poor guy. There was a lot to be jealous about when it came to me.

She stepped into the room, and Carter followed.

"We're supposed to be diplomats," she said. "Sleeping with the ambassador's wife is not diplomatic. The whole point of presenting ourselves as a triple was to get on his good side."

I shrugged. "How do you know members of a triple don't enjoy the occasional double?" Ha. I smiled. "Or line drive at an away game? Quinta seemed to enjoy herself."

"I know because it's not in the intelligence briefing," Gina said.

I snorted. "And that's totally accurate."

She looked a little less livid.

"And, anyways, I was, uh, doing something, doing some spy stuff." In recent weeks I'd been trying to do a little research into what spies were supposed to do. "What's it called? I was developing her as an asset. Yeah! An asset!" I grinned. "She's my asset; she likes me."

What had she said right before we drifted off to sleep? It was something important.

"Oh yeah?" Gina said. "If she's an asset, what'd you learn?"

"I learned where the super-top-secret FTL drive factory is."

Their mouths hung open.

Oh yeah. "And I learned the Quihiri and the sldkfjfoisut are mortal enemies." Technically, I hadn't learned all that from Quinta, but I had learned it.

"Wow," Carter said. "That's pretty good." He turned to Gina. "You gotta admit, that's pretty good."

Her face relaxed. "That isn't in the intelligence briefings." She stared at me. "I keep forgetting you're really Jack."

I decided to take that as a compliment. I had skills, but I wasn't a big jerk. "Thanks."

Carter stepped forward. "Can you take us to the super-secret factory? Is it nearby?"

"Terrans? Where are you?" came from the atrium. "We brought you some food. Terrans?"

This was followed by some muttering on the part of the Quihiri. I may have heard the words 'security' and 'alert.'

Gina twirled and glided out of the bedroom into the atrium. "We're here. We're here. Thank you for the food. We appreciate your generosity."

Carter followed her like a trained puppy. "Yes. And thank you for the lovely accommodations."

I glanced around the bedroom. Something felt off. Something was missing. Something about morning... Oh, right.

166

I needed to brush my teeth. And record my memories. I didn't want to forget what had happened last night. But I didn't have my gear here because we hadn't known we'd be staying here.

Since I'd been cloned, I hadn't missed one day of recording. I wasn't going to be caught memoryless again. Without my memory gear, I felt unsettled.

I followed Gina and Carter out into the atrium.

A large Quihiri flanked by two smaller ones stood holding overflowing trays of food, seafood, fruit, and some plants. We hadn't met this triple yet.

I didn't recognize all the food, but there was a lot of it. Perhaps after a triple spent the night together (as the Quihiri thought Gina, Carter and I had), they needed to fortify themselves? It sounded good to me.

The large one jerked back when he saw me. "I didn't mean to interrupt at an inopportune moment." But his color was blue, which I knew meant he was pleased. So, he was truly pleased to interrupt?

His two companions were green--which I knew meant horny. Of course, they were. Maybe Quinta had told them about our tryst?

"What?" Gina glanced over at me. "Jack," she said. "Go get dressed."

"Yes, ma'am." I saluted her and started jogging over to the other bedroom.

Once inside, I quickly got dressed, pulled my fon out of my pocket and called Ted.

He answered right away. "Oh, thank God, Jack. Are you all right? You just disappeared. What happened? You didn't get kidnapped again, did you?" Aw. He was worried about me. He must care.

"I'm okay," I said. "Thanks for asking. We're VIP guests of the Quihiri ambassador."

"We?" he asked. "Who's we?"

"Gina and Carter and me," I said. "The Quihiri think we're a triple."

"You slept with Gina and Carter!" he said, sounding more than a little upset. Clearly, we needed to have a talk about the status of our relationship.

167

"Relax," I said. "I didn't sleep with Gina and Carter, or only part of the time. I slept with Quinta."

"Who's Quinta!" he shrieked.

"Relax," I said again. "She's a Quihiri."

"What!" he yelled. Apparently, telling people to relax didn't make them relax.

Carter took a step into the bedroom. "What are you doing? Get out here." He stepped back out.

I quickly told Ted what I'd discovered about the FTL factory and the Quihiri/sldkfjfoisut situation.

"Wow," he said. "Tell me more."

"I don't have time to explain, Ted. I'm with Gina and Carter at the rehearsal space--the Quihiri call it the Magnificent Atrium. Please bring me some memory-recording gear."

"But, but--"

I sighed and resisted the urge to tell him to relax again. "At some point, the Quihiri will have to let the rest of the cast and crew in here so we can rehearse--just make sure you're with them."

"I am in the cast," he said, sounding insulted.

"Great," I said. "It should be easy then. Just bring me a memory recorder. Dr. Sharma probably has some extras."

He didn't answer right away. For some reason, I thought he might be about to say something like, 'I'm not your errand boy!'

"I appreciate your help, Ted," I said. "You are very important to me. Please. I need your help."

"Well ...I ...I, okay," he said. "I'll be there as soon as I can. But you didn't answer my questions. Are you all right? What's happening?"

"I'm about to have a breakfast feast. Bye for now." I hung up, cutting him off as he started to sputter something else.

The Quihiri triple had set up breakfast for my triple on a table near the stage in the front of the room. In the back, more Quihiri were setting up a bigger table with more food.

Gina was enthusiastically helping herself to food. As she put it on her plate, it looked a lot like Terran sushi. I didn't know if she was really hungry or if she was being diplomatic.

Wait. Why would she be really hungry? I glanced at Carter. What had they gotten up to after I left them?

Why did I care?

Let it go, Jack. I was all about live and let live. Or maybe I was all about love the one you're with. Or...

"Jack?" Carter said. "Are you all right?"

I shook my head. "Sure. Just hungry." I grabbed a plate and started piling on. I sniffed the plate; it smelled like sushi--fresh fish, but not fishy--if that made any sense.

The three Quihiri were just standing there watching us. And, yeah, it was a little creepy.

"You guys should join us." I pointed at the feast. "Are you a triple? Join us." I glanced at Gina and Carter. Despite myself, I did want to be in their good graces. "Join our triple." Look at me, the diplomat.

All three of them turned blue and then green.

Gina and Carter turned red. Ha. Apparently, Quihiri weren't the only ones that showed emotions with skin color.

"Ah..." Gina said.

I sat down next to her at the table.

She grabbed my arm and pulled me closer to her. She whispered in my ear. "You may have just asked them to mate with us."

I shrugged. "Whatever." I must admit I was curious. How did octopi mate?

"We are honored by your offer," the large Quihiri said. "But we will merely keep you company while you partake in your meal."

I smiled at the littlest octopus. I glanced at Gina.

She shrugged, the color in her face fading.

I smiled at the littlest octopus-like creature again. "Come sit next to me, little one."

She turned bright neon green but sat down next to me and put some food on her plate.

"Do you know my friend Quinta?" I asked. "The ambassador's wife?"

"Oh, no," the little one said. "She's much too exalted for me to know. Why?" She turned to me. "Do you know her?"

Gina was chatting with the large Quihiri on the other side of her but keeping an eye on me. I couldn't decipher her current expression.

We passed a pleasurable meal. The food that looked and smelled like sushi tasted like sushi. No doubt Gina would lecture me at some point that it was fish-like creatures and not actual fish. Whatever.

Even better, I was on my way to developing another asset. The little neon-green Quihiri sat next to me, not eating and not saying much. I was starting to think these little Quihiri were cute. I was also wondering how they mated. And why they didn't want to eat with us.

I surreptitiously took out my fon and looked up octopi mating practices. From what I could tell, it was all pretty bizarre. I guess that made sense since they weren't mammals. Did Quihiri mate like Terran octopi? I didn't know.

Gina gave me a look that said, 'What's wrong?'

But the larger Quihiri said something to her, so she had to turn and give him her attention.

"Is there anything we can do to make you more comfortable?" he said. "The ambassador assigned my triple to take care of your triple, Captain."

"Thank you. We need to start rehearsing," she said. "We need to be able to come and go to bring our equipment and cast and crew here."

Carter, sitting across the table from her, nodded. "Yes. We are eager to put on a wonderful show for you."

She elbowed me.

"Yes. Wonderful. Show." I felt discombobulated. "Sing. Act. Me."

All five of them turned and looked at me.

"*Taci, e trema al mio something,*" I sang. I couldn't quite recall the line.

"Oh. Are you Don Giovanni?" the little Quihiri asked.

I stared at her. "Uh."

"Are you licentious?" the other little Quihiri asked.

Who knew Quihiri had such good vocabularies?

"Oh, yes," Carter said, sort-of laughing. "He's licen-tious. Ver-y." He made a strange expression.

I glared at him, feeling even odder.

Now the big Quihiri was a bright green color. "Do you want to mate?"

"Uh..." How could I agree before I knew what I was getting into? (Look at me. I was getting wiser and wiser all the time.) "Could you be more spec-if-fic a-bout what is in-volve-d?" My mouth felt a little numb.

"What Jack means to say is we would be hon..." Gina said. "But, a-las we can-not." She was talking unusually slowly.

"Ah," the large Quihiri said, color fading to pink. What did that signify? "Just as well; I believe some of your crew are here."

The large Quihiri said something I couldn't hear to the two smaller ones. They moved away from the table.

A crowd of Terrans burst into the atrium, led by Ted.

"Jack! Jack!" He ran up to me and threw his arms around me.

But I couldn't lift my arms to hug him back.

"What is the meaning of this?" the large Quihiri asked. "Are you not a triple?"

I couldn't talk. I couldn't move.

Chapter Twenty-Six

In the Magnificent Atrium on Quihiri, I couldn't move. I could breathe fine but couldn't talk or manipulate my limbs. What was going on? Panic was right around the corner--all the more terrifying since there was no sign of it in my body.

Ted was hugging me.

I tried to breathe deeply, to smell his unique Ted smell, but I couldn't.

He pushed me to arm's length and looked me in the eyes. "What's wrong? Why aren't you hugging me back?"

Without moving my head, I checked out Carter and Gina still sitting at the table; they weren't moving either.

Members of the *Shakespeare* crew brought in various instruments and props, setting them down near the door when the Quihiri ushered them to the large buffet. The room was bustling. I even spotted old Bill from the cargo bay with the anti-gravity dolly bringing in some larger containers.

In the meantime, the Quihiri who'd brought the food were leaving.

'Hey!' I thought. 'We're in trouble here! Pay attention!' But I couldn't speak. I thought words but couldn't move my lips, tongue or jaw. At all. *And thus the whirligig of time brings in his revenges.*

The only person paying attention to us was Ted.

It was super frustrating to be frozen and surrounded by people but unable to communicate with them. Why didn't they notice?

Out of the corner of my eye, I saw our host Quihiri triple glide through the doorway. They weren't acting particularly guilty or moving particularly quickly.

Was it possible our paralysis was accidental? Could it be a coincidence?

The other crewmembers shouldn't eat the food until we were sure. But how to tell them?

I had a feeling Old Jack the spy would say there was no such thing as a coincidence.

'Hey! The food might be dangerous!' Sadly, no one heard my mental message.

Ted touched Gina on the shoulder as she still sat at the table.

She didn't move.

In the meantime, the *Shakespeare*'s crew had started eating the food laid out in the buffet. Oh no.

Ted looked over my frozen triple. He pulled out his fon and punched a button. "Commander Lu, something's wrong. Jack and Captain Gomez," he glanced at Carter, "and first officer Nillion seem paralyzed." He listened for a moment. "There aren't any Quihiri in the immediate vicinity." He listened some more. "I don't know. But, sir, Jack told me earlier he'd made some important discoveries." He listened and then said, "Yes, sir."

He hung up. "Lu and a security squad and Dr. Sharma are coming ASAP." He put away his fon. "He said we should avoid causing a diplomatic incident if possible in case this is some kind of mistake."

Gina widened her eyes a little. But if that meant she agreed or disagreed, I couldn't tell.

We needed to stop the crew from eating anything. 'Stop. Don't eat.' But I hadn't developed ESP in the last few moments.

Ted looked me in the eyes and then hugged me again. Even though I couldn't hug him back, it felt nice. Mentally. I couldn't feel it physically. "I'm sorry this is happening to you," he said softly. I liked Ted. He was a good guy.

After a few minutes, Commander Lu burst in with a security squad, followed by Dr. Sharma. They ran right over to my triple, ignoring the other crewmembers now enjoying breakfast.

Lu took one look at Gina and me and Carter and nodded. "Good job, Ted." He glanced at the stage and the other *Shakespeare* crewmembers (who still weren't paying attention to us) and frowned. "Very good job, Ted."

Dr. Sharma poked me with some kind of medical device that looked like a cross between a fon and a small gun. I didn't feel it.

He typed a little on the machine's keypad and then grunted. "Yeah, you guys have been given a paralytic. I can synthesize a few doses of antidote." He punched some buttons and then poked me with his machine again. He went and poked Gina and Carter as well.

Where had the Quihiri gone? Would they come back? Had this all been some horrible accident?

I did not think so. Darn. Cynicism must be contagious. I must have caught some from Gina or someone.

Maybe we needed to go to battle stations or something. But I couldn't speak to suggest it.

After a few moments, I got an unpleasant pins-and-needles feeling in my upper arm that started spreading throughout my body. It was like a bunch of tiny worms were crawling around inside me. I rubbed my arms and legs briskly, trying to get rid of it. "*Mwah, mwah...*" I cleared my throat. "I can talk. I have something important to say! Battle stations!"

Gina and the Terrans near me gave me an annoyed look.

"What do you want to do, Captain?" Lu asked Gina. "Do you think it was an attack?"

"Yes." She frowned. "But as far as attacks go, it was pretty subtle. Why didn't they just kill us?"

Carter walked around the table and peered at me. "Maybe they were trying to kidnap us."

Ugh. What was it with me and kidnapping? I was like catnip to kidnappers that liked catnip. I didn't want to be kidnapped again. "Why would they do that? We're already on their planet."

"Some kind of power play?" Gina said. "Could there be different factions at work here?"

"That disagrees with the intelligence on the planet," Carter said.

I snorted.

Gina looked thoughtful.

"Wait a minute. Shouldn't we be doing something?" I asked. "Something defensive? Something offensive? Battle stations! Something with weapons, anyway."

"Captain?" Lu said.

"I'm starting to doubt the intelligence reports for Quihiri," Gina said. "There's something going on here we're not getting. Let's get back to the ship."

"Everyone?" Lu asked.

"Hey," I said. They were forgetting something. The breakfast buffet was poisoned.

"No," she said and turned to Carter. "Can I leave you in charge? We need to get the scenery, props, and instruments set up so we can start rehearsing, or at least look like we're going to start rehearsing. We need to at least try to maintain our cover."

"Isn't our cover blown?" I asked. They ignored me.

"Ma'am," Carter said. You can depend on me." He turned and started walking to the stage.

"Wait a minute!" I yelled.

They all looked at me.

"This is important!" I'd gotten distracted there for a second with all the kidnapping talk. "How did we get poisoned? It was probably the food, and the rest of the crew is eating!" I pointed at the buffet, still surrounded by *Shakespeare* crewmembers.

"Shit," Gina said, face slack. "We should have figured that out. The poison must be interfering with our thought processes somehow." She pointed at Commander Lu. "Evacuate the crew immediately. Don't let them eat anything else."

"Yes, ma'am," Commander Lu said. "Ted, you're with me."

"We need someone to show us how to get out of here," I said.

Gina nodded. "In the meantime, Sharma, start checking them out and treat them if they show any signs of poisoning."

"I think I need to investigate this poison more if it's affecting your cognitive abilities," Dr. Sharma said. "I can call some junior medical personnel to treat people."

"All right." She pointed at me, Sharma and Carter. "Back to the ship.

The four of us walked for the door.

"Dr. Sharma, I hope you know your way out of here," Gina said. "They led us on quite a circuitous tour yesterday."

Had that been a nefarious plan, too? Wow. The Quihiri were sneaky.

"Yes, ma'am," he said.

Back on the ship, I convinced Gina we all needed a break before meeting to discuss these latest developments. For my part, I was going to brush my teeth and take a shower. I don't know what they were planning to do with their minutes of freedom.

At my cabin, the door snicked open. I sighed in relief as I stepped inside. Home sweet home. The door closed behind me.

I stripped and stepped into my little bathroom. I started brushing my teeth and spied my memory gear hanging on a hook on the wall. Thank goodness. I needed to record my memories from last night.

I put down my toothbrush and picked up my recording device. It resembled a cap with a bunch of electronics in it. I accessed the memory app on my fon and started it.

For a moment, I got lost in the memory of the silvery-lit deserted embassy and then the amazing yellow-gold sun seemingly inside the factory.

I finished, hung the gear on the wall and picked up my toothbrush again.

"Jack?" Addie said.

"Ack!" I jumped and dropped my toothbrush.

"What's wrong?" she asked. "You seem jumpy."

I'm sorry to say I'd forgotten all about her. And baby Slid. What was going on with my brain today?

Bad, Jack. "Er, hi, Addie. How are you and baby Slid doing?"

"Fine," she said with a grayish tinge to her cloud. "You didn't answer my question. Is something wrong?"

I knew gray meant she was sad or worried--and no wonder, we were parked at the planet of her sworn enemies.

As I looked at her, it hit me that Addie's species and the Quihiri both communicated emotions through their colors. And little Quinta had also said their species were enemies.

Even in my limited existence, I knew the opposite of hate was love. Why, exactly, were they enemies now? Had they been something else before?

"Jack?" she asked.

I picked up my toothbrush and asked, "What's the history

between the sldkfjfoisut and the Quihiri?" and resumed brushing. Checking myself out in the mirror, I looked good, even though I could use a shave. I should see Dr. Sharma about an update to my facial depilatory.

She didn't immediately answer. When I glanced over at her, she looked distinctly gray and gloomy.

"Why do you ask?"

I shrugged exaggeratedly. "*Mwah, mwah,*" I said with my mouth full of toothbrush and toothpaste.

"Do you know something?" she asked. "What do you know?"

Ah ha. There was something to know.

If I could trust her. Which I didn't think I could. Right?

I shrugged again.

She didn't answer.

I spat toothpaste in the sink and stowed my brush. I turned and leaned back against the sink, crossing my arms in front of me. "I can't help noticing both you and the Quihiri are very colorful. It seems significant."

"How did you figure that out?" she whispered.

"I paid attention," I said.

"But..."

"Come on, Addie, spill," I said and pointed at Slid under my bunk. "You owe me."

"You have to swear you won't tell anyone," she said, floating closer to me.

I shook my head. I didn't trust her. "I'm not promising that."

Now she was black at her core. I knew that meant she was upset. I could give her a minute to calm down.

"Just a sec." I wanted to remember what I'd just figured out. I grabbed my memory gear, held it to my head, and flipped the switch. After a couple of seconds, it beeped. I put it back near the medicine cabinet.

"Spill," I said.

Addie floated right up to me, leaning into me. "We may have a common ancestor," she whispered, "but you didn't hear it from me."

I leaned away from her. "I knew it! I knew it was something like that."

"How did you know?" She sounded sad and looked gray and black, her cloud roiling. "No other Terran has ever figured it out."

"No other Terran is as awesome as me. The color thing really gives it away." I reached into the shower and turned it on. The small room filled with fog as steam billowed out.

"But Terrans don't know about that," she said in her quiet voice.

I stepped inside the tiny stall, and the hot water started massaging my aching muscles. Getting paralyzed apparently gave you aching muscles.

"Addie?" I called out.

She didn't answer me.

I poked my head out of the stall, but she'd left.

When Gina, Carter, and I reassembled in the captain's ready room, I couldn't help smiling at my triple. I felt much better physically after my shower. And I felt good mentally after figuring stuff out about the sldkfjfoisut that no other Terran knew. Yay, me.

"What's that smile, Jack?" Carter asked. The ready room was a fancy conference room. Gina had decorated it in a pretty girly fashion with muted rose walls, flowers, and soft lighting.

"You need a shave," Gina said.

"I think it looks sexy." I touched my stubbly cheek.

She frowned. I figured she was thinking whisker stubble was against regulation.

I leaned back in my chair, grinning. "So, not only did I find the super-secret FTL drive factory, and find out the sldkfjfoisut and the Quihiri are enemies..." I smiled broadly. "I also found out they have a common ancestor."

"No," Carter said. "They're from opposite sides of the galaxy."

I held up a forefinger. "So you think, but you think wrong."

"It's impossible, Jack," Gina said. "It goes against all our data on the galaxy."

"The data's wrong," I said. "Think about it. It makes sense. They both change colors based on their emotions. And the sldkfjfoisut and the Quihiri hate each other. You only hate people you know."

"We are kind of the new kids on the block, galactically," Carter said, corners of his mouth turning down. "What if they're trying to trick us?"

"No," Gina said, shaking her head. "That would mean all the species have been lying to us."

"Or, the Quihiri and slids have tricked the other species," I said.

Gina continued. "And if they all lied about where a species is from, they could be lying about anything." She paused. "I need to contact TCC command."

"Wait a minute," Carter said. "How do we know this new info is reliable? What if the new info is false? Where'd you get it?"

"I got some of it from Quinta, a very cute little Quihiri," I said. "And I got some of it from Addie."

"Where is she?" Gina asked. "I'd like to hear this from her own mouth, so to speak."

"Yes," Carter nodded.

"I'm not sure where she is," I said. "She was in my cabin, but I don't think she is anymore."

He was already typing on his fon. "No sign of her on internal sensors."

"That doesn't necessarily mean anything," I said. "She was on the ship for a while before we knew it. Check if Slid is still in my cabin."

Carter typed and then shook his head. "According to sensors, Slid is gone, too."

"That can't be right." I stood up and ran to my cabin.

When I got there, and the door opened, I could tell immediately that no other life form was there. The cabin felt utterly empty in a way it hadn't for a long time. I went in and went through the motions of checking under the bed.

The box was empty.

Slid was gone.

Chapter Twenty-Seven

Back in the captain's ready room, Carter and Gina sat at the table-- they looked like they'd been arguing. It was odd to see agitated faces in the calm, flower-filled setting.

I sat, flummoxed. Where had Addie and little Slid gone?

"Are you sure they're gone, Jack?" Gina asked.

"I'm sure they're not in my cabin," I said. "But I'm not sure they're off the ship."

"They don't show up on sensors," Carter said.

"I think Addie can avoid being sensed when she wants to," I said. Initially, I'd thought she was a ghost. In my defense, I wasn't familiar with noncorporeal entities--or whatever we were supposed to call them.

Intimidating Gina was frowning. "We need to figure out how to update sensors."

Handsome Carter nodded. "Yes. But I'm not sure this is the right time." He looked around the table. "We're in the middle of a mission, right? Possibly surrounded by something..."

The intimidating woman frowned some more. "Wait. What were we talking about?"

"Sensations?" I said. We'd been talking about something more important. "Addie. Slid." I started to think about some sensations I'd had with Addie but shied away from them. Now was not the time.

"Huh?" the handsome middle-aged man said.

"Addie. Slid," I said. "I think they're some kind of people." I couldn't concentrate. "I think they're missing. I think they're important, somehow." I shook my head.

"What do you want me to do again?" the handsome middle-aged man said.

The intimidating woman frowned. "What were we talking about?"

They both looked at me. Was I in charge? That sounded good. I smiled.

Unfortunately, if I was in charge, I didn't know what we were supposed to be doing.

That didn't seem too in-charge-y. I lost my smile.

The woman cleared her throat. "Who are you people? What's happening here?"

She must not be in charge, either.

That left the man. I stared at him.

He stared back at me, then his eyes moved to his ring. He held up his hand, looking at it.

The woman held up her hand. "I have one too. They match."

Aw. I wanted a pretty matching ring. But I didn't say that. "That seems significant." I nodded in what I hoped was a wise way.

The matching-ring couple stared at each other.

The woman said, "What's your name?"

The man said, "What's your name?"

What was my name? I couldn't remember. Surely I had a name. "I think something's wrong," I said. "What's my name? Do you know my name? *What's in a name? That which we call a rose by any other name would smell as sweet.*"

The couple turned to face me at the same time.

Why had I said that?

The man said, "Huh?"

The woman said, "I don't know my name."

The man said, "What's my name?" He looked scared now. "I don't know anything."

I didn't know anything, either. I didn't remember anything. How long had I been sitting here in this room? What was this room? I stood up and walked the perimeter. Then I went over to a vase of flowers, poking at them. Were they real? They felt real.

"I don't know anything," the woman said, on the verge of crying. "I don't remember anything."

I didn't remember anything either, but I wasn't as freaked out as I might have expected. I wasn't as freaked out as these two, anyway.

"Something is amiss. We need information." The flowers were not informative. I patted my pockets.

I found a fon and pulled it out. There were some texts and messages addressed to someone named Jack Jones. "I think my name is Jack Jones!"

"How do you know?" the woman asked.

I held up my fon and shook it.

The woman and man started patting their pockets, quickly finding their own fons and accessing them.

I continued skimming texts and messages. "I think we're on a spaceship! I think it's called the *Shakespeare*!" A spaceship sounded super cool.

When I looked up from my fon, the man and woman were still engrossed in theirs.

"I'm going to investigate the ship!" I said.

The man looked up. "But won't you get lost?"

"Huh." I scrolled through the apps on my fon. "Locator and map app!"

The woman winced. "Stop yelling."

I turned on the map and location app. An internal map of the spaceship appeared. "A map of the spaceship!"

The man said, "Stop yelling."

On the little map, there was a small red dot labeled, 'You are here,' attached to a dashed red line. "I'm going to retrace my steps!"

The woman didn't look up. "Yes. Please get out of here."

I shrugged. Her loss.

I walked over to the door and stepped out.

The location app led me through the spaceship's halls. The walls all had colorful murals painted on them. There was one with a beautiful woman with flowing hair standing on a balcony, looking down on a beautiful man with flowing hair. There was one with a man holding a spooky skull. They were fun.

I didn't pass any other people--which was a shame because I wanted to ask someone who knew what was going on: what is going on?

Eventually, I ended up in front of a closed door. The red-dashed line indicated I'd been in that room. I took a step forward, but the door didn't open. I put my hand on the small panel next to the door.

It whooshed open.

I walked inside. The cabin was diminutive, with what looked like a standard bed, chair, desk and a tiny bathroom attached. Over the desk were a bunch of pictures of some old guy with several different other unfamiliar-looking people. Darn. This must be the cabin of the old guy.

What had I been doing here earlier?

I paced around the cabin, looking for clues. No clues.

I threw caution to the wind and thoroughly searched the cabin. Under the bed was an old-school box, but it was empty. Curious.

The only interesting things I found were some data cubes in the desk drawer. And how interesting could they be? There'd been no effort to hide them. I hadn't looked at them yet, but I guessed that was a logical next step.

This whole thing had been a letdown. Why had I even been in here? I sighed.

I had to pee.

I ducked into the little bathroom and used the facilities.

As I washed my hands, I noticed a kind of cap hanging on the wall. I dried my hands and picked it up. It had a bunch of electronics.

In my pocket, my fon pinged. When I looked at the screen, it said, 'Ready for Memory Upload?'

Ha. That was a good one since I had no memories to upload. I looked at my grinning face in the mirror. At least Jack Jones was a handsome young man--with a nice grin.

But wait a minute. If this could upload memories, maybe it could download memories, too.

I accessed the app's menu. Sure enough, 'Memory Download' was an option. Yay! I rocked! I was awesome! I was, like, a detective or a spy.

I put the cap on my head and started the memory download.

Holy shit. The whole thing hit me like a ton of bricks.

Moments ago, I didn't know anything about myself, and now I knew everything. I knew about my many friends and lovers, my ship, my planet, and my mission.

I paused for a moment savoring the wonder that was me, staring at myself. I was a great singer, musician and actor. I was an excellent friend and lover. I was just plain excellent.

"Handsome devil." I even looked good in the little memory cap. "And I don't care what people say. I'm a wonderful spy." I figured out what was going on, didn't I?

I was a very good spy…

We were under attack! This whole memory thing had to be an attack by the Quihiri. It had to be associated with the weird food and the paralysis, right? "Ack!"

I might be the only Terran who knew what was going on. I had to save the day! Lucky for the rest of the galaxy, I was the man for the job!

I hung my memory cap back on the wall.

But where to start?

I sat on my bed for a second. How had we lost our memories? I hadn't known such a thing was possible--wiping memories right out of a person's head. And why had we retained some stuff, like language and how to use technology? It was all very mysterious.

Maybe I wasn't the best spy in the galaxy after all.

I needed help. The only person I knew for sure that was on the ship now that hadn't eaten the food in the Magnificent Atrium was Dr. Sharma. I needed Sharma.

Before I left my cabin, I backed up all my memories on one of the data cubes and hid it under my bed.

Out in the hall, walking to the med bay, I didn't pass a soul. This was not good. Hadn't Gina ordered all the crew back to the ship? Where were they? Not here.

It was eerie.

I started running.

Inside the med bay, Dr. Sharma sat at his desk.

I ran over to him. "Oh, thank God, Dr. Sharma," I said. "I need your help! We're under attack."

Dr. Sharma didn't answer me.

Dr. Sharma didn't move.

I examined him and could barely make out his chest rising

and falling as he breathed. "Can you move?"

He didn't answer me or move---which I interpreted meant he couldn't answer or move.

I needed that gadget he'd used on me earlier. Luckily it was there in front of him on the desk.

I shot him with it.

After a few moments, he shifted in the chair. "Thank you," he said. "Are you a doctor? Something's wrong with me. I don't know who I am. Can you help me?"

My spirits sank. I needed a knowledgeable Dr. Sharma, not an ignorant Dr. Sharma.

And why was the timeline different for him? Gina, Carter and I had remembered who we were when we were unparalyzed.

Why, how, had Sharma even been paralyzed?

But buck up, Jack. The galaxy needs you.

"I can help you," I said. "We need to find your memory gear. It looks like a funny little cap."

I searched under his bed, under a cozy-looking afghan, under his pillow, basically under the whole slumber area.

He didn't have a memory cap hanging on the wall in his personal bathroom, either. "Darn it."

"Did you say something?" he called out.

"Nope," I called back. "Just keep looking."

Eventually, standing in front of a drawer, he said, "I think I found it." He held it up. "Is this it?"

"Yes." I darted over to him, taking the cap. "You should probably sit down."

He sat.

I put the cap on his head.

"Give me your fon."

He gave me his fon, and I found the memory app. I selected 'Memory Download' and started it.

After a few minutes, he looked into my eyes. "Jack! You got away from the kidnappers!"

Damn. He was weeks behind the times.

I smiled weakly. "Yes."

This did not bode well for the rest of the crew.

This did not bode well for the rest of the galaxy.

Chapter Twenty-Eight

As we sat in the empty med bay, I filled Sharma in on the events of the last few weeks.

He nodded periodically.

I wound down and said, "Do you understand?"

He frowned. "No. And a lot of the stuff you just told me was pretty unbelievable and, frankly, inappropriate. Why do you think I care who you have sex with?"

He made a good point. "Let's put a pin in the sex talk," I said. "What do you think we should do now?"

"I don't want to put a pin in the sex talk," he said. "I want to forget the sex talk."

"Fine. Forget it! Forget the sex." I jumped up. "We're under attack! Are you going to help me or not?"

He gave me a long, measured look. Finally, he said, "Of course, I will help my crew if they're under attack. It's not even a question."

I said, "*If it were done, when 'tis done, then 'twere well if were done quickly. If th' assassination could trammel up the consequence, and catch with his surcease, success....*"

He said, "What are you talking about?"

"If this was an assassination attempt, they moved too slow," I said. "We're about to be successful, trammel up the bad guys. I think we're about to get back the upper hand. We should give Gina and Carter their memories back first. And then we can move on from there. However, I'm not sure who else is on the ship. It seems pretty empty."

"An empty ship is not protocol," Dr. Sharma said, frowning again.

"No." I was a bit discombobulated that the Quihiri had

disrupted us so thoroughly. "I think we have to be very, very careful. If we tip our hand to the Quihiri that we know they attacked us, we might lose our advantage. Clearly, this isn't the first time they've had their way with Terrans--so to speak."

"I think you're right," he said. "This drug is very effective on humans. It was possibly developed specifically for this purpose, to control us and our information."

He stood. "I need to get a bunch of doses of the anti-paralytic ready. We might need a dose for everyone in the crew."

"Okay," I said. "You do that. I'll get Gina and Carter their memories back and bring them back here, and we can regroup." I realized I didn't truly know how the memory gear worked. "Are the memories stored in the cap or in a person's fon or what?"

"The default is to store them in the cap's memory," he said. "But you can store backups wherever you want, in your fon, or whatever."

So, I needed everyone's individual cap. Check.

I took a step toward the door, but something was nagging me. I stopped. "Hey, wait, how did you get paralyzed? You didn't eat the food on the surface, did you?" He didn't eat anything that I saw. He didn't do anything on the planet that could paralyze him, that I saw.

That meant he must have been attacked on the ship, right? Uh oh.

Dr. Sharma was already pushing buttons on his med dispenser. He stopped. "I don't remember."

"Right." Damn. "This is very sneaky. Pernicious. If you got dosed on the ship, there might be other dosed crew members on board." I pondered things for a moment. "There must be Quihiri on the ship that dosed you, somehow."

"Must be." He turned to face me. "Be careful, Jack."

"Do you have any weapons in here?" I asked.

He walked to the wall and pressed a panel. It levered open, revealing some weapons-looking devices. He pulled a couple out. "Of course. This is a spy ship." He held them out.

I took them, but then I didn't know where to put them. "Do you have any kind of holster?"

"No," he said. "And it would blow your cover as a memoryless moron, wouldn't it?"

187

"True," I said. "Do you have any kind of jacket or anything I could borrow?"

Sharma glanced around the room. "All I've got in here are a bunch of those gowns people wear when getting treatment."

"You mean those ugly things?" I shuddered a little. "No thanks." I wouldn't be caught dead in one of those--talk about unflattering. I'd much rather parade around nude. Focus, Jack.

"Well, that's all I've got," he said.

"What about your personal clothes?" I asked.

He shrugged. "Pants. Shirts. In my size. I don't think they're going to help." Sharma was about the same height as me but much, much heftier, to put it politely, and, of course, I would.

And then it hit me. "Take off your doctor's coat."

"But you're not a doctor," he said.

I raised my eyebrows and curled my lip as if to say, 'Really?'

He shook his head a little. "Sorry." And started shrugging out of it.

I put down the guns, put on the white lab coat, and filled the pockets with guns. The pockets were huge, so the guns didn't even peek out. "This works." I approached the door. "Be careful, Dr. Sharma."

"You too, Jack."

I entered the hall. Seeing it so uncharacteristically empty was spooky; it seemed to stretch on forever like some Mobius strip. I shook off the feeling.

I ran to Gina's cabin, not seeing anyone (not even nefarious Quihiri) on the way, and searched it for her memory gear. I found it in a little cabinet in her bathroom. I guessed great minds thought alike.

Now all I needed was to find Gina. I'd hoped she might be here in her cabin. Shoot.

How to find her? I sat down on her bed.

I got out my fon and looked at it. The map/locator app helped me figure out where I'd been. I thought back to the events in my short life. When I'd first gotten my fon, Jack's fon, the map/locator app had been off, and right after I turned it on, people started shooting at me.

Maybe none of that had been a coincidence.

I accessed the app. There was a setting to locate other

188

people. Sweet! I turned it on and said, "Locate Gina Gomez."

My fon said, "That user has implemented privacy features."

Well, damn. Damn, that my good idea couldn't help me find Gina, and damn, that I could have been using privacy features this whole time and didn't know it.

I said, "Implement privacy features." A little lock icon appeared in the upper right of the screen.

I bounced on Gina's bed a little and glanced down. "Comfy." This mattress was much nicer than mine. Focus, Jack. If I was Gina, where would I be? Bounce. I wished I could just ask her. Hey, I could!

I called her on the fon.

She answered, "Hello? Who is this?"

"Hello, Gina," I said, beaming from ear to ear. We were going to beat these nefarious Quihiri yet.

"You don't sound like a Gina," she said. "You sound like a man."

"No," I said. "You're Gina."

Away from the fon, she said, "This guy says I'm Gina."

In the background, I heard Carter say, "Does he know who I am?"

"He's Carter," I said.

She said, "He says you're Carter."

"How does he know?" Carter said in the background.

This wasn't getting us anywhere. "I was just with you in the ready room. I'm Jack. Just tell me where you are," I said. "I can help you guys."

Gina said to Carter, "He wants to know where we are. Should we trust him?"

"Hell, if I know," Carter said.

"I'm your friend. Hell, I'm your husband," I said. "You can trust me. Just tell me where you are!"

"We're in a room with a bunch of screens and computers and a big chair in the middle," she said. "I think it's the bridge. Do you know where that is?"

"I know where that is," I said. "Stay put. I'll be right there."

I ran to the bridge. Thankfully, it wasn't far.

I opened the door and ran in.

They both pointed guns at me.

189

"Oh, it's the kid from earlier," Carter said.

They lowered their guns.

"You didn't mention you're a doctor," Gina said.

Somehow they both looked younger, more innocent than I was used to. Except for the guns.

"What?" I glanced down at the white lab coat with bulging pockets. "Oh, right. I'm not a doctor."

"You shouldn't impersonate one, then," Carter said, frowning.

I resisted the urge to pop him in the nose. I turned my attention to Gina, pulling her memory cap out of one of my pockets. "Here." I handed it to her. "Put this on your head and give me your fon."

"I'm not sure we should trust a doctor-impersonator," Carter said.

Gina shrugged. "What do we have to lose at this point? A fake doctor's better than nothing."

My fingers flew over her fon, accessing her memory app. "I'm not a fake doctor." I found the Memory Download. "Forget the doctor stuff! I'm not a doctor."

I looked up at Gina. She'd put on the cap and stood there staring at me. "You better sit down. This thing packs a punch." I led her to the captain's chair. It seemed appropriate.

I pressed the Memory Download button.

She closed her eyes, swayed and then jerked back and forth a few times. Then she opened her eyes.

"Jack?" She glanced at Carter. "Carter? What's going on?" She glanced around the bridge. "Why is the bridge empty? Did we reach Quihiri?"

Hurray. She was only missing about a day or two of memories.

"Yes," I said. "We reached Quihiri. We're under some kind of attack from the Quihiri. They poisoned us and stole our memories. Besides Sharma and you two, I don't know where the rest of the crew is. We need to get Carter back his memories and then meet up with Sharma in the med bay to regroup." I paused to take a breath. "I think there are hostile Quihiri on board. If we meet any, I think we need to play dumb."

Gina and Carter were both staring at me with their mouths

hanging open.

"A memory attack?" Gina finally said. "I've never heard of such a thing. Are you sure?"

"Yes," I said. "I'm sure. Or are you saying you don't have a hole in your memories?"

She paused for a moment, presumably perusing her memories. "Shit," she whispered. "I don't know when we got to Quihiri, and I don't know what happened after that."

"Yeah," I said. "Who knows how many times they've done this to Terran crews? And why?"

"Shit." She looked over at the communications array. "This is an act of war. We need to warn Earth."

Carter's head bobbed back and forth, watching both of us in turn like it was a tennis match.

"I think we should hold off for the moment," I said. "Right now, we have the element of surprise. I'd like to get more of the crew in their right minds before we risk letting the Quihiri know we've figured it out."

Gina nodded. "I agree." She pointed at Carter. "Let's do Carter. Do you have his cap?"

Look at me, super mature, not even giggling at her suggestion to do Carter together. "No," I said. "Sorry. I didn't have time to find his cabin."

"Well, come on," she said, gesturing at us. "I know where it is." Of course, she did. They were married.

She ran out the door, and the two of us followed her a short way down the hall. She stopped in front of a cabin next to hers. Duh. That made sense.

Carter just stood there.

Gina made an exasperated sound and then grabbed his hand and pressed it against the sensor plate.

The door whooshed open.

We all went inside.

"Where's your memory gear?" Gina asked him.

Carter shrugged and gave us a look like he had no idea. "I have no idea."

I refrained from stating the obvious: he doesn't remember.

After tossing the whole cabin, we finally found his memory cap in the secret weapons panel on top of a nice stash of guns and such.

"Why keep it in here?" Gina asked.

"I have no idea," he said.

"It's valuable?" I said. I knew only too well what happened when one's memories were deleted.

She shoved the cap on Carter's head, pushed him down on his bed and grabbed his fon. After a few moments, she said, "Here we go."

Carter closed his eyes and jerked back and forth on the bed. Then he opened his eyes, looked at Gina, and smiled. "Hey, babe," he said in a bedroom voice.

A furrow appeared in the middle of Gina's forehead. "Hey," she said slowly. I didn't know her super well, but I was guessing that was her worried look.

Then, Carter seemed to realize they weren't alone. He stared at me. "Who the hell are you?"

Chapter Twenty-Nine

In Carter's cabin, Gina and I were staring at Carter. We'd restored his memories, and he still didn't know what had happened in the last few months. Not keeping memories up-to-date had to be against regulations, didn't it?

I was shaking my head. He had no idea who I was? Poor him. However, I'd learned my lesson from regaling Sharma with my tales of adventure. Shorter was better. Huh. This might be the first time that was true.

I smiled and said, "Hi, I'm Jack. I'm a new crewmember." I glanced at Gina. She was still frowning a lot. "We're under attack from the Quihiri."

"The Quihiri?" he asked, clearly surprised. "But why? How? Where?"

I cut him off. "We landed at Quihiri because we think they're the source of the FTL drives. They attacked the *Shakespeare* crew somehow with a memory wipe."

Gina went to Carter's weapons stash and extracted four electromagnetic guns and a couple of holsters. She checked if the guns were charged.

"I don't understand," Carter said. "I don't remember any of that."

"When did you last back up your memories?" Gina handed Carter a holster; he took it absentmindedly and started putting it on.

"Just now," he said. But of course, that's what he would say; he'd lost all the memories between then and now. "Gina, babe." He looked at her. "What's going on?"

"What he said," she said.

Carter turned back to me and stared. "Why should we trust

an ...ensign we don't know who's impersonating a doctor?"

"I'm not impersonating a doctor!" I said. I'd be happy to lose this lab coat. "Hey, is there another holster in there?"

"No." Gina shook her head and handed Carter a gun.

He put the gun in his holster. I had holster envy. He said, "Gina?"

She said, "We should trust him because I'm the captain, and I said so." Nice.

"So, we need to meet up with Sharma in the med bay," I said. "Carefully. There may be hostiles on the ship."

Carter took another gun from Gina. "So, it's shoot first and ask questions later?" he asked.

"Or, maybe we should play along and pretend we don't have our memories if we run into any Quihiri?" I said.

Gina looked thoughtful. Finally, she said, "I don't think we should risk them attacking us with the memory weapon again. We don't know what it is or how it works." She glanced at me. "Do we?"

"Not for sure," I said, mind churning. "We were paralyzed by something. And then, after a short time, we lost our memories. It wasn't simultaneous." Was memory-loss a side effect of the paralytic? Or was paralysis a side effect of the memory attack? Or were the two things unrelated? "Sharma might know more. Since he knows about drugs and stuff."

"Let's get to the med bay," Gina said, pulling her two guns out of the holster. "And for now, shoot first, ask questions later."

Carter pulled out his two guns., squinting. "I don't know what it is about you, but you seem familiar, Jack."

I said, "Huh, imagine that," and pulled my two guns out of my lab coat pockets. I felt myself frowning. Drawing out of pockets wasn't nearly as cool as drawing from a holster.

Safeties off, check. Set on stun, check.

Gina opened the cabin door, stuck her head out, looked both ways, and said, "Come on."

As I stepped into the hall, I said, "*Cry havoc and let slip the dogs of war--*"

Both Gina and Carter said, "Shh!"

The three of us ran down the hall more quietly than I would have thought possible. It was a little surreal, with the dramatic mural characters looking down on us, cheering us on.

Where was the crew?

When we turned the corner near the med bay, I saw a Quihiri right there in the hall approaching the med bay. It was wearing a purse or something. In a fluid motion, I shot it.

Gina and Carter each also shot it in a fluid motion. Three shots at once were very loud.

Where were the other two members of its triple? I looked around but didn't see any other Quihiri.

We ran to the Quihiri. Gina felt for a pulse. "Well, shit," she said. "It's dead." She turned to glare at me. "You should have put your weapon on stun."

"My weapon was on stun," I said indignantly.

Gina turned her glare on Carter.

He shrugged and said, "Stun."

"Apparently," I said, "three stuns at once is bad for your health."

Dr. Sharma poked his head and then his gun-toting hand out of sick bay. His scared expression morphed into relief and then irritation. "You shouldn't have killed her. We need intel." He waved us inside. "Get in here. And bring her."

Gina strode after Sharma without another look at the Quihiri.

Carter said, "Ensign," pointed at the dead creature, and followed the other two humans.

I put my weapons back in my pockets. I leaned down to pick up the Quihiri. As my hands touched her octopussy flesh, I felt sad. Did she have little baby Quihiri that depended on her? Did she have a husband and another husband that she'd leave widowers?

I cradled her in my arms and stepped into the med bay. How did we even know she was nefarious? What if she'd just been in the wrong place at the wrong time?

Inside, Carter was talking. "How do we even know if it's a she?"

Dr. Sharma indicated I should put her on one of his examination tables. "The females are generally smaller," he said. "But you're right; I don't know for sure."

"She feels like a she to me." I set her gently on the table.

"Let's focus," Gina said. "We're under attack." She looked at Dr. Sharma. "Where's the crew?"

He shrugged. "I have no idea."

Gina turned her attention to me. "Jack? Do you know?"

"I don't know. We could check the security feeds," I said. "But I think they're on the planet. We should try to get everyone back to the ship as soon as possible--if they can come back. They're in danger on the planet." If that was even where they were. They could be anywhere. In any kind of shape. Shit.

All this uncertainty was freaking me out. I was going to assume the crew was down on the planet, alive, and not locked up or anything until I heard otherwise. It made a certain amount of sense if this was a plot the Quihiri had used before--erasing memories of visitors.

I needed to calm down. Calm, I was calm. "I think we should assume the Quihiri have successfully done this before--wiped the memories of a spaceship crew. It's sneaky."

"I don't understand what's going on," Carter said.

Gina touched his shoulder. "I know, honey. Just be quiet." Ouch.

"It would be much easier to treat everyone back here on the ship," Dr. Sharma said. "And it's a controlled environment. Even if there are some hostile Quihiri on the ship, there'd have to be a limited number of them."

"I agree with you guys," she said. "Let's get everyone back here. But how?"

Carter said, "Can I talk?" He continued talking. "Don't they have comms? Can't we order them back to the ship?"

I'm calm and rational. "We don't know if everyone has comms," I said. "They should. But they probably don't know the way back to the ship if they've lost their memories."

"And judging by what happened to us, they probably can't move," Dr. Sharma said.

"I'd just as soon keep the Quihiri in the dark about the fact that we've figured out their plot as long as possible," Gina said. "Right now, we have the element of surprise. And a lot of the *Shakespeare* crew will probably get hurt if we start shooting."

"Yeah," Carter said. "Since they can't move and all, and there's a whole planet of Quihiri."

"Okay," I said. "I'm hearing that we need a sneaky way to get folks back to the ship, and we need a sneaky doctor to help them do so." I held up my hand. "I volunteer to be the sneaky doctor." What the heck? I was dressed for it already.

"No," Dr. Sharma said. "I should go."

"No," Gina said. "You're too valuable. Let Jack go."

Because Jack wasn't valuable? Ugh. I did not like the sound of that.

"What about the sneaky reason?" Carter said.

"The Quihiri probably don't know much about our culture," I said. "What about if the crew has to return for a mandatory birthday party for Gina?"

"That's Captain Gomez to you, Ensign," Carter said, bristling.

"They may not know a lot about us, but I'm guessing their intelligence knows if it's my birthday or not," Gina said. Darn. A fake birthday party sounded kinda fun.

"Ooh," I said. "What about some kind of religious thing?"

"A religious thing is a good idea," Dr. Sharma said. "Species steer clear of each other's religious practices."

"There aren't many Terran religious holidays in summer," Carter said. The *Shakespeare* followed Earth's calendar, but it was far from summer now.

"It's fall," Gina said.

Carter looked surprised.

We all stared at each other for a few moments. We were wasting time. "It's a fake holiday. We can make something up. Today is ...All Saints' Day."

"That's a real holiday, and today isn't the day, is it?" Carter asked.

"It doesn't matter!" I said. "Okay, the plan is: we'll order the crew back to the ship over comms for the special mandatory All Saints' Day celebration. I'll go down to the surface, unparalyze anyone who needs it and lead everyone back to the ship. You guys access the security feeds to find the Quihiri on the ship and then go and stun them. And look for other *Shakespeare* crew onboard and unparalyze them as needed."

"Gee," Dr. Sharma said. "Is that all we have to do? Search the ship for hostiles, shoot them, find our people and help them?"

"Yeah," I said. "There's three of you. Divide and conquer." Three people sounded like more than enough to me.

All I had to do was go down to a hostile planet and save over a hundred people without getting caught by enemy natives. I briefly considered asking for help, but I knew more people would make it more difficult to sneak around. And we didn't exactly have a wealth of human resources at the moment.

I unloaded one of the weapons from my pocket and held out my hand for the medical gun. "Gina, send the message over comms--and say it's automated."

Dr. Sharma gave me the medical gun. "The anti-paralytic is loaded up and ready to go."

Gina started to say something but just nodded.

"And then we need to be ready to take off as soon as everyone's on board, okay?" I said. "Be ready."

"Wow," Carter said. "You are very bossy for an ensign."

I didn't have time to explain things to him. My mind was racing. I needed a way to show the crew back to the *Shakespeare* in that labyrinthine Quihiri building without necessarily showing them in person. I glanced back towards Sharma's personal quarters. "Can I borrow some yarn?" While we were tossing his cabin looking for his memory gear, I'd discovered Sharma was a knitting aficionado.

"Why?" he asked.

"Bread crumbs," I said.

Understanding lit his eyes, and he nodded and darted off.

"I don't understand what's going on," Carter said again.

"*Shh*, honey," Gina said.

I innocently strolled through the Quihiri compound, trailing yarn behind me. I'd tied one end to a handle near the *Shakespeare*'s external door; the large skein sat in one of my big lab coat pockets, unraveling behind me.

I tried to keep a blank, memory-less look on my face. I clutched a stun gun in my other pocket. Calm, stay calm.

Over comms, I heard, "All *Shakespeare* personnel report to the ship's galley for our mandatory All Saint's Religious Observance." Gina did a good impression of a robot; if I hadn't known it was her, I would have thought it was a machine talking.

"All *Shakespeare* personnel report to the ship's galley for our mandatory All Saint's Religious Observance." This whole flimsy scheme only worked as long as the Quihiri thought their evil wipe-the-Terrans-memories plan was working.

So far, I hadn't come across any sentients--neither Quihiri nor humans.

I made it all the way to the Magnificent Atrium without seeing anyone. The ease of it was making me uneasy.

I took a deep breath at the atrium and pushed open one of the doors.

Inside, a bizarre sunny frozen tableau greeted me. All the humans stood as still as statues in the middle of whatever they'd been doing. Most of the crew were still clustered around the buffet table. The orange sun shining through the glass ceiling made the space seem cheery and totally at odds with crewmembers in distress. It was disconcerting. I became more uneasy.

Focus, Jack.

Quickly, I scanned the room, looking for Quihiri.

I saw only *Shakespeare* crewmembers. Only by carefully scrutinizing them could I make out the faint rise and fall of their chests as they breathed. A few humans were separated from the main group, on stage or across the large atrium.

But time was of the essence. Sneak attacks only worked as long as they were sneaky. I pulled out the medical gun near the door and shot the first crewmember I could reach with the anti-paralytic. He immediately shuddered and blinked. "What's happening? Who are you?" He paused for a moment. "Who am I?"

So, memory loss, check. Darn it. The whole paralyzed-slash-memory loss timeline was confusing.

I stepped to the next crewmember. "You're an important crewmember on the Terran ship the *Shakespeare,*" I said to the first guy as I shot the second guy.

The second guy blinked and shuddered. I held up my hand to stop him from speaking.

"I know both of you are confused. You're human. You're crewmembers of the Terran ship the *Shakespeare*. I need you two to tell everyone to follow the yarn back to the ship after I unparalyze them. It's an order." I was guessing everyone would have lost their memories.

"Yarn?" the second guy said.

"What?" the first guy said.

"For the super important All Saint's Day observance," I said. "You just heard that message, right?"

They still looked confused but nodded.

I shot a third guy.

"I'm counting on you two," I said. "You've got your orders. It's an emergency. Hurry! Get everyone back to the ship! Follow the yarn!"

The third guy shuddered and blinked. "What--"

I ignored him and moved on, shooting all the people near the buffet table.

The first two guys must have been successful because crewmembers jogged out of the atrium, staring down at the yarn on the floor.

I finished everyone near the buffet, ran up to the stage, and started injecting.

Blink. Shudder. "What--"

I cut off the cute female crewmember. "Go see those men near the door for your orders."

Running from person to person, I cleared the stage.

I stopped to catch my breath for a moment and scanned the large atrium.

Where were Eva and Ted? And Security Commander Lu?

More importantly, where were the Quihiri?

Chapter Thirty

In the Magnificent Atrium on Quihiri, I'd unparalyzed all the humans near the buffet and on the stage. There were a couple of stragglers over on the other side of the large room. Hopefully, it was Ted and Eva. I wasted no time getting over to the stragglers, but I didn't recognize them. Darn. I shot the first one.

Blink, shudder. "What--" the first crewmember said.

I held up my hand. "Just a sec." I shot the other one.

Blink, shudder. "Who--" the second crewmember said.

"You guys are important crewmembers on the Terran ship the *Shakespeare*. You need to report to the two crewmembers near the door for your orders." Yay, crewmember one and two were still loitering by the doors to the atrium. "And tell them they have fulfilled their mission. Tell them their new orders are to follow the yarn back to the ship."

"Yarn?"

"What?"

"Go!" I pointed at the door. "It's an emergency. Go!"

After hesitating for a few moments, they ran to the door area. After conferring, the four of them ran out, watching the ground.

Why hadn't I found Ted and Eva? And Commander Lu? I scanned the space, my uneasiness ramping up to fear. What if something had happened to them? Something worse than being paralyzed and losing their memories. Focus, Jack.

I hadn't checked the rooms off the atrium yet. I knew from personal experience at least a few of them were bedrooms. Most of the doors were partially open. Off the bat, I couldn't think of a reason why Ted, Eva, and Lu would go into a bedroom together... but I, of all people, couldn't fault them if they had.

I sneaked towards the first door. "*The raven himself is hoarse that croaks the fatal entrance of Duncan under my battlements,*" I whispered."*Come, you spirits that tend on moral thoughts, unsex me here, and fill me from the crown to the toe topful of direst cruelty.*" It was a measure of the direness of the situation that I could quote 'unsex me' without balking.

I reached the first door and slowly poked my head into the opening. Nothing. I took one step inside and looked around. Yep. Nothing.

I left and crept to the next door. I slowly poked my head into the opening. I saw Ted, Lu, and Eva lying on the bed, not moving. And a Quihiri! The Quihiri was on the bed with them. The Quihiri sat up.

"Ack!" I ducked back behind the doorway.

"*Fill me from the crown to the toe topful of direst cruelty!*" I exchanged my medical device for a stun gun. I rushed into the room, cruelly pointing the gun at the Quihiri.

"Jack!" the Quihiri said, holding up her tentacles. "What are you doing? Don't shoot." Her color roiled red, black and gray with a few spangles of green.

The Quihiri looked and sounded very familiar. And she didn't have a weapon.

I stepped closer. I recognized the cute pattern of freckles on her face. "Quinta!" I lowered my weapon, and she lowered her tentacles. "What are the Quihiri doing? Why are you here with my crewmembers?"

She pointed a tentacle at the trio lying on the bed. "I was trying to protect them. They're a triple, right?"

I didn't know what the trio would think of being classified as a triple, but I was guessing they wouldn't be happy. "Ah, okay?"

I realized being frozen was not a good defensive move if the cruelty hit the fan. I got the medical gun and shot Ted, Lu, and Eva with the anti-paralytic.

"I hadn't had a chance to bring any others in here yet," Quinta said.

The Terran trio was blinking and shuddering.

Quinta continued talking. "I heard a noise in the Magnificent Atrium--maybe that was when you came in?--and I decided to hide, too. I know it wasn't brave of me, but--"

Commander Lu pulled out his gun and pointed it at Quinta before sitting up.

She turned all red and flowed off the bed.

"What the hell is going on here?" Lu asked, jumping out of bed.

I stepped around the bed just in time to see red Quinta flow into the teeny tiny space underneath.

Ted and Eva both sat up. They both drew their weapons.

I froze for a second. What if they didn't remember me? What if all the good times, affection, and love between us were gone?

What if they thought I was the enemy?

"Don't shoot," I said.

Eva got off the bed. "So, we're under attack? By the Quihiri?" She leaned down to peer under the bed and then straightened up again. "Who are you? Doctor..." She narrowed her eyes. "You seem pretty young to be a doctor."

She might remember me once she got her memories back. No, she'd definitely remember me. Who wouldn't remember me?

Ted scrutinized me. "What's going on? It looks like we're on Quihiri, but why don't I remember how I got here? And why am I in bed, doctor?" He looked me up and down and then grinned. It was a sexy grin.

I grinned back for a split second. But I couldn't think about myself or my interests right now.

Ted got off the bed. Darn.

"What was that message about All Saints Day?" Lu had gotten out his fon and pressed at least one key.

Shoot. What if the Quihiri were monitoring our communications? I grabbed Lu's fon and turned it off.

If looks could maim, the look he shot me then would put me in maim-city. Heck, it'd put me in the hospital in maim-city.

"*Shh*," I said. "My name's Jack. We're all crewmembers together on the Terran ship the *Shakespeare.* We are under attack from the Quihiri. But so far, they haven't figured out that we've figured it out. Don't use your fon. We have to assume comms and fons are being monitored."

"Yeah, they are," a muffled voice from under the bed said.

"The Quihiri that brought you here, Quinta, is trying to help us," I said. "Right, Quinta?"

"Yes," she said.

Both Eva and Ted holstered their weapons. Darn, I still had holster envy.

I put the medical gun back in one of my big pockets.

"Why are the Quihiri attacking us?" Eva asked.

No explanations were forthcoming from under the bed.

"I think the best thing is to get back to the ship as soon as possible," I said. "You all need to get your memories back."

"I'm not going anywhere until I get some answers," Lu said.

"Why is Quinta helping us?" Ted asked.

"Yeah," Lu said, finally holstering his weapon.

"Yeah," Eva said, leaning down again.

"Quinta?" I asked. "We won't hurt you if you come out."

"Promise?" she asked.

"Yes," I said. "I promise. No Terrans will hurt you."

She slithered out, her red color fading to pink.

"Why are you helping us, honey?" I asked.

"It's wrong what the Imperial Council's doing," she said.

"Imperial Council?" Lu said. "What Imperial Council?

"What are they doing?" Eva said.

"Huh?" Ted said.

"Maybe we should continue the discussion on the *Shakespeare*," I said.

"I'm not sure I should go with you," Quinta said. "It could be very bad for me."

I was torn between trying to convince her to help us and trying to protect her. I didn't like the sound of that 'very bad.' She'd tried to help three humans, two of my dearest friends, without thought of herself. She went against her whole species for us. She was a hero. I had to blink back a tear.

"Come with us," Lu said. "We'll protect you!"

"Definitely," Eva said.

But could we protect her? We didn't know what was going on.

Ted took a step towards the door. "Well, I'm going back to the ship. Wait. How do I get there?"

"Follow the yarn," I said.

"Yarn?" he said.

"Just do it," I said.

He ran out the door. Phew. That was one less person I needed to worry about.

"What do you think, Jack?" Quinta asked. "Can you protect me?"

"I'm not sure," I said.

Lu shook his head. "We need intel."

Eva exhaled.

"But I'll sure try," I said.

"Okay," Quinta said. "Let's go. We'll probably move faster if you carry me."

"Okay," I said and held out my hands. "Eva, Lu, go ahead. Go as fast as you can; go like the wind."

They didn't need to be told twice and immediately ran out the door.

Quinta jumped into my arms. I tried not to think about the dead not-moving Quihiri I'd held in my arms earlier. It wasn't an omen. Nope. Not at all.

I jogged out of the bedroom, holding sweet little Quinta.

I couldn't see Ted at all, and Lu and Eva were way ahead of us. Good. I wanted all of them to be safe.

I ran along the yarn, holding precious cargo. I ran and ran. I started getting a little winded. Darn it! My pace definitely decreased.

We got to within about a hundred yards of the ship. I couldn't see Ted, Eva, or Lu ahead of us any longer. The *Shakespeare*'s exterior door was closed. That seemed like a good idea--no need to make it easier for evil Quihiri to get on the ship. The others must have made it back. Thank goodness.

"Oh, no," Quinta wailed. "There's Quihiri over there!"

Sure enough, there was a large contingent of them down a side hallway. We didn't have time to get into the ship. The contingent hadn't spotted Quinta and me yet. But I didn't want her to be hurt when they did. I'd promised to try to protect her. I would protect her.

I set her down.

"What are you doing?" she sputtered. "They'll catch us!"

"That's the idea," I said. "I'm your prisoner. You captured me."

I flicked my fon. "*Shakespeare*, take off immediately."

Gina answered, "We're waiting for you. We'll open the door. Hurry! You can make it!"

The Quihiri flowed towards us. Ominously.

"No," I said into my fon. "Go! Go! Go!"

In moments I was surrounded by Quihiri.

Octopi, er, octopi-like creatures, were creepy when they were trying to be menacing. I shivered. It was surreal to be endangered in what seemed like an average--albeit with a lot of groups of threes--office building. I tried to remain calm.

The largest (I thought it was her husband, but I wasn't sure) said, "Quinta, what is the meaning of this?"

"He is my prisoner," she said, pointing a tentacle at me. "I captured him."

Many sets of eyes swiveled toward me. Their cold octopus-like orbs made my skin crawl. Maybe I was a little speciesist, after all.

"Yes," I said. "I am her prisoner. She captured me. Yep. Captured. Totally captured."

Largest Quihiri said, "But how? You don't have a weapon. He's much larger than you."

Quinta looked at me with fear in her eyes. She started turning black and gray.

That did seem like a problem. Think fast, Jack. "Uh, no weapon?" I said. "That's not what you told me! What about your stinging tentacles? You told me you had stinging tentacles. You tricked me."

"Yes," she said, her color brightening a little. "I threatened him with my fictitious stinging tentacles."

Burble, burble, burble. The crowd of Quihiri made sounds that I could only assume were laughter. *Burble, burble, burble.*

"Good job, little Quinta." The largest Quihiri caressed her head with one of his tentacles. Husband, check.

She turned blue. "What's going to happen to him?"

"To the dungeons with him!" Largest Quihiri said.

Uh oh. I didn't think this through.

All the Quihiri took up the chorus. "To the dungeons with him!"

I didn't like dungeons.

206

"To the dungeons!"
"Dungeons! Dungeons! Dungeons!"
They led me away.

Chapter Thirty-One

It turned out the Quihiri dungeons had very fine metal mesh walls. That made sense. Even the Quihiri couldn't flow through such tiny spaces.

It also turned out the Quihiri dungeons were located off the giant FTL drive factory I'd discovered earlier. Considering the Quihiri wanted to keep their FTL drives tip-top secret, this did not bode well for my survival.

But I tried to keep my spirits up. I was Jack Jones, interstellar singer-spy! If anyone could escape from this, I could.

I hoped the *Shakespeare* had gotten away safely.

I hoped Quinta wasn't in trouble.

But all this stewing wasn't getting me anywhere. I knew just the thing to keep my spirits up. I started singing. "Whenever I feel afraid, I hold my head up high and whistle a happy tune..."

I sang and watched the FTL drive factory through the mesh. The factory goings-on made a lot of noise, so no one paid my singing any attention. Darn.

On the other hand, the torture and interrogation hadn't started yet, so yay!

The secret FTL drive factory was still a cavernous warehouse-type space filled with Quihiri workers dollying featureless white spheres from one place to another.

In the middle, they had one of the spheres open. I quit singing as I strained to see what was happening. A Quihiri stood over the open sphere, connecting it to some machine, which I was guessing was a computer. He did something with the machine, and a portal opened across from me in the back of the warehouse with a whoosh.

A green-yellow sun shone through it. Wow. *Let the sunshine in.* Everything looked a bit sickly in the green-yellow light.

The Quihiri nodded and disconnected the sphere. The room's typical orangeish light became noticeable again. The Quihiri tester closed up the drive. He pointed at it, and another Quihiri took it to the growing stockpile in the back of the large room.

Yet another Quihiri brought him another sphere. Tester-Quihiri repeated the process: he opened up the drive and connected to his computer. He did something with his computer, but no portal opened. He tried again. He seemed annoyed, waving his tentacles around and turning black with reddish spots.

Another Quihiri rushed up and took the offending drive away. He dollied it in a different direction than the first one went. To the trash? Hmm. I was apparently watching some kind of quality control testing for the FTL drives.

My mind was tingling with mystic crystal revelation. My special skills didn't seem to work with the *Shakespeare*'s new FTL drive. Maybe they worked in the shuttle because the shuttle's FTL drive was defective in some way...

I stared at Tester-Quihiri as he started working on another drive.

Maybe my special skill could work here in the FTL drive factory.

Was it *easy to be hard*? Apparently, I'd started humming the songs from "*Hair*." *Don Giovanni* wasn't exactly hummable.

Well, the only way to prove or disprove my hypothesis was to test it. My hypothesis was: my special skill worked when a defective FTL drive was active.

Tester-Quihiri hooked up a new drive and manipulated his computer.

An amazing portal opened up, and friendly-yellow sunlight flooded the room. Sunlight that reminded me of Earth and my beautiful home sun.

....*And love will steer the stars*...

An FTL drive was active. Quick, use special skill! "My cell is unlocked! My cell is unlocked!" I ran to the door and tried to open it. Nope. Still locked.

Whoosh. The portal closed. Orange light.

Dammit! If I was honest with myself, I'd have to admit I

thought that might actually work.

Next time it might, right?

I stared at Quality-Control-Quihiri, and every time he hooked up a drive, I said, "My cell is unlocked! My cell is unlocked!" and ran to the door and tried to open it.

And every time: nope. Still locked. *Whoosh*. The portal closed. Orange light.

I spent hours running back and forth in my cage. Very unfortunately, the door was on the opposite side from the factory.

Quality-Control-Quihiri left, and a different one took his place. And the saga continued.

Eventually, I must have fallen asleep because I woke up on the floor, face pressed against the mesh.

I had a horrible crick in my neck, and I was super-thirsty. "Hey, water! I need some water!"

No one brought me any water. That had to be against the Geneva Convention or the intergalactic version of that. One of these days, I'd have to actually study some documentation.

I went back to staring at the Quality-Control-Quihiri.

He hooked up a drive.

"My cell is unlocked! My cell is unlocked!"

A portal did not open. No foreign sun shone in the room. Oh, wow! This might be it! This drive didn't work right. "My cell is unlocked! My cell is unlocked!" I ran to the door and tried to open it.

It opened!

I ran through it right into a small gray cloud.

"Mark me," the cloud said in a high soft voice.

"Ack!" I jerked back into the cell and fell to the ground.

From my spot on the floor, I stared at the cloud. Earlier on the *Shakespeare,* I'd met what I thought was a ghost and it had said, 'Mark me.' But it hadn't been a ghost then, and I was guessing it wasn't a ghost--or a small cloud--now. "Addie?" I asked. "Is that you?"

"Are you Jack?" the cloud said. It didn't sound like Addie. Plus, she would recognize me. "I'm here to rescue Jack."

"I'm Jack," I said, sitting up. "Who are you?"

"I don't think you are Jack," it said. "Jack's supposed to be in dire trouble. In the dungeon. You're not in the dungeon."

"I am Jack," I said. "I promise." I pointed at the cell. "This is the dungeon." I waved my hand around. "Technically, I'm in the dungeon." The door was wide open, but I was in the dungeon.

"Prove you're Jack," it said. "Sing something."

I cleared my throat and then sang, "*I believe in love. I believe in love. I believe in love.*"

"Huh," it said. "Maybe you are Jack."

This was taking far too long. I stood up. "Whatever. I need to get out of here."

Another cloud, a bigger cloud, floated into the area. "What's taking so long?" it said in Addie's voice.

"Addie?" I said.

"Of course it's me," she said. "Let's go already." She turned and stormed away.

The little cloud followed after her. Obediently. Ding, ding, ding. My brain was a little slow when I was so thirsty.

"Hey, are you little Slid?" I asked.

"Of course it's me," little Slid said, imitating his mom exactly.

I snickered. "Nice to meet you." We glided or walked, as the case may be, down the hall of the dungeon area.

I didn't see any Quihiri. "Where are the Quihiri?"

"Preparing for war," Addie said.

"Preparing for war," Slid said.

Crap.

We passed prison cells in a pool of water. "Wait," I said. "I need water."

Addie stopped abruptly. Slid stopped abruptly.

"Sorry, Jack," Addie said. "I forgot you're still a corporeal sentience. Of course, you need water. There should be some over here." She floated over to what looked like a faucet and turned it on.

Beautiful, gorgeous, delicious water streamed out. I stuck my whole head under it. Brr. It was cold. I eagerly gulped it up.

Slid made a giggling sound. "Boy, you really like water," he said.

He was cute. I shot him a grin.

"Humans need water to survive," Addie said. Her color darkened to black. She reminded me of a storm cloud--which I was guessing meant she was upset.

"What?" I asked.

"I don't think they ever expected you to leave that cell," she said.

"Oh no," I said.

"Oh no," Slid said.

I shivered, and it wasn't just because of the cold water.

"We need to go," she said. "Quickly, now. Follow me." She turned and glided down the hall.

"Gotta go," Slid said. He floated after her, and I ran after him.

We all zoomed right up to three closed doors.

Addie did a complicated knock on one of them. I strained forward, trying to figure out how a cloud knocked on a door. I wanted to ask her, but I figured now wasn't the time.

A complicated knock answered back, and then, the middle door opened. Quinta was on the other side. "Good. Finally," she said. "I was getting worried."

"Are you all right?" Addie asked.

"So far," Quinta said.

Addie, Slid, and I quickly moved through the door. The lighting on the other side was muted.

"Thanks, Quinta," I said. "And thanks, Addie and Slid; I really appreciate your help." They'd saved my life. "I owe you. Please let me know if I can ever do anything for you." I paused for a moment. "Uh, why are you helping me? Isn't it dangerous for you?" Okay, that probably wasn't a cool spy thing to say, but I wanted to know.

In the dim light, Quinta looked a little sparkly.

"We'll discuss it later," Addie said. "We don't have time to chat right now. We need to go." She turned to Quinta. "Did you see anyone?"

"No." Quinta shook her head, looking still more sparkly. Did octopi sparkle? I didn't think so. Did octopi-like-creatures sparkle? I had no idea but asking about sparkling probably fell under the category of chatting.

The four of us ran or floated or slimed (as the case may be) down the dim industrial hallway.

I couldn't resist asking, "Where are we going?"

Addie said, "*Shh.*"

Slid said, "*Shh*."

We zoomed and zoomed through one hallway after another, passing no Quihiri. I may have been imagining it, but Quinta seemed to get more and more sparkly.

Finally, we stopped in front of a single door. Addie did something to it, and it opened, revealing what looked like a *Shakespeare* shuttle. "Come on," she said. "We don't have much time."

Slid and Quinta, and I ran inside.

The shuttle didn't just look like a *Shakespeare* shuttle; it looked like my *Shakespeare* shuttle--with my special FTL drive in the front.

Addie closed the door. "You can fly this thing, Jack, can't you?"

"Yeah." I made my way to the pilot's chair. "But you flew it here, didn't you? Why do you need me?"

She didn't immediately answer me. Instead, she and Slid surrounded Quinta.

Quinta was definitely more sparkly now. "I can't hold it in anymore," she said.

"You don't have to, honey," Addie said. "Take off, Jack."

I turned my attention to flying the shuttle. Soon, we were flying away from the Quihiri planet.

A beeping noise erupted from the pilot's console. What was that? I leaned over and examined it. It said: 'Warning!'

"FTL away, Jack!" Addie said. "Now! Now! Now!"

"We're too close to the planet," I said. But I realized the beeping noise was attached to a warning that said, 'Warning! Weapons lock on shuttle.'

I engaged the FTL drive, and we FTLed away. To where I did not know.

And then the shuttle seemed to explode with light.

Chapter Thirty-Two

On my shuttle, I may have just blown up. My hands touched my chest. So, I still had a chest; it hadn't blown up. That was good, at least. That was a step in the right direction.

I couldn't really see. My eyes were watering and filled with bright spots. I rubbed my eyes, and my sight started coming back. I looked around the shuttle.

"What happened?" I asked. I could see Addie and Slid, but no Quinta. "Oh, no! What happened to Quinta?" I jumped out of the pilot's chair and ran to the back of the shuttle. "Quinta?" She wasn't there; she wasn't anywhere. "Oh no. Did she ...blow up? Is she dead?"

A rainbow-colored cloud in front of me said, "No. I'm here." It used Quinta's voice.

"Wait," I said. "What's happening?" I realized there was a lot more cloud in here now than just Addie and Slid. I took a step closer to the new cloud. "Quinta?"

"Yes," the Quinta-cloud said. "It's me." It sparkled.

Slid giggled.

"The former-Quihiri Quinta is now a sldkfjfoisut," Addie said.

"What?" I said.

"I told you we evolved from the Quihiri," Addie said. "Well, it's still happening."

"What?" I said.

"My grandmother was a Quihiri," Addie said. "She evolved to become a sldkfjfoisut. And now Quinta has taken the evolutionary leap. Welcome, child."

"Is this like a caterpillar and a butterfly?" I asked.

Addie said, "Well, we don't like being compared to insects, but yes." She was shading gray.

"I still don't totally get it," I said. "Do all Quihiri turn into, ah, smoky sentients?"

"No," Addie said. "Not every Quihiri will make the evolutionary leap. It's a genetic mutation that not everyone has. But their descendants might have it."

"The Quihiri don't like it," Quinta said. "I didn't know what was happening to me. The doctor said I was sick. He gave me drugs, maybe to suppress it?"

"Yes," Addie said. "I'm afraid so. The Quihiri race will go extinct if everyone evolves."

"The doctor said my illness could be fatal," former-Quinta said. "But Addie told me the truth. I don't know what I would've done if I hadn't met her."

Addie turned black again. "Let's just say the Quihiri don't let Quihiri evolve into sldkfjfoisut."

Former-Quinta turned black, too.

Slid turned black. I hoped he was just copying them and didn't understand what they were talking about. Murder was too dire for a toddler, even a sldkfjfoisut toddler.

My mood was black. "*This naked villainy!*" Darn it. I couldn't think of a good quote. "*Demi-devil ...this thing of darkness*... is going down!"

I glanced out the window, seeing nothing but the black of space. Of course, there was the little matter of having no idea where in the galaxy we were.

I didn't like the idea of being so far away when the *Shakespeare* was in trouble, possibly fighting for its life. All my friends were in danger--possibly dead already, for all I knew. "Do you guys know anything about the *Shakespeare*? Did they get away?"

"We don't know," Addie answered.

Addie and Slid continued to crowd around former-Quinta, congratulating her and generally sparkling at her.

For her part, she sparkled back. I guessed they were all too excited about her transformation to remain black for long.

I still felt black. I sat down in the captain's seat. Where the hell were we? Looking out the window didn't tell me anything.

Think, Jack. I stared at the front console.

To use a shuttle, you had to program in a course. And the

215

FTL drive had its own nav system. Who'd used the shuttle last? Probably Addie and Slid to get away from the *Shakespeare*, but they hadn't needed to use the FTL drive to do that since the ship was near Quihiri at that point. "Addie, did you use the FTL drive?"

"No, Jack," she said, not seeming to pay me attention.

When I glanced back, they were changing shapes, solidities, and whatnot. It looked fun.

I accessed the FTL drive's navigation system, staring at the coordinates. It was just a bunch of numbers, so no help there.

Who had used the FTL drive last? Think, Jack. I pressed my fingers on my forehead. So much had happened. I stared at the console.

Of course, I could fire up the FTL drive again and use my special skill to find out who'd used the drive last...

Ding, ding, ding. "*Be not afraid of greatness! Some are born great!*"

"What?" Addie said.

"What?" former-Quinta said.

"What?" Slid said.

They all floated towards me.

"I figured it out. I was the last person to use the FTL drive," I said.

"Okay," former-Quinta said.

"What should I call you?" I asked her. "Are you still Quinta? Or do you want to be called something else?"

"It is traditional to take a new name in the glorious naming ceremony," Addie said. "Of course, humans generally can't pronounce our names."

"You can still call me Quinta, Jack," Quinta said. "Thanks for helping me, by the way."

I nodded. I was pretty great, saving myself and the three of them and all.

"What were you saying?" Addie asked.

"What?" Slid asked.

"I was the last person to use the FTL drive," I said. "I used it in the *Shakespeare*'s shuttle bay to move just a fraction of an inch."

"Why is that important?" Quinta asked.

"I'm trying to figure out where we are," I said. "So, since we didn't change the FTL settings, we should have ...moved less than an inch." That obviously wasn't the case. "Shoot."

"So, you're saying you have no idea where we are?" Addie asked.

Yes. "No," I said. "I'm figuring it out." How did that *Whenever I feel afraid* song go? Fake it 'till you make it?

"Okay," Addie said.

"Okay," Slid said.

Quinta sparkled some more. "I know you will. I have faith in you, Jack."

They floated to the back of the ship.

So, we should have moved about an inch. That wasn't what happened. What was different? Ah ha. I'd never FTLed so close to a planet before--what effect had that had? Some kind of gravity effect did something.

As a first hypothesis, if we hadn't jumped very far, maybe we were still in the Quihiri system?

I accessed the sensors, looking for stars and planets. Ding, ding, ding. A few parsecs away, out of visual range, I detected what appeared to be the Quihiri planet and sun. Ah ha. "We're still in the Quihiri system," I said.

"Okay," Addie said. The other two echoed her. Boy, non-corporeal sentiences, or whatever we were supposed to call them, really liked the word 'okay.'

"I'm going back to Quihiri to see what's happening. And don't say 'okay.'"

Addie had said, "O--" but then she shut up.

"Don't worry, I'll sneak up on them so they don't attack us," I said. I could come up behind one of the Quihiri moons so they wouldn't detect us. I set in a course through regular space at high speed.

Sitting in the captain's chair, I strained to detect something, anything, through the front window. But they didn't call it 'space' for nothing. There was nothing to see--just blackness all around.

My pulse raced, and I leaned forward in the chair, willing the ship to move faster.

I was worried about the Quihiri going to war. What did that entail?

I was worried about my ship and crew.

Finally, in the distance, I saw a small round object.

Soon I was approaching Quihiri's largest moon. I flew right up near it and skimmed the surface, sneaking to the rim. I peeked us over the rim of the moon, giving a view of the planet and nearby space.

The *Shakespeare* was under attack! It hadn't gotten away after all. Many small Quihiri ships were firing on the *Shakespeare*. At least none of the large Quihiri ships were attacking the *Shakespeare*.

"Oh no! This wouldn't stand. *The words expressly are a pound of flesh.*"

Why hadn't they gotten away when they had the chance?

I accessed comms. "*Shakespeare*, this is shuttlecraft one. Why didn't you leave the system? Leave!"

The comms squawked, and then I heard Carter's voice. "Jack? Is that you? How did you escape?" In the background, I could hear a lot of yelling.

"Some sldkfjfoisut helped me." Hey, I said it. "But that's not important now. You guys need to leave the system."

Over comms, I heard a loud bang, and an alarm went off. "We can't," Carter said. "Somehow, they disabled our FTL drive. I guess when we were parked on the planet, and everyone was incapacitated."

"So, fix it!" I said.

"Bello's working on it, but so far, no joy." *Bang. Crash.*

Something tugged on my shoulder. It was Addie. How did she do that when she was made of smoke? "Look!" She said, and an amorphous arm pointed as two very large Quihiri ships materialized out of FTL-space. Right in front of the *Shakespeare*.

I distinctly heard Carter gulp over comms. "Shit." He disconnected.

I jumped up. "Shit!"

"You have to help them, Jack," Addie said.

I needed to help them. Every second counted.

I knew I needed to use my special skill. I knew it might not work, but I had to try.

I reached for the FTL drive controls, mind racing. I flipped it on, implementing the less-than-an-inch flight plan. "The shuttle is back on the *Shakespeare*!"

The view instantly changed from the black of space to gray walls and a red flashing light. We shook back and forth, as presumably, the *Shakespeare* shook back and forth.

I implemented the flight plan again. "The *Shakespeare* is back in Earth orbit!"

The shaking stopped. It must have worked. The *Shakespeare* must be back at Earth. The sudden calm was delightful. I breathed in deeply, savoring the moment.

The comms squawked again. Carter said, "Jack? Where are you? Did you do something? What did you do?"

"I saved the day," I said.

But over comms, I heard, "Oh, no! Earth is under attack! Battle stations! Battle stations!"

Earth was under attack? No! That was a worst-case scenario.

I ran back to the shuttle door, opened it, and ran out. I ran down the halls, dodging crew members running to their battle stations, through the flashing red lights, all the way to the bridge.

I ran onto the bridge.

There spread out in front of me on the viewscreen, in all its beautiful blue-and-white-marble glory, sat our home planet. Under attack! By several huge Quihiri ships!

"Oh no!" I collapsed against the door frame, panting.

I needed to use my special skill. "All the Quihiri weapons stop working!"

Everyone turned around to look at me.

"Jack?" Carter asked. "Where'd you come from?"

Gina stood. "Jack? What are you doing?"

In the meantime, the Quihiri weapons hadn't stopped working. Volley after volley streaked down towards the planet, towards billions of defenseless humans.

Chapter Thirty-Three

Planet Earth was under attack! The wonderful cradle of humanity. It floated outside the bridge like a fragile blue-and-white-swirled glass orb. My breath caught in my throat as missiles shot toward it.

"Battle stations! All weapons systems online!" Gina said. "Fire at will on the Quihiri ships!"

"*There's a tide in the affairs of men*," I whispered.

The flashing red lights quieted as the ship's interior was bathed with a steady and alarming red light.

Commander Lu had a grim expression, but his fingers were flying on the weapons console. "Take that! And that! And that!" He fired a bunch of stuff at the Quihiri ships.

The red light made everyone look like they had a bad sunburn.

The Quihiri ships took some damage. It was like they were surprised we'd appeared and hadn't even considered an Earth ship could show up. They stopped firing at Earth for a moment.

Three of the Quihiri juggernauts abruptly turned and flew toward the moon.

"All right!" Carter said, and the other bridge crew joined him, cheering.

Me and Gina did not. I figured the Quihiri were going to hide near the moon as I'd just done with my shuttle and the Quihiri moon.

"They're probably just taking cover on the other side of the moon," she said. Maybe she did know what she was doing as captain.

"Yeah," I said, nodding. We were on the same page.

The other two juggernauts turned around and pointed their

weapons ports at us. Shit. I gulped.

"Maximum power to shields," Gina said. "Lu, fire on those ships!"

His fingers started flying again. On the viewscreen, I saw various missiles flying from our ship and smashing into the Quihiri ships.

"Yes!" I raised my fists into the air.

But within moments, the *Shakespeare* started jittering in space. We must be taking fire as well. The artificial gravity flickered each time we were hit, causing the movement.

Damn. How long would the shields hold? Old Jack would know that. For the first time, I wished I knew what the original Jack knew.

My blood thundered in my ears. My first space battle!

"There's a message from the surface." Carter turned to face Gina. "Do you want to take it in your ready room?"

"No," she said. "Here. Put it on speaker."

"Oh, thank God you're here, *Shakespeare*," a worried voice wafted over the room. "How did you know we were under attack?"

"We don't have time to chitchat," Gina said. "Who am I speaking to?"

"I'm Lieutenant Singh, Captain Gomez," he said.

"Earth needs to scramble all its defensive forces immediately," she said. "Where are the ships? And what's happening with the planetary defense shield?"

The *Shakespeare* moved a little as if beginning a stately promenade. That wasn't good. Movement meant damage to the ship.

We all needed to pitch in to protect Earth, including me. I had a brainstorm. Quinta was recently a Quihiri and married to the ambassador. She might know something that could help us.

I went to an empty comms station and called the shuttle. "Quinta? Addie? Are you guys there?"

After a few moments, I heard, "This is Addie. We're here."

"Quinta? Can you come to the bridge? You might have some information about the Quihiri weapons or defenses that would help us."

In the meantime, on Earth, Singh said, "It was a surprise

attack; the shield wasn't on maximum. I put it on maximum immediately, but its strength is mostly depleted."

Quinta said to me over comms, "Okay."

Addie said, "We'll be right there." We closed the connection. I turned my attention back to Gina.

She said to Singh, "Ships?"

"We called them all in," he said. "The ones we've been able to reach said their FTL drives aren't working." Now he sounded scared. "But they're on their way."

"Keep doing what you're doing, Singh," she said. "Try to bolster the defense shield. Launch any ships available from the surface ASAP. The Quihiri have declared war on Earth. They're the ones who make the FTL drives, and they've disabled them."

Singh gasped. "Oh no."

"You need to send out an announcement to the galaxy," she said. TCC had an extensive almost-light-speed communication system.

"Yes, ma'am," Singh said.

Addie, Slid, and Quinta floated onto the bridge. "What's happening?" Addie asked quietly, black and gray swirling in her physique.

Slid and Quinta imitated her coloration.

I said to the trio, "As you can see..." I pointed at the large Quihiri ships. "The Quihiri ships are attacking us. Quinta, do you have any information that might help? About weapons or defenses or anything?"

"Maybe," Quinta said, color brightening a little.

I surveyed the bridge. Who was the least busy? Carter.

I ran over to him, gesturing for Quinta to follow me. "Carter, this is Quinta," I said to him.

His brow furrowed.

"She used to be a Quihiri," I said. "She used to be married to the ambassador."

"What are you talking about?" he said, face turning even redder. "We don't have time for this, whatever it is."

"It's true," Quinta said. "I was married to the Quihiri ambassador. He's bad. What they're doing to the rest of the galaxy, trying to take over, is bad. I can help." She morphed back into the traditional Quihiri shape. Now she looked like a threetentacled, three-legged, three-eyed octopus creature again.

Now Carter's eyes bugged out of his head. "Uh. Okay. If you can assist us, good."

"Good." I felt good that I'd helped at least a little.

My brain jump-started. What was I doing loitering on the bridge? I'd be much more helpful by using my special skill. "I'm going back to the shuttle bay. Keep me on comms."

I headed for the door of the bridge. My first instinct had been right. I needed to try to disable the Quihiri weapons. Obviously, that didn't work from the bridge. I needed to return to the shuttle and fire up my FTL drive again. Hopefully, my FTL drive wasn't disabled.

I ran and ran through the ship. Every sunburned-looking crewmember I passed had a grim look on his or her or its face.

Addie and Slid floated right with me. I hadn't known they could float so fast. I glanced at Addie. I didn't know much of anything about them. "Can you help with this at all?"

"I'm not sure," she said. What the heck did that mean?

"Try to think of something," I said. We entered the hallway off the shuttle bays.

I almost ran right into Ted standing there in the hall. I stopped for a moment to catch my breath.

He smiled and pointed at me. "Hey, you're that guy from the surface that saved us all, right?" His smile got brighter.

Crap. He didn't remember me? "Did you download your memories?" I asked.

"Yes." He nodded.

That meant his saved memories were incomplete? My spirits sank like they were stuck in a gravity well. Focus, Jack. No time for sad spirits. "No time for chitchat," I said. "Come with us if you want to help."

He followed us.

I ran back into the shuttle and up to the FTL drive in the front, sitting in the captain's chair and buckling in. It was a relief to get out of the red light.

I turned on the drive and inputted the one-inch flight path. I initiated the drive.

Nothing happened except an alarm went off. "Shit!" A red light blinked on the front console.

Addie and/or Slid obscured my view of the panel with their smoky bodies. Unless it was actual smoke. Fire? Oh no. I whipped my head around, trying to account for smoky creatures. There did seem to be too little smoke behind me.

"Move, please," I said. "I need to see the console."

The smoke floated back behind me. Phew.

"What's happening?" Ted asked.

"I'm going to implement the FTL drive to use my special skill." I flicked on the FTL drive, programmed a millimeter jump and initiated it.

"What skill?" Ted asked. I ignored him for the moment.

Nothing happened.

"Aren't we awfully close to the planet to use an FTL drive?" Ted stuck his arm in front of my face, pointing at the blinking red light. "What's that red light?"

"What's that red light?" Slid said.

"Who said that?" Ted said, looking around the small shuttle.

I punched the blinking button.

I couldn't remember who knew what at this point. "Ted, these are sldkfjfoisut."

"Door ajar. Warning. Door ajar," the shuttle said.

"I don't understand,' Addie said. "How can a door be a jar?"

"Who said that?" Ted said.

I whipped my head around again. The shuttle door was wide open. "Dammit!"

"Language," Addie said.

"Language," Slid said.

"Introduce yourselves," I said, punching the button to close the door. It closed with a thud. The alarm stopped beeping. The red blinking light stopped blinking.

In the background, I was vaguely aware of Ted conversing with Addie and Slid.

I initiated the FTL drive again.

Nothing appeared to happen. Was it working? My special skill had worked most of the time with this FTL drive.

It worked all the time, except when it didn't work. If there was a rhyme or reason to when it worked and when it didn't, I hadn't discovered it. Dammit.

"Did that do something?" Ted asked.

Slid said, "Did that do something?"

Then the whole ship moved a little--including us sitting in the shuttle in the shuttle bay--as if the *Shakespeare* was beginning to waltz. Not good.

"Shit!" Carter said over comms. "Hull breach on deck five! Evacuate deck five!" Also, over comms, we could now hear a loud alarm blaring. It made it difficult to think.

Focus, Jack.

Basically, I needed to run the FTL drive and make a wish. If the FTL drive still worked and my special skill worked, it would come true. I needed to save lives on the *Shakespeare* and Earth.

I ran the FTL drive. "The hull breach on deck five is fixed!" I said.

Immediately, the loud klaxon over comms stopped.

"Huh," Carter said over comms. "There's not a hull breach on deck five. Belay the evacuation order."

"Did you do that, Jack?" Addie asked.

The ship waltzed more energetically. Uh oh.

What next?

I tried the drive again. "The Quihiri's weapons don't work!" Nothing seemed to happen.

I accessed comms. "Carter, are we still being fired upon by the Quihiri?"

The ship tangoed.

"Duh," Carter said over comms.

"Dammit!" I pounded my fists on the arms of the captain's chair.

"Lang--" Addie said.

"Quit saying that!" I said. "In fact, everyone shut up!"

The sldkfjfoisut floated back away from me, maelstroms of swirling red and black.

Ted had jerked back as well. "Rude much?" he said.

The *Shakespeare* salsa-ed.

Was my special skill working or not? I pointed at Ted. "Kiss me. Now."

He took a step back. "I'm not sure I feel like kissing you now. You're acting like kind of a jerk."

"It's an order," I said. "Kiss me now."

Ted stared at my collar. "We're the same rank. You're an

ensign, the same as me. I don't have to follow your orders."

My blood was boiling with frustration. Did my special skill work or not?

"Please, young man," Addie said. "Ted, was it?"

Ted nodded.

"I know it doesn't necessarily make any sense, but please just kiss him," she said.

Ted shrugged, took two steps, leaned in and planted a juicy one right on my lips.

Mmm. Instantly I felt less like throttling something. "Mmm." I pulled him closer as my body started to get other non-throttling-related ideas.

Addie cleared her throat (so to speak). "Jack."

I gently pushed Ted away. So, special skills not working right now. On the bright side, I felt much calmer. Maybe I'd be able to think a little better now.

"Wow," Ted said, face flushed.

"Jack!" Gina said over comms. "We're in trouble. If you're going to do something, you better do it."

The ship started hip-hopping.

I didn't know what to do but try engaging the FTL drive and wishing again. And again and again, until it worked.

How often didn't it work? How long did the effect last? Why, oh why, hadn't we done more experiments with this earlier when we had the chance?

I initiated the drive. "The Quihiri weapons don't work!"

I couldn't tell if anything had happened or not.

"Kiss me!" I said.

Ted leaned in and gave me a smooch. I felt it. I didn't say dammit, but I really wanted to.

The ship jumped up and down as if performing a gymnastic floor exercise at the intergalactic Olympics.

"Jack!" Gina said over comms.

I initiated the drive. "The Quihiri weapons don't work!"

"Jack?" Gina said. "Did you do something?"

I didn't feel any *Shakespeare* movement.

"I don't know," I said. "Did I?"

"The Quihiri stopped firing," Gina said.

Faintly over comms, it sounded like the people on the

bridge were cheering.

And then the *Shakespeare* shook a little.

The bridge crew groaned.

Had I stopped the Quihiri weapons only momentarily?

Chapter Thirty-Four

On the *Shakespeare,* we were under attack by the dastardly Quihiri.

I said, "The Quihiri weapons don't work for a hundred years!"

The *Shakespeare* started break-dancing. "Dammit!" I pounded the arm rest. My blood thundered in my ears. So, the Quihiri weapons were still operational. My special skill didn't work that time. I was starting to panic.

I initiated the FTL drive. "I can think clearly. I can think clearly."

Suddenly, I could think clearly.

"What's happening?" Ted asked.

"What's happening?" Slid asked.

"Shush," I said. "Please be quiet, all of you."

It appeared that when I initiated the FTL drive, I got one wish--if it worked. So, logically, I should keep initiating the FTL drive and making wishes. Sometimes it would work. Sometimes it wouldn't.

"Jack!" Gina yelled over comms. "Do something!"

Then the shuttle was thrown on its side. Ted was thrown against the wall, and he grunted as he hit. I couldn't see what was happening with Addie and Slid. The shuttle lost its artificial gravity. I didn't move from where I was strapped into the captain's chair. Ted floated up.

"Hull breach in the shuttle bay!" Gina yelled over comms.

The shuttle floated out of a large hole in the *Shakespeare*. Through the front window, I saw only the black of space. Gee, a giant hole in the shuttle bay was not good.

I started initiating the FTL drive repeatedly, saying,

"Emergency bulkheads initiated in the shuttle bay. Emergency bulkheads in the shuttle bay. Emergency bulkheads in shuttle bay."

"Emergency bulkheads in shuttle bay," Gina said. "Good. Thanks, Jack."

"The *Shakespeare*'s shields are at one hundred percent," I said. "Shields at one hundred percent."

"Shields at one hundred percent," Carter said over comms.

"Thank God," Gina said.

When I looked out the window, I realized we were drifting farther and farther away from the *Shakespeare*.

I also saw one of the Quihiri ships getting closer and closer.

Our radio crackled with static. A Quihiri said, "Jack Jones, you are detected on the shuttlecraft. Prepare to die, number one enemy of the Quihiri people!" The voice sounded a lot like Quinta's husband. Yikes. Was he jealous of me on top of everything else?

"I'm scared," Slid said.

I was starting to feel scared and panicky. But I wasn't about to say it.

The Quihiri ship launched what looked like a very large missile straight at us--the type of very large missile that would totally destroy a little shuttlecraft.

"Oh no!" Ted yelled, staring out the window and pointing.

We needed to get out of here. We didn't seem to have time to fly away through regular space. "We four are all safe and sound ..." Definite panic. "Where?" I turned to Ted. "Where should we go?"

"Ashland, Oregon!" he yelled.

I was still implementing the millimeter FTL drive flight plan over and over.

"We are safe and sound in Ashland, Oregon," I said. "We are in Oregon. Oregon. Oregon. Oregon."

"I'm scared," Slid said in a small voice.

"*Shh*, honey," Addie said. "It'll be okay."

There was a bright light and then ...darkness.

Was that it? Had we blown up? Had we died? If so, it was surprisingly anticlimactic.

I reached up and touched my chest. Chest, check.

And I seemed to be lying awkwardly on a concrete floor--so that went against being dead. It also went against still being on the shuttlecraft. Belatedly I realized I should have wished we and the shuttle were all safe.

"I'm scared," Slid said.

"I know, honey," Addie said. "Here." She brightened her body, glowing with a soft light.

We were in a strange windowless room with metal supports and what appeared to be a wooden ceiling. Unfortunately, it strongly resembled a jail. So, definitely not on the shuttle; check.

"We're all safe and sound," I said.

"How do you know?" Ted asked.

When I'd said, 'We're all safe and sound,' I'd been making a wish, trying to use my special skill again. But...the shuttle was probably blown up--along with the special FTL drive. My special power was gone, maybe for good.

Looking at Slid, I resisted the strong urge to say, 'I'm scared.' Or cry.

Buck up, Jack. You're not blown up. You're with friends. You're handsome. You're an excellent singer. You're a superspy. I felt a little better.

Then, a trap door in the ceiling opened. Light streamed in, revealing a man wearing strange-looking leather shoes, hose, a codpiece, and a linen shirt. He appeared to be holding a doublet.

I felt my mouth fall open. Had we traveled in time somehow? How? I couldn't talk.

"*The more I have. For both are infinite,*" the man said.

The man took a step down the ladder. Yes, he appeared to be from the sixteenth century. Were we in the sixteenth century? But did they have the word 'infinite' back then?

A woman appeared wearing a long linen smock. She followed the man.

What was happening?

From the open trap door, applause thundered above us.

"Hurry up," the woman said. "I have to pee."

The man said, "*Courage, man; the hurt cannot be much,*" as he continued climbing down the ladder.

The woman seemed unhappy with that.

"Oh, my God," Ted said. "I know where we are."

"Where?" Slid said.

My brain still wasn't working a hundred percent.

"We're at the Oregon Shakespeare Festival!" he said. "In Ashland, Oregon. It's where I'm from."

"You're from a Shakespeare festival?" Addie said. "Earthlings are strange." I got a sense of a shaking head which was a good trick since she didn't have a head.

But I had to agree. Ted was from a Shakespeare festival? It explained a lot.

"Maybe you guys should try to keep a low profile," I said to Addie and Slid. "Until we get a handle on things here."

"Hey," the man, no, the actor, said, walking past us. "You guys aren't supposed to be down here. And what's with the smoke? Have you been smoking down here? Not cool. That's a fire hazard. I should report you to the safety officer."

"Out of the way!" The woman ran past us, holding up her plain gown.

"Wow," Ted said. "You're Liam Lightning, aren't you?" He looked like he wanted to lick the guy from head to toe.

Truth be told, I couldn't blame him. He was gorgeous. Of course, not quite as gorgeous as me, but still pretty gorgeous. I wasn't jealous, though.

The actor stopped, grinned, and brushed his hand through his-- I'll admit it--very nice brown locks.

I had to stop myself from saying, 'Wow.'

Addie whispered in my ear, "I'm not sure about this guy." I tried not to jerk back or swat her away. She was supposed to be incognito, after all.

"Do I know you?" the actor asked, smiling at Ted.

"It's Ted--" he started to stay.

"Oh, Teddy!" Liam smiled and clasped Ted on the shoulder. "You understudied for me in the Scottish play. When was that?"

"Yeah, Teddy, right. You remember me? Wow." He looked like a deer caught in headlights. "It was two years ago. But I was just a student intern."

"Didn't we have a moment, the two of us?" Liam handed Teddy, er, Ted, his doublet.

Ted took it, gulping. "Yes."

"Remind me what happened." Liam waved his hand in the

231

direction the woman had gone and started walking.

Ted followed along, clutching the doublet to his chest.

I just stared. Gee, don't mind us. Don't mind that planet Earth is under attack. It's not like it's an emergency or anything.

Assorted muted conversations drifted down from the open trap door.

"What now?" Addie asked.

I glanced around the small space. It was empty but for the three of us. "You probably shouldn't talk when Earthlings are around unless you want to draw attention to yourselves."

"Why?" Slid asked. "What's wrong with Earthlings?"

"Earthlings aren't familiar with your species," I said. "But we're getting off the point. We need to get back to the battle. Earth is in danger!"

I paused. Huh. Why wasn't it more battle-y here if Earth was under attack?

I accessed my comms. "*Shakespeare*? TCC? Earth command?" No one answered. Oh no. Did that mean they were all dead? I started shaking.

Wait. That didn't make sense. No one here was even worried. It was more likely the comms weren't working. Or TCC was too busy to answer.

"I wonder," Addie said, sparkling silver a little. "Maybe TCC doesn't need us. I'm not happy about putting little Slid in such a dangerous situation."

"Hey," Slid said. "I'm not a baby."

"Yes, you are," Addie said. "And, Jack, without access to your special FTL drive, you've lost your power, haven't you?" She glowed gently.

"Well, yeah," I said. "But they still need me. I'm an important member of the *Shakespeare*'s crew."

"Without your special power, aren't you basically a wet-behind-the-ears eighteen-year-old on his first mission?" she asked. "I mean, sorry. Personally, I like you very much. Obviously." She pointed at Slid.

She had an impressive facility with Earth idioms. "Uh..." I said.

"Do you have any skills at this point?" she said.

I sang, "*I'm very well acquainted with matters mathematical.*

232

I understand equations, both the simple and quadratical... For my military knowledge, though I'm plucky and adventury."

"Do you have any non-entertainment-related skills?" she said.

"Of course!" I said. "I'm a good lover. I'm good with a gun and all manner of other weapons--probably. I'm a good spy." I was a good spy. "Hey, I was the one who uncovered the Quihiri evil plot. Me. No one else in the whole galaxy. And I helped you and Slid. And Quinta."

"You're right," she said. "You're very valuable. But there's the little matter of the Quihiri thinking you're their number one enemy." Some black swirls entered her torso area. "At this point, you might be better off lying low."

I drew back. "*Done to death by slanderous tongue.*"

"What does that mean?" Slid asked.

"I'm not hiding," I said. "And, anyway, we need more information. Why is there a play going on here when Earth is under attack?"

Ted ran back into the strange little room. "Liam says we can watch the show from back stage!" He wasn't acting like a TCC officer.

"Let's go," Addie said.

"You want to watch the play?" I asked.

"We're not going to get any information sitting under the stage," she said.

"Oh, right," I said. "Let's go."

We followed Ted out into a cluttered, dark hallway. It was strewn with props, scenery, spare lights, and a lot of black fabric. I sighed. It reminded me of the *Shakespeare*.

Was she even still up there? Were any of the crew still alive?

I rushed up behind Ted as he hiked up a ramp.

"These are the vomms, short for vomitoriums," he said.

I stopped short and felt Addie and/or Slid run into my back. "What?" I said.

Addie said, "What?"

Slid said, "What?"

Ted said, "They're these neat tunnels that connect the theaters. They have three theaters here--"

233

I was slightly fascinated but said, "Ted, focus. We're TCC officers. Earth is under attack. We need to help. At least we need some information. Is the battle still going?"

"Oh, right," he said. "We should be able to access the news backstage. Come on." He led us through more cluttered corridors.

When we got backstage, everyone was clustered around a large TV screen. Blaring out from the TV in a robotic voice was an announcement. "This is an emergency alert. Planet Earth is under attack."

Everyone was looking at each other with skeptical expressions and muttering like this was some kind of weird joke.

I also heard, "I can't believe fon service is down. That's never happened before, has it?" No wonder no one was accessing their fon.

The robot said, "To repeat, planet Earth is under attack. Take shelter immediately. Earth is under attack. Take shelter immediately."

"Dammit," Slid said in a little voice.

"Language, Slid," I said.

Over the theater comms system, a man said, "Attention, please. The remainder of the show is canceled. I guess..." He paused. "I guess planet Earth is under attack. Take shelter immediately."

Then, from the audience area, we heard screaming and feet stamping.

A lot of screaming.

Chapter Thirty-Five

Backstage at some Shakespeare festival on Earth, people were screaming.

"Oh, my God!"

"Oh no!"

"*Aagh!*"

"What should we do!" The people (all humans by the looks of them) all milled around, no one doing much of anything.

Ted was alternating between gazing lovingly at the Lightning guy and looking alarmed.

"Do something, Jack," Addie whispered in my ear.

I jerked back. I didn't think I'd ever get used to a cloud talking to me. But she was right. Milling around and muttering or yelling wasn't going to help anyone.

"Hey!" I said, loudly. "Attention please!"

They did not pay attention to me. They seemed to be panicking. Who knew thespians were so flighty?

"Jack," Addie whispered.

My brain whirred. I needed to speak their language. Luckily, I did. I nudged Ted. "Say, *'if we should fail.'*"

"Huh?" he said.

"Say, *'if we should fail,'* loudly."

He shrugged and said, "*If we should fail?*" at the top of his lungs.

I jumped on top of a crate and yelled. "*We fail?*" I flourished my arms. "*But screw your courage to the sticking place and we'll not fail!*"

Now I had everyone's attention.

"We need to evacuate to some safe shelter," I said in a more reasonable tone. "Surely, you have one? A nuclear bomb shelter?"

Everyone jolted.

Oops, too far, Jack. "A tornado shelter," I said. "We need someplace safe underground. Where is the tornado shelter?"

"No tornado shelter," the Liam guy said, "but we do have a sub-basement. But it's full of props and stuff."

"Is it underground?" I asked. I'd never been on a planet while it was attacked from space but I was guessing the further away we were from space, the better."

"Yeah," he said. "It's pretty far underground."

I nodded wisely. "Let's all decamp to the sub-basement." I pointed towards the house. "Get the audience members."

A couple players darted through the partially opened curtain and then darted back. "They've all gone."

"All right," I said. "Follow me and Liam to the sub-basement." I jumped off the crate. "*Lay on, MacDuff.*"

Liam started marching back the way we'd come, towards below stage. I didn't stare at his fine derrière. Nope, not at all.

It looked like most of the cast and crew were still here and they all fell in behind me and Liam. Were they checking out my fine derrière? No doubt.

"Who are you, again?" Liam asked, turning and checking me out thoroughly. I'm sure he was impressed with what he saw.

I said simply, "You can call me Jack." Yes, I was modest among my many excellent qualities. I braced myself for the barrage of compliments sure to be forthcoming.

But Liam just said, "Huh," and turned and led us all through below stage, down a small dark hallway, down some dark stairs, down another dark hallway, and down more dark stairs. Everything was crammed full of scenery, props, and assorted theatrical flotsam.

It all reminded me of the *Shakespeare.* I really hoped she and her crew (and Quinta) were okay.

The sub-basement was definitely underground. We kept going down and down. He finally stopped in what appeared to be a huge warehouse, crammed full of old sets, costumes and whatnot.

He looked at me in the dim light. "What now?"

"Let's make ourselves comfortable," I said. "And wait for the all-clear." Hopefully, there'd be an all-clear. I didn't see how the resources of the whole planet couldn't overcome a few Quihiri spaceships.

On the other hand, they were super evil.

I checked my fon. It showed an emergency alert to take shelter. Check.

I looked around for Addie and Slid. It was so dark I couldn't tell if they were down here with us or not. "Can we get more light?" I asked.

Liam said, "This is it," and flourished his hands at the few dim electrical lights.

"Look for candles, prop lights, whatever," I said. "And some chairs. Let's make ourselves comfortable."

Two lovely young women approached me. One of them was the bladder-challenged, but gorgeous, actress from earlier. I didn't know who the other one was but she had a clipboard.

"Greetings, lovely ladies." I gave them my sexiest smile.

They faltered a bit in its majestic exuberance. Poor things.

Clipboard-woman was the first to recover. "Who are you? Do you know what's going on?"

"I'm Jack." I flourished. "I'm glad to meet you, Miss...?"

"I'm the P.A.," she said.

"Nice to meet you, Miss P.A." I chuckled a little at my own joke.

"No. It's not my name; it's my title. P.A., production assistant," she said.

"I know what a P.A. is," I said. Good grief. What did she think? I was a wet-behind-the-ears eighteen-year-old? As the group turned on more lights, I looked around for Addie. Did the area near the door look cloudy? I nodded slightly in that general direction.

The cloud bobbed up and down and threw out a faint sparkle in reply. Addie, check.

I turned back to the P.A. In her defense, I did resemble a wet-behind-the-ears eighteen-year-old. "I'm an officer in the TCC, the Terran Cultural Committee."

"Oh, thank God," she said. "Do you know what's going on? Why are the fons out?"

"Earth is under attack by a hostile species, the Quihiri," I said in a low voice.

The beautiful P.A. and the beautiful actress both gasped.

"We should be totally safe here underground," I said. "I'm sure the Terran fleet has it under control." I hoped the Terran fleet had it under control. With the FTL drives out of commission the Terran fleet was pretty small at this point.

"I'd be happy to give you both a hug, if it would comfort you," I said generously.

They shrugged and then complied briefly. For the couple seconds when they were in my arms, I felt much better.

The group finished setting up more lights and found a bunch of chairs and sofas for us to all sit on.

We all sat.

"Now what?" the P.A. said.

"We need a distraction," I said, brain zinging again. "What was that show you were doing? It looked fun. Maybe you should do that." I pointed at an empty space in the middle of the group.

"I do need a distraction," the beautiful actress said.

"I want to see Liam in the show," Ted said from right next to me. He gazed across the large room at the actor in question.

I jumped a little, not knowing he was there.

The P.A. nodded. "Let's do it." She gestured at the large empty space in the middle. "Let's resume the show," she yelled.

A bunch of men in various stages of dress and undress stepped forward and sang, "*Shall I compare thee to a summer's day? Thou are more lovely and more temperate. Rough winds do shake the darling buds of May, and summer's lease hath all too short a date. Too short a date.*" Aw. I wanted to sing.

Liam pulled an old couch into the middle of the space.

He and the beautiful actress flopped down on it and started making out.

Huh?

The actress said, "*I would not have thought it. There is something better than a play.*" She seemed out of breath.

The audience grinned.

Liam said, "*There is?*"

She said, "*Even your play.*"

They made out some more. I examined the crowd. They seemed pleased. This was apparently part of the show.

I knew for a fact sex-play was not part of Shakespeare's works (unfortunately). What was this?

"*Well, perhaps better than Two Gentlemen of Verona*," Liam said, nuzzling her neck.

Ha. I knew *Two Gentlemen of Verona* was a Shakespeare play. So this was a play about Shakespeare plays? How meta. Very neat.

"*And that was only my first try*," the actress said, giggling. Somehow she made the giggle seem dirty and sweet at the same time. Wow. I wanted to get to know her better.

I sidled up to Ted. "Do you know what this play is?"

He nodded, staring at Liam, entranced. "I always wanted to play Viola."

"Well, what is it?" I finally had to ask.

"*Shakespeare in Love*," he said.

Ah ha.

The troupe continued to be engrossed with the play.

I stepped ever so slowly back toward the door and Addie and Slid. When I got near them, I stopped. "Addie? Are you all right? Is Slid all right?"

"Yes," she whispered. "We're fine. But what is this show? Is it appropriate for a child?" I could hear the irritation in her voice.

"*Shakespeare in Love*," I said. "It's fine. Don't worry." Frankly, I was a little impressed with myself. I'd managed to distract her from her real problems enough to worry about if a play was too racy for her child.

"What are they doing on the couch?" Slid asked.

"It's just a grown-up thing, honey," Addie said. "You don't need to worry about it."

The three of us stood (or floated) there watching for a few minutes. It was a nice show.

"What are you doing now?" Addie asked.

"Watching the show." I pointed at the actors.

"Is this what you should be doing?" she asked.

Eek. Good point. Earth was under attack.

But Addie's earlier remarks were still ringing in my ears. Was I valuable without my special skill? I hated to admit it, but I was not as valuable without it as I was with it.

"Are we in danger here?" she asked.

I glanced around. I couldn't see how we would be in danger in a basement in tiny-town Oregon. "No." I smiled at her encouragingly. "So, you have successfully protected little Slid. Good for you."

She bobbed up and down, giving the impression of a nod.

She was satisfied, but I was not satisfied. I wanted to be out doing something, saving something. Saving the world!

The group laughed at something on the impromptu stage. And, hey, if a dingy dark basement in the middle of an attack could be a stage, the bard really knew what he was talking about.

I needed to get out of here and go save the day. What if my special FTL drive hadn't been destroyed? I needed to know for sure. I glanced at Addie and Slid. I couldn't ask them to help me; it was too dangerous.

The only person I could ask was Ted, so Ted it would be. I wasn't entirely sure what was going on with this version of Ted, however. What did he remember?

I elbowed my way through the crowd. Sure enough, Ted was still staring lovingly at Liam and his antics. I was starting to get a little irritated. I mean, the Liam guy was sort of good-looking and sort of talented, but he was no Jack Jones, right?

I tugged on Ted's sleeve. "Ted."

"*Shhh*," he said.

"Ted, we need to go," I said.

He looked at me with disappointment in his eyes. "Really?"

"Yes," I said. "We're TCC officers, not tourists. We need to report for duty."

"Aw, really?" he said.

People around us said, "*Shh*."

Geez, he was distracted. I grabbed his arm and led him to the stairs. "First of all, we need transportation." My mind was racing. What about a shuttle? Could we go into orbit and look for my FTL drive?

"What kind of transportation?" He seemed to be coming to his senses.

"We need a shuttlecraft," I said. "Do you think there's one of those in town?"

"Yes." He said. "I know there is. How do you think I ended

240

up in TCC after growing up here? There's a TCC outpost here. We visited it on a school field trip." At least he remembered that.

"Take me to it, Ensign," I said in a commanding voice.

"Okay, eh, sir," he said. "Right this way." He led me up the stairs.

Addie and Slid floated unobtrusively behind us. Darn it. I thought they were going to stay where it was safe. If I argued with them about it, they would stop being unobtrusive.

Of course, if the planet was destroyed they wouldn't be safe. So maybe it was a moot point.

Once we got away from the crowd, I asked the cloud following us, "Are you sure it's safe to come with us?"

"I'd rather be with TCC officers than with random humans," Addie said.

We all kept following Ted until we ended up outside a large theater complex. In the sun. It was still daytime. We'd been inside in the dim lighting so long it seemed bizarre.

An emergency alert was blaring from some kind of outdoor sound system. "This is an emergency alert. Earth under attack. Take shelter immediately," it said in a robotic voice. It wasn't exactly reassuring.

I squinted, looking up. I couldn't see any sign of any attack. "Ted, which way to the shuttle?"

He pointed down a hill. "This way. Near City Hall."

The streets seemed empty; it was a little eerie. As we walked quickly down the hill, I said, "So, what do you remember from the Quihiri planet and all that?"

"I woke up in bed with Commander Lu, who I guess is my boss, the head of all security on the *Shakespeare*. But I don't know how we got there or why this woman, Eva, was there, too. Awkward. I mean I'd assume relations between officers and their commanders would be frowned on." He glanced at me. "Wouldn't you?" He paused. "You're not my commander, are you?"

"Yes." Before he could question me further, I added, "We're on special assignment. What else do you recall about the *Shakespeare* or anything?"

"You rescued us, told us to follow the yarn." He grinned a little. "That was pretty brilliant, by the way."

My heart was sinking. My guess that he'd lost a lot of

memories was seeming more and more likely.

"So, we went back to the ship and were all ordered to go back to our cabins and download our memories. I did so, but I didn't recall anything about the *Shakespeare*. My last memories were of my academy graduation."

Unkindest cut! I didn't know that Ted was my true love, but we'd definitely had something between us. I guessed 'had' was the operative word.

"So, then on the ship, Commander Lu was briefing us on what happened, and then we were under attack, and then I guess, some prisoner Quihiri in sick bay escaped, and we were chasing it around, and that's when I ran into you outside the shuttle bay."

Wait. So that little Quihiri we'd stunned wasn't dead? I didn't know if I should be relieved or worried.

We arrived at some buildings and a TCC shuttle sat right there, out in the open. We all walked, or floated as the case may be, straight for it.

"So, you don't remember anything about your time, your service, on the *Shakespeare*?" I asked.

"Nope." He shook his head. "Why?"

I opened the shuttle door with my security code (it didn't have a DNA scanner) and then turned and met Ted's eyes for a moment. There was no recognition there. Suddenly, I did feel fifty-plus years old.

Addie and Slid entered.

"Did something important happen?" he asked.

I sighed heavily. Oh, Ted, so much happened. But now wasn't the time to get into it.

From inside the shuttle, Slid said, "Do I still have to be quiet?"

"No, honey," Addie said. "You did great, by the way. I'm really proud of you."

Ted and I stepped inside. "The important thing is we're on special assignment," I said. "I'm your commanding officer, Ted, and we need to get up to orbit and search for the shuttlecraft we came here on."

"But, eh, didn't that blow up or something?" he asked.

It might have blown up, but if it didn't blow up I needed it.

242

Earth needed it. I strapped into the pilot's seat.

He strapped into the co-pilot's seat. "Isn't the battle still going on? There are bombs and missiles and stuff up there, aren't there?"

I flipped on the shuttle and remembered to close the back door. "Probably. But we're TCC officers. It's our duty. It's our duty to protect the people of Earth if we can."

I turned to him and forced a smile. "What's the worst that could happen?"

Chapter Thirty-Six

I was getting ready to take off from Oregon in a TCC shuttle with my troupe of merry sentients Ted, Addie, and Slid.

Suddenly, the shuttle clanged with a loud banging sound. Oh, no! Were we under attack?

Ted said, "Oh no! Are we under attack?"

Geez, he was excitable. "Relax, Ted." I accessed the sensors. "Scan for hostile forces." I couldn't take defensive actions because shuttles didn't have any defensive actions--as I knew only too well from before.

Addie bobbed closer. "What did you do to the shuttle, Jack?"

"Do?" I asked. "Why do you think I did something?" It was like she thought I could wreck a shuttle when it was just parked on the ground.

Clang. Clang. Clang.

The shuttle's computer said, "There's someone knocking on the back door."

"Relay external sound," I said to the ship's computer.

Clang. "Teddy? Teddy? Where are you going? Someplace safe?" Clang. "Take me with you."

Ted unbuckled. "That's Liam!" He jumped up. "Open the door."

I did not make a move to open the door. This all seemed a bit odd. Liam had been safe underground. Ted was great and all, but why was this actor so desperate for him all of a sudden?

"Jack..." Addie whispered in my year.

Ted made an exasperated sound, punched the door release on the console, turned, and ran to the back door.

"I don't think this Liam is what he appears," Addie said.

"I'm way ahead of you." I was suspicious of Liam because he was suspicious--not because he was so handsome.

I rummaged in the storage compartment for a weapon, pulling out a gun. I double-checked that it was loaded. It was.

In the meantime, the door had opened. "Liam, what are you doing here?" Ted asked. "It's not safe. Go back to the basement. What about the show?"

I held the gun behind the captain's chair.

Slid hid behind Addie. Addie resembled faint haze--it was her most insubstantial look yet. She whispered, "We're going to play the 'be quiet' game again, Slid."

Liam laughed as he strolled into the shuttle. "Who cares about the show?"

My gaze shot back to him. This guy wasn't a thespian. No thespian would say that. He was just going through the motions. Very suspicious.

"What about the show must go on?" Ted asked, seemingly flummoxed.

"I care about you, Teddy," Liam said.

"*Whuh...*" Ted took a step back. "What do you mean, you care about me? I'm nobody." He took another step back.

"You're not nobody." Liam took another step inside the shuttle, smiling and putting his hands in his pockets. With his perfect male physique, it was charming. "You're a TCC officer, aren't you?" There wasn't a microgram of fat on him. How often did this guy work out, anyway? I glanced down. I had some micrograms. Maybe I should go to the gym more. Focus, Jack.

Ted took another step back. "Yes." He furrowed his brow. "Why are you here, Liam?"

"Shoot him, Jack!" Addie whispered a little too loudly.

Now it was Liam's turn to take a step back. "Who said that?"

"I said it." I pointed the gun at him. "Put up your hands."

"Of all the people I cozied up to over the years, I can't believe it's little Teddy that ends up being important." Liam did not put up his hands. Instead, he pulled out a fon. "I've secured TCC agent Ted Allen."

I did not like this guy. He hadn't secured anyone. Who was he talking to? And why did his fon work?

"Why does your fon work?" Ted asked.

245

Liam listened for a moment and then said, "I don't know. Some lackey named Jack." Now he turned to stare at me.

"Shoot him!" Addie whispered.

"What's your last name, Jack?" Liam asked.

"I'm in charge; not you." I gestured with the gun. "This is your last warning." Why didn't he care that I had a gun on him?

He listened some more and then said into the fon, "I don't know." He pointed at me. "Sing something, Jack."

I shot him. The gun's report was very loud in the small space.

But the bullet passed right through Liam and on out the still-open shuttle door. He seemed to dissolve into some kind of pixels for a few seconds and then rematerialized.

"He's a shapeshifter!" Addie said. "I knew it!"

In the meantime, Ted had fallen back, landing on one of the chairs. His eyes were as wide as Saturn's rings.

I closed my mouth, which I discovered had been hanging open. I punched the button on the console to close the back door behind Liam. This Liam-creature must have something to do with the Quihiri attack. I couldn't let him get away.

Liam glanced back at the closing door and then turned and smiled at us. "Homo sapiens are so stupid. What do you think you can do to me?"

"Electromagnetic gun!" Addie whispered.

"Who said that?" Liam asked.

I had seen a ray gun in the storage compartment. "Ted! Cover him!"

Ted stumbled up and took the conventional gun from me.

I quickly opened the storage compartment and pulled out the ray gun. I pointed it at so-called Liam.

He looked a little nervous for the first time. Yay. I'd finally wiped that smug look off his face.

"Ted, take his fon," I said.

He did so. "What are you?" Ted asked the creature, still clearly shaken.

"Ted, strap in," I said. "We're taking off." I kept so-called Liam covered with the ray gun.

Ted sat in the seat next to him and put on the seat belt.

"Here, Ted. Keep him, er, it, covered." I handed him the

246

ray gun and took the mystery fon and the regular gun from him. I made a note of the number 'Liam' had called and turned the fon off. "We're going to TCC headquarters where they can interrogate this spy or whatever he is."

So-called Liam did not look happy. But then he made a big show of sighing and then sitting down in a seat and strapping in.

I scanned the skies and didn't see any missiles or anything. What was happening with the battle? I tried using the shuttle's comms to call TCC. No go. They were jammed like the fons.

"Shuttle, do you detect any dangers?" I asked the shuttle computer.

"Insufficient data," the shuttle said in a robotic voice.

Still scrutinizing the sky, I initiated the flight sequence and we took off. What were the chances we'd fly into a missile or something? Not great, I was thinking. Hoping.

"What do you mean you cozied up to people over the years?" Ted asked, voice shaking.

"Why do you think I'm so amazingly handsome and charming?" Liam-thing asked.

He was sadly mistaken if he thought he was charming. I glanced back at him as we reached cruising altitude.

Wow. He'd totally changed his features. Now he had a big bulbous nose, flushed skin, beady eyes. Ha! I knew he'd been too handsome to be real. I knew it! No one could really be more handsome than me.

Ted had an expression like he'd made love to excrement. Poor guy.

"I said homo sapiens were stupid. Not that I was stupid," Liam-monster said. "What do you think? I'm going to spew all my plans like some kind of melodramatic Shakespearean villain?"

Did he just insult the bard?

"Are you sure about this, Jack?" Addie whispered in my ear. I struggled not to jerk in surprise. I nodded.

"What if he wants to be taken to TCC headquarters?" she asked. "What if that's his plan?"

I felt like I was in a little over my head, but I didn't want to admit it. "Can you try calling TCC on his fon and ask them what we should do?" I asked her. I didn't know if his fon could call TCC. And I still didn't understand how a cloud could manipulate physical items.

She extruded an arm of mist towards the fon on the empty seat next to me. The misty arm solidified and punched some keys on the fon.

Very faintly I heard, "Why does this fon work? Who is this?"

"Hold it up to me," I said. "This is Jack Jones. I've captured a prisoner in cahoots with the Quihiri. His fon works." I continued flying us to Paris.

Addie said, "Cahoots?"

Slid whispered, "Cahoots?"

The guy on the fon said, "Cahoots?"

"In league!" I said. "I captured a bad guy in league with the Quihiri. Should I bring him in to headquarters?"

I glanced back at Liam-thing.

He was staring at me, mouth hanging open. His facility with human expressions was impressive. It made me wonder how long he'd been undercover here. It was a measure of the severity of the situation that I didn't snicker at the thought of how he'd worked undercover.

The guy on the fon said, "This is above my pay-grade. Let me go get someone. Just a minute."

"I thought Jack Jones was in custody," Liam said. "Or dead."

Ted looked confused. "Why do you know Jack?" Oh, poor Ted.

"Jack Jones is the most famous Earthling of all," Liam said. That was more like it! "And promiscuous! I can't believe we could have made love and I missed out. I can't believe I let him slip through my fingers." I tried not to imagine what those not-really-fingers might have been able to do.

"What do you mean, the most famous?" Ted asked.

"Are you saying you don't know, little Teddy?" Liam-thing said. "Jack Jones is the most talented and famous singer in the galaxy. And he's supposed to be the best super-spy of all time." All true.

But... he may have been laying it on a bit thick. Did he think I'd get distracted and stop and have sex with him?

"Jack," Addie whispered. "You can't stop and have sex with him." She paused. "Even though shapeshifters are the best lovers in the galaxy."

"Not helping," I said through gritted teeth.

"This is Lieutenant Singh," a man on the fon said. "Jack Jones? We thought you were on the *Shakespeare*. What's happening?"

We were passing over the Atlantic. "I'm in a TCC shuttle. I've captured a prisoner, a shapeshifter. He's been impersonating a human named Liam Lightning. He has some kind of special tech which still works. Obviously. What do you want me to do with him?"

"We need to interrogate him," Singh said. "And get a look at that tech. Bring the fon and him to headquarters, exterior landing zone. A shapeshifter, huh? We'll be ready. I've gotta go." He hung up.

Darn. I wanted to ask how the battle was going. I wanted to ask if the *Shakespeare* was still up there.

As the west coast of France came into view, I sped up.

I said loudly, "Coming in for a landing." More quietly I said, "Addie, Slid, you guys stay in the ship where it's safer." I didn't know if Liam-thing had deciphered there were two other life forms on board, but if there was a chance he hadn't, I wanted to keep them safe.

Paris was strangely silent. Unlike the last time I'd flown in here I didn't see any people or vehicles moving about. The streets were silent. The Seine was silent. The park near the Eiffel Tower was still green and beautiful--but empty. I guessed all the people were hunkered down.

Several large artilleries near TCC headquarters were shooting energy beams into the sky. So, battle still raging; check.

We zoomed down for a landing and I parked in front of the Eiffel Tower. As soon as the engine turned off a phalanx of black-clad soldiers bearing pulse rifles ran towards the ship. Good. This Liam guy wasn't going to get away. I punched the back door controls on the front console and stood up.

A deep *zoom, zoom, zoom* noise came from outside.

Ted gestured at Liam with the ray gun and Liam walked out with his hands up. Ted followed closely behind.

As soon as they got outside, Liam said, "Help! They kidnapped me. I'm a Terran citizen."

One of the soldiers said, "Drop your weapon."

Oh, good grief. I grabbed the fon and ran out of the shuttle. Ted had dropped his ray gun and both Ted and Liam now had their hands up.

But Liam looked different again. Now he looked just like me. "Hey! Quit impersonating me," I said. Although he did look very good.

The *zoom, zoom, zoom*, was much louder out here. Some kind of force field flickered around the artillery batteries as they shot into the sky.

The phalanx of soldiers surrounded us, pointing their pulse rifles at our heads.

"Drop your weapon!" one said. He was glaring at me. "Hands up."

"It's a fon," I said.

"Drop it!" He jabbed his rifle in my direction.

I dropped the fon.

It was a little disconcerting to have so many rifles pointing at a person. I swallowed. "He's our prisoner." I pointed at Liam. "He's a shapeshifter."

Liam pointed at me and said, "No! He's the shapeshifter!"

The soldiers shifted on their feet, obviously confused.

"No," Ted said, "Liam's the shapeshifter. I swear. Me and Jack are TCC officers."

Liam glanced at me and smiled.

Uh oh. *That one may smile, and smile, and be a villain.*

"The shapeshifter's still on the shuttle," he said gleefully.

Oh no. Poor Addie and Slid. I wasn't entirely sure what TCC would do with a couple of former-Quihiri. But maybe TCC didn't know they used to be Quihiri?

The slightly older soldier gestured with his rifle. "Check it out, Devi. Double-time."

Another one of the soldiers ran into the shuttle. Maybe he wouldn't find them.

"I found it!" Devi yelled. "There's some kind of noncorporeal sentient here."

"Bring it out," the commanding officer yelled.

Addie floated out of the shuttle, gray-colored with black swirls. The soldier followed her closely pointing at her with his pulse rifle. I was guessing even noncorporeal sentients didn't do well when hit by electromagnetic pulses.

I scrutinized her as she bobbed to my side. I didn't see any sign of Slid. Did that mean he was still hidden in the shuttle? Or maybe Addie had hidden him somehow in her body? Neither option sounded good for the little guy.

I cleared my throat. "Addie didn't do anything. This isn't right. I'm the one who talked to Singh. I'm Jack Jones. I'm a famous TCC officer."

"Yeah," Ted said. "Famous throughout the galaxy."

Liam snorted. "Yeah, right."

"We don't have time for this shit," the commanding officer said. "Put them all in holding--with electromagnetic fields--and we'll sort it out later. Pick up the fon or whatever it is."

Well, he got one thing right. We didn't have time for this shit.

I scowled at Liam-monster. *All the infections that the sun sucks up from bogs, fens, flats, on him fall, and make him by inch-meal a disease!*

They marched us into TCC headquarters with pulse rifles at our backs.

Chapter Thirty-Seven

The TCC officers marched me, Addie, Ted, and loathsome Liam all the way down to the detention level underneath headquarters. It was sort of amazing how similar detention centers looked all over the galaxy, all nondescript halls, empty walls, and doors to cells.

On the detention level, the former-Jack-Jones super-singer and super-spy, and his buddy Noah, seemed very, very surprised to see us march past. Especially since there appeared to be two of me. Luckily, the cells were airtight--which, now that I knew about shape-shifting energy beings, made much more sense--so I couldn't hear anything they said. I'm guessing it wasn't totally flattering.

The officers kept the pulse rifles pointed at our backs the entire time. We all stopped in front of some empty cells.

I shot a glance at Addie. She looked like thick smoke with swirls of black and red writhing through it. Why didn't she escape? Couldn't she just wisp away like she'd done in the past? Was Slid inside her? Or had she left him unprotected and alone back on the shuttle? I wasn't sure which was worse.

For his part, I think loathsome Liam did something to his hair to make it more shiny. His skin tone seemed slightly tanner and more healthy. When the officer pointed into the empty cell with the rifle, Liam sidled right up to him and whispered something into his ear. As I looked at the duo, I swear Liam's eyes got slightly larger and sparkled. Competing against a shapeshifter in the romance department clearly wasn't a fair fight.

The officer, a thirty-year-old man, smiled and blushed.

I had a sudden strong desire to know exactly what Liam had

said to him.

Ted looked blatantly jealous. Since he now knew Liam was a bad guy, this mystified me.

Liam saw me looking and smiled smugly at me. It was weird seeing such a smirky look on my own face. I would never make that expression.

A second officer approached them. "What's the holdup? Get the perps into the cells."

Liam turned the full force of his smile on this second officer. His teeth were the whitest white I'd ever seen.

The officer's stern look evaporated.

Liam said, "I'm a valuable TCC officer, fellas. Why don't you let me buy you a beer and then we can see what happens?" More quietly he said, "My talent as a singer doesn't compare to my talent as a lover. Surely, you've heard about me. Don't you want to find out if the rumors are true? I promise you'll have the time of your life…"

I couldn't believe it. Was the cad using my own tactics against me?

The two officers seemed to be considering Liam's offer. He appeared quite accomplished at using sex to get his way. Was that his mission in Oregon?

Old Jack was flailing his arms around dramatically inside his cell. The officers with guns glanced at him and Liam's spell was broken.

Both officers pointed inside the empty cell with their rifles.

"Aw," Liam said, stepping inside.

What grown man said 'Aw?' Still, I had to admit the jerk had a certain something.

I watched Ted and Addie go into their cells, wishing we were incarcerated together. "*There is special providence in the fall of the sparrow*!" I yelled out.

Addie definitely looked heartened at my outburst. Ted looked confused.

Looking annoyed, the officers were not enamored with me. They put me into a cell across the hall from Old Jack.

The door clanged shut. The force field went up. My spirits went down at the same time I sat down on the cot. Why did I seem to end up in cells so much lately? I stared at the prisoners I could see across the hall: Old Jack, Addie, Ted, loathsome Liam wearing my face. Surely this would all be resolved quickly.

Surely.

The officers turned on a dime and marched away.

We all sat on our respective cots staring at one another.

The lights flickered, the ground shook slightly, and a layer of dust or something fell from the ceiling. Was the battle still raging? Had TCC headquarters been hit?

Liam winked at me.

I felt my blood pressure rise. I was gonna get that guy if it was the last thing I did. And I couldn't believe I'd gotten my friends Ted and Addie into this position. I needed to get all of us out of here. And where was Slid?

Old Jack started gesticulating again. It looked like he was pounding on the wall of his cell and staring at me. He made a long pound and a short pound and a long pound and so forth. It looked very dramatic, but I couldn't hear a thing. Eventually, he stopped. He seemed disgusted with me, scowling and pulling at his gray hair. He needed a haircut.

We sat. Time dragged.

On the bright side, the lights didn't flicker again. The ground didn't shake again.

I may have fallen asleep.

The next thing I knew, beautiful Captain Gina Gomez was leaning over me.

"Gina!" I said. "Thank God you're okay. Is the battle over? Is the *Shakespeare* all right? Is the crew all right? Did we save Earth?"

Gina pressed her lips into a thin line. "This is him."

The TCC officer (the blusher from before) standing next to her frowned. "Are you sure? They look exactly alike. Ask him the question."

She shrugged. "What did we do in the mud springs of planet Geryon 876 d?"

I groaned. "I don't know. Why won't you tell me? I'm guessing it was pretty great."

"This is the imposter!" the officer said, shaking his rifle a little.

"No," Gina said. "This is him, the real Jack."

"How could a man not know what he did with his wife and two other women in the mud springs of Geryon 876 d?" the officer asked.

"The answer to that question is a long story," Gina said.

"You and two other women!" I said. "You're killing me, here, Gina. Come on, please tell me, pretty please."

"That other guy told a long elaborate tale," the officer said.

"I'd like to hear that tale, too." My brain, and okay, possibly another area of my body, was tingling. "Did Liam seem to enjoy the tale?"

"What does that have to do with anything?" she asked.

"I don't think someone could be that good a seductress if he didn't enjoy it," I said.

"Seducer. But maybe so," she said, nodding.

The officer said, "Yeah. I buy that."

Something Addie had said on the shuttle inspired me. "I have a plan," I said. "We need his intel. I'm going to seduce him."

She leaned back and snickered. "Why am I not surprised?"

"Okay," I said. "You guys menace me like you don't believe me. And then put us in the cell together." I held up a finger. 'But first you have to tell me what's happening with the battle. Is the *Shakespeare* okay? Is Earth okay? And please release Ted and Addie and take them back to the ship." I took a breath. "Don't forget to look mean."

The officer started grimacing and growling. Personally, I thought he was over the top but the poor guy was no actor, so I guess he did his best.

Gina frowned dramatically and said, "The battle's over. The Quihiri ships FTLed away when the other TCC ships in the system finally arrived and joined the fight. The *Shakespeare* sustained some damage and injuries but casualties were minimal. Earth's planetary defenses held--just barely. Some surface areas including TCC headquarters here sustained damage and as I understand it, there were thousands injured."

So many injured? So many people suffering? So many families worried about or mourning loved ones? My heart broke.

Focus, Jack. Now was not the time for mourning. Now was the time for fighting. "I'm glad the Quihiri ran away like the sneaky evil cowards they are," I said. "But that was just the opening salvo. They're still nefarious."

"I think you're right," she said. "We haven't heard the last of them. We need to know what they're planning next and this shapeshifter guy seems to know something."

Old Jack started silently pounding on his cell wall again.

Gina glanced his way.

"I don't know what's up with Old Jack," I said. "He seems very riled up."

"How many guys named Jack are down here, anyway?" the TCC officer asked.

Gina watched Old Jack for a few moments, cocking her head to the side. "It's Morse code, Jack."

"Ohh…" I said. "That makes more sense than him just going cuckoo." At least I couldn't see myself just going cuckoo.

She watched his gestures. "He demands to talk to us. He says he's got information."

I perked up. Maybe he'd tell me about the mud springs of Geryon 876 d.

Focus, Jack!

The TCC officer did something with his fon. The force field on Old Jack's cell went down, leaving the metal bars.

Old Jack grabbed the bars and shook them. "What the hell's going on! Don't tell me you cloned me again!"

The officer gasped.

Gina pointed at the gasper. "That's classified, officer. Don't speak a word of it to anyone."

Yay, Gina. She was still trying to protect me.

"What we did or didn't do is no business of yours, prisoner." Gina gave Old Jack her evil-eye stare.

He took a step back.

It made me wonder what else I didn't know about Gina.

"If you have information, spill it," she said. "Quickly."

"Is Earth under attack?" he asked.

"Yes." She nodded curtly.

"Is it the Quihiri?" he asked.

"Why would you say that?" she asked.

"I was investigating the Quihiri," he said. "They invented the FTL drive and they manufacture them on their home world." That would have been nice to know months ago. Had he admitted that earlier? Sadly, I wasn't privy to the interrogations of Old Jack.

In the meantime, the officer gasped again.

Gina just pointed at him and he shut up and took a step back.

She turned back to Old Jack. "And?"

He looked surprised she didn't react more strongly.

"I have a special secret FTL drive in the cargo hold of the *Shakespeare*," he said, like it was some kind of huge prize.

"And?" Gina said.

Now Old Jack looked rattled. "You know about that?"

"What do you think went on a few months ago when we captured you?" I asked. "The shuttle had an FTL drive. Where do you think that came from?"

"No." He shook his head. "There's another one."

I had to use all my considerable acting skills not to gasp.

Gina met my eyes. Her acting skills were also apparently very impressive because she didn't react either.

The TCC officer looked afraid to react.

"And?" Gina said again.

Now Old Jack looked disappointed. "You knew about that one? I thought it was my ace in the hole."

The TCC officer said, "If you had an ace in the hole, why didn't you use it to try to reduce your sentence? Why use it now?"

"Earth is under attack!" Old Jack said. Maybe we weren't so different after all.

"Do you have anything else?" Gina asked.

"Yes. I was investigating the Quihiri. There's a secret stash of data cubes on the wall over the doorway to the secret tunnels off my cabin," he said. We already knew about that, too. "The uh, decryption key is 'mud springs of Geryon 876 d.'"

Dammit. I really need to get to Geryon 876 d some time.

But wait a minute. I didn't know that decryption key. Was it possible there was more data on those cubes?

"Is that it?" Gina asked with a sigh.

"Yes," he said.

She turned as if to go.

"Gina?" he said.

257

"What?" she asked.

"It's nice to see you," he said softly. "I miss you."

She said only, "Force field back up, officer." But as she turned away, for a nano-second her expression said she missed him, too. Aw.

Bam. My face was shoved to the left as her palm slapped it. I put my hand up to my stinging cheek. "What was that for?"

"I needed to hit a Jack," she said in a growly voice. More calmly, she said, "It was your plan. We're menacing you."

The TCC officer pulled his hand back to slap me.

I dodged out of the way.

Gina yelled, "Horrible traitor to Earth! Evil! Yadda yadda yadda!" and waved her clenched fists around.

The officer followed suit, yelling, "Yadda yadda yadda!" and waving his rifle around.

As far as menacing went, I wasn't impressed. But I screwed my face into an angry expression and yelled, "You promised to release Ted and Addie!"

"I know!" she yelled back. "I will! I'll look for the secret FTL drive back on the ship! Where are the data cubes?"

"In my desk drawer in my cabin," I yelled. "Maybe you should flicker and then turn out the lights like TCC's under attack!"

"Good idea!" Then, she said to the officer, "Now force him into the fake Jack's cell and yell something like 'traitor!' or similar."

He grabbed my arm and yelled, "Good idea!"

"But be quick," I yelled. "He could shapeshift out!"

"I know!" the officer said. He started dragging me out of the cell and across the hall to loathsome Liam's cell.

I tried to focus on the task at hand. I needed to convince Liam the Earthlings didn't believe or trust me. I needed to convince Liam I was on his side, or at least might be on his side. I needed to convince Liam I was sexy and I thought he was sexy. I was guessing that last one wouldn't be hard. The goal was to gain his confidence.

The officer quickly removed the force field, opened the physical door, and shoved me inside.

"But, I swear, I'm the real Jack Jones! I'm human!" I said.

258

"But, I swear, I'm the real Jack Jones! I'm human!" he said, the cad.

"As far as I'm concerned, you're both traitors," Gina said.

The officer closed the door. "Maybe they'll fight it out," he said, and put the force field back up.

Wait a minute. What if Liam decided to make war rather than love? Ugh...I hadn't thought this plan through sufficiently.

I turned and stared at him. "Uh, you're very handsome."

Behind us, Gina let Ted and Addie out of their cells. They both seemed agitated, gesturing energetically at me. She shook her head and led them down the hall.

Liam smirked.

I was trapped in a very small space with an evil shapeshifter. Gee, what could possibly go wrong?

Chapter Thirty-Eight

Liam, the shapeshifting bad guy, glided towards me in the holding cell in the basement of TCC headquarters, a smirk on his face.

I held my ground with some difficulty. My plan was to befriend him and get info out of him, one way or another. I smiled.

He stopped right in front of me. "Boo!"

I flinched--but just a bit.

"That's what I thought," he said, nodding. "Now that you know what I am you don't think I'm handsome." Since he looked identical to me I did think he was handsome. "You're scared of me," he said. This was true, and fear and sexy-times did seem somewhat incompatible.

If I'd ever had any acting chops now was the time to use them. I smiled some more. "Not true." I gave a flourish with my hand. "*Shall I compare thee to a summer's day?*"

"Yeah, right," he said. I was getting a sad vibe from him.

I continued. "*Thou are more lovely and more temperate.*"

He morphed his features into the pathetic fellow he appeared to be on the shuttlecraft and sighed as if it was a relief. Did shapeshifting tire a person out? Were certain shapes harder to maintain than others?

I kept going. "*Rough winds do shake the darling buds of May, and summer's lease hath all too short a date.*"

He frowned and I definitely got a sense that he felt sorry for himself.

"What's wrong, Liam?" I asked softly.

"My name's not Liam."

"Well, what's in a name?" I smiled some more. "Tell me your

name. I'd like to know it."

"It's Quigley."

Was that a Quihiri name? Why? He didn't look like a Quihiri. "Nice name." I smiled. My jaw was getting a little tight at all the smiling. "I accept all sentients and appreciate them all equally. You can show me your true form if you like."

He stared at me for a few moments and I got the distinct impression he was thinking, 'How stupid do you think I am?'

"I'd like to see the real you."

He sighed.

The two of us didn't move for a moment.

Then, he morphed into a slaggy octopus-looking creature. It was as if a mottled gray-and-black human-sized octopus had partially melted. I immediately guessed what had happened to him. The Quihiri had tried to stop his metamorphosis into a sldkfjfoisut and had only been partially successful.

I had to use all my acting skills not to draw away. "Nice to meet you at long last, Quigley."

"I know you're wondering what's wrong with me." He looked me up and down. "But I appreciate you not running away screaming, like the rest of my triple did."

"I don't run away screaming," I said. I quickly scanned my memory. At least I hadn't recently.

"I got a disease," he said. "I guess it's like human cancer. My cells went crazy, growing out of control. The docs on my world tried to help me and they gave me a bunch of experimental drugs and treatments. And this was the hideous result." He indicated his body with one of his tentacles. "The shapeshifting was a side-effect of the procedures. It was best that I leave the Quihiri home world."

"I don't think you're hideous." I did feel a little sorry for him--not because of how he looked, but because the Quihiri, his own species, had lied to him. They'd done quite a number on him. It was cruel. Now, I disliked the Quihiri even more than I had before, and that was saying a lot.

He nodded. "Yeah, you humans are pretty stupid. That's why I've had such an easy time of it here, spying on you all." He straightened, giving off a proud vibe. "I'm an important part of the advance team for the Quihiri war." Sadly, he was the stupid--or, at least, gullible--one, being duped by the Quihiri.

I took a step closer and patted one of his tentacles. "And what's the Quihiri goal? Why did they start a war?"

"They have a good reason, an altruistic reason," he said. "They're going to eradicate my disease from the galaxy. In the future no one will ever have to suffer like I suffered."

"Huh?" That was not at all what I was expecting him to say. "Uh...what?"

He nodded. "Yes. Our scientists believe all species are susceptible to the disease. For example, I mentioned human cancer. We think you are just one mutation away from getting what I got."

My mind was reeling. I had to sit. I sank down on the floor. Could it be possible the human race was on the verge of transforming into some kind of energy-based sentiences?

Could it be possible the Quihiri were trying to eradicate the human race?

"I know. It's pretty amazing, right?" he continued, oblivious to what I was thinking. "The Quihiri are the saviors of the galaxy."

The depths of the Quihiri deceptions were amazing. "You better not be saying the Quihiri are trying to wipe out the humans," I said in a low gravelly voice.

"Uh, no." He physically backed up. "I don't think that's the plan. No. The Quihiri want to save the humans and the other species from the disease."

Save? Save was not the word I would use. I looked up at the poor sucker, shaking my head. "No."

"What?" he said.

"You better sit down." I pointed at his cot.

He sat on his cot. "What?"

"I'm sorry to tell you, you didn't have an illness," I said. "You were evolving into an energy-based sentience, one of the sldkfjfoisut. Your people, the Quihiri, tried to stop a natural process. Their so-called medicine injured you. Your people hurt you."

"No." He shook his head. "That's crazy. You're wrong! I've never heard of anything like that. If that was true, we'd know about it on Quihiri."

"I'm guessing Quihiri doesn't have a free press," I said.

"What's a free press?" he asked.

"People who have the right to investigate things independently and report the results without any oversight from the government or other groups."

"You mean, like, the news?" he asked. "We have news. The news bureau puts out all kinds of news every day."

I shook my head. That didn't sound like a free press.

Focus, Jack. "The point is: your people hurt you. They're not good guys. They're bad guys. And now they're trying to hurt the rest of the galaxy. You need to tell me their nefarious plan."

"I don't believe you. You're just trying to trick me. The Quihiri would never hurt me. No way. You're wrong. You're totally wrong."

He doth protest too much. "Think back to when your transformation first started happening. Did it feel wrong? Did you feel sick?" I asked.

He was silent for a few moments. "Well, no. But the rest of my triple said I was sick. And they're my triple." He paused. "Or at least they were." He definitely gave off a sad vibe now.

"Aw." I stood up and wrapped my arms around him. "It's their loss, Quigley. Their loss."

He made snuffling sounds like he was crying. Poor guy.

After a while he pushed me away. "I'm okay now."

I sat next to him on the cot. "I promise you what I said is true. I can introduce you to a Quihiri, Quinta, that just transformed." She must still be up on the *Shakespeare*.

"Quinta? Part of the ambassador's triple?" he asked. "I know her. Are you sure she got sick?"

"It's not a sickness," I said. "It's an ...upgrade. She's doing great. Better than ever."

"I'm not saying I believe you, but I'd like to see Quinta." He glanced at me. "But, wait. You mean she's here on Earth? Is she a prisoner, too?"

"Nope." I shook my head. "Not a prisoner. She's working with the humans against the Quihiri. The Quihiri tried to hurt her too, but I wouldn't let them."

He looked at me a long moment. Finally, he said, "If Quinta confirms what you said, I'll tell you what I know."

"Excellent!" I said.

263

"Now I regret calling humans stupid," he said. "On the other hand, if you guys had used enhanced interrogation techniques it would have been immediately apparent that I'm not human." Enhanced interrogation? What century did he think this was? We weren't barbarians.

He continued. "When bio matter leaves my body, it reverts to my natural form." Frowning, he indicated his gray-and-black octopus-like torso with one of his tentacles. "Now, it's a kind of disgusting gray-black goo."

"Aw. You're not disgusting Quigley." I put my arm around him. All sentients had something to offer. I couldn't hate him. I felt too sorry for him.

Ted reappeared in the hallway with Quinta in her cloud form.

Quigley jumped up off his cot and glided to the edge of the cell. His figure shimmered as he tried to make himself look more like a typical Quihiri. After a few moments he succeeded. Mostly. Was it difficult to look typical? Clearly I had no idea how shapeshifting worked.

I joined him near the door.

Ted pressed a button outside on the wall. "This is Quinta. She'd like to say something to you, ah, Quigley."

Wow. That was fast. So, we were definitely under surveillance. Check.

Quinta flowed into the cell.

"Hi, Ted," I said to Ted in the hall, but he had already closed the door.

Quinta easily morphed back into her Quihiri form. "Quigley?" she asked. "Is that you?"

Quigley started crying. He wiped his eyes with his tentacles. "How do I know that's you Quinta, and not some trick?"

"If I was a trick how would I know what we did together in junior high, just the two of us?" she said in a jaunty teasing tone. "There was no third anywhere in sight."

"*Shhh!*" Quigley said, looking around. "I thought we agreed never to speak of that."

I grinned. Love really did make the worlds go round. "*Love is a smoke raised with the fume of sighs.*" The quote seemed particularly relevant.

"Is it really you, Quinta?"

"Yep." She nodded.

Tears streamed down Quigley's face.

I put my arm around him.

"Is it really true what Jack said?" he asked. "We were supposed to change into these new …beings?"

"Yep." She morphed into a pretty pastel-colored cloud with sparkles and then after a moment morphed back.

"I can't do anything like that." Quigley seemed very shaken. "So, the Quihiri lied to us? My triple? Your triple? Everyone?"

"I don't think the average Quihiri knows what's going on," Quinta said. "Your triple might not know. But my triple must know. They're at the highest level of government." She sounded tigerish.

"I…all this…what I did…" He waved his tentacles around, seemingly at a loss for what to say. "I…" Finally, he turned to me. "I'm sorry, Jack."

"I'm sorry, too, Quigley," I said. "But we'll make it right."

The TCC must have been listening in (duh) because at that point Commander Wu of the *Assyrian* walked down the hall to the cell and opened the door.

Ted straightened from where he'd been leaning against the wall.

"Hey, good-looking," I said to Commander Wu.

He gave me a fierce look.

I quailed but only on the inside. Maybe that was an inappropriate thing to say to a TCC commander but he made me nervous. A little. Okay, a lot.

"Hey, good-looking," I said to Ted.

He didn't answer me.

"I'm here to escort you, this Quinta creature and the prisoner Quigley to the *Shakespeare*," Wu said.

The *Shakespeare*? Hallelujah! I couldn't wait to get back home. I started singing, *"Hallelujah. Hallelujah. Hallelujah…"*

Wu touched his ear. "Shut up, Jack."

How could he ask me to shut up? I was just getting warmed up.

He looked at me. "First, Gina wants you to get the location of the other FTL drive out of the other Jack." He pointed at Old Jack's cell. "She can't find it. They searched the entire cargo

265

bay."

"Okaay..." I said. "But haven't all you security guys interrogated him already? Why would he tell me anything?"

"You could always try to kiss him," Ted said, smirking.

"Ensign, draw your weapon and cover this Quigley creature," Wu said.

Ted hopped to it.

I walked over to the front of Old Jack's cell and stared inside. Somehow, I didn't think I could woo the information out of him. Woo. Heh, heh. I glanced back at Wu.

I looked at Old Jack some more and tried to imagine myself in his position. What would I want more than anything? Companionship, definitely companionship. But somehow I didn't think that was on the menu.

I pondered for a few more moments. I had it: music.

"Can we bribe him?" I asked Wu.

"No," Wu said. "Crooks don't get rewarded for their crimes."

"I just meant could we get him some music?" I asked.

He appeared to consider. Finally, he said, "Sure." He lowered the force field on Old Jack's cell.

"Jack," I said. "Where's the second secret FTL drive?"

"I thought you knew about it," he said in a growly voice.

"Oh, we knew," I said convincingly. "Gina's just having trouble locating it."

"Why should I help you? You get to fly around the galaxy and I'm stuck in here."

I resisted the urge to say, 'Well, you made your own bed, didn't you?' Instead, I said, "I'm prepared to offer you--"

"A pardon?" he said quickly, stepping up to the edge of his cell. "Reduced sentence? Leniency?"

"I'm prepared to offer you music," I said.

"Aw," he said, looking at the floor. After a few moments he looked up. "What kind of music?"

"Whatever you like," I said. "We'll give you a whole library."

He stared at me. "You seem to be telling the truth. Okay, it's hidden in a large container of supplies labeled 'Rice' in the cargo space, and is in fact in the middle of a bunch of rice."

Huh. Not a bad hiding place.

"We should be able to detect it inside a bunch of rice," Wu

said with a skeptical look on his face.

"I have a special shielding device that hides its technological components," Old Jack said.

Commander Wu was already talking into his comms. "Yes, that's right. It's in a box of rice." He glanced at me and Old Jack. "Well, I'm guessing it's a big box." He paused. "Okay. We'll be there soon. Wu out."

"When do I get the music?" Old Jack asked eagerly.

Wu stepped to the wall. "You don't." He put the force field back up.

How rude! I glanced at Old Jack. He looked like someone had just murdered his cute, cuddly little puppy. Poor guy. "Hey!" I said. "That's not fair! We made a promise to him."

Wu was unimpressed with my outburst. "Come on, you four," he said. "We're going to the *Shakespeare*. We've got a war to finish."

I did not want to get on his bad side. I was guessing the others didn't either because we all fell in line.

How the heck did you finish a war?

Chapter Thirty-Nine

As I stepped onto the *Shakespeare* from the *Assyrian*, taking in its dramatic murals and crewmembers rushing to and fro, tears pricked the corners of my eyes. *I was home.* Wu had actually managed to get his ship inside the *Shakespeare*'s largest bay. I wouldn't have predicted it would fit.

The ship seemed to be extra crowded with the crew of the *Assyrian* on board.

Several areas of the *Shakespeare* were undergoing repairs, poor baby. On the bright side, it looked like she was in good hands.

In the hall outside the shuttle bays, Wu looked at Ted and said, "Ensign, escort the prisoner to the brig," gesturing at Quigley.

Still pointing his weapon at Quigley, Ted nodded. "Let's go."

In a small voice, Quigley said, "Jack?"

"Hang in there, Quigley," I said. "Ted will take good care of you, and I'll come visit." I knew Ted was a good person and if he didn't remember our times together we'd just have to make new memories.

With one last lingering look, Quigley glided down the hall in front of Ted.

Wu turned and walked off somewhere.

For my part I really wanted to get back to my cabin and do my morning ablutions.

Quinta's blue-gray cloud started darkening. "What should I do, Jack?"

"Perform your morning ablutions?" I said. "Do you have any? Or do you want to get breakfast? What do you eat?"

"I am feeling a mite peckish," she said. "But I'm not one

hundred percent sure what to do about it."

"Why don't you come with me to my cabin?" I said. "Addie and Slid are probably there. They can help you out." They'd stayed with me before when they were on the ship.

Quinta sparkled a little. "Good idea. We should tell them about Quigley, too."

But back at my cabin, when I entered I didn't see any sign of Addie or Slid. I saw my bed and my desk and all the rest of my stuff. *Home.*

"Addie?" I asked. "Slid? Are you here?"

Quinta followed me closely.

I closed the door behind us.

Slid flowed out from somewhere. "We're here. We're here."

Addie also flowed into the room. From a tiny opening to the secret tunnel? "Hello, Jack. Hello, Quinta."

Quinta got dramatically more sparkly. "Hi!"

"Hi!" Slid said and sparkled, too.

I smiled, feeling warm inside. I was glad my sldkfjfoisut friends were safe and there for each other.

"Wait until I tell you what's been happening," Quinta said.

I got an amused vibe from Addie.

"I'm so glad everyone is okay," I said.

"We're glad, too," Addie said, sparkling a little.

"We're glad, too," Slid said, sparkling a little.

I wanted to hug them. But how did one hug smoke-creatures? So I just stood there and smiled at them for a few moments.

"What about breakfast?" Quinta asked.

"What about breakfast?" Slid asked.

"You guys sort out breakfast." I waved my hands around. "I'm taking a shower. Even someone as wonderful as me needs a shower and a new uniform after a few days of adventures, boisterous battles, turning enemies into friends and whatnot."

"And we should check on Quigley," Quinta said.

"Sounds good," Addie said.

"Sounds good," Slid said.

I started pulling off my uniform and stepped into my tiny bathroom. Naked, I turned on the shower and stepped into the water. I let the water sluice over me. "*Ahhh.*" There had been

269

a few moments there when I wasn't sure I'd ever get to take another shower. I should have had faith that the good sentients would win out, that good would defeat evil. We'd had some setbacks, but goodness had prevailed in this solar system, anyway. And me and my friends would just have to make sure it did in the rest of the galaxy, as well.

When I came out of the shower, my visitors were elsewhere--too bad for them. I brushed my teeth, recorded my memories and felt much better for doing so. I wasn't going to forget a nano-second of my daring-dos.

As I stepped out of the bathroom, I felt back to my normal awesome self.

There was something I needed to do... It had to do with the mud springs of Geryon 876 d. Oh, right. Old Jack's encrypted data cubes.

I sat at my desk, opened the drawer, and pulled out the cubes. I tried the new decryption key 'mud springs of Geryon 876 d' on the first one. Nothing happened. "Aw."

I tried out the key on the second one and a new file seemed to blossom into existence. "Now that's more like it!" I opened the file. It was a vid of Old Jack, lines on his face, lips turning down, skin gray.

"If you're reading this, Gina, something has gone badly wrong," he said. "I'm probably dead." There was a catch in his voice. "I'm sorry to leave you alone, honey. You are, were, the love of my life." Light shone off his eyes as if they were filled with tears.

He cleared his throat. "So, I've got a lead on a potentially very dangerous situation, dangerous for me, dangerous for the crew, dangerous for all Terrans and the rest of the galaxy, for that matter." He sighed and ran his hand through his too-long gray hair. "There's some kind of civil war brewing on Quihiri. I don't know why. I don't know when. But my sources say the crew of the *Shakespeare* is particularly endangered. They might be kidnapped. There might even be some bombs planted on the ship. I know I should have told you about this earlier, Gina, but it's all rumors and innuendo. But I'm going to do it tomorrow night when we get back to Earth. I've got a special dinner planned, er, I did. I guess I don't have anything now ...since I'm dead."

He cleared his throat again. "Anyway, I hope you find this before it's too late." The vid ended.

I sat at the desk for a moment, stunned. Could my kidnapping and Daniel blowing up all be related to a Quihiri civil war? Was that what we were embroiled in right now? Some kind of Quihiri civil war?

Why hadn't Old Jack told his interrogators about the civil war months ago when he was taken into custody? Could he be scared? Could that be why he faked his death?

My comms trilled. No doubt the crew was all waiting for me with bated breath so we could finish this whatever-it-was. "I have some important new information for you, Gina."

She growled. "That's Captain Gomez to you, Ensign."

I swallowed my pride. Accolades weren't important. Awards weren't important. Compliments weren't important (darn it). Saving the galaxy was important. "Yes, ma'am, Captain Gomez. How can I help?"

She growled some more. "Well, apparently, that old bastard lied to us. We searched every millimeter of the cargo hold. No secret hidden FTL drives."

Yikes. My spirits sank. We couldn't take the battle to the Quihiri if we couldn't get to the Quihiri.

But one of my special skills was thinking like Old Jack. If the drive was there, I could find it. "I'll be right there. Are you in the cargo hold?"

"Yeah." She ended the call.

I ran over to the cargo bay. I even remembered to put on my pants first.

I did think Old Jack had told the truth. Deep down, really deep down, Old Jack was a good guy. Yes, he'd made mistakes, but he wasn't evil.

In the cargo bay, Gina stood fuming next to Commander Bello and Olivia, who both held special scanners. "Well, check it all again," she said. The three of them were dwarfed by the large assortment of large boxes, many with mysterious alien markings on them.

Bello nodded. "Yes, ma'am."

Olivia looked annoyed. I was glad to see I wasn't the only one she got annoyed with.

"Greetings, all," I said. "Are you glad to see me?"

They just looked at me.

"I'm glad to see you," I said. I was glad. "I'm glad you survived the battle and everything. Do you, ah, remember me?"

Olivia nodded, still looking annoyed. Darn. If there was one person I'd like another chance to make a first impression with...

Bello said, "All senior officers keep their memories up to date." Darn. Another person who I'd rather didn't recall exactly everything about me.

"We're busy, Jack," Gina said in a growly voice.

"Okay." I nodded. "I hear what you're saying. No time for chitchat."

Commander Wu jogged into the cargo hold. "We're all squared away, Captain Gomez. The *Assyrian* is onboard. We're ready to leave orbit. All the Quihiri ships left the solar system, and we need to pursue them to their home system." He glanced around. "You haven't found the drive yet?"

"No," Gina said, pausing for a moment to glare at me.

"We will totally find it," I said. "Never fear. Jack is here." I grinned a little.

Gina pointed at me. "You better." She turned to the door. "Come on, Wu. Let's go to the bridge." They stalked out.

Olivia and Bello stared at me some more.

My stomach growled. Awkward. "So, you searched everywhere already?" I asked.

"Yes," Bello said.

Stomach growl.

"I believe you," I said. I did believe them. They were competent. "And you didn't find any big boxes of rice?"

"Nope," Bello said.

I wracked my brain. I had faith in Old Jack. He wouldn't lie when the fate of the galaxy was on the line. My stomach rumbled. I was a mite peckish myself. Ah ha! "Where do foodstuffs go from here? Where do they go before we get them in the mess hall?"

Bello frowned. "The kitchen, of course."

I held up a forefinger. "I have a feeling I know where the secret FTL drive is."

The three of us decamped to the kitchen.

Bello opened some storage compartments, and the two of them started scanning in earnest.

I spied a very large box saying 'Rice.' "What about this one?" It was about three feet square; the drive could fit inside it.

Both Bello and Olivia scanned it.

"The scanner says it's rice," Olivia said.

"Supposedly, Old Jack had some special tech that can make a secret FTL drive look like rice."

They looked at me like they didn't believe me. I sighed. I knew I looked good, but they were doing entirely too much looking at me and not doing their jobs.

I grabbed the box and pulled the top up. Inside I saw ...rice. I tilted the box over and started pouring rice on the floor. Eventually, when there was a very large pile of rice on the floor, I saw some decidedly not-rice-looking stuff. "Ha! *Oh Lord that lends me life, Lend me a heart replete with thankfulness*!"

Olivia and Commander Bello examined the inside of the box.

He nodded. "Good."

She smiled broadly. "Yay!"

I grabbed her and kissed her smiling face. For a glorious instant, she kissed me back. Yay!

Bello cleared his throat as he took out his comms. "Get an anti-grav dolly to the kitchen." He paused. "Yes, the kitchen."

Olivia stepped away from me, seeming embarrassed. Aw. I was guessing no more kisses would be forthcoming from her. At least not right now.

"I'm going to go look for my friend Eva," I said. "I'll meet you in engineering." I ran out of the kitchen and down to the gym.

Running into the gym, I yelled, "Eva? Eva? Are you here?"

She stepped out of her office. "Jack? What's wrong?"

I ran right up to her, and we went inside and closed the door. "I just wanted to make sure you were all right."

She studied me. Then, she held out her arms for a hug. We embraced, and it was heavenly.

"So, you remember me?" I asked. "You remember all our times together?"

"Yes. And I'm all right," she said. "Are you all right?"

"I'm all right, too," I said, eyeing her couch. We kissed

tenderly, and one thing led to another as we got lost in each other. I totally lost track of time.

My comms clicked. "Jones?" Bello asked. "Where are you?"

"I'm coming," I said into comms.

Eva sat up, grinning. "No pun intended. What are you supposed to be doing?"

"Helping to install the new FTL drive," I said.

"There's a new FTL drive?" she asked. "How?"

I waggled my eyebrows as I rearranged my clothing. "Old Jack."

"That old son of a gun." She shook her head. "Does it work?"

I took a step for the door. "We're about to find out. Come on." I gestured her towards me.

The two of us jogged over to engineering. I caught glimpses of Gina, Carter, Wu, Bello, and Olivia. But as soon as we entered, the lights flickered and went out. Everyone gasped, groaned or cussed, as the case may be.

And then the lights came back on. Bello grunted and then said, "I hope that's it, then. Is the power core fully repaired?"

A crew member I didn't know said, "Yes, sir."

Gina said into her comms, "Bridge, take us out of orbit."

Bello looked at me. "There you are, Jones. Do you want to do the honors?" He pointed at the drive.

They'd successfully removed the old drive and placed the new drive in its location. "Do you mean hook it up?"

Bello nodded. He seemed nervous. I glanced around the room. Frankly, everyone seemed nervous.

"Sure." I nodded as I knelt near the drive. "*There is special providence in the fall of a sparrow.*"

I reached for the wires but couldn't help looking around the room first. My friends and I had been through a lot: we'd discovered the Quihiri FTL drive factory, escaped from Quihiri despite their best evil efforts, rushed back to Earth in the nick of time to save it, and uncovered the Quihiri's nefarious plans for all the sentients in the galaxy. I was proud of us.

But it would all be for naught if I couldn't get this FTL drive to work so we could get back to Quihiri, defeat them, and, hopefully, fix all the FTL drives.

Eva patted my back. "Go ahead, Jack."

"You can do it, Jack," Gina said and smiled.

Olivia smiled and nodded.

And, oh yeah, if this didn't work, I wouldn't get my special skills back.

Of course, even if the drive did work, there was no guarantee I'd get my special skills back. But that would be okay. I'd discovered along the way I had a variety of special skills.

And taking in the hopeful faces of the sentients surrounding me, I realized my friends, my loved ones, were my greatest strength.

I smiled. "*Once more into the breach, dear friends, once more.*"

I connected the wires.

Extra-Solar Planets

The words extrasolar or exosolar mean outside our solar system. As you know, we live on a planet called Earth which orbits a star we call the sun. Together, the sun and the eight planets that orbit it are called our solar system.

Scientists know our solar system formed when a cloud of atoms and molecules in outer space was brought together because of the gravitational force. This cloud collapsed into a disk called the protoplanetary disk. Then, clumps of matter in the disk were attracted to each other because of gravity--eventually forming the sun in the center with the planets surrounding it. Thus, to summarize, all you need to make a solar system is matter in outer space, gravity and a lot of time.

For thousands of years, humans have known there are many, many stars in the sky. We know this because they give off light and energy so we can see them in the night sky. The current estimate of the number of stars in the universe is 100 billion. Presumably, each of these stars formed when a cloud of atoms and molecules in outer space was brought together because of gravity. Thus, it is theoretically possible that each of these stars has its own solar system of orbiting planets. In other words, it is theoretically possible that billions of exoplanets exist.

Scientists decided to look for these exoplanets many years ago. Unfortunately, it is much more difficult to detect a planet than a star because planets do not give off light.

We can see the planets in our solar system because they're relatively close, and they reflect the light of our sun.

There are two main methods of detecting exoplanets: radial

velocity and transit photometry. Most confirmed exoplanets have been found using these methods.

Radial Velocity uses the idea that a star moves a little bit when a planet orbits it because of the gravitational pull of the planet. Hence, this method is also called the wobble method. This tiny movement, or wobble, is detectable in the light given off by the star. Light actually has a range of energies which scientists call different wavelengths. This range of light wavelengths is also called a spectrum, and the wavelengths correspond to different colors. When a star moves towards an observer, its spectrum appears slightly more energetic or blue. When a star moves away from an observer, its spectrum appears less energetic or red. Thus, the radial velocity method looks for star spectra with regular patterns of blue shift, red shift, and so on. Scientists can then infer a planet orbits this star.

Transit photometry detects exoplanets by measuring the tiny decrease in light as a planet passes in front of a star, blocking its light. If such dimming is measured at regular intervals and lasts for a fixed period of time, scientists infer an exoplanet is there orbiting the star.

There are two additional methods of detecting exoplanets: gravitational microlensing and direct imaging.

Gravitational microlensing uses Einstein's theory of General Relativity to find exoplanets. General Relativity says gravity bends spacetime itself and thus makes light rays bend. Microlensing works when two stars are aligned in a straight line from Earth. The light from the farther star is bent by the closer star in a particular way. When the closer star has an exoplanet, the planet's gravity bends the light and temporarily produces a third image of the farther star. This third image appears as an increase in the far starÕs brightness. Scientists can detect this temporary brightness spike and know it points to the existence of an exoplanet.

Direct imaging is exactly what it sounds like: taking a picture of an exoplanet. This method only works for exoplanets that are close enough to take a picture of and simultaneously block the light from the star it orbits.

As of early 2018, approximately 3600 exoplanets have been confirmed, with approximately another 4900 candidates yet to be confirmed.

The next great mystery is: do any of these exoplanets harbor life? We're still investigating...

What about visiting some of these exoplanets to check them out for ourselves? Sadly, the speed of light makes this impossible.

For more information and details about these and other topics, check out the Physics Is Fun website: www.physicsisfun.net

Thank you for reading *A Jack in the Dark.* I hope you enjoyed it!

- For more info about me or my work, please visit my author's website, http://www.lesleylsmith.com/. Sometimes, I post links for free fiction downloads!
- Please check out the Physics Is Fun website www.physicsisfun.net for lots of information about fun physics topics.
- Reviews help other readers find books. I appreciate any and all reviews.
- A sneak peek at my next book, *Quantum Mayhem*, follows.

−Lesley L. Smith

Quantum Mayhem
Chapter One

I was working in my office in the Gamow physics tower when I was interrupted by a call on my cell phone.

The caller was my roommate, Ben Willis, aka hot cop (I really needed to quit thinking of him like that since I had a boyfriend). "Hey, Ben. What's up?"

"Hey, Madison," he said. "Are you busy?"

I looked at the stack of papers to grade on my desk and my giant to-do list on the pad of paper next to it. But Ben was a pretty awesome roommate; I owed him a lot. "Depends. . . I might not be busy if you need help with something."

"The police chief up in Nederland called," Ben said. "He said he has a situation that might call for the quantum cop." Ben was developing a reputation as the first line of defense when it came to quantum crimes. I'd discovered how to affect reality using quantum physics; unfortunately, others had deciphered how to commit crimes using this knowledge.

Damn. Since I was the quantum cop, I definitely needed to help him. "When can you pick me up?"

"I'm next to the south door with my bike." We'd ridden his awesome motorcycle to crime scenes before.

"Sweet! I'll be right down." I almost--but not quite--ran down the many stairs. I was excited about solving a quantum crime and serving justice and not at all about hugging Ben as we zoomed up mountain roads on a beautiful fall day.

Outside, the weather was unseasonably warm and pleasant for the beginning of November. The sun shone brightly, and a light breeze blew colorful fallen leaves across the sidewalk.

Ben stood right outside the exit on his bike, on the sidewalk.

Around thirty, he did that sexy, shaved-head thing that some guys did. He looked as hot as ever in his sexy leather jacket, all muscles, not an ounce of fat on him. Darn it.

He smiled under his mirrored shades and saluted as he saw me.

"Where are we going?" I asked.

"Caribou, Colorado," he said. "A former silver-mining town, a ghost town. It's up in the mountains, near Nederland. Should be a fun ride today." He handed me a helmet.

The drive up to Caribou was fun. Correction: it was wonderful. We motored up the highway like NASCAR racers-- at least it felt like it. A few Aspen trees still clutched their sunny yellow leaves, and the various pines stood majestically as we zoomed by.

I had my arms wrapped snugly around Ben, and I leaned into his back. The roaring wind was a powerful presence hammering at us. But in the bright sunshine, it just felt exciting as we drove up and up the mountain.

Eventually, we drove up a dirt road, seemingly in the middle of nowhere, and Ben turned off the bike. We were in a vast empty meadow filled with brown grass and the skeletons of last summer's flowers, surrounded by snow-sprinkled mountains. Pretty.

A man standing next to a battered pickup truck waved to us. He wore a warm-looking jacket with a shearling collar. If I had to guess, based on his sparse white hair, craggy face, and worn hands and neck, I'd say he was pretty old.

"Ben," he called out. "Thanks for coming. Is this the physics lady?" He pointed at me.

I nodded as I got off the bike. Standing there next to the bike, my body still vibrated from the ride.

The temperature was a little cooler than down the hill in town, so the warm sun on my skin felt good.

"Yep," Ben said. "This is Professor Madison Martin, the quantum cop. Madison, this is Chief Goodwin of Nederland." He stowed the two helmets.

"Nice to meet you, sir," I said, holding out my hand.

We shook, and he frankly looked me up and down. I couldn't tell what his conclusion was. At least he didn't say I

281

didn't look like a physicist, or I did look like a soccer mom, which was what people usually said.

"Ben, here, told me you were the quantum cop," the Chief said. "But not how it all works. Can you help me out?"

"Sure." I nodded. "Quantum physics is the physics of very tiny things."

Ben joined us. "The short version, Madison." He said that like I was going to get carried away talking about physics. He knew me pretty well.

"Suffice it to say, the universe follows the rules of quantum physics," I said. "Basically, everything can be described as a probability, and it takes a human mind to collapse the probability wavefunction and instantiate a reality."

"What?" the Chief said.

Ben interrupted. "The bottom line is if you really understand this, you can control reality. It's like a superpower. Or magic." I didn't like the words 'superpower' or 'magic,' but Ben and I had had this conversation before.

"Can you do the physics magic, Ben?" the Chief asked him.

"I'm trying to learn," Ben said. "It's a little tricky, but hopefully, I'll get it soon." He glanced around. "Anyway, What's the trouble here?"

Chief Goodwin waved his hand around. "You're looking at it."

I examined the beautiful mountain meadow with a narrow dirt road and lots of dried grasses and wildflowers. Some kind of bird of prey glided over us under the enormous indigo sky. "I don't see anything," I said. "I mean, it's pretty and all, but. . ."

"Exactly," the chief said. "The town is gone. There were a bunch of old wooden structures and some stone buildings and foundations."

I started getting a bad feeling. Stuff disappearing did sound like quantum shenanigans. But I shouldn't jump to conclusions, right?

Ben shook his head and scowled as he unzipped his leather jacket and shrugged it off. He placed it on the bike's seat. Underneath, he had on a form-fitting black t-shirt. Good thing I'd stopped thinking of him as the hot cop because I might have been distracted.

"Granted, they were old and rundown and all, but still," Goodwin said. "This is a historic site. It's not right." He paused. "Did you know a prospector named Conger discovered gold downstream in 1861 and followed the gold right up Coon Trail Creek to here?"

He knew a lot of history for a chief of police; I was impressed. "I did not know that. Neat," I said. "Is there still gold around here?" I looked around; I wouldn't mind seeing some gold in its native habitat. Or silver, for that matter.

The two men glanced at me with downturned lips and then continued their conversation.

"Who reported it?" Ben asked.

"Some scientist types," Chief Goodwin said. "I think they said they were archeologists. From the university." He looked to me. "Do you know them?"

Archeologists? Why would I know them? It wasn't like every one of the thousands of university employees knew everyone else. "Gosh, no. I can't say that I've had the pleasure."

"Anyway," Ben said. "Did they give you any other info?"

"Yeah," Goodwin said. "They sent me some pictures." He swiped his phone and held it out in front of him. "This is what the place looked like just a few days ago. They were studying it."

Ben and I stepped to his phone and squinted, trying to see the image.

Goodwin swiped.

I could barely make anything out in the bright sunshine. "Can you email us those pix?"

He nodded and started typing. "Crap. Not enough signal. Usually, it's decent around here. Can I send them later?"

"Sure," Ben said.

"So why do you think it was quantum stuff?" I asked.

"Come on." The chief turned and started walking away. We followed him.

Our shoes crunched on the stones and gravel in the dirt road. We left the road and walked up what seemed to be a dirt walkway. But it ended abruptly at nothing.

Goodwin pointed. "The biggest stone building was here."

There was no building now. I crouched down on the walkway. It ended suddenly in a packed dirt rectangle covered with piles of sand. I carefully poked one of the piles of sand. "It feels like sand." I turned around to face the two men who stood behind me. "Are you sure there was a building here recently?"

"Yes." Goodwin held out his phone.

I stood and squinted into the screen. An old stone building was centered in the picture, and the tree in the picture looked exactly like the physical tree about ten feet from the foundation. Tree, check. Building, not so much. "Huh."

Ben leaned over and checked out the picture and then the tree.

"Okay," I said. "So that is weird. But it's not necessarily quantum mayhem." It was very probably, but not totally necessarily, quantum mayhem.

"There's more." Goodwin pointed at another space in the clearing. We followed him over there. A dirt walkway led to a pile of sawdust. Goodwin swiped and held out his phone.

Sure enough, the picture showed a rickety wooden structure with a familiar background. Again, there was no sign of the building presently--with the exception of the sawdust.

I got a chill, and I didn't think it was from the wind that had sprung up.

"There's a whole bunch of these piles of sawdust," Chief Goodwin said.

"Is it quantum stuff, Madison?" Ben asked.

"Can't be sure." I was pretty sure. I shrugged. "Anything else?"

"Oh, yeah." Goodwin led us over to another open space.

As we approached, this time, the ground seemed to be covered in something shiny. We walked right up to it and stared at mounds of shiny goo. "What was this?"

"A bunch of trees and plants and stuff," Goodwin held out his phone again and showed us a picture of a bunch of trees and plants and stuff.

I crouched down next to the goo. I didn't want to touch it. It looked slimy, glistening in the sun.

I stood. "Okay, you're convincing me." Darn it.

"We should take a sample," Ben said.

I took a step back. "Knock yourself out. I don't do goo."

Ben took a small plastic evidence bag and latex gloves out

284

of his jeans pocket and scraped some goo into the bag.

"Anything else?" I asked Goodwin.

"Yeah. It's a little further away." He pointed at a path through the grass.

The three of us tramped along, not saying anything.

I didn't know why they were quiet. I was quiet because I was mystified. Why come out in the middle of nowhere and wreck everything? Why destroy a whole town? What was the point?

After several minutes, Chief Goodwin stopped abruptly. I almost plowed into the back of him. He pointed down. "Look."

"Look at what?" There was nothing there. Literally. It was a giant hole in the ground.

"This is where the mine was," he said. "It used to be a relatively small opening, with a wooden structure and a warning sign blocking it." That was not what it looked like now.

Now, it almost looked like a modern-day strip mining operation had taken place here. Or maybe a huge sinkhole. Or a quarry. The point was there was an extremely big hole in front of us.

"I'm guessing it wasn't like this before?" Ben asked.

Goodwin held out his phone. I could just make out a small, rickety-looking wooden structure about the size of an outhouse with a big sign, 'Danger. Do not enter.' There were no holes in the ground visible in the picture.

I crouched down next to the gaping chasm.

"Be careful!" both men said.

I jerked at the loud voices.

Ben added, "Don't fall in."

"I won't," I said. "Unless you guys startle me again." I leaned over the edge, and the edge of the hole looked weird, kind of spongy. "Gloves?"

Ben handed me some latex gloves.

I put them on and carefully touched the edge of the hole. The earth felt spongy.

It felt familiar. Crap. It felt like holes that had been made in the past, using quantum mechanics to collapse the probability wavefunction. That was a mouthful, so I called it q-lapsing.

In the past, similar holes in things like bank vaults had been

285

made by criminals, technically my criminal former students. I frowned. Would this never end?

I stood and pulled off the gloves. "Okay, you totally convinced me. Something quantum happened here."

"So, can you catch them?" Chief Goodwin asked.

Ben and I glanced at each other. It was unlikely with so little info. "Uh, we'll try," I finally said.

Ben said, "Maybe I should take more samples."

Chief Goodwin departed with instructions to call him as soon as we identified the bad guys.

I resisted the urge to tell him not to hold his breath.

Ben scurried around, taking samples of spongy earth, sawdust, and sand.

As the sun started to go down, I sat on a big rock and thought. Who knew how to q-lapse? Me, my boyfriend Andro Rivas, my grad student Alyssa Long, FBI agent Lisa Baker, the physics department secretary Nancy Hernandez, and my former students Griffin Yin and Arjun Chatterjee.

Everyone else was dead. Sigh. Knowing how to q-lapse was not good for your health--even disregarding the possibility of an aneurysm if you did it too much.

About a year ago, I had been trying to teach other FBI agents how to q-lapse until one of them turned evil. Could yet another agent have figured it out?

There was also a minor chance my current quantum mechanics students had figured it out even though I'd been extra careful this year.

And then there was the pesky issue of the webpage controlreality.org that basically explained how to control reality using quantum mechanics. So, technically, there were potentially thousands, if not millions, of people who knew about q-lapsing. I needed to get rid of the webpage if it was back. I took out my phone but, like Chief Goodwin, couldn't access the web.

Ben stomped up. "Gee, thanks for helping."

I tapped my forehead with my finger. "I am helping. I'm trying to figure out who could have done this."

"I guess that makes sense." He placed a bunch of evidence bags into the inside pocket of his leather jacket and started putting it on.

The sun was slipping behind the higher peaks. The temperature was dropping quickly as the sun set.

"So, what'd you figure out?" he asked.

"I'm still working on it," I said.

"What do you think happened here?" he asked. "What was the point of all this? Of destroying a ghost town?"

"I wish I knew." All I knew was it wasn't good. I shivered.